continued ...

Opening Atlantis

"An interesting, alternative version of our own world.... Turtledove's development of it allows him to look not only at political but also geographical and evolutionary differences between his world and our own." —SF Site

"Imaginative." —Don D'Ammassa

"I enjoyed this book.... The exploration and in some cases defiling of this new land [are] interesting.... I look forward to the further adventures of the Radcliff(e)s." —SFRevu

"The book itself is quite readable: Each vignette is based around a military conflict, and the author has his usual eye for appropriate detail and ear for authentic historical attitudes. Turtledove has been generally unwilling to warp his characters to the point where they are twenty-first-century Americans in funny clothes, and keeps to that tradition here: The viewpoint characters judge themselves by their standards, not ours ... makes for a more internally consistent novel." —Collected Miscellany

"The unchallenged master of alternative history touches on a common myth in his latest retelling of the history of the world.... Turtledove's many fans and anyone interested in the Atlantis mystique should enjoy this." —*Library Journal*

"Showcases Harry Turtledove's ability to write a believable alternate historical thriller.... Fans will appreciate a different take on the legend of Atlantis." —Alternative Worlds

"Turtledove's strengths—detailed settings and backgrounds, and complex yet realistic characters inhabiting them—are all on display here.... I'm looking forward to seeing Victor Radcliff establish the United States of Atlantis." —Books Well Read

"The true charm of this novel lies in its clever depiction of modern humanity wreaking havoc on a pure and beautiful land. In this subtle social commentary, Turtledove bares some sharply intense views about colonization, war, and ecology.... The reader is challenged to disregard their previous assumptions and beliefs as they read, a recurring trait in Turtledove's writings." —Curled Up with a Good Book

"This is classic Turtledove, the wizard of 'If,' treating us to solid historical conjecture and the finely spun storytelling that typifies one of the most prolific and consistently entertaining novelists in science fiction today.... It's a little bit like Michener.... Alternate history is great mind candy and almost no one does it better than Turtledove. He is a prodigious writer.... [He] edifies while he entertains. That, of course, is a functioning definition for all sci fi, with alternate history a particular laboratory for historical speculation. So do check out Atlantis and any other of Harry Turtledove's engaging alternate worlds."   —Scifi Dimensions

"The world building, while created with some similarity to history, is just phenomenal. The characters are well-drawn, and as the centuries pass their relation to the original settlers is easily seen. If you're looking for the usual fantasy or paranormal tale of Atlantis, you won't find that here between these covers. What you will find is an action-packed adventure bound to intrigue any reader who dares to wonder what might have been if the world were a slightly different place."
—Darque Reviews

End of the Beginning

"Chilling.... A plethora of characters, each with his or her own point of view, provides experiences in miniature that combine to paint a broad canvas of the titanic struggle."
—*Publishers Weekly*

Days of Infamy

"[*Days of Infamy*] is a gripping book that makes it clear just how lucky the United States was to have things go its way in 1941; it's a read worthy of an all-nighter."
—*Sacramento News & Review*

Ruled Britannia
A *San Francisco Chronicle* Best-of-the-Year Selection
A *Locus* Recommended Read

"Sprinkled with literary jokes, peopled with a lively supporting cast, and filled with engaging plot reversals, *Ruled Britannia* is a smart, enjoyable exercise in 'what-if.'"
—*San Francisco Chronicle*

ALSO BY HARRY TURTLEDOVE

BY HARRY TURTLEDOVE WRITING AS DAN CHERNENKO

THE UNITED STATES OF
ATLANTIS

HARRY
TURTLEDOVE

A ROC BOOK

ROC
Published by New American Library, a division of
Penguin Group (USA) Inc., 375 Hudson Street,
New York, New York 10014, USA
Penguin Group (Canada), 90 Eglinton Avenue East, Suite 700, Toronto,
Ontario M4P 2Y3, Canada (a division of Pearson Penguin Canada Inc.)
Penguin Books Ltd., 80 Strand, London WC2R 0RL, England
Penguin Ireland, 25 St. Stephen's Green, Dublin 2,
Ireland (a division of Penguin Books Ltd.)
Penguin Group (Australia), 250 Camberwell Road, Camberwell, Victoria 3124,
Australia (a division of Pearson Australia Group Pty. Ltd.)
Penguin Books India Pvt. Ltd., 11 Community Centre, Panchsheel Park,
New Delhi - 110 017, India
Penguin Group (NZ), 67 Apollo Drive, Rosedale, North Shore 0632,
New Zealand (a division of Pearson New Zealand Ltd.)
Penguin Books (South Africa) (Pty.) Ltd., 24 Sturdee Avenue,
Rosebank, Johannesburg 2196, South Africa

Penguin Books Ltd., Registered Offices:
80 Strand, London WC2R 0RL, England

Published by Roc, an imprint of New American Library, a division of Penguin
Group (USA) Inc. Previously published in a Roc hardcover edition.

First Roc Mass Market Printing, December 2009
10   9   8   7   6   5   4   3   2   1

Copyright © Harry Turtledove, 2008
All rights reserved

I

*V*ictor Radcliff didn't like to go into Hanover or New Hastings or any of Atlantis' other seaboard towns. Too many people crowded too close together to suit him in places like that. He lived on a farm well to the west, more than halfway out to the Green Ridge Mountains. Whenever he found—or made—the chance, he ranged farther afield yet.

But towns were sometimes useful. He had a manuscript to deliver to a printer in Hanover. Unless he cared to buy a printing press himself (which he didn't) or to stop writing (which he also didn't), he needed to deal with the men who could turn his scribble into words someone besides himself and the compositor could understand.

His wife kissed him when he left. "Come home as soon as you can," Margaret said. "I'll miss you."

What might have been lay not far below the surface of her voice. They'd had two boys and a girl. None of the children saw its third birthday. Without Victor, Meg had a lonely time of it. Adam would have been fourteen now. . . .

"I'll miss you, too." Victor meant it, which didn't keep him from plunging into the trackless swamps and forests of western Atlantis as often as he could. A lot of Edward

Radcliffe's descendants—those who still kept the *e* on the
end of their surnames and those who didn't—still had the
restless spirit that came down from the Discoverer.

No doubt Edward had it, for without it he never
would have started the English settlement in Atlantis.
On sea and land, his descendants through his sons—and
others through his daughters, who didn't wear the family
name any more—had kept it through more than three
centuries now.

"Give my regards to all the cousins you see," Meg
said.

"There'll be a swarm of them," Victor replied. Radcliffs and Radcliffes had thrived here as they never
would have in England. Without a doubt, old Edward
had known what he was doing when he decided this was
a better land than the one he'd left behind. Englishmen
thought of Atlanteans as colonials, and looked down
their noses at them. Atlanteans thought of Englishmen
as straitjacketed on their little island, and felt sorry for
them.

Someone knocked on the front door. "That will be
Blaise," Margaret said.

"Not likely to be anyone else," Victor agreed.

He opened the door. It *was* Blaise. "You are ready?"
the Negro asked, his English flavored both by the French
he'd learned as a slave farther south and by the tongue
he'd grown up speaking in Africa. He and Victor and
two copperskins from Terranova had escaped French
Atlantis together. Victor didn't know what had become
of the men from the west. Blaise had stuck with him. The
black man had been his sergeant during the war against
France and Spain, and his factotum ever since.

"I'm ready," Victor said.

"Let's go, then. It will be good to get away." Blaise
had two boys and two girls. He and his wife had buried
only one baby. With the genial chaos in his household,
he probably meant what he said. He made sure this trip
wouldn't be for nothing: "You have the manuscript?"

"Put it in my saddle bag half an hour ago," Victor replied. "I won't be the kind of author they make jokes about—not that kind of joke, anyhow."

"Good." Blaise lifted his plain tricorn hat from his head for a moment. "I'll bring him back safe, Mrs. Radcliff."

"I know you will." Meg smiled. "I don't think I'd let him go if you weren't along."

"I'm not an infant, Meg. I have been known to take care of myself," Victor said, a touch of asperity in his voice.

"I know, dear, but Blaise does it better." No one could deflate you the way a wife could.

Victor left with such dignity as he could muster. He swung up onto his horse, a sturdy chestnut gelding. Blaise rode a bay mare. Stallions had more fire. They also had more temper. Victor preferred a steady, reliable mount. Blaise had come to horsemanship late in life. He rode to get from here to there, not from a love of riding. A temperamental horse was the last thing he wanted.

They rode off Victor's farm and down a little, winding side road toward the highway east. It had rained a couple of days before—not a lot, but enough to lay the dust and make the journey more pleasant.

Fields were broader than they would have been in England. Most of the crops were the same, though: wheat and barley, rye and oats. Here and there, farmers planted a field in Terranovan maize, but English farmers were doing that these days, too. Horses and cattle and sheep cropped grass in meadows, as they might have on the home island. Chickens and ducks and Terranovan turkeys strutted and waddled across farmyards.

Apple orchards and groves of peaches and plums and walnuts grew among the fields and meadows. Lettuce and cabbage and radishes, turnips and parsnips and carrots flourished in garden plots. Dogs barked and played. Cats sauntered or snoozed or sat by woodpiles waiting for unwary mice. Again, everything was much the way it would have been in England.

Only in the unsettled stretches did Atlantis remind Victor of what it must have been like before Englishmen and Bretons and Basques first began settling here. Pines, and even a few redwoods, made up the woods in those stretches. Barrel-trees, with their strange, short trunks and sheaves of palmlike leaves sticking off from the top of them, showed themselves here and there. All manner of ferns gave the native forest an exuberant, bright green understory.

A bird called from the woods. "An oil thrush!" Victor said. "They're getting scarce in settled country."

Oil thrushes were plainly related to the brick-breasted birds Atlanteans called robins. That name irked Englishmen, who applied it to another, smaller, bird with a red front. It seemed natural to Victor, though; he'd used it all his life. Oil thrushes were much larger: easily the size of chickens. They had wings too small to let them fly and long beaks they thrust into soft ground in search of earthworms. Their fatty flesh gave them their name. Settlers rendered them for grease to make soap or candles. And ...

"Good eating," Blaise said. "They're mighty good eating."

"Do you want to stop and hunt?" Victor Radcliff asked.

As if to tempt a yes, the oil thrush called again. Like a lot of Atlantean creatures, the flightless birds didn't know enough to be wary of men. But, reluctantly, Blaise shook his head. "I reckon not," he said. "We know where our next meal's coming from. I do like that. Don't need to take the time."

"Sensible. I was thinking the same thing." Radcliff laughed at himself. "Funny, isn't it, how often we think *He's a sensible fellow* means the same thing as *He agrees with me*?"

Blaise laughed, too. "Hadn't looked at it like that, but you're right, no doubt about it."

Victor's good humor faded faster than he wished it would have. "No wonder Englishmen don't find Atlanteans sensible these days, then, and no wonder we don't think they are, either."

"What can we do about it? Can we do anything about it?" Blaise was, above all else, a practical man. Victor supposed anyone who'd been a slave would have to be.

"I don't know," Victor answered. "Along with seeing my manuscript off to the printer, finding out whether we can do anything makes me put up with going to Hanover. I won't have to wait for the news to come out to the farm."

Blaise looked at him sidelong. "Thought you liked it there."

"I do," Victor said. "God knows I do. But Edward Radcliffe came here three hundred years ago so he wouldn't have lords and kings telling him what to do. They seem to have forgotten that in London." Air hissed out between his lips. "Some people in Hanover seem to have forgotten, too."

They came into the little town of Hooville as afternoon neared evening. Only an antiquarian—of which there were few in Atlantis—would have known it was named for the Baron of Hastings in the mid-fifteenth century. The sun going down toward the Green Ridge Mountains cast Victor's long shadow, and Blaise's, out ahead of them.

Hooville had three or four shops, three or four churches, and several streets'—or rather, rutted lanes'—worth of houses. Most of the streets in Hanover and New Hastings and other prosperous coastal towns were cobbled. No one in Hooville had seen the need, or, more likely, cared to spend the money.

A boy took the travelers' horses. Victor tipped him a penny apiece for them. The boy grinned, knuckled his forelock, and made the broad copper coins disappear.

Smoke and noise greeted Victor and Blaise when they walked into the tavern. The taproom was nearly full. A pockmarked man raised his tankard in salute. "Here's to the major!" he called.

"To the major!" Mugs rose. Men drank. A dozen

years earlier, Victor had been the highest-ranking officer from the English Atlantean settlements in the war against France and Spain. He saw several people here who he knew had fought under him. Some he knew by name. Others were just familiar faces.

"And here's to the major's shadow!" shouted the fellow who'd hailed him before. Amidst laughter, the topers drank again. Blaise smiled, his teeth white against his dark skin. What he thought was anyone's guess. But, as a practical man, he must have known he couldn't keep people from noticing and remarking on his blackness.

"Let's get us something to drink," he said.

"Now you're talking," Victor replied. They made their way over to the tapman and ordered mugs of flip. The potent mix of rum and beer, sweetened with sugar and mulled with a hot poker, went a long way toward letting a man forget he'd been in the saddle all day—or, if he didn't forget, at least he didn't mind so much.

"Something for your supper, gents?" By the way the tapman said it, he was stretching a point to include Blaise in that, but stretch the point he did. Nodding toward the big fireplace, he went on, "My brother-in-law shot a wild boar this morning, so if you hanker for pork. . . ."

"Bring it on, sir, bring it on," Victor said expansively: the flip was hitting him hard. Blaise nodded. Victor lifted his mug on high. "And God bless your brother-in-law, for turning an ugly beast into a fine supper."

"Good to think God will bless him for something," the tapman said. But then, men who spoke well of their brothers-in-law were few and far between.

The cheap earthenware plates were locally made. So were the pewter forks. Victor and Blaise cut the pork with their belt knives. They drank more flip and listened to the Hooville gossip. Part of that was the inevitable local scandal: So-and-So had run off with Such-and-Such's daughter, while Mr. Somebody was supposed to be paying entirely too much attention to Mrs. Someone Else.

Mr. Somebody had some sympathy among the Hoovilleans. "Can you blame him, when the body he's stuck with is cold as Greenland winter?" a well-lubricated fellow asked.

"How do *you* know?" cried another drinker, and everybody laughed.

Sooner or later, though, the talk veered toward politics, the way it did in any tavern sooner or later. "Major, how come England thinks it can tax us here?" somebody asked Victor. "Doesn't the king recollect our grandsires crossed the ocean to get away from all that nonsense?"

As far as Victor knew, *his* many-times-great-grandsire came to Atlantis because of the cod banks offshore. Men still fished those banks today, even if the man-sized monster cod the old chronicles talked about had grown rare. But cod weren't what this fellow was talking about. Radcliff had to pick his words with care: "The king recollects that he spent a pile of money keeping the French from taking these settlements away from us. He wants to get some of it back."

"He's got no right to do it the way he's doing it, though," the man insisted. "England can't tax us, not in law. Only we can tax ourselves."

"That's how we see it. England sees it differently." Again, Victor spoke carefully. Ordinary people could talk as free as they pleased. No one cared about them. But chances were somebody in this crowded room would report *his* words to the English authorities . . . and someone else would report them to the local leaders squabbling with those authorities. He didn't want either side to conclude he was a traitor.

He didn't want the two sides banging heads, either. Whether he could do anything to stop them might be a different question.

Another man banged his mug down hard on the tabletop in front of him. "Me, I'm damned if I'll buy anything that comes from England, as long as she's going to play these dirty games," he declared. "We can make do with what we turn out for ourselves."

"That's right!" someone else shouted. Heads bobbed up and down. Support for the latest boycott ran strong.

A hundred years earlier, the settlers couldn't have done without England. The mother country made too many things they couldn't make for themselves. No more. Oh, some luxury goods, furs and silks and furniture and fripperies, still came from across the sea. But Atlantis could do without those, even if certain rich Atlanteans—some of them Radcliffs and Radcliffes—still pined for them.

"D'*you* buy English, Major?" asked the man who'd said the king had no right to tax Atlanteans.

A hush fell. Everyone waited on Victor's answer. He passed it off with a laugh, or tried to: "What? This far inland? I didn't think they let English goods get past the coast."

When the laugh rose, it was an angry one. England might think of the Atlantean settlers as bumpkins one and all. The rich merchants in the seaside towns resented what the English thought of them—and thought the same thing of their inland cousins.

"You can't win. No matter who you are, you can't win," Blaise said. The color of his skin gave him uncommon authority on such questions.

"Someone will have to win, I think," Victor said later that evening, hoping the mattress he'd lie down on wouldn't be buggy.

"Mm—maybe." Blaise still didn't sound convinced. "When he wins—if he wins—will he be happy in the end?"

Victor said the only thing he could: "I don't know." He blew out the candle he'd carried from the taproom. It was guttering towards an end anyhow. The landlord wasn't about to waste a quarter of a farthing by giving a customer any more light than he absolutely had to. Darkness fell on the bedchamber like a cloak. Victor fell asleep before he found out whether the mattress held bedbugs—but not before Blaise, whose first snores he heard as darkness came down on them.

*   *   *

By the time Victor and his colored companion got to Hanover, they were both scratching. One inn or another—or, more likely, one inn *and* another—*had* proved buggy. Victor was more resigned than surprised. Blaise was more apt to complain about big things than small ones.

Hanover was a big thing, at least by Atlantean standards. With about 40,000 people, it claimed to be the largest city in Atlantis. Of course, so did New Hastings, farther south. And so did Freetown, south of New Hastings. Croydon, north of Hanover, also had its pretensions, though only locals took them seriously.

Down in French Atlantis, Cosquer might have been half the size of the leading English settlement towns. Of course, most of the people who'd flocked there since the end of the war came from one English settlement or another. The same held true for the still smaller St. Denis, south of Cosquer, and for New Marseille, smaller yet, on the west coast of Atlantis. As for Avalon, north of New Marseille, it wasn't a pirates' nest any more, but it remained a law (or no law) unto itself. Nobody could say how many people lived there, which suited those who did just fine.

None of Atlantis' leading cities would have been anything more than a provincial town in England or on the Continent. Even Terranova to the west, settled later by Europeans, boasted larger human anthills than any here. Of course, the Spaniards, who dominated the richer parts of the western continent, built on the wreckage of what the copper-skinned natives had done before they arrived. Atlantis was different. Atlantis was a fresh start.

Cross-topped spires dominated Hanover's skyline. Churches here and farther north were Anglican or belonged to one of the sterner Protestant denominations. Officially, New Hastings and points south were also Anglican. Unofficially, Popery thrived there. The southerly English settlements in Atlantis were a lifetime older than the Reformation. Kings had always had trouble enforcing their will here. Sensible sovereigns didn't try too hard. Victor's mouth tightened. George III and his ministers seemed unwilling to stay sensible.

Along with the spires, masts in the harbor reached for the sky. Some of them were as tall as any church steeple. Not only merchantmen lined the quays, but also English frigates and ships of the line. Redcoats garrisoned Hanover. The locals had, and did not enjoy, the privilege of paying for quartering them.

When the travelers rode into town, more English soldiers were on the streets than Victor Radcliff remembered seeing since the war. Then, the redcoats and English Atlanteans fought side by side against France and Spain. They were comrades-in-arms. They were friends.

The redcoats in Hanover neither looked nor acted like friends. Their faces were hard and closed. They carried bayoneted muskets, and stayed in groups. When they went by, locals called insults and curses after them—but only from behind, so the soldiers had a hard time figuring out who'd done it.

Instead of going straight to his printer, Victor called at the house of Erasmus Radcliff, his second cousin once removed. The Discoverer's family had flourished mightily in English Atlantis, and no doubt Radcliffs and Radcliffes and other kinsfolk with different surnames were busy helping to turn what had been French Atlantis upside down and inside out. Erasmus, these days, headed the trading firm William Radcliff had brought to prominence a hundred years before.

He looked like a prosperous merchant: he wore a powdered wig, a velvet jacket the color of claret, and satin breeches. He had manicured hands, an exquisitely shaved face, and a gentleman's paunch. His eyes were a color somewhere between blue, gray, and green, and as warm as the Atlantic off the northern reaches of Iceland.

"Yes, it's very bad," he said as a servant with the map

of Ireland on his face brought in ale and smoked pork for him and Victor—Blaise was taking his refreshments with the house staff. "I always think it can get no worse, and I always find myself mistaken."

"Hanover has not the feel of a garrisoned city, as it did when I was here year before last. It has the feel of an occupied city." Victor raised his mug. "Your health, coz."

"And yours." Erasmus Radcliff returned the compliment. They both drank. Victor praised the ale, which deserved it. Erasmus waved the praise aside. "You would know what occupation feels like, wouldn't you, from your campaigns in the south? Well, by God, here we find ourselves on the wrong end of it. How dare the Crown treat us like so many Frenchmen?" His voice was soft and mild, which only made the indignation crackling in it more alarming.

"We cost England money," Victor answered. "In their way, King George's ministers are merchants, too. They want to see a return on their investment."

"If they so badly want money of us, let them ask our parliaments for it," his cousin said. "London has no more right to wring taxes from Hanover than Hanover has of taxing London: the difference being that we presume not, whereas London does."

"The other difference being that London can put soldiers into Hanover, whereas we cannot garrison London," Victor said dryly. Erasmus Radcliff's response to that was so comprehensive, so heartfelt, and so ingenious that Victor stored it away for future reference. But he asked a blunt question of his own: "Dislike it as you will, coz, but what do you propose to do about it?"

Erasmus sent him a look filled with dislike—and with reluctant respect. "Damn all I *can* do about it, as we both know too well."

"Oh, indeed." Victor Radcliff nodded. "And since we know it, what's the point to so much fussing and fuming?"

"Do you know of the newfangled steam-driven engines they're using in England to pump water out of coal mines?" Erasmus asked. When Victor nodded, his cousin went on, "They have a valve that opens when the pressure from the steam inside grows too great. Absent this valve, the boiler itself would burst. All Atlantis curses England. By cursing, we harmlessly vent our steam. Did we not, this island might explode. Or will you tell me I'm mistaken?"

"I'll tell you you may be," Victor replied. "For 'all Atlantis' does not curse England. Much of Hanover may, but Hanover, however loath you are to hear it, is not Atlantis. It never has been. Please God, may it never be. As things stand, most of Atlantis is content with England, or at least resigned to her. Were it otherwise, the explosion you speak of would have come long since."

His cousin seemed even less happy than he had a moment earlier. Erasmus, Victor judged, didn't care to hear that Hanover and Atlantis weren't synonymous. Few Hanoverians did. *Pity*, Victor thought, *because it's true whether they care to hear it or not.*

"That it has not come does not mean it will not come," Erasmus said at last. "These valves can fail. These steam-driven engines can blow up. I have heard of several such misfortunes. And when they do . . . When they do, Victor, things are never the same afterwards for anyone who chances to stand in the way."

Victor eyed him. Was Erasmus hiding a message there? Victor laughed at himself for even wondering. If Erasmus was hiding a message, he was hiding it in plain sight.

"Way! Make way there!" bawled the teamster atop the brewery wagon. He cracked his whip above the four big, strong horses hauling the cask-filled wain. Then he cracked it again, this time in front of the nose of a man who didn't step aside fast enough to suit him.

The man swore, but flattened himself against the side

of a building nonetheless. He wore a knife on his belt—
who didn't?—but a man with a belt knife was even more
disadvantaged against a bullwhip than against the rapi-
ers some gentlemen still carried to mark their status.
You had to be able to judge when picking a fight made
sense and when it was only foolishness.

Victor Radcliff had stepped to one side as soon as the
teamster started shouting. The heavy wagon clattered
past, iron tires banging and sparking on cobblestones.
Puddles from the last rain lingered between the stones
and in the holes where a few of them had come up. The
wagon wheels splashed passersby, but not too badly.

A sign hanging above a small shop creaked in the
morning breeze. CUSTIS CAWTHORNE, PRINTING AND PER-
SUASIONS, the neatly painted letters proclaimed. The
breeze carried the smells of sea and smoke and sewage:
like any other town, Hanover dumped its waste into the
closest river, for ultimate disposal in the ocean.

Manuscript under his arm, Victor ducked inside. A
bell over the door jangled. The shop was gloomy inside. It smelled of wood and paper and sweat and ink.
A harassed-looking 'prentice fed sheets into a press,
one after another. A printer worked the lever again
and again. Another 'prentice stacked the newly printed
broadsheets.

Custis Cawthorne watched the work from behind the
counter. "There'll be a mistake somewhere," the printer
said mournfully. "There always is. Perfection, they say,
is for the Lord alone. They don't usually know what
they're talking about, but when it comes to printing I'm
persuaded they have a point. . . . And how are you, your
Radcliffishness?"

"I thought I was pretty well, till I set eyes on you,"
Victor replied.

Cawthorne gave back a sepulchral smile. He was tall
and thin and stooped, with a fringe of white hair clinging
to the sides and back of a formidably domed skull. "You
do me too much honor, sir," he said. "Of course, when it

comes to honor I hold with Falstaff, so any honor would be too much. Is that the latest effusion from your goose there under your arm?"

"Maybe I should pluck you for quills next time—you seem prickly enough and to spare," Victor said.

"And here I was going to do *you* an honor." Cawthorne stared reprovingly over the tops of his gold-rimmed spectacles. They were of a curious design he had devised himself. A horizontal line across each lens separated weaker and stronger magnifications, so he could read and see at a distance without changing pairs.

"A likely story," Victor said. "More likely, you were about to set some libel against me in type."

"Oh, any printer from Croydon down to the border of Spanish Atlantis could do that," Custis Cawthorne said dismissively. "But no—I had something new and interesting and perhaps even important to tell you, and did you want to hear it? It is to laugh."

"Go ahead. Say your say," Radcliff replied. He laughed at himself. "Why should I waste my time encouraging you? You'll do as you please anyhow. You always do."

" 'Do what thou wilt'—there is the whole of the law. Or so said a wiser man than I." Cawthorne might have been—probably was—the wisest man in Atlantis. By mentioning someone he reckoned wiser, he reminded his audience of that truth. "Because you make yourself so obnoxious, I ought not to tell you."

"Fais ce que voudrais," said Victor, who also knew his Rabelais.

He surprised the printer into laughter by knowing. To hear Custis Cawthorne guffaw, anyone would think him fat and jolly, not a somber-seeming beanpole. Victor didn't know how he brought forth such a sound from that narrow chest, but he did.

"I shall do exactly that," the printer said after guffaws subsided to chuckles. "Hear me, then. When that indifferently written drivel of yours—"

Victor bowed. "Your servant, sir. Plenty of rope for all the critics to hang themselves." That was from Rabelais, too.

"If you were my servant, I'd thump you the way you deserve. As things are, all of Atlantis has that privilege," Cawthorne said. Before Victor could ask him what he meant, he went on, "Here is the honor I propose giving you: setting your work with the first font of type made on this side of the Atlantic. We not only speak English in Atlantis, we write it and we print it . . . with or without let or hindrance from the so-called mother country."

"So-called?" Victor raised an eyebrow. "Your ancestors did not come from England?"

"There was a Cawthorne aboard the *St. George*, which you know as well as I," the printer said. "But a proper mother knows when her offspring is grown and ready to set out on his own. She does not garrison soldiers on him to keep him from leaving home."

"If I were an Englishman, I would clap you in irons for that," Victor said.

"If you were an Englishman, I would despair of Atlantis," Custis Cawthorne replied. "But since, by the favor of Providence, you are not, I still have some hope for us. And I also have *some* hope of turning your manuscript to print without too much butchery along the way. Multifarious as your flaws may be, you do write a tolerably neat hand."

"I hope you will not do yourself an injury, giving forth with such extravagant praise," Victor said.

"Nothing too serious, anyhow," Cawthorne said. "And a good thing, too, for a visit to the sawbones is likelier to leave a man dead than improved."

He had a point. Doctors could set broken bones and repair dislocations. They could inoculate against smallpox—and, in Atlantis' towns, they did so more and more often. That scourge still reared its hideous head, but less often than in years gone by. Doctors could give opium for pain, and could do something about diarrhea and constipation. Past that, a strong constitution gave you a better chance of staying healthy than all the doctors ever born.

Victor doled out such praise as he could: "They do try."

"And much good it does them, or their sorely tried patients," Cawthorne said.

"Are you done insulting me and physicians?" Victor asked. "Can I make my escape and let you get back to reviling your 'prentices and journeymen?"

"I do less of that than I like these days," Custis Cawthorne answered. "Good workers are hard to find. Even bad workers are hard to find. The good ones would sooner set up for themselves, whilst the bad ones try to squeeze more money out of an honest man than they're worth."

"Did some honest man tell you that?" Radcliff asked innocently.

"Ah! A fellow who fancies himself a wit but overestimates by a factor of two," the printer said. "You had better go, all right, before I thrash you in a transport of fury."

"I'm leaving—and quivering in my boots." The bell rang again as Victor went out onto the street.

Custis Cawthorne's voice pursued him: "If you think you're quivering now, where will you be in five years' time?"

On my farm, working and writing, Victor thought. *I hope.*

"More brandy?" Erasmus Radcliff inquired.

Victor was feeling what he'd already drunk, but he nodded anyway. His cousin poured for both of them with becoming liberality. "Your health," Victor said, a little blurrily.

"And yours." Erasmus drank. "Whew! After the first swallow numbs your gullet, the rest doesn't taste quite so much like turpentine."

"We don't make it as well as they do in Europe," Victor agreed. "But it will leave a man wobbly on his pegs, which is a large part of the point to the exercise. We can live with this."

"You can, perhaps," Erasmus Radcliff said. "I find myself compelled to, which is not the same thing. If England treats us unjustly, our only recourse is to refuse intercourse with her, which keeps us from importing anything finer than this . . . firewater, I believe, is the term they use in Terranova. I could easily trade with France or Holland and once again have a source of fine brandy . . . save that the Royal Navy would impound or sink my ships if I presumed to try. This leaves me with nothing to do, nothing whatsoever."

"What do you want from me? I can't change anything about it," Victor said. "No one in London will listen to me, not to the extent of changing set policies because I ask it. The policy is to squeeze all the revenue England can from Atlantis. It is the same policy England uses wherever she rules."

"Yes, I know, but most places have to put up with it, because they needs must buy some large proportion of their necessities from the mother country," his cousin replied. "That is no longer the case with us. We can subsist on our own, and England pushes us toward demonstrating the fact with every ill-advised tax she tries to ram down our throats." He drained his glass and filled it again. He would be crapulent come morning. Now . . . Now he seemed determined. "What we have here may not always be as good, but we can make do with it."

"I suppose so." Victor also drank more; he couldn't let Erasmus get too far ahead of him. "Custis Cawthorne said he would print my latest from type cast here in Atlantis, not brought from England."

"Yet another example," Erasmus agreed. He paused, then went on, "You do realize that, if my fellow settlers keep me from trading with England whilst the English prevent me from dealing with anyone else, I shall in due course commence to starve?"

Victor Radcliff looked around the well-appointed office where they drank. Whale-oil lamps lit it almost as bright as day. Some strange and almost obscene fetish from the South Pacific shared pride of place in a cabinet of curiosities with a bejeweled elephant from India and the mineralized skull of a long-snouted creature from southern Terranova. None of those would have come easy or cheap. Neither would Erasmus' desk, a triumph of marquetry in multicolored wood.

"I concede the eventuality, coz, but it does not strike me as imminent," Victor said.

"Perhaps not. Then again, I am more fortunate than many in similar straits," Erasmus replied. "Not everyone has so much to fall back on when times get hard."

No sooner were those words out of his mouth than someone started pounding on his front door. The octagonal window in the office rattled in its frame at the insistence of the blows. "That doesn't sound good," Victor said.

"A knock in the nighttime is never good news," his cousin said, and he could only nod.

The pounding stopped as abruptly as it had begun. One of Erasmus' servants brought a plainly dressed man who smelled strongly of horse into the office. "Mr. Mitchell, from Croydon," the servant said. And so it was: Richard Mitchell was a leading goldsmith in the northern town, and a leading light in the struggle to turn Atlantis against the mother country. His pamphlet called *Where Now?* was banned wherever the English could seize it.

"For God's sake, Radcliff, give me a drink," he said. Without a word, Erasmus did. Mitchell, a squat, powerfully built man, gulped it. "Ahh!" He seemed to notice Victor for the first time. "What? You here, too? Just as well! It's started up north."

"What do you mean?" Victor and Erasmus asked together.

"They heard we had guns. They marched to get them. They did, too, or some of them—but we gave them a black eye and a bloody nose in the getting. It's war up there, Radcliffs—war, I tell you! And it will be war here, too, war all through this land, unless you're a pack of spineless poltroons." He slammed down his mug. "Fill it up again! Atlantis and liberty!"

II

$\mathcal{V}$ictor Radcliff looked at the English soldier. The redcoat, standing on a Hanover street corner, glowered back. He carried a flintlock musket; with its long bayonet, it was about as tall as he was. He had pale blue eyes, yellow hair, and pimpled skin almost pink enough to belong to an albino.

Had he known who Victor was, he might have tried to seize him. If the Atlantean settlements had risen against the unloved and unloving mother country, they would need someone to lead their soldiers. Without false modesty, Radcliff knew he had more practice at that than any other man born on this side of the ocean. No doubt some English officers knew it, too, but the knowledge hadn't trickled down to this spotty young fellow.

He just disliked being looked at. "Move along, you," he growled in a clotted, barely comprehensible Northern accent.

"Yes, indeed." Victor touched the brim of his hat. "I never argue with a man with a gun."

"Damned well better not," the redcoat said. Victor thought that was what he said, anyhow; he swallowed so many vowels, it was hard to be sure.

What Blaise swallowed was a chuckle. "Oh, no, you

never argue with men with guns," the Negro said. "Not much, you don't."

"Hush." Victor looked back over his shoulder. To his relief, the redcoat was paying attention to a pretty girl crossing the street, not to him any more. "You don't want to give him ideas. He's liable to come up with them on his own even if you don't."

"Him?" Blaise didn't bother hiding his scorn. "He wouldn't know an idea if it walked up and honked in his face."

By such idioms did the Atlantean distinguish himself from the Englishman. The irony was that honkers had grown rare on this side of the Green Ridge Mountains. The enormous, flightless gooselike birds were, like oil thrushes, unlucky enough to hatch from the egg without fear of man. As settlers advanced, honkers retreated: or rather, they died in place, and their haunts grew ever scarcer and more remote.

Custis Cawthorne had written a pamphlet arguing that land should be set aside so honkers and other native productions of Atlantis could have somewhere to survive. It struck Victor as a good idea; most of Custis Cawthorne's ideas were good. That didn't mean it was likely to happen. People wanted to grab land, not set it aside for anything.

Somebody shouted from a second- or third-story window: "The Devil fry all murdering English dogs!"

"There! There he is!" Victor might not have known just where that cry came from, but the young English soldier pointed like a hunting dog. At *his* shout, four more redcoats charged out of an eatery. When they saw where he was pointing, they rushed in.

A pistol shot rang out. Other gunshots answered it. A redcoat lurched from the building, right hand clutched to left shoulder. Blood welled out from between his fingers, brighter than the dyed wool of his coat.

More gunshots boomed. Victor heard the crash of breaking furniture and several voices high and shrill with pain and fury. A couple of minutes later, the other three redcoats came out dragging a wounded local. The man was bloodied and battered, but he had no quit in him. His head came up. "Atlantis and freedom!" he called in a great voice.

One of the redcoats hit him in the face. "Shut up, you bloody big-mouthed bastard!"

"Shame!" a woman screeched.

"Atlantis and freedom!" the prisoner cried again.

This time, the English soldier clouted him with his musket butt. The local went limp in the other redcoats' arms. "Shame!" the woman said again.

"Maybe you'd better let him go," a bareheaded, shock-haired 'prentice said, his hands balling into fists.

"Maybe you'd better bugger off, sonny," a redcoat answered. He had a corporal's stripes on his sleeve and a scarred, weasely face that warned he'd give trouble no matter the mess in which he found himself.

"Maybe I'd better not." The 'prentice set his feet. Several other Atlanteans ranged themselves behind him.

More English soldiers came out of the cookshop. The sun glittered off the sharp edges of their bayonets. "Last chance, boy," the corporal said, not unkindly. "Otherwise, we'll stick you and we'll gut you and you'll end up dead never knowing why."

"What do we do?" Blaise asked in a low voice.

"Try to keep the town from blowing up," Victor answered. "The time's not ripe."

No matter what he thought, his opinion turned out not to be the one that counted. One of the men behind the bushy-haired 'prentice stooped to grub a cobblestone out of the ground. He flung it at the redcoats. It caught a soldier in the ribs. He said "Oof!" and then "Ow!" and then "Fuck your bleedin' mother!"

A split second after the curse passed the redcoat's lips, muskets leveled at the crowd of Atlanteans. "Fire!" the corporal shouted. Triggers clicked. Descending hammers scraped flints on steel. Sparks fell into flash pans. The guns bellowed, sending up clouds of acrid gunpowder smoke.

Most of them bellowed, anyhow: flintlocks were imperfectly reliable. The English soldiery's muskets were also imperfectly accurate. Some of the shots went wide; one of them shattered a window well off to the side of the crowd. But men screamed. Men fell.

And men who didn't scream or fall hurled more stones at the redcoats. One of them had a pistol, which he discharged. The ball hit the weasely corporal in the arm. What he said made the other soldier's obscenity sound like an endearment.

The sound of gunfire brought more redcoats at the run. More Atlanteans boiled out of houses and shops. The two sides hurried towards each other like lodestone and iron. The Englishmen had discipline and firearms and bayonets. The Atlanteans had fury and whatever makeshift weapons they could snatch up and numbers. The fury kept them from fleeing when the redcoats shot and stuck some of them. What the Atlanteans did to a couple of redcoats they managed to grab ...

A paving stone sailed past Victor Radcliff's head. He ducked, as automatically and uselessly as a man did when a musket ball came too close for comfort. If it was going to hit you, it would before you could do a damned thing about it.

There were fights to join and fights to stay away from. This struck Victor as a fight to stay away from. He'd faced more dangerous enemies with qualms no worse than those of any reasonably brave man. When he had, though, he'd done it with some purpose in mind. If this mêlée had any point at all, he couldn't see it.

He pulled Blaise into a narrow, stinking alley. He didn't know where it went, but it led away from the madness that had kindled here. "They are liable to tear this whole big place down," Blaise said mournfully.

"That they are," Victor agreed. "They're liable to tear Atlantis apart while they're doing it, too."

"What can we do?" the Negro asked.

"Get away. Live through this. See what happens next. Try to shape what happens next. Have you got any better ideas? If you have, spit 'em out, by God. I'd love to hear 'em."

But Blaise shook his head. "If we gonna get away, we better do it right now," he said. That struck Victor as one of the best ideas he'd heard in a long time. The two of them wasted not a moment using it.

Hanover writhed under martial law. The redcoats strode through the streets by squads. When they went by ones or twos, or even by fours or fives, they were much too apt to be mobbed. Rocks and crockery and the contents of chamber pots came flying out of upper-story windows.

Blaise had already escaped the city. He and Victor had gone their separate ways precisely because they were known to stick together. Blaise had got away clean. Victor'd expected nothing less. Englishmen—Atlanteans, too—had trouble taking black men seriously.

And now it was time for Victor to get away himself, if he could. Coming into Hanover, he'd worn the clothes of a prosperous farmer, which he was. Leaving the city, he was by all appearances a down-at-the-heels shoemaker. He even rode a swaybacked nag, the kind of horse such a man would have if he had any horse at all.

The English had checkpoints west of Hanover. They also had men scattered between the checkpoints. If you got caught trying to sneak out, you landed in real trouble. Things at the checkpoints were supposed to come closer to routine.

They'd better, Victor thought. Up ahead of him, the redcoats were searching a fat man's carriage. The fat man didn't like it, and let them know he didn't. "I'm a loyal subject of good King George! It's not right for you to treat me like a common criminal," he said.

"Everybody's a loyal subject ... when he talks to us," said the underofficer in charge. "Find anything, Charles?"

"No, Sergeant. He's not a smuggler, anyhow," said a soldier, presumably Charles. "Do we strip him to his drawers?"

"No. I expect he's clean." The sergeant nodded to the fat man. "Pass on, you."

"Strip me to my drawers?" the fat man spluttered. "You'll win few friends playing such games."

"And do you think we care?" the sergeant said. "If you settlers weren't in revolt, we wouldn't have to worry about keeping you from sneaking guns out of Hanover. If you haven't got guns, who cares if you're friendly or not? Now get going, or we *will* find out if your linen's clean."

Still spluttering, the fat man rolled on. The soldier called Charles gestured Victor Radcliff forward. "And who are you, friend?" he asked.

No friend of yours, Victor thought. "My name is Richard Saunders," he replied. Some Radcliffs and Radcliffes favored the English; the clan was too large to have uniform opinions. But if the redcoats knew they had hold of Victor Radcliff, they'd never let him go.

"Well, Saunders, what are you doing coming out of Hanover?" the sergeant asked. "Where are you bound?"

"I'm heading for Hooville," Victor answered, which was true, although he wouldn't stop there. Then he blossomed into invention: "I was seeing my solicitor. My uncle just died childless, and looks like I'll have to go to law with my cousins over his property and estate." He tried to seem suitably disgusted.

The sergeant and Charles and the rest of the redcoats put their heads together. "Are you loyal to his Majesty, King George III?" the underofficer demanded fiercely.

"Of course I am." Victor lied without compunction. As the redcoat had said to the fat man, who would tell George's soldiers no?

And the English soldiers' crooked grins said they understood the likely reason for his answer. "Then you won't mind if we search you?" the sergeant asked.

"Yes, I'll mind," Victor said. "Not much I can do about it past minding, though, is there?"

"Too right there's not, friend." Charles used the last

word to suggest anything but its literal meaning. "Why don't you get down from that sorry piece of crowbait you're riding?"

"Sam's a good horse," Victor protested. The redcoats laughed. In their boots, he would have laughed, too.

They patted him down and looked inside his saddle bags. They found nothing to make them suspicious—Victor wanted to look as harmless as he could. The sergeant still seemed unhappy. "You've fought in war," he said, and it wasn't quite a question.

Victor nodded. "I fought the French here, back about the time your beard sprouted."

The English underofficer scratched at a side whisker. "We were on the same side then, England and Atlantis."

"I am on England's side still," Victor Radcliff said once more.

"Yes, of course you are." The sergeant didn't believe it, not for a second. But he had no real reason to disbelieve it, no proof Radcliff was anything but what he claimed. He looked unhappy, but he jerked a thumb toward the swaybacked horse. "Climb on your old screw and get out of here."

"Obliged." Victor pretended not to notice his reservations. When he mounted Sam, the deep curve in the horse's spine left the stirrups only a few inches above the ground. He pressed his knees against the animal's sides and flicked the reins. Away Sam went. He'd get where he was going, but he wouldn't do it in a hurry.

Don't look over your shoulder, Victor told himself. He didn't want to give the redcoats any more chances to see his face. Sam ambled along. The soldiers could still call him back. They could, but they didn't. The road swung around behind a stand of native pines. Only then did Victor breathe easier.

He was riding a better horse by the time he came to Hooville. Someone took Sam back to the farm where he'd labored for a lot of years. Maybe his role in helping Victor escape Hanover would be celebrated in songs and paintings in years to come. He couldn't have cared less. All he got out of it were a couple of carrots.

Blaise waited in Hooville. "Good to see you," he said when Victor rode in. "I wasn't sure I was going to."

"Well, neither was I," Victor said. "But here I am. They didn't know they had me in their hands, and now they don't, and so they won't."

"Custis Cawthorne is loose, too. He's on his way to New Hastings," Blaise said.

"Good for him—and that's the right place for him to go, too," Radcliff said. New Hastings held fewer loyalists than any other town in English Atlantis. Other places might be noisier in their disapproval of the mother country, but it ran deeper and wider there than anywhere else.

"Not everybody's going to get away, though. The redcoats do hold Hanover," Blaise said. "What can we do?"

"Right now? I don't quite know. If this is truly war . . ." Victor Radcliff no doubt looked as unhappy as he sounded. If this was truly war, Atlantis stood alone against the mightiest empire in the world. "If this is war, I see only one advantage on our side."

Blaise raised an eyebrow. "Well, that's one more than I see."

"Oh, we've got one." Victor waved to the barmaid for another mug of flip. He'd drunk enough that he should have felt it, but he didn't, or not very much. As she set the mug in front of him, he went on, "We're a long way from England. She can't move quickly against us, and she won't find it easy or cheap to ship soldiers across the sea."

After a moment's consideration, Blaise said, "Huzzah."

Victor wondered whether the Negro had been so sardonic in the African jungles where he grew up, or whether Blaise had learned it from him. If the latter was true, as he feared, then he had a lot to answer for. Sar-

donic or not, the Negro had a point with his sour accla-
mation. Atlantis had merchantmen and fishing boats to
oppose the Royal Navy, farmers to face professional soldiers. She was short of gunpowder, and even shorter of
firearms. And she was short of people—and how many
of the ones she had would take England's side?

"What will the French down south do?" Blaise
asked.

"Good question," Radcliff said. French Atlantis had
passed under English rule only a dozen years before.
Since then, the more numerous English-speakers had
flooded into lands formerly barred to them. Would the
older settlers rise against King George, or against the
interlopers disrupting their way of life?

"Have you got an answer?" Blaise seemed surprised
to discover his mug of flip was also empty. He waved for
a refill, too.

"Only *We'll have to see*," Victor replied.

The barmaid didn't come back for Blaise as fast as
she had for Victor. Was that because he was servant, not
master? Because he was black, not white? Or only because she had other orders to fill first? Sometimes you
could read too much into things that in fact carried no
great meaning. Sometimes you could miss meanings in
things that seemed ordinary at first.

Blaise brushed two fingers of his right hand against
the dark skin of his left forearm. Victor had seen Negroes use that gesture before. It meant, *You did that because of my color*. His factotum knew what he thought,
then. And he knew what he thought of Victor's comment
as well: "Is that good enough?"

"No," Victor said honestly. "But it's what we've got."

When he came to his farm, he found a delegation from
the Atlantean Assembly waiting for him. The settlements had tried protesting to England one by one, only
to learn that the mother country didn't want to listen to
them. Then they'd all joined together, thinking Atlantis

might be heard if only it spoke with a single voice. Thus far, the evidence was against them.

Isaac Fenner had red hair and ears that stuck out from the sides of his head like open doors. He was a solicitor from Bredestown, a few miles up the Brede from New Hastings, and spoke for the older city as well.

Matthew Radcliffe, from Avalon on the west coast, was bound to be some sort of cousin of Victor's, but neither had set eyes on the other before this meeting. The westerner was short and stocky; he looked travel worn. One of the farm cats had taken a liking to him and fallen asleep on his lap. He absently stroked its back while sipping rum punch.

Everyone called Robert Smith, from Croydon in the north, Uncle Bobby. He'd carried the name since he was young. Victor didn't know why; he wondered if Smith did himself. Uncle Bobby was also drinking rum punch, with the single-minded diligence of a man who needed it.

From the south came two men: Abednego Higgins and Michel du Guesclin. Maybe Higgins stood for the English-speakers down there and du Guesclin for the Frenchmen, or maybe things had just worked out that way. They were both very tall, the one broad-shouldered, the other slim as a rapier. Du Guesclin, Victor knew, was somehow connected to the Kersauzon family, as prominent down there as Radcliffs and Radcliffes were in English Atlantis.

As soon as Victor came inside and saw them, Margaret said, "They want to talk to you."

"Well, I expected they could find rum and something to mix it with somewhere closer than here," he answered.

His wife sent him an exasperated look. "No. They want to talk to you about something important."

"I was afraid they did." Victor Radcliff was also afraid he knew what the gentlemen of the Atlantean Assembly wanted.

"You aren't going to throw them out?" Despite the way Meg said it, it wasn't really a question.

Victor sighed. "No, I suppose not." As if in ironic counterpoint to that, Matthew Radcliffe raised his mug in salute. Abednego Higgins tossed a well-gnawed chicken bone onto the platter from which he'd taken it when it was meatier. The gentlemen from the Assembly did not expect to be sent on their way. With another sigh, Victor stepped past his wife and nodded to them. "Hello, my friends," he said, wondering how big a lie he was telling.

Radcliffe from Avalon raised his mug again. Du Guesclin, full of French politesse, bowed in his seat. Uncle Bobby grabbed the bull by the horns, saying, "Do you recall what the Discoverer did when the Black Earl tried to tax him without his leave?"

"Yes, I recall," Victor answered. Every schoolchild in English Atlantis knew what Edward Radcliffe had done when the exiled Richard Neville, Earl of Warwick, tried to set himself up as king in Atlantis. What had happened then helped shape Atlantean history for the three hundred years between that day and this.

But Robert Smith went on as if Victor hadn't spoken: "He died, that's what he did. He died fighting tyranny, and his sons put it down for good." That was the story schoolboys learned. Some people said what had actually happened was more complicated. Victor Radcliff didn't know; he hadn't been in New Hastings back in 1470.

Isaac Fenner was descended from the first man to die in Atlantis (and, if some tales were true, from the girl the Black Earl had taken as his bedwarmer, maybe even from Neville himself). He said, "The damned Englishmen still haven't learned their lesson. They think they can tax us as they please. Do we let them get away with that? Do we let them make us into slaves?"

Both du Guesclin and Higgins shook their heads at that rhetorical question. They owned slaves: copperskins from Terranova to the west and Negroes like Blaise brought in to do hard work in a climate not well suited to white men. Maybe that gave them extra cause not to want to be enslaved themselves. Maybe it meant they feared their own bondsmen would rise against them given even half a chance. Maybe they had reason for such fears.

"We are in arms around Hanover—you've seen that for yourself, Radcliff," Uncle Bobby said. "And we are in arms in Croydon, too. We rose before Hanover did." He spoke with a northerner's pride: doing anything ahead of Hanover and New Hastings mattered a lot up there.

"What has this got to do with me?" Victor asked, much in the way, almost eighteen centuries before, Jesus had said, *If it be possible, let this cup pass from me: nevertheless, not as I will, but as thou wilt.* Jesus must have known it wouldn't be possible. And, in the same way, Victor knew what it had to do with him. If Jesus could hesitate, he thought he was entitled to do the same.

Now Smith spoke as to a child: "We are at war with England, Victor. The settlements have armies. We need to join them into one army, into an Atlantean army. We need a man under whom they will be glad to combine, a man who can command them. Who else but you?"

During the war against French Atlantis, France, and Spain, Victor had been the highest-ranking Atlantean soldier fighting alongside the redcoats he was now expected to oppose. Wasn't one war enough for one man? "I should sooner stay here on my farm and live as an ordinary private person," he said.

As if activated by some clockwork mechanism, the delegates from the Atlantean Assembly shook their heads in unison. "If you sit on your hands here, we'll lose," Abednego Higgins said bluntly.

"Il a raison," Michel du Guesclin agreed. He continued in accented English: "I can think of no other English man the French of the south will follow."

"Do you want to let the Discoverer down?" Matthew Radcliffe added. "If we lose this fight, England will do to Atlantis what the Black Earl, damn him, tried to do to New Hastings. Come on, coz! Isn't fighting those bastards from across the sea in your blood?"

In the last war, the men from across the sea had been allies, and vital allies at that. They hadn't sought to ram taxes down the Atlanteans' throats, not then. Afterwards, though ... Afterwards was another story, as afterwards so often was.

Up until a little more than a century before, Avalon had been a pirates' roost. Did Matthew Radcliffe carry some of the freebooters' blood in his veins? Victor wouldn't have been surprised. His distant kinsman certainly seemed ready, even eager, to brawl.

"This won't be the Battle of the Strand, one fight and it's over," Victor warned. "This will be a war like the last one—worse than the last one, unless I miss my guess. England won't want to let us go our own way."

"No. She wants us to go her way, and she aims to drag us along if we don't care to follow on our own," Isaac Fenner said. "Is that what you have in mind for Atlantis till the end of time, Radcliff? Is that why your forefathers first took folk away from the greedy kings and nobles on the other side of the sea?"

There were days when Victor Radcliff wished he sprang from a less illustrious family. This was one of those days. People expected things from him because of who his forefathers were. He could have done without the compliment, if it was one.

"England is the greatest kingdom in Europe. England is the richest empire in the world," he said. "Even if she runs short of her own soldiers, she can buy poor men from the German princes to do her fighting for her. We are ... what we are. Can we fight her and hope to win?"

"Can we bend the knee to her and look at ourselves in the glass afterwards?" Matthew Radcliffe returned. "You are our best hope, coz, but you are not our only hope. We aim to fight with you or without you."

"Chances with you are better than without you, though," du Guesclin said.

"They are," Abednego Higgins agreed. "We need a general we can all respect. If anybody in Atlantis fills the bill, you're the man."

I've never been a general. The protest died before Victor let it out. What Atlantean had? He'd led a good-sized force of soldiers in the field, which put him one up on almost everyone else who opposed England.

"You gentlemen are mad," he said: one last protest.

Uncle Bobby stood up from his chair to bow. "We are, sir. We are," he agreed. "But it's a grand madness. Will you join us in it?"

Victor looked around. He'd been comfortable here ever since coming home from the war against France and Spain. He'd wanted to live out the rest of his days as a gentleman farmer, not as a man of war. But, if Atlantis called on him, what could he do but answer the call?

He sighed. "Join you I will. I note that it was our idea, not mine. May none of us ever have cause to regret it."

"Oh, I expect we will, sooner or later—probably sooner." Abednego Higgins was a man of melancholy temperament. Victor wasn't, or not especially, but he suspected the same thing.

But then all five men from the Atlantean Assembly crowded around him, pumping his hand and slapping his back and telling him what a lion, what a hero, he was. If he'd believed a quarter of what they told him, he would have been sure he could run every redcoat out of Atlantis by day after tomorrow at the latest.

Fortunately—or, odds were, unfortunately—he knew better.

News from the east came slowly. That was one of the reasons Victor Radcliff had settled where he did. More often than not, he was happier not knowing. His livelihood didn't depend on hearing things before other people could.

If he was going to take up the sword again, though . . . "Must you do this?" Margaret asked. She hadn't wanted him going off to fight the French Atlanteans and their overseas reinforcements, either, and they weren't even married then.

"If I don't, someone else will—and worse," he said. "The settlements are going to rise up against England. No, they've already risen up, and they won't quiet down till they win or till they're too beaten to fight any more. The redcoats have pulled out of New Hastings."

The redcoats had pulled out of New Hastings more than two weeks before. He'd only just got the news. That was one of the reasons he needed to travel east. Farming might not depend on the latest news. War did.

"What difference does it make to you whether King George orders Atlantis about or we make our own mistakes?" his wife demanded.

"I don't want anyone across the sea telling me how many pounds I owe on this farm," Victor said. "If some Englishman can do that, he can take it away from me, too."

"So can a honker from New Hastings," Meg retorted. Properly speaking, only people from New Hastings (and perhaps Bredestown) were honkers. Englishmen were in the habit of using the name for—or against—anybody from Atlantis.

"At least I have some say in what those people decide," Victor said. "London won't pay attention to me. London never pays attention to Atlantis, not unless someone else is trying to take it away . . . or unless Parliament decides it needs to squeeze money from us."

"Whether London takes it or we do, the money's gone," Margaret said.

Victor grunted. "I should like some choice in where it goes. London will use it to pay fat, sweating soldiers to tyrannize over us. Whereas if we spend it ourselves, we'll—"

"Use it to pay fat, sweating soldiers to keep England from tyrannizing us," his wife broke in.

He stared at her. Such sarcastic gibes were usually his province. He couldn't even tell her she was wrong, because she was much too likely to be right. If Atlantis was to cast off the mother country's yoke, it would need to assume the trappings of other nations. He said the most he felt he could say: "They'll be *our* soldiers, not redcoats or those German barbarians from Brunswick and Hesse and God knows where."

"Oh, hurrah," Meg said. "Do you think they'll come cheaper on account of that?" He didn't answer, mostly because he thought no such thing. Understanding as much, Meg gave him a knowing nod. "I see."

"What would you have me do?" Victor asked. "Tell the gentlemen of the Atlantean Assembly that I've changed my mind and will not fight for them? They will carry on regardless, the only difference being the greater likelihood of their defeat and our subjection."

"I would have you—" Margaret Radcliff broke off, tears filling her eyes. "What I would have you do doesn't matter. The only thing that matters is what Atlantis would have you do. Atlantis would have you carry on till you catch a musket ball in your teeth, and then proclaim you a fallen hero to rally more fools to the cause."

Again, she was much too likely to know what she was talking about. As patiently and calmly as he could, Victor said, "I don't intend to get shot, Meg."

"Who does?" she retorted. "But the graveyards fill up even so. *Died for his country, much too young*, the tombstones say. I want you to live for your country."

"If you think I want anything else, you are very much mistaken," Victor said. "But Atlantis is my country. Shall I pretend I have not got one, or that I care not who rules here?"

"No-o-o," Meg said slowly, in a way that could mean nothing but *yes*. Then she sighed a wintry sigh. "It may be necessary, Victor, but that makes it no easier for me."

"I'm sorry. By God, I *am* sorry. I wish England weren't doing any of this. I'd like nothing better than to live here in peace and bring in my crops every fall," Victor said. "But life gives what it gives, not what you like."

He wished he could talk about passing the land down to their children. To say anything along those lines, though, would only dredge up pain older and deeper than any about his marching off to war. Losing children young was hard on men, but harder on the women who bore them.

They both knew how the argument would end. He would leave the farm and lead whatever armies the Atlantean Assembly scraped together against the ferocious professionals from the mother country. He'd served with those professionals in the war against the French Atlanteans and France and Spain. He knew their virtue, their unflinching courage, their skill. Fighting alongside such men was a pleasure. Fighting against them would be anything but.

He rode out the next morning. Meg saw him off, biting her lip and blinking against more tears. Blaise's wife seemed no more enthusiastic about his military venture.

Once out of reach of the farmhouse, Victor asked, "Did you have fun getting ready to go on your way?"

"Fun?" Blaise rolled his eyes. "I don't know if I would call it that. Stella wanted me to stay right where I was. You know how women are."

"I have some idea, anyhow," Victor said. "I'd better, after all these years. But the thing needs trying. I don't believe anyone can do it better than I can, and you will help me a great deal. Even with you, I do not know if it can be done. I do know it would be harder without you."

"I thank you," Blaise said. "I tried to explain this to Stella. 'He needs someone to take care of him,' I said. 'No one can do that better than I can,' I told her. She did not want to listen to me. Not even when I talked about freeing the colored folk down in the old French settlements did she want to hear me."

Victor Radcliff grunted uneasily. Freedom from England for the white man was one thing. Freedom from the white man for the black was something else again. *One thing at a time*, Victor thought, and rode on.

III

*N*ew Hastings struck Victor as old. The first English settlement in Atlantis had more than three hundred years of history behind it now. Next to London or Paris, Rome or Athens, that was but the blink of an eye. Next to anywhere else on this side of the Atlantic, it seemed as one with the Pyramids and the Sphinx.

The church and some of the buildings nearby dated from the fifteenth century. The church had originally been Catholic, of course. How could it have been anything else, dating as it did from before the Reformation? Anglicanism and sterner Protestant sects predominated in Atlantis these days, but not to the extent they did on the other side of the ocean. England had needed many years to take a firm grip on these settlements. Now, wanting to make it firmer yet, she had a war on her hands.

Soldiers' encampments dotted the fields outside of town. The men in them wore whatever they would have worn at home. They carried whatever muskets they happened to own. None but a few veterans of the fight against French Atlantis had the faintest conception of military discipline. But they were there—till the terms for which they'd enlisted ran out, anyhow.

And they were enthusiastic. They cheered Victor whenever he showed himself among them. They fought under a crazy variety of flags: some showed honkers, others fierce red-crested eagles. Real honkers and the eagles that preyed on them—and on men—were rare almost to extinction in this long-settled part of Atlantis. They were growing scarcer everywhere, from what Victor had heard.

That was the least of his worries. Turning enthusiastic militiamen into real soldiers was a bigger one. Keeping those militiamen fed well enough to fight might have been a bigger one yet. And dealing with the Atlantean Assembly towered over all of the others.

It was, Victor supposed, as close to a native government as Atlantis had. But it wasn't very close. Atlanteans had never liked being governed: that was one of the reasons they or their ancestors came to Atlantis in the first place. It was one of the reasons they fought England now. And it was one of the reasons the Assembly was what it was and wasn't anything more.

It couldn't tax. It could ask the settlements for money to support it and what it did, but couldn't compel them to give it any. It decided things by two-thirds majority vote. If fewer than two-thirds of the settlements voted in favor of any measure, it failed. If two-thirds or more did vote for it, it passed—but still wasn't binding on the settlements whose delegations voted no. It wasn't quite the Polish *liberum veto*—but it wasn't far removed, either.

With an organization like that, the Atlantean settlements seriously proposed to beat the greatest empire the world had seen since Roman days. That struck Victor as madness—a glorious madness, maybe, but madness even so.

It struck Blaise the same way. "You know the English, they are going to fight," he said when he and Victor got settled into their room at an inn not far from the old redwood church.

"Well, yes," Victor agreed, splashing water from the basin onto his hands and face. Whiskers rasped under his chin. He hadn't shaved coming down from his farm.

Unless he was going to grow a beard—something only frontiersmen did in Atlantis—he needed to take care of that. He went on, "We wouldn't have come here if they were just going to sail away."

"But this Atlantean Assembly ... This militia ..." Blaise's African accent made the words sound faintly ridiculous. By the way he shook his head, that was the least of how he felt about them. "They are a *joke*. If they had to decide to go to the privy, they would shit themselves halfway there."

Victor snorted, not because he thought the Negro was wrong but because he thought Blaise was right. "They're what Atlantis has," he said.

"I know," Blaise replied. "This is what worries me. Maybe you should go home and not tell the English you were ever here."

"Too late for that," Victor Radcliff said. "We are going to fight them. The way things are, we cannot avoid fighting them. We have a better chance if I do what I can than if I don't. I had to explain all this to my wife before we set out."

"I know," Blaise said again. "I had to explain to my wife, too. I know what England has. Now I see what we have. I think I was a fool." He didn't say he thought Victor was a fool; that would have been rude. Whether he thought it or not was a different question.

"No one is keeping you here against your will. You were a slave in French Atlantis. You are no man's slave now—certainly not mine," Victor said. "If you do not care to be here, you may leave. You may surrender to the English and tell them everything you know. Chances are they'll make you an officer if you do."

"Thank you, but no," Blaise replied with dignity. "Atlantis is my land, too, now. I do not want to leave it. My roots here are not as old as yours, but they are firm. I want to make this place better if I can."

Victor Radcliff held out his hand. "In that we are certainly agreed." Blaise clasped hands with him.

*　　　*　　　*

The Atlantean Assembly met in the church, it being the building in New Hastings best suited to containing their number. On Sundays, most of the Assemblymen worshiped there. Some few, from New Hastings and points south, were of the Romish persuasion, and found other ways and places to commune with God as they saw fit. And from Croydon in the north came Benjamin Benveniste, the Assembly's one and only Jew.

Some people said he was the richest man in Atlantis. Others, more conservative, called him the richest man not a Radcliff or Radcliffe. Benveniste would always laugh and deny everything. Victor didn't know if the Jew was wealthier than some of his own merchant kinsmen. He was sure Benveniste had more money than he did himself.

"What difference does it make?" Benveniste replied when another Assemblyman asked him just how rich he was. "The more I have, the more others think they can take from me. Wealth is a burden, nothing less."

The other Assemblyman was from New Grinstead, a backwoods town with not much wealth and not much else. Wistfully, he said, "I'd be a donkey if it meant I could carry more."

"Chasing money too hard will make an ass of anyone," Benjamin Benveniste said—a shot close to the center of the target.

"Well, what does that make you?" the other Assemblyman said.

Benveniste sent him a hooded glance. "A patriot, sir—if you will let me be."

"We have room for everyone here," Custis Cawthorne said before the man from the backwoods could reply. "Why, look at me—they have even made room for a scurrilous printer. Next to that, what does it matter if you're Christian or Jew or Mahometan?"

Plainly, several people thought it did matter. None of them felt like antagonizing Cawthorne, though—he could be as scurrilous in oral debate as he was when setting type.

"I am able to care for myself, Custis," Benveniste said.

"I didn't do it for you." Cawthorne sounded surprised. "I did it for Atlantis."

"Ah." The Jew nodded. "Well, that I have no trouble with."

By easy stages, the debate drifted around toward formally appointing Victor Radcliff commander of the Atlantean forces in arms against the British Empire. Nothing the Atlantean Assembly did seemed to move very fast. When men from all the settlements came together to protest to the mother country, that was one thing. When they aimed to conduct a war against that mother country, it was liable to be something else again.

Victor wondered if telling the Assemblymen as much would do any good. He decided it would only put their backs up. He would have to work with them for—how long? Till the war was over, one way or the other. If it was the other . . .

"We have to win," Custis Cawthorne said. "If we lose, they will hang us *pour encourager les autres*. Do I say that correctly, *Monsieur* du Guesclin?"

"If you mean it ironically, then yes," replied the man from what had been French Atlantis. "Otherwise, you would do better to say *pour décourager les autres*."

"Getting my neck stretched would certainly discourage *me*," Cawthorne said, "but I was alluding to the eminent Voltaire's remarks about the reason why the English hanged Admiral Byng."

Several Assemblymen smiled and nodded. So did Victor Radcliff, who admired Voltaire's trenchant wit. But a storm cloud passed across Michel du Guesclin's darkly handsome features. "Speak to me not of that man, if you would be so kind. He believes not in God nor in the holy Catholic Church."

"Look around you, *Monsieur*," Cawthorne advised, not unkindly. "I will not speak of any man's belief in God save my own, and then only with reluctance, but you will find precious few of Romish opinions here in New Hastings."

"Oh, I understand that. But you are Protestants from the cradle, and so I can partly forgive your views since you know no better," du Guesclin said with what was no doubt intended for magnanimity. "This thing of a Voltaire, however, knows and, knowing, rejects. For this he is far worse. God will have somewhat to say to him when he is called to account."

"He may render unto God the things that are God's," Cawthorne said. "What we're engaged in doing here is ciphering out how not to render unto Caesar the things Caesar thinks are his." He turned and nodded to Victor. "How do we best go about that, General Radcliff?"

How many men had gone from major to general while skipping all the ranks in between? Victor couldn't think of many. But Cawthorne's question would have perplexed a man who'd held every one of those ranks—Victor was sure of it. "I have no detailed answer for you, sir, not knowing what the enemy will attempt," he said. "In general, we should do our best to keep him from holding and occupying our leading towns, and not allow him to split Atlantis so he can defeat in detail our forces in the various parts."

"As always, the Devil is in the detail." Cawthorne's eyes twinkled behind his spectacles, so that he looked like a skeleton pleased with itself. Several Atlantean Assemblymen groaned or flinched at the pun; those who'd missed it looked puzzled. Still smiling slightly, Cawthorne went on, "And they are now strongest at Hanover?"

"Yes, and at Croydon," Victor Radcliff replied. "We must do everything in our power to keep their two armies from joining forces."

"That seems sensible," the escaped printer said. "Nevertheless, we will try not to hold it against you."

Before Victor had to respond to that, Matthew Radcliffe asked him, "How do you view the situation in the west?"

"Through a glass, darkly," Victor told his distant

cousin. A ripple of laughter ran through the Assembly. He wondered why; he meant it. "I have visited Avalon and New Marseille only once—most of my life has passed on this side of the Green Ridge Mountains, as you well know. I understand the importance of holding all we can there, but I would be lying if I said I had any certainty as to ways and means."

An Assemblyman he didn't know said, "It sounds as though we have too much to do and not enough to do it with."

It sounded that way to Victor, too. Admitting as much would probably result in the army of the National Assembly getting a new commander on the instant. With a shrug, he replied, "Sir, I can but promise my best effort and full dedication to victory. I do not believe it will come swiftly. Anyone who does, in my view, has charged his brier with something stronger than pipeweed." He got another laugh for something he didn't intend as a joke.

After more questions and more back-and-forth among the illustrious Assemblymen—they all thought they were, anyhow—they finally got around to calling the question. No one voted against putting Victor in charge of their makeshift army, although several Assemblymen abstained. If things went wrong later, they could say it wasn't their fault.

If things went wrong later, chances were what they said wouldn't matter a farthing's worth.

Somewhere close to two thousand men had gathered outside of New Hastings. Victor's first order of business was to give them the rudiments of drill, so they could—with luck—perform as an army, not a mob. Veterans from the war against French Atlantis had some notion of marching and countermarching and deploying from column to line and other such mysteries.

Understanding them well enough to teach them to men who had no notion they existed, though . . . In the whole encampment, Victor found two men he trusted with the job. One was a deserter from the redcoats, a barrel-chested sergeant who'd fallen in love with an Atlantean barmaid and changed sides because of her. Tim Knox had a manner that brooked no argument and a voice that carried halfway to Hanover.

The other drillmaster was Blaise.

A few people objected to taking orders from a Negro. Victor had seen that in the last war, too. After Blaise knocked the stuffing out of a couple of the grumblers, the rest of the men stopped complaining. Blaise took it all in stride. "In Africa, my clan wouldn't want to do what a white man said, either," he remarked.

"Had you ever seen a white man before you were brought to the coast and sold?" Victor asked him.

"Once. A trader. He died of a fever in our village," Blaise said. "We took what he had—iron needles and little shears and the like. The women were so happy!" He smiled at the memory.

"Poor trader wasn't," Victor Radcliff said.

"True." Blaise nodded. "You white men have learned all sorts of tricks we don't know: everything from those good needles—ours are bone, and not so slender—to books and guns and ships. But you have not got the trick of staying healthy in our country."

Radcliff had heard the same thing from men who dealt in slaves off the African coast. They'd sounded irked, not—relieved?—the way Blaise did. Victor had another question for Blaise, one that mattered more than how Africans thought about white men: "Are we ever going to make soldiers out of these militiamen?"

"Maybe," Blaise said. "Chances are, about the time their enlistments run out."

"Ha!" Victor said, not that Blaise was kidding. Since the war that swallowed French Atlantis, militias had sadly decayed. There was no one left to fight—the Spaniards in the south weren't going to cause trouble, so why worry about drilling? Unless Hanover went to war with New Hastings, people in Atlantis could live in peace, and they did.

And, because they did, most of them didn't know the first thing about soldiering. Even the young men who took up arms against England weren't thrilled about learning, either.

"Do the best you can, that's all," Victor said. "If we can keep our armies in the field for a while—and if we can keep the same people in them—the men will pick up what they have to know."

"If we can't, we lose," Blaise said.

Radcliff nodded. "I know. I figured that out, too. Quite a few people in the Atlantean Assembly haven't yet."

"But they are supposed to be the smartest men in Atlantis," Blaise said.

"So they are," Victor agreed. "And if that isn't a judgment on all of us, I don't know what would be. One more thing, too." He waited till the Negro made a questioning noise, then went on, "In their infinite wisdom, they're the ones who chose me for chief general. Makes you wonder, eh?"

Blaise said not a word.

The courier rode into the encampment outside of New Hastings five minutes after Victor Radcliff had sat down to half a fat roasted capon with starberry sauce spooned over it. The green sauce, tart and sweet at the same time, came from one of Atlantis' few native berries, a product of the thinly settled southwest. It went well with chicken, and even better with greasier fowl like duck and goose.

A sentry let the courier into Victor's tent, making him pause with a bite halfway to his mouth. "Yes?" he said.

"Sir, the English are coming," the courier said, and then, "Could I have a bite of that? I'm powerful hungry."

Victor liked white meat better than dark. He tore off the drumstick and handed it to the newcomer. As the fellow started to eat, Victor demanded, "*Where* are the English coming?" The courier had interrupted his supper; he saw no reason not to return the disfavor.

"Wumbumpf," the courier said with his mouth full—that was what it sounded like, anyhow.

"Would you care to try that again?" Victor asked.

The man swallowed heroically. "Weymouth," he managed, and took another bite, this one even bigger than the last.

"Ah," Victor said. That did make sense—an unpleasant amount of sense, in fact. Weymouth was a small coastal town that lay between New Hastings and Hanover, closer to the latter. Victor would have said the English were welcome to the place—if ever a town had a fine future behind it, Weymouth was the one—if only it didn't have a sizable arsenal. He couldn't afford—Atlantis couldn't afford—to lose the tons of powder and lead bars stored there.

As things were, he wasn't sure how much he could do about it. If the enemy started out closer to Weymouth and moved first . . . Maybe he should just send as many wagons as he could, and hope to salvage at least part of the military supplies.

"When did they march?" he asked. "How fast are they going? Is anyone trying to hold them back?"

"Powerful *thirsty*, too," the courier said. At Victor's shouted order, he got a mug of beer. He drained it at one long, blissful pull, his Adam's apple bobbing up and down as he swallowed.

Then he told Victor what he knew. General Howe wasn't moving south very fast. He didn't think he needed to, even though loyalists had told him about the armory. He didn't believe the Atlanteans had an army that could fight his. He also didn't believe they would even if they could.

Militiamen and enthusiastic volunteers between Hanover and Weymouth were doing their best to make him think twice. They were shooting at his men from behind fences and from the woods. They were blocking the roads with barricades of rocks and fallen trees. One enterprising group had dammed a roadside stream and turned the roadbed to water and mud. No, the redcoats weren't making good time.

Which meant it behooved the Atlanteans to hurry if they wanted to hold Weymouth. Victor set them in motion the morning after he got the news the English were advancing on the town. He wanted to leave New Hastings at the crack of dawn. In fact, the army started marching more than two hours later.

The column straggled much more than it should have, too. Men fell out whenever they grew tired or got sore feet. At every stream and pond, militiamen splashed water on their faces. When sergeants and officers screamed at them to keep going, the soldiers yelled back. As far as they could see, they were in this because they felt like it, or for a lark. That the war and what came from it might be important didn't seem to have entered their heads.

They might have advanced ten miles by the time they halted for the evening. A properly trained army would have gone twice as far. Seeing that, Victor was almost ready to despair.

"If they get there before us—" he groaned.

"Then we don't stop them," Blaise finished for him. The Negro grunted with relief as he took off his boots. "I've got sore feet myself. I'm more used to riding than to marching."

"Good for you!" Victor said, snapping his fingers. "You've reminded me of something, anyhow."

"What's that?" Blaise examined his heels and the balls of his feet and the bottoms of his toes.

"I can send horsemen ahead of the main body. Maybe they'll keep the redcoats out of Weymouth till the rest of us get there." Victor scowled blackly. "Or maybe they'll stop at every tavern along the way, drink rum, pinch the barmaids, and never get there at all. Christ, maybe they'll ride off toward the Green Ridge Mountains after butterflies! Nobody knows till I try it—I'm sure the dragoons don't."

"I don't ... think ... they'll go chasing butterflies, General." Blaise spoke with exaggerated care, as if humoring a lunatic.

Victor Radcliff felt fairly lunatic just then. "Well, maybe not," he allowed. Though he had no enormous confidence they would do what he wanted, he summoned the leaders of the mounted infantry and gave them their orders.

"You're sending us off as a forlorn hope, then," said a bright young captain named Habakkuk Biddiscombe.

"Forlorn hope" was what people called the advance parties who tore up the abatis in front of enemy earthworks. Those parties got the name because not many of the men in them usually lived through the attempt. Radcliff shook his head. "No, Captain. I want you to delay the redcoats, yes. But I don't want you to throw away your men's lives or your own doing it."

"You want us to fire and fall back, then," another officer said.

"Yes!" Victor nodded gratefully. "That is exactly what I want of you."

"The only way we can fire and fall back is to get well north of Weymouth before we meet the enemy," Habakkuk Biddiscombe said. "We'd best commence straightaway if we are to have any hope of gaining so much ground."

"Bless my soul," Victor murmured. *Someone* grasped the essence of the situation, then. Radcliff made himself nod. "I couldn't have put it better myself, Habakkuk."

"In that case, let's get moving." Captain Biddiscombe herded the other officers of dragoons out of Victor's tent. A few minutes later, some loud and profane swearing came from the mounted infantrymen. A few minutes after that, aided by a waxing gibbous moon, they rode out of the camp, heading north.

"Can they get there soon enough to do any good?" Blaise asked.

"I don't know," Victor answered. "I do know they have a better chance setting out now than they would if they left tomorrow morning. And I think—I don't know yet, but I think—Captain Biddiscombe will get everything they have to give from them, and maybe a little more besides. An officer like that is worth his weight in gold."

"And maybe a little more besides?" Blaise's voice was sly.

"Yes, by God!" Victor nodded. "Every once in a while, maybe a lot more besides."

Victor ordered the buglers to wake the army before sunrise, so the men could start marching at first light. By the groans and oaths that greeted the horn calls, the buglers won no friends doing it. In an army that elected most of its officers and underofficers, friendship was important. Victor didn't care. As far as he was concerned, getting to Weymouth was important. Everything else could wait.

Militiamen gnawed hard bread and gulped tea or coffee or beer. The army drove some unhappy beeves with it, too. The cooks knocked a few of them over the head, just enough to leave everybody dissatisfied with the portion he got.

Victor Radcliff was certainly dissatisfied with his portion. "This is some of the most odious beef I ever had the misfortune to eat," he said.

"Better than no beef at all," Blaise said, grease running down his chin. "Better than slave rations, too. And we won't work as hard when we fight as I did out in the fields. Sergeants don't have whips, either."

"Do you feel the lack?" Victor inquired, not altogether ironically.

"Only every now and again," Blaise answered—also not altogether ironically. He took another bite of beef. He had better teeth than Victor did. Dentistry wasn't quite hell on earth, but it came close. Even after heroic doses of brandy and opium—or of laudanum, which combined the two—losing a tooth hurt like blazes.

"As long as your men fear you worse than they fear

enemy musketry, they'll hold the line," Victor said. "That's what we need."

Blaise's wave took in the Atlantean army's encampment. "Can we fight the redcoats with troops like this?" he asked. "Seems to me we had better men when we took on the French settlers. And we had England to back us up then, too—we didn't go against her."

"The second is true, of course," Victor said. "As for the first . . ." He shrugged. "This is a raw force. No one would say any different. But as soon as the men gain some experience—"

"Their enlistment time runs out, and they go home," Blaise broke in.

"That isn't what I was going to say, dammit!" Victor burst out, which made it no less true. He sighed and took a careful bite of his tough, stringy beef. "Before long, we shall have to improve our system of recruitment. In the meanwhile, what choice have we but to do the best we can with what the Atlantean Assembly, in its infinite wisdom, has seen fit to give us?"

"If we lose a few times, how well we fought won't matter." Yes, Blaise was ruthlessly pragmatic.

Again, Radcliff thought his comment altogether too likely. Still . . . "The first few times, I would not be completely discontented with any result that demonstrates we can confront English soldiers on terms approximating equality. Our men need to believe that—and so does the enemy."

"If it be true," Blaise said.

"Yes. If." Victor Radcliff might not have admitted that even to his wife. As much to raise his own spirits as for any other reason, he went on, "The last time around, you will recall, we fought not only French settlers but also French regulars. We did well enough against 'em, too. I see no reason we can't do the same against King George's redcoats. Am I overlooking anything?"

"Only that, when we fought the French, all these settlements joined together against them," the Negro said.

"How many settlers now aim to fight on King George's side?"

Victor grunted uncomfortably. He'd already talked about loyalists. He knew too well that this fight would split families. It had already split some. Custis Cawthorne's press and his formidable wit were at the Atlantean Assembly's disposal. Richard Cawthorne, his eldest son, was royal governor of Freetown, south of New Hastings. Richard was not the man his father was. But he was, by all accounts, capable and conscientious: a good enough servant for the king.

"Not many settlers who aim to fight for King George are in camp with us here," Victor said, again trying to buck himself up.

"Nooo," Blaise said, which sounded like agreement but was anything but. He found another unpleasant question to ask: "But how many of 'em are hotfooting it off to General Howe, to tell him how many men we've got and how they're accoutered? By the time we fight, he'll know everything about us except the holes in our stockings."

"Well, it's not as if we won't know as much about his men," Radcliff replied. Patriots came south with word of Howe's movements and of his regiments. And more than a few redcoats, having come to Atlantis, wanted nothing more than to strip off their uniforms and either join the Assembly's army and take aim at their former comrades or to go off into the wilderness where neither side would trouble them again.

"How soon before we meet him?" Blaise asked.

"Two or three days," Victor said. "Three, I hope: that will mean our skirmishers are making his march a misery. It will also mean we've passed through Weymouth and saved what's in the arsenal. We won't get powder from England any more, either."

"Not unless we take it from the redcoats' baggage train after we beat them." Blaise understood how war worked, all right.

"I hope we can do that. I expect we will, some of the time. But we are going to have to make our own, too. If we need to depend on what we can steal, we're ruined," Victor said.

From horseback, he urged his men to hurry north. Every so often, a horseman would come down and tell him where General Howe's army was—or rather, where it had been when the horseman rode off to report on it. Victor had to calculate how long it had taken each rider to come from one army to the other. That told him about where the redcoats were at any moment, and about how fast they were coming.

"Whole countryside's in arms against 'em," one scout told him. "They've got to battle their way past every copse of trees and every stone fence within range of the road to Weymouth."

"Good," Victor said. He scowled at the map he held open between his knees. How much nonsense would his horse put up with before it tried to buck him off onto his head? If he was doing his sums correctly, Howe and the Englishmen ought to be about . . . there. He did some more sums in his head. Then he blinked in sudden glad surprise. "By God! We really may get to Weymouth ahead of them! Who would have believed it?"

"Way they go stealing anything that ain't nailed down, no wonder everybody wants to take a shot at 'em," the Atlantean scout said.

"Well . . . yes." Victor Radcliff hid as much of a smile as he could. The redcoats' thievery was far from unique. The French Atlanteans had robbed just as enthusiastically in the last war. So had the English Atlanteans, come to that. Soldiers in the Atlantean Assembly's army—his army—were bound to plunder, too. Victor dared hope they would mostly steal from farmers who favored King George. Sometimes, though, it didn't do to inquire too closely.

Heavy wagons carried hogsheads of gunpowder out of Weymouth and down toward New Hastings. The Atlantean soldiers moved off the road to let those wagons by, where all the other traffic had had to move aside for the army's sake. Other wagons brought muskets and lead away from the redcoats. Victor was glad to see them. Even if Weymouth fell, the precious munitions stored there wouldn't fall into English hands.

His men burst into cheers when they entered Weymouth. Victor felt like cheering himself—he'd got there ahead of General Howe. He wondered how long it had been since Weymouth heard much in the way of cheering. The town stank of cod. With Hanover to the north and New Hastings to the south, it would never get very big or very prosperous. A lot of the shops hadn't been painted or spruced up for a long time. *Why bother?* the shopkeepers seemed to say.

Some of them came out into the street to clap as the Atlantean army went by. Barmaids handed out mugs of beer and kisses. Church bells clanged. Dogs yapped as if possessed.

Not all the locals seemed delighted to see the settlers in arms. One weathered fellow, a cigar clamped in his jaws, looked more as if he was counting them than applauding them. Would he slip off and tell General Howe what he knew, as Victor's scouts had been doing for him? The chances seemed good. Both sides in this fight would have plenty of spies.

With the arsenal evacuated, Victor could have let Howe have Weymouth. Sooner or later, though, the Atlanteans would have to fight. If they let the redcoats march here and there unhindered, they weren't an army at all—they were only playing at being one. Victor looked for favorable ground on which to make a stand.

He found what he wanted about five miles north of the town. A stout stone wall led from the road to the beach. A grove of apple trees off to the left covered that flank. All he had to do was barricade the roadway and he would block the redcoats' path and force them to fight.

Axes rang out among the apples. Men and oxen dragged fallen trees to block off the space between the grove and the stone wall. Victor set up his fieldpieces where they could rake the oncoming English soldiers. He wished they didn't burn so much powder at every shot. Yes, he'd got that store out of Weymouth, but even so. . . .

The sun was setting in the direction of the Green Ridge Mountains when he got the position strong enough to suit him. That was just as well; scouts said Howe's men were only a few miles away. The Atlanteans ate at their posts. They bragged about what they would do to the enemy come morning. And then, like any innocents, they slept.

IV

 rums and fifes woke the Atlantean rebels with the eastern sky going from gray to pink. The men staggered out of tents and uncocooned from tight-wound blankets. They yawned and rubbed their eyes and swore sleepily. It was as if they only half remembered—or didn't want to remember—what lay ahead.

The cooks served bread and meat and coffee. The men might have hit their wives if they'd got food like that at home. Here, they ate without complaint. They seemed glad to get any food at all. Gnawing on a chunk of half-raw beef between two slabs of badly risen bread, Victor remembered from the way his belly'd pinched in campaigns gone by that they were right to be glad.

Up ahead, musketry in the distance said farmers and hunters were still harassing the redcoats. They weren't even militiamen, and had no connection to the Atlantean Assembly or anyone but their neighbors. If Howe's men caught them, the usages of war said they could hang them. But catching *francs-tireurs* wasn't easy. All they had to do was hide their firelocks, and then they were just men ambling down country tracks. Shoot at redcoats? The idea would never once cross their minds!

Victor stepped out in front of the abatis to survey the ground once more. The English would have to charge uphill to come at his men. That would make things harder for them, too. He nodded to himself. He wanted to make things as hard as he could for the enemy, because he knew the redcoats were better soldiers than his own men were.

A fieldpiece boomed. Maybe Howe's troopers had got a good shot at some of their tormentors. Maybe they just wanted to scare them off. Victor thought they had a pretty good chance of doing it, too. Men who'd never had cannon aimed at them found it terrifying. Radcliff had faced field guns before, and he wasn't enthusiastic about it, either.

Here came the redcoats. Mounted men rode out ahead of the main column on foot. When the riders spied the obstruction ahead, they wheeled their mounts and galloped back to report the news.

"Won't be long now, men!" Victor called to his own army. "Pretty soon, we'll give the damned English what they deserve!" The Atlanteans raised a cheer. They didn't know what they were getting into, not yet. Pretty soon, they'd find out. They would never be the same again, neither the ones who died nor the ones who lived.

Watching the redcoats deploy from column into line, Victor tried to fight down his jealousy. He'd put the Atlanteans through their evolutions in the fields outside New Hastings. He knew how raw they were. Seeing those same evolutions performed by professionals for whom they were second nature rubbed his nose in it.

Lines perfectly dressed, regimental banners and Union Jacks waving in the breeze off the ocean, the English troops advanced. Victor looked nervously out into the Atlantic. To his vast relief, he saw no warships. Their fire could have enfiladed his line and made him fall back, and he had no answer for them.

Three hundred years earlier, a fishing boat with a few swivel guns helped in the Battle of the Strand. Blasting Sir Richard Neville off his horse made sure Atlantis would have no native kings. Naval gunnery had come a long way in those three centuries. And now the artillery was on the king's side.

"Come back, General!" someone called from behind the abatis. "You don't want to make yourself a bull's-eye for them."

Victor's uniform wasn't so resplendent as all that. He would have felt embarrassed—to say nothing of weighted down—by all the gold braid and medals and buttons English generals wore to declare who they were. But a man standing out in the open in front of his side's works was bound to be a target. Victor picked his way back through the abatis' tangled branches. It wasn't easy; that was why the obstruction was there.

Thinking of the way the opposing general dressed reminded him of something. "Riflemen—aim at their officers!" he shouted. "The more of them we kill, the better off we are."

He didn't have that many riflemen. Most of the ones he did have came from the backwoods, where every shot had to count. A rifle was accurate at three or four times the range of a smoothbore musket, but was also slower to reload and quicker to foul its barrel.

An Atlantean field gun roared. Victor watched the ball kick up dirt in front of the English line and bound forward. It bowled over two redcoats like ninepins. Other soldiers smoothly stepped forward to take their places. More Atlantean guns fired. Enemy fieldpieces replied. A rending crash said a ball smashed a gun carriage. That cannon was out of action for the rest of the battle.

Enemy bugles blared. The soldiers in the first two ranks brought their muskets down to the horizontal. Their bayonets flashed in the sun. Barbarians facing the Roman legions must have known that shock of fear as the legionaries' spearheads all glittered as one. It had lost none of its intimidation over the centuries between Caesar's day and Victor Radcliff's.

The bugles blared again. Here came the redcoats, at a

steady marching pace. The first ranks' muskets probably weren't even loaded. General Howe wanted them to win with the bayonet. If they got in among the Atlanteans, chances were they would, too. Only a few of Victor's men had the sockets and long knives that turned muskets into spears. The rest would have to fight back with clubbed guns or with knives.

A cannon ball tore through the redcoats' ranks. Injured men fell or fell out. Others moved up to replace them. The soldiers knew getting killed or maimed was all part of the job. They didn't get excited about it—unless it happened to them.

Atlantean riflemen started firing. A captain or major, his epaulets proclaiming his rank, clutched at his shoulder and went down. Another officer fell a moment later, and then another. The ones who remained kept coming. English officers weren't professionals like the men they led. That didn't mean they lacked courage, though. On the contrary—a man who showed fear in front of his fellows was hardly a man at all.

"Wait till you can see what they've got on their buttons. Then blow 'em all to hell!" a sergeant shouted to the musketeers he led. Good advice: their guns weren't accurate much farther out than that.

"Now!" someone else yelled, and a blast of fire ripped into the English soldiers. Redcoats staggered. Redcoats stumbled. Redcoats screamed. Redcoats fell.

And the redcoats who didn't stagger or stumble or scream or fall came on. Another volley tore into them, and another. The third one was noticeably more ragged than the first. By the time it came, the enemy was almost to the wall and the abatis. The blast of lead proved more than even the bravest or most stoic flesh and blood could bear. Sullenly, the redcoats drew back out of range, now and then stopping and stooping to help a fallen comrade.

Cheers rose from the Atlanteans. "We whipped 'em, by Jesus!" somebody cried, which set off new rejoicing.

Knowing the men his army faced, Victor wasn't so

sure. And damned if the redcoats didn't re-form their lines and make ready to come at the Atlanteans again. Their field guns turned on the abatis across the road. The fallen trees might hinder soldiers, but they didn't keep out roundshot. A man hit square by a cannon ball turned into something only a butcher would recognize. And a man speared by a branch a cannon ball tore loose was in no enviable situation, either.

A few Atlanteans couldn't stand the cannonading and fled. They were raw troops, men who'd never come under fire before. Most of the new men stood it as well as any veterans. Victor was proud of them. He was also astonished, though he never would have told them so.

On came the Englishmen again. This time, they sent fewer troops against the stone wall and more against the area protected by the abatis. This time, too, they stopped and delivered two volleys of their own before rushing the Atlantean field works.

Bullets snapped past Victor's head. A wet *thud!* said a man next to him was hit. The Atlantean clutched his chest and crumpled to the ground, his musket falling from his hands. Victor snatched up the firelock. He aimed at a redcoat pushing through the abatis—a man from Howe's forlorn hope. If the gun wasn't loaded . . . *What do I lose?* he thought, and pulled the trigger.

The musket bucked against his shoulder. The redcoat went down, grabbing his leg. Victor had aimed at his chest. With a smoothbore, you were glad for any hit you got. Another man from the forlorn hope fell, half his jaw shot away. But the English soldiers were making paths their friends could follow.

And follow the redcoats did. Some of them fell. More stepped over corpses and writhing wounded and set about doing what they knew how to do: massacring amateurs who presumed to stand against them. The Atlanteans were brave. In close-quarters fighting like that, it probably did them more harm than good. They rushed forward, clutching any weapons they had—and the redcoats emotionlessly spitted them with their bayonets.

The Englishmen had the edge in reach, and they had the edge in training, and they used both without mercy.

Victor might have fed his whole force into the fight, as a man fed meat into a sausage grinder. The Atlanteans would be gone . . . and they would have gone down. He saw as much, a little more slowly than he might have. "Back!" he yelled. "Fall back!"

The Atlanteans obeyed him with more alacrity than they'd ever shown marching north from New Hastings. They'd had enough—they'd had too much—of the horrible redcoats. Watching them break away from the English troops, Victor tasted gall. He wondered if the rebellion would smash to bits at the first test.

"Form ranks!" he shouted, hoping they would. "Give them a volley!" he added, praying they would. "Show them you're not whipped!" he said, fearing they were.

And damned if the Atlanteans didn't obey him again. The ranks weren't neat enough to delight an English drillmaster's heart. The volley was on the ragged side, too. But it was enough to knock the redcoats back on their heels. They'd come after the settlers, aiming to break them all at once—and they'd got a nasty surprise.

"Withdraw fifty yards and give them another one," Victor commanded. The men he led did as he told them to. This volley was fuller, thicker, than the one before. More English soldiers went down.

Now the redcoats, seeing that they couldn't force a decision with the bayonet alone, began loading their muskets again, too. They rebuilt their own battle line with marvelous haste—and much bad language from their sergeants. And they traded several volleys with the Atlanteans, both sides banging away at each other from less than a hundred yards. That was warfare as it was practiced on the battlefields of Europe: organized mutual slaughter.

More bullets cracked past Victor Radcliff than he could keep track of. None of them bit. He had no idea why not: either God loved him or he was luckier than he deserved. He'd begun to think he was luckier than he deserved in the men he led, too. They stood up under that pounding as well as the redcoats. Oh, a few men slipped off toward the rear, but only a few.

Victor told off several companies of New Hastings troops to serve as his rear guard. No settlement, not even Croydon in the north, despised royal authority more than New Hastings. Having disposed of one would-be king on their own soil, New Hastings men had little use for anyone else who tried to tell them what to do.

They held off the redcoats and let the rest of the army fall back toward Weymouth. Then they too broke free. General Howe showed little appetite for the pursuit: less than Victor would have in his place. Maybe that said something about him. Maybe it said something about what the Atlanteans had done to his army, even in defeat.

Victor Radcliff looked around for Blaise. He found the Negro with a bloody rag wrapped around the stump of his left middle finger. "Stupid thing," he said. "Hurts like a mad bastard, too." He looked more angry than stunned, as wounded men sometimes seemed.

"Get some poppy juice from the surgeons," Victor told him. "It will dull the pain a little, anyhow."

"Plenty need it more than I do," Blaise said.

"Plenty need it less, too. Go on. That's an order," Victor said. What point to being a general if you couldn't tell a sergeant what to do?

Blaise's "Yes, sir" was as mutinous an acceptance as Victor had ever heard. But it was an acceptance. He'd take what he could get. He hadn't beaten the English, but he'd given them a better fight than they must have dreamt of in their wildest nightmares. He'd take what he could get there, too. The retreat went on. He had no choice about taking that.

The Atlanteans fortified Weymouth. If General Howe wanted to break into the seaside town with men shooting at him from behind barricades and out of windows and ducking back around corners, he was welcome to try. So Victor thought, anyhow.

His men also seemed ready for another crack at the English. "Hell, yes! Let 'em come," one of them said. "We'll give 'em a bloody nose and whip 'em back to their mamas."

General Howe, unfortunately, didn't seem inclined to play Victor's game. His warships, perhaps slowed by contrary winds, arrived two days later. They lay off-shore and bombarded the town. The Atlanteans' field guns fired back, but that was more to make the men feel better than for any other reason. Three- and six-pounders couldn't reach the men-of-war and might not have been able to pierce their thick oak timbers even if they had.

When a ball from a twenty-four-pounder hit a house or an inn, on the other hand, the building was likely to fall down. And when a ball from a twenty-four-pounder hit a man, or several men . . . what happened after that wasn't pretty. The gravediggers got more work than the surgeons did.

The ships were still there the next morning. As soon as the sun climbed up out of the Atlantic, they started cannonading Weymouth again. They fired slowly and deliberately, one roundshot every few minutes. Again, the Atlanteans returned fire, but with no great hope of success. They fearfully awaited each incoming cannon ball.

Flash and smoke came first. After them—but well after, proving sound traveled slower than light—came the boom from the gun. Victor had the displeasure of watching each roundshot arc through the summery air toward Weymouth. Then another crash would announce more destruction.

The slow, steady bombardment had a horrid fascination to it. Victor almost forgot to breathe as he waited and tensed himself before each new explosion. He hoped each round would fall harmlessly, yet feared each one would not. Surgeons and dentists worked as fast as they could, to get the agony over with in a hurry. The Royal Navy here operated in just the opposite way. Their officers wanted the Atlanteans to suffer for a long time.

Victor Radcliff figured that out right away. The Royal Navy officers also wanted something else: they wanted to use the deliberate cannonading to blind the Atlantean rebels to everything else that was going on. They got what they wanted, too. Along with everyone else in Weymouth, Victor spent the day staring fearfully out to sea, bracing himself for the next thunder from a gun.

"Sir? General Radcliff, sir?" By the exaggerated patience in the man's voice, he'd been trying to draw Victor's notice for some little while.

"Huh?" Victor said. In less than a minute now, one of the guns on the fleet out there would speak. What else mattered next to that?

He found out. "Sir, we've had a deserter come in. You'd better hear what he's got to say about General Howe's army."

"General ... Howe's army?" Victor said slowly. He realized that, confident in the works in and around Weymouth, he'd almost forgotten about the redcoats. And he belatedly realized that wasn't the smartest thing he could have done.

He blinked, then blinked again, like someone coming out from under the spell of that French charlatan, Mesmer. Flash! *Boom!* A roundshot bigger than his clenched fist flying through the air, swelling, swelling ... *Crash!* The Royal Navy did its best to keep him bemused.

But he'd been distracted. Pulling him back under the spell wasn't so easy. "All right. Bring this fellow to me."

He'd seen a lot of English soldiers like this one. The two chevrons on the fellow's left sleeve proclaimed him a corporal. He was short and skinny and pockmarked. He had two missing front teeth. His pale eyes wouldn't light on Victor. He looked like a man who would cheerfully murder for the price of a pot of ale. He also looked like a man who would keep coming forward no matter what any opponent tried to do to his battle line.

"Well?" Victor said.

"Well, it's like this, your Honor," the corporal said in a clotted London accent. "General 'Owe, 'e's moving inland, around your bloody flank. 'E aims to get between you and New 'Astings, 'e does."

"Sweet suffering Jesus!" Victor said. That would put him—and the Atlantean Assembly—in a very nasty spot . . . if it was true. He eyed the deserter. "And you came in to tell me this because . . . ?"

Flash! *Boom!* Flying roundshot. *Crash!* The redcoat hardly seemed to notice, let alone get excited. "Why, your Honor? I'll bloody well tell you why." He brushed his chevrons with a scarred hand. "On account of over there I'll be an old man by the time I make sergeant, if I ever do. I took the king's shilling to keep from starving. Well, I've done that, any road. But if I want to make summat of myself, if I want to be a lieutenant, say"—like a lot of Englishmen, he pronounced it *leftenant*—"I've got a better chance 'ere than I ever would've there. And so I lit out, I did."

Lots of Englishmen came to Atlantis because they thought they could do better here than in the cramped, tradition-filled mother country. This corporal wasn't the first deserter from Howe's army: nowhere near. But none of the others had brought such important news. "What's your name?" Victor asked him.

"Pipes, your Honor," he answered. "Daniel Pipes."

"All right, Pipes. I'm going to send out riders to check what you've said." Victor feared he knew what they would find. The deserter's news had a dreadful feel of probability to it. He went on, "If they show you're telling the truth, you're Sergeant Daniel Pipes on the spot. How high you climb after that is up to you."

The redcoat stiffened to rigor mortis–like attention. His salute might have been turned on a lathe. A couple of watching Atlantean soldiers sniggered. That kind of stern discipline was what they were fighting against. But Victor knew it had its merits in winning wars.

"Much obliged, your Honor!" Pipes said.

Flash! *Boom!* Victor watched the cannon ball come in. *Crash!* "I think we're the ones obliged to you," he said. How big a march had General Howe stolen? How much bigger would it have been if not for Daniel Pipes?

Radcliff sent out the riders. He'd let the ships distract him, but he wouldn't make that mistake any more. What other mistakes he might make ... he would discover only by making them.

A new question rose in his mind. How often could he count on help from English deserters? That brought up another new question. How often would Atlantean deserters help the enemy? He knew he'd already lost some men to desertion. He hadn't thought till now about how much it might mean.

Flash. *Boom!* Pause. *Crash!* Screams followed this shot—it must have come down on a building with people inside. Victor swore. No wonder the Royal Navy had been able to mesmerize him for a while.

The next roundshot missed him by only about twenty feet. "Nasty thing," Pipes observed. He hadn't flinched as the big iron ball bounded by. Neither had Radcliff. It wasn't the same as a bullet snapping past. Victor didn't know why it wasn't, but he was sure of the fact.

A couple of hours went by. The bombardment went on. He thanked heaven the cannonading hadn't started a fire in Weymouth. That was nothing but luck, as he knew too well. Fire was any town's biggest nightmare. Once it took hold, it was next to impossible to quell.

Hoofbeats clopped on dirt as a horseman trotted in. "Well?" Victor called.

"They're moving, all right," the scout answered. "Heading around our left flank. But I think you can still pull out all right."

"That's what she said," Victor remarked, and the horseman laughed.

His men weren't sorry to leave Weymouth. Who in his right mind would have been? He marched away from the little seaside town as quietly as he could. The longer the Royal Navy took to realize he was gone, the better. *Boom!* ... *Crash!* (He couldn't see the flash or the flight of the ball any more. The sound, though, the sound pursued.)

"Can those ships do this at New Hastings, too?" Blaise asked.

"We do have forts there, but I don't know if they would stop them," Victor answered.

"Mm-*hmm*," the Negro said, a fraught noise if ever there was one. "How are we ever going to win the war, then?"

That was a better question than Victor Radcliff wished it were. "Most of Atlantis is out of the range of the Royal Navy's guns," he said. That was true. He was less sure how helpful it was. If the Atlantean Assembly's army couldn't safely stay by the coast, the enemy gained an important advantage.

Atlantis had ships of its own, as befit a land that made much of its living from fishing and whaling and slaving and trading with the mother country (and, when the mother country wasn't looking, trading with other people, too). Some of them went armed. Piracy wasn't what it had been in the wild days of Avalon, more than a hundred years before, but it wasn't dead, either. How many carried enough guns to face a Royal Navy frigate? Any? Victor knew too well none could face a first-rate ship of the line.

"If Howe comes at us and the ships come at us, can we hold New Hastings?" Blaise persisted.

"We can try," Victor said. That didn't sound strong enough even to him, so he added, "We have to try." Blaise nodded and didn't say anything more. It was less of a relief than Victor had thought it would be.

General Howe's skirmishers pushed toward the coast. The Atlantean army's skirmishers pushed them back and took a few prisoners. They hauled one of them in front of Victor Radcliff. The redcoat acted more aggrieved that he'd been caught.

"What are you buggers doing marching along down

here?" he said. "They told us you were still back in bloody Weymouth."

"Well, you've learned something, then, haven't you?" Victor answered.

The prisoner scowled at him. "What's that?"

"Not to believe everything you hear," Victor said blandly. What the redcoat said then wasn't fit for polite company. The Atlanteans gathered around him laughed. He seemed even less happy about that. The Atlanteans thought he got funnier as he got louder.

General Howe began pressing harder on the Atlantean army's flank. That was a problem Victor could deal with, though. A small rear guard sufficed to slow down the redcoats and let the rest of his men get ahead of them on the road down to New Hastings.

He wondered what would happen when he got there. By now, the Atlantean Assembly would know he hadn't held Weymouth. Would they take his command away from him? He shrugged. If they did, they did, that was all.

The next interesting question would be whether he could hold New Hastings. It certainly had better works than Weymouth did. But, like Weymouth, it was a seaside town. If the Royal Navy wanted to lie offshore and bombard it, Victor didn't know how he could respond.

He shook his head. That wasn't true. He knew how: he couldn't. He didn't like that, but he knew it.

And if he lost New Hastings, the echo of its fall would reverberate throughout Atlantis. If New Hastings came under the redcoats' boots . . . Would the rest of the land think the fight was still worth making? Victor really had no idea about that.

Nor did he want to find out. The best way to keep from finding out would be to hold New Hastings. He hoped he could.

Another rider came in from the west. "They're starting to turn in on us for true, sir," he reported.

"They would," Victor said, and then, "Did you see any fence or stone wall that runs more or less north and south? Something we could fight behind, I mean?"

"Plenty of 'em," the man answered. "These New Hastings folk, they're as bad as the people up by Croydon for walling themselves away from their neighbors." By the way he talked, he came from somewhere close to Freetown, well to the south of New Hastings. He could sneer at New Hastings folk as much as he wanted, but his own settlement held a far higher proportion of men loyal to King George.

He wasn't, though—and he'd given Victor Radcliff the answer the Atlantean commander wanted to hear. "Good," Victor said. "If they want to charge us across open country, they're welcome to pay the butcher's bill."

They'd done that north of Weymouth, and come away with a victory anyhow. Victor hoped General Howe didn't care for what he'd paid to get his victory. He shouted orders, swinging the Atlantean army out of its retreat and off to the west to face the redcoats again.

He also sent more horsemen out ahead of his infantry. He wanted them to lead the English army straight toward his. That way, he wouldn't—he hoped he wouldn't—get taken in the flank.

Once he'd set things in motion, he turned back to the courier who'd brought word of Howe's swing. "Take us to one of these fences."

"Glad to do it, General." The man brushed the brim of his tricorn with a forefinger—probably as close to a salute as Victor would get from him.

The first fence to which he led the Atlanteans wasn't long enough to let all of them deploy behind it. Victor didn't want them out in the open trading volleys with the redcoats. The English were better trained than the settlers. They could shoot faster, and could also take more damage without breaking. And, if it came down to a charge and hand-to-hand fighting, all the redcoats had bayonets.

And so they went a little farther northwest, and found a stone wall that seemed perfect. It was more than a mile long, and almost chest high. If the musketeers steadied their firelocks on top of it as they shot, they were likely to do better than smoothbores commonly could, too.

Sheep grazed in a broad meadow on the far side of the fence. They looked up in mild surprise as the Atlanteans took their places. They didn't know enough to run. If General Howe declined this engagement, Victor Radcliff suspected a good many of his men would enjoy a mutton supper tonight.

But Howe did not decline. Victor saw the rising cloud of dust that marked the redcoats' approach. He listened to occasional pistol shots: those would come from the two sides' horsemen skirmishing with one another. Some of the Atlantean mounted soldiers wore green coats. Others were in homespun, and had only weapons and determination to mark them as fighting men.

They took refuge at either side of the Atlantean position. The English horsemen, by contrast, recoiled when they saw the enemy in arms in front of them. They didn't push the attack—nor would Victor have in their place. Instead, they rode back to give their commander the news that the rebels were waiting for them.

Howe's infantry came out onto the meadow not quite half an hour later. Victor peered at them through a brass spyglass. A golden reflection caught his eye. He had to smile. There stood an English officer—General Howe himself?—staring back through a telescope almost identical to his own.

Victor didn't much like what he saw. He hoped the enemy general was even less happy with what his spyglass showed him.

Field guns unlimbered and deployed to either flank of the redcoats. English artillerymen opened fire. Maybe they hoped the cannonading would terrify their raw opponents. A couple of balls slammed against the stone wall but didn't break through. Then one took off the head of a tall soldier who was looking out at the martial spectacle in front of him. His corpse stood upright, fountaining blood, for several seconds before it finally fell.

Even Victor thought that might be plenty to frighten

his men. But it didn't seem to. "Did you see Seth there?" one of them exclaimed.

"Didn't know he had so much blood in him," another replied.

"Sure went out in style, didn't he?" the first man said, nothing but admiration in his voice. In spite of himself, Victor Radcliff smiled. The Atlanteans were turning into veterans in a hurry.

General Howe's men were already veterans. Without fuss or wasted motion, they swung from column to line of battle, staying out of range of both muskets and rifles as they took their places. Victor ordered his handful of field guns into action. They knocked over a few redcoats. The rest kept on with their evolutions as if nothing had happened.

Drums and fifes moved the Englishmen forward. The field guns cut swaths in their advancing ranks. They closed up and kept coming. Victor wondered if they would charge with the bayonet again. He hoped so. He didn't think they would be able to stand the gaff if they tried.

But Howe proved able to learn from experience. Having suffered from one charge, he had the redcoats halt about eighty yards from the fence that sheltered the Atlanteans. The first rank went to one knee. The second stooped to fire over their shoulders. The third stood straight.

"Fire!" Victor yelled, and the Atlantean volley went in before the English soldiers could start shooting. Redcoats crumpled. Redcoats writhed.

And redcoats opened fire. Musket balls smacked the stone fence. And they smacked soft flesh. Atlanteans screamed. Atlanteans reeled back, clutching at themselves.

The first three ranks of redcoats retired and began to reload. The next three stepped forward. The first of them went to one knee. The second stooped. The third stood straight. They all fired together. Then they retired and also began to reload. Three more ranks of English soldiers delivered another volley. By that time, the first three ranks were ready to fire again. They did. Then the regulars charged.

They'd taken casualties all through their volleys—the Atlanteans had blazed away at them, too. And Victor's men—those of them still on their feet—delivered a couple of more ragged volleys as the redcoats rushed at them. A few fieldpieces fired canister into the English soldiers. The sprays of lead balls tore holes in the redcoats' ranks. They came on regardless.

At the wall, they stabbed with their bayonets, driving the Atlanteans back. Then the Englishmen started scrambling up and over. More of them got shot doing that. Once they dropped down on the east side, they lashed out with those bayoneted muskets. Again, at close quarters Victor Radcliff's men had no good answer for them. Guts spilled out onto the trampled, bloodstained grass.

"Back!" Victor shouted. "Back! Form lines! Give them a volley!"

He wondered if the farmers and cobblers and millers and ropemakers and horse dealers would listen to him. They'd faced the redcoats twice now, and been forced from strong positions both times. Why *wouldn't* they want to break and run after that?

They didn't. Not so neatly as their foes would have done it, they drew back fifty yards, formed up, and gave Howe's men a volley. Fire rippled up and down their ranks. Any English sergeant worth his stripes would have screamed at them for such ragged shooting. Some of the Atlantean sergeants did scream at them.

Victor was just glad they'd fired at all. "Give them one more!" he yelled. "One more, and then fall back again!"

This volley was even more ragged than the one before had been. The Atlanteans remained in order, though: a force in being. They'd hurt the redcoats, too. Victor could see a lot of dead and wounded English soldiers on both sides of the wall. He could also see a lot of dead and wounded Atlanteans.

The army that held the field was the one that won the battle. So it had been in ancient days, and so it was still. General Howe's army would hold this field, as it had held the one north of Weymouth—as it now held Weymouth itself.

"They aren't so tough," somebody not far from Victor said as the settlers withdrew. "Give us big old knives on the end of our firelocks and we'll make 'em sorry—just see if we don't."

"Damn right, Lemuel," the fellow next to him replied. They both nodded, as if to say, *Well, that's settled.* Victor had lost two battles and one town. All of a sudden, he didn't feel nearly so bad.

V

*N*ew Hastings again. Victor Radcliff had hoped he wouldn't see it so soon. He'd *hoped* he wouldn't see it at all. He'd dreamt of driving the redcoats before him as if he embodied the Horsemen of the Apocalypse. Why not drive them back to Hanover? Why not drive them out of Hanover? Out of Atlantis altogether?

Well, now he knew why not. General Howe's soldiers were better trained than his. The Royal Navy had cost him more trouble than he'd expected, too.

And so . . . New Hastings again.

He went to the ancient redwood church to report his two failures to the Atlantean Assembly. Those worthy patriots would already know he'd lost two battles. If anything outran the wind, it was rumor.

But the forms had to be observed. The Assemblymen were his superiors—the only superiors he had. They were as much of a government as the rebellious settlements had. Here and there, English governors persisted. Nobody said much about that to Custis Cawthorne.

Stolidly, Victor told the Assembly what had happened. "We did succeed in removing the munitions from Weymouth before English forces reached the town," he said.

"Did you succeed in removing Weymouth itself?" an

Assemblyman asked. His name, if Victor remembered rightly, was Hiram Smith. He came from New Marseille, in the far southwest.

"Unfortunately, no," Victor answered.

Smith went on as if he hadn't spoken: "I think you did, sir. You removed it from free Atlantis and returned it to King George."

A low ripple of laughter ran through the church. A split second later, it came echoing back from the high, vaulted ceiling. "Mr. Smith, you may have your sport with me if it please you," Victor answered, not showing the rage that griped his belly. "We did, I believe, what we could do with what we had. The men showed themselves to be uncommonly brave. They fought hard and spiritedly, holding their ground well against professional soldiers and retaining their morale even when fortune failed to smile on them. True, they did not triumph, but even in defeat they cost the enemy dear, and they remain both willing and able to fight again when called upon to do so. Any deficiencies in their conduct must accrue to me, not to them."

Custis Cawthorne rose and straightened. He made something of a production of it, as he made something of a production of most things. Looking out over the tops of his spectacles at the gentlemen of the Atlantean Assembly, he said, "My friends, I should like to propose a resolution concerning General Radcliff."

"Say on, Mr. Cawthorne," said redheaded Isaac Fenner, who held the gavel. "You will anyhow."

"Your servant, sir." Cawthorne dipped his head in Fenner's direction. "Be it resolved, then, that we imitate the Roman Senate. After the Battle of Cannae, the worst defeat Rome ever knew, the Conscript Fathers voted their official thanks to the surviving consul, Caius Terrentius Varro, because he had not despaired of the Roman Republic. Let us confer the same honor upon General Radcliff for the same reason."

"It is so moved," Fenner said. "Do I hear a second?" He heard several. Cawthorne's motion swiftly passed.

Fenner nodded to Victor Radcliff. "You see? We do not despair of you, and may you never have cause to despair of us."

"Thank you. And thank you all." Victor was more moved than he'd imagined he would be. "Let me also say I hope and pray we suffer no defeat worse than these two, for they truly were close, hard-fought struggles."

"We have shown King George and his ministers that we can confront their minions in arms," Custis Cawthorne said.

"We have not shown that we can beat them," Hiram Smith put in.

"That may not prove necessary," Cawthorne said. "As long as we stay in the field, as long as we fight, as long as we annoy, we drain England's treasury and make her people despair of victory. Sooner or later—God grant it be sooner—they will tire of trying to force us to an allegiance we detest. There are more ways to win a war than by gaining glory on the battlefield."

"None surer," Smith said. "None quicker."

Isaac Fenner nodded to Victor. "What are your views in this regard, General?"

"Winning in the field is victory," Radcliff replied. "Not losing in the field . . . may eventually be victory, depending on our continued resolve and England's eventual impatience. I prefer to win. If forthright victory eludes me, I will do what I can to maintain the fight."

"That seems reasonable," Fenner said judiciously.

"Try it anyway," Custis Cawthorne added.

"As always, Mr. Cawthorne, your sentiments do you credit," Fenner said.

"Credit is all very well, but cash is better," the printer replied. "As we are discovering to our dismay."

Isaac Fenner's large ears twitched. Cawthorne had struck a nerve. The Atlantean Assembly had no sure power to tax. It could ask the parliaments of the several settlements for cash, but they were under no obligation to give it any. If they didn't—which happened much too often—the Assembly paid with promissory notes, not gold or silver. The war was still young, but merchants already traded those notes at a discount.

"Have you gentlemen any further need of me?" Victor asked. "I thank you for the great honor you have conferred upon me, but I believe it would be best if I returned to my troops and saw to the defenses of this city."

"I think we've finished with you." Custis Cawthorne looked around the Assembly. Seeing no dissent, he went on, "And I am glad today's resolution pleases you. It is, after all, worth its weight in gold."

The full force of that didn't strike Victor till he'd left the old church. Then, belatedly, it hit him like a ball from a forty-two-pounder. He staggered in the street and almost bumped into a woman in a lacy bonnet. She sent him a reproachful glare as she sidestepped.

"Your pardon, ma'am," Victor said. The woman only sniffed and hurried away. Victor shook his head, still chuckling under his breath. "That old reprobate! He ought to be ashamed—except he has no shame at all."

Blaise looked at his hands. They hadn't been soft before. Even so, they were blistered and bloody now. "I dug in front of Nouveau Redon," he said. "Since then, I forgot how much of soldiering is pick and shovel work." Missing one finger couldn't have made things any easier. He rubbed grease on his abused palms. By his expression, it didn't help much.

A privilege of being a general was not having to imitate a mole. Victor Radcliff clucked when that figure of speech crossed his mind. England had moles. So did the mainland of Europe, and so did Terranova. Atlantis had none, nor any other native viviparous quadrupeds but for bats. In their place, burrowing skinks went after worms and underground insects here.

His ancestors had left England more than three centuries before. Habits of speech from the mother country still persisted, though. He wondered why.

"Sometimes the spade is as useful as the musket," he said, trying to clear his mind of moles.

"Sometimes being on the wrong end of the one hurts almost as much as with the other," Blaise replied tartly.

He might have been right about that. Whether he was or not, fieldworks would help the Atlanteans hold General Howe's army away from New Hastings. Victor worried less about the Royal Navy here than he had up at Weymouth. Unlike the smaller town, New Hastings already had seaside works to challenge warships. They'd been built to hold off the French, but no law said they couldn't fire at men-of-war flying the Union Jack.

Afterwards, Radcliff remembered he'd had that thought only a few minutes before the distant thunder of cannon fire from the coast made him jump. "Big goddamn guns," Blaise remarked.

"Aren't they just?" Victor said, and ran for his horse. The beast stood not far away. He untied it, sprang up onto its back, and rode for the shore as fast as it would carry him.

Sure as the devil, English frigates and men-of-war tried conclusions with the coast-defense batteries. If they could smash the forts and silence the guns, they would be able to bombard New Hastings at their leisure. The men-of-war carried bigger guns than any the forts mounted.

But the star-shaped forts had walls not of oak but of bricks backed by thick earth. Their long twelve-pounders could shoot as far as any warship's guns. And they could fire red-hot shot, which was too dangerous to use aboard ship. If a red-hot ball lodged in a man-of-war's planking . . .

Somewhere right around here, all those years ago, Edward Radcliffe and his first party of English settlers had landed. They'd killed honkers and fought against red-crested eagles. Now, reckoning themselves Englishmen no more, their descendants fought against redcoats and Royal Navy alike.

Crash! A big cannon ball from one of the English ships smashed bricks in a fort's outer wall. But the earth behind the bricks kept the ball from breaking through.

Cannon inside the fort bellowed defiance. Gray smoke belched from their muzzles. They might well be using the powder saved from Weymouth. At least one ball struck home. Victor could hear iron crashing through oak across close to half a mile of water. He hoped it was a red-hot roundshot, and that the English warship would catch fire and burn to the waterline.

None of the Royal Navy vessels out there did. He might have known they wouldn't. That would have been too easy. They went right on exchanging murder with the seaside forts.

And one of them noticed the lone man on the strand. Maybe a seagoing officer turned a spyglass on Victor and noticed he was dressed like an officer. Any which way, two or three cannon balls whizzed past him and kicked up fountains of sand unpleasantly close to where he stood.

He wasn't ashamed to withdraw. One man armed with sword and pistol was impotent against a Royal Navy flotilla.

Or was he? One man with sword and pistol was, certainly. One man armed with a working brain? Victor smiled to himself. He could almost hear Custis Cawthorne asking the question in just those terms.

More than a hundred years before, the pirates of Avalon had discommoded a fleet of Atlantean, English, and Dutch men-of-war with fireships. A few fishing boats were tied up at the piers that jutted out into the sea. The wind lay against them, though. Whatever Victor came up with, that wouldn't work.

Despite the cannonading, Atlantis' flag still flew defiantly over the forts: the Union Jack, differenced with a red-crested eagle displayed in the canton. From a distance, it hardly looked different from the flag the enemy flew. *We need a better banner*, Victor thought, *one that says right away who we are.*

He suddenly started to smile again. "By God!" he said. Better banners came in all sorts—or they might.

Victor shouted for runners and sent the young men to the forts. Before long, a new flag went up over them, as well as over the city as a whole. No doubt the officers of the flotilla could make out what that flag meant: it warned that yellow fever was loose in New Hastings.

That flag told a great, thumping lie. The yellow jack hardly ever came this far north. It broke out in Freetown now and again, and more often down in what had been French Atlantis. But, while Atlanteans knew that, Englishmen might well not. The warning of flags wouldn't keep the Royal Navy from bombarding the forts. It might prevent a landing by Royal Marines.

And it might make General Howe think twice about assailing New Hastings. No general in his right mind would want to expose his troops to yellow fever. Howe would think the Atlantean rebels were welcome to a town stricken by the disease. He might even think it God's judgment upon them. Whatever he thought, he would think staying away was a good idea.

That much Victor foresaw. He didn't tell the men of the Atlantean Assembly that the flags lied. Sometimes the less you told people, the better—or more secret. Some of them rapidly discovered pressing business well away from New Hastings. They preferred risking capture by General Howe to the yellow jack.

Isaac Fenner came up to Victor and said, "I had not heard this plague was among us."

"Neither had I." Victor didn't care to use the lie direct, even if the lie indirect troubled him not at all.

The current speaker of the Atlantean Assembly raised a gingery eyebrow. "I . . . see. So the wind sits in that quarter, does it?"

"It does," Radcliff replied. "And I will add, sir, that your discretion in this regard may keep it from swinging to some other, less salubrious, one."

"Salubrious, is it?" Fenner's eyebrow didn't go down. "You've been listening to Custis again."

"Better entertainment there than in most of the taverns," Victor said, "and less chance of coming away with a chancre or anything else you don't want. You may tell him, sir. I rely on his discretion."

"Then you must believe all is for the best in the best of all possible worlds," Fenner said.

"I do believe that, candidly," Victor said, and the speaker winced. Victor went on, "Whether the same may be said for the world in which we find ourselves may be a different question."

"So it may," Isaac Fenner agreed. "Cawthorne's experience, as he will tell you at any excuse or none, is that three may keep a secret—if two of them are dead."

"I should hate to impose such terms on the illustrious members of the Atlantean Assembly, however tempting that might be," Victor said. Fenner grunted laughter. Victor added, "Do tell him. I don't want him haring out of town and risking his freedom for nothing."

"I shall do that." Fenner glanced off to the northwest, where General Howe's redcoats hung over New Hastings like a rain-filled thunderhead. "And I trust that, if the need for us to hare out of town *should* arise, you will tell us in good time so we can tend to it without undue difficulty."

"You have my word," Victor said. He wouldn't have minded if the Englishmen caught and hanged a few Atlantean Assemblymen. Nor would he have been surprised if Fenner also had a list of men he reckoned expendable. Comparing the two—and, say, Custis Cawthorne's—might have been interesting, to say nothing of entertaining. *After the war is won*, Victor told himself.

He smiled to himself. Doing anything at all after the war was won would be very fine.

Maybe rumors of disease in New Hastings gave the redcoats pause. Maybe Howe would have gone after Bredestown any which way. The English commander seemed to like moving inland and then turning back toward the coast.

Word of the deployment toward Bredestown reached Isaac Fenner as soon as it reached Victor Radcliff. That was no great surprise: Fenner came from Bredestown, and people from the threatened city naturally appealed to the man who represented them.

Fenner came to the camp outside of New Hastings to confer with Victor. "Can you save Bredestown from the tyrant's troops?" he asked.

"I'm ... not sure," Victor said slowly. "Even by trying to do so, I risk losing that town and New Hastings both."

"In what way?" Fenner asked, his tone leaving no doubt that anything Victor said would be used against him.

Sighing, Victor answered, "That Royal Navy flotilla still lies offshore. If we march up the Brede toward Bredestown, the enemy is bound to learn of it. What save the fictitious fear of the yellow jack then prevents him from landing a force of bullocks and sailors and seizing New Hastings before we can return? If the seaside forts fall, as they may well from a landward assault, nothing hinders the English warships from adding their weight of metal to the small arms the marines and sailors will have to hand. Under these circumstances, I fear *nihil obstat*, to use the Popish phrase."

"If we were to save Bredestown from the redcoats ..." Like a lot of men from the city up the Brede, Fenner thought it was at least as important as New Hastings. Few people not Bredestown born and bred shared that opinion.

Victor didn't. Instead of coming out and saying so, which would have affronted the speaker of the Atlantean Assembly, he replied, "We have no assurance of holding Bredestown even with all our forces collected in it. And I would rather not do that if I can find any alternative."

"Why not?" Fenner asked sharply.

"Because it lies on the north bank of the Brede," Victor said. "I have never yet seen a manual of strategy advocating taking a position on a riverbank if there is danger of being pushed back, which would be the case there."

"What difference does it make?" Fenner said. "Several bridges span the stream at Bredestown."

"No doubt, sir. But if we have to try to cross them in a hasty retreat, under fire from the enemy's guns . . ." Victor's shudder was altogether unfeigned. "Meaning no disrespect, but I would prefer not to have to essay that."

"Would you prefer Bredestown to fall into the blood-dripping hands of King George's butchers, then?" Isaac Fenner's voice and the temperature of his rhetoric both rose dramatically, as if he were making a closing argument in a court of law.

That didn't impress Victor Radcliff. "I know who the enemy is," he said. "I surely fought alongside a good many of the redcoats now opposing us when we conquered French Atlantis. They are not fiends in human form—although I may have to qualify that opinion if they import certain copper-skinned mercenary bands from Terranova."

"Do you suppose they would?" Fenner asked anxiously.

"If they use mercenaries at all, I think them more likely to bring in German troops: Braunschweigers and Hessians and the like. Germans are better disciplined and better armed." Victor paused. "On the other hand, copperskins cost less. That will matter to his Majesty's skinflint ministers, even if not so much to him."

"Confound it!" Fenner said. "You are telling me Bredestown *will* fall, and we can do damn all to stop that. If we can't beat the damned Englishmen, why did we go to war against them?"

"Because the other choice was submitting to tyranny and oppression," Victor said.

"It looks as though we must submit to them anyhow," Fenner said.

"You gentlemen of the Atlantean Assembly determined to take arms against King George. You summoned me from a peaceful life as farmer and author to lead them," Victor said. "If now you repent of your determination or you would sooner have some other commander, you need but say the word. I assure you, I will return without complaint and without regret to the life that late I led."

"We entrusted you with command on the belief that you would lead our troops to victory against the redcoats," Fenner said. "Instead, we have suffered two sanguinary defeats. We face the loss of Bredestown. The safety even of New Hastings is far from assured."

"Your Excellency, I will say two things in response to that." Victor Radcliff ticked them off on his fingers: "First, I strongly believe General Howe's victories to have been far more bloody than our defeats. He held the ground after both encounters, but paid a high price for it. And second, sir, mark this and mark it well—the only assured safety's in the grave. Anything this side of it is subject to time and chance."

The speaker of the Atlantean Assembly sniffed loudly. "If you made as good a general as you do a philosopher, Mr. Radcliff, I would face the coming struggle with the utmost confidence."

"I, on the other hand, knowing my limits as a philosopher, would face it with trepidation verging on terror," Victor replied.

"Your limits as a general are what concern me," Isaac Fenner said. "We cannot simply abandon Bredestown to the redcoats. The Atlantean Assembly deplores the moral effect such an abandonment would have on Atlanteans and on Terranovans and Europeans favorable to our cause."

"For the reasons I just outlined to you, your Excellency, holding it seems unlikely, and all the more so unless you intend to risk New Hastings," Victor said. "Or has the Assembly some clever stratagem in mind by which both towns may be preserved in our hands?"

"We hope and trust, sir, that you are the repository

of such stratagems," Fenner answered. He scratched his chin, then leaned close to Victor. "May I rely on your discretion here?"

"If you may not, sir, you chose the wrong general."

Fenner grunted. "A point—a distinct point. Very well, then. This is for your ears and your ears alone, do you understand?"

"Say on," Victor told him.

"If Bredestown must be lost, then it must." Fenner looked like a man with something sour in his mouth. Visibly pulling himself together, he continued, "But Bredestown must not be seen to be cravenly lost. We must not appear incapable of fighting for it even if we prove incapable of holding it. Does that make any sense to you at all, General?"

"Whatever our weaknesses may be, you do not care to advertise them to the world," Victor said slowly.

"That is the nub of it, yes." Isaac Fenner sounded relieved. Victor got the feeling that, had he failed to divine it, he would have returned to the retirement of which he'd spoken. The head of the Atlantean Assembly went on, "So—can you bloody Howe's men before you pull away?"

"I can try, sir," Radcliff answered.

"That is my home, you know. I shall rely upon you to make them pay a high price for it," Fenner said.

"I'll do what I can, sir," Victor said. That satisfied Fenner, which was fortunate, because Victor knew (whether the speaker did or not) he'd promised nothing.

Bredestown lay twenty miles up the river from New Hastings. Victor thought it was the second-oldest English settlement in Atlantis, but wasn't quite sure— Freetown might have been older. He knew some restless Radcliffe had founded it. In those long-vanished days, twenty miles inland were plenty to get away from your neighbors. If only that were still true now!

Victor marched his field artillery, his riflemen, and a

regiment's worth of musketeers up the Brede from New Hastings. He left the rest of his force behind to make the Royal Navy think twice about landing marines. The enemy admiral wouldn't be sure he hadn't left the whole army behind. The enemy general wouldn't be sure he hadn't brought everyone along. Neither of them would be able to talk to the other, not quickly or conveniently. And so, taking advantage of their uncertainty, Victor could do what Isaac Fenner wanted.

Whether that was a good idea . . . he'd find out.

As the redcoats advanced on Bredestown, riflemen harassed them from trees alongside the road. Victor made sure all the snipers he sent forward wore the green coats that marked uniformed Atlantean rebels. General Howe had started hanging snipers captured in ordinary coats. He'd sent the Atlanteans a polite warning that he intended to treat such men as *francs-tireurs*. Victor's protest that not all Atlanteans could afford uniforms and that green coats were in short supply fell on deaf ears.

Under the laws of war, Howe was within his rights to do as he did. And Victor knew some of the snipers *were* plucky amateurs, not under his command or anyone else's but their own. He also knew hanging them was more likely to make Atlanteans hate England than to make them cower in fear. If General Howe couldn't see that for himself, he watered the rebellion with the blood of patriots. The more he did, the more it would grow.

The redcoats came on despite the snipers. The riflemen who obeyed Victor Radcliff's orders fell back into Bredestown. They went on banging away at the enemy from the houses on the northern outskirts of town. If the Atlantean Assembly wanted Victor to fight for Bredestown, he would do his best to oblige that august conclave.

General Howe went on learning from some of his earlier battles. He didn't send his men against Bredestown in neat rows, but in smaller, more flexible storming parties. *If this is the game you're playing*, he seemed to say, *I can play, too*.

And so he could . . . up to a point. But Victor had posted more riflemen in some of the houses closer to the Brede. As the redcoats pushed deeper into Bredestown after cleaning out the first few houses there, they got stung again.

English field guns unlimbered. A couple of them set up too close to their targets. Riflemen started picking off the gunners before the cannon could fire. The redcoats hastily dragged the guns farther away.

Cannon balls could knock houses down. A roundshot smashing into a wall sounded like a pot dropped on cobbles. Through his spyglass, Victor watched the redcoats cut capers when their artillerymen made a good shot. After a while, the riflemen fell silent.

That had to be what General Howe was waiting for. Satisfied he'd beaten down the opposition, he finally formed his men in neat lines and marched them into Bredestown.

Closer and closer they came. At Victor's orders, the surviving riflemen—a larger fraction than Howe would have guessed—held their fire. He wanted the redcoats to draw near. General Howe might have learned something from his earlier fights, but he hadn't learned enough.

Several houses in Bredestown concealed not riflemen but the meager Atlantean field artillery. The guns were double-shotted with canister. Half a dozen musketeers standing near Victor fired in the air to signal the field guns to shoot.

They roared as near simultaneously as made no difference. The blasts of lead balls tore half a dozen great gaps in the English lines. Even from close to half a mile away, Victor heard the screams and moans of the wounded and dying.

He'd hoped such a disaster would give the redcoats pause. He knew it would have given him pause. But he'd reckoned without the English soldiers' doggedness.

They stepped over their dead and injured comrades, re-formed their lines, and trudged forward once more.

Two or three of the Atlantean guns fired again. Fresh holes opened in the ranks of General Howe's men. Again, the redcoats re-formed. Again, they came on. Teams of horses pulled some of the field guns back toward the Brede. Victor realized he would lose the rest—and lost guns were an almost infallible mark of a lost battle.

"Dammit, I didn't intend to win this one," Victor muttered. But he hadn't intended to lose cannon, either.

"What's that, sir?" Blaise asked.

"Nothing," Victor said, which wasn't quite true. Up till now, everything had gone the way he'd planned it. The field guns had taken such a toll among the redcoats, he'd started to hope they would cave in. If you let your hopes take wing like that, you commonly ended up sorry afterwards.

Victor did, in short order. His riflemen and musketeers fought from house to house, but they were outnumbered. And, he discovered, the redcoats didn't seem inclined to take prisoners in this fight. Anyone they caught, they shot or bayoneted. He didn't like the reports he got on that, but he also didn't know what he could do about it.

Some of the smoke that rose from Bredestown had the fireworks smell of black powder. More and more, though, brought a fireplace to mind. Dry timber was burning. How much of Bredestown would be left by the time the fight for the place was over?

A runner came back to him. "Colonel Whiting's compliments, sir," the man panted, "but he doesn't know how much longer he'll be able to hold his position. The redcoats are pressing pretty hard."

When Dominic Whiting said the enemy was pressing pretty hard, any other officer would have reported disaster some time earlier. From what Victor had seen, Whiting liked his rum, but he also liked to fight. Not only that, he was good at it, which not all aggressive men were.

"My compliments to the colonel, and tell him he's done his duty," Victor said. "I don't want him getting cut off. He is to retreat to the bridges over the Brede. Tell him that very plainly, and tell him it is an order from his superior."

"Yes, sir. I'll make sure he understands." The runner sketched a salute and hurried away.

Victor Radcliff sighed. When General Howe told one of his subordinates to do something, he could be confident the man would jolly well do it. Discipline in the English army wasn't just a matter of privates blindly obeying their sergeants. It ran up the whole chain of command.

An Atlantean officer would obey his superior . . . if he happened to feel like it, if he thought obeying looked like a good idea, if Saturn aligned with Jupiter and Mars was in the fourth house. He wouldn't do it simply because he'd got an order. If Atlanteans didn't love freedom and individualism, they never would have risen against King George. They wanted to go on doing as they pleased, not as someone on the other side of the ocean wanted them to do. A lot of the time, they didn't want to do as someone on *this* side of the ocean wanted them to do, either.

How were you supposed to command an army full of dedicated freethinkers, anyway? *Carefully*, Victor thought. It would have been funny—well, funnier—if it didn't hold so much truth. You could tell a redcoat what to do. He'd do it, or die trying. If an Atlantean didn't see a good reason for an order, he'd tell you to go to hell.

To Victor's relief, Dominic Whiting did see a reason for the order to fall back. So did his subordinate commanders. If he couldn't get his majors and captains to obey, he had as much trouble as Victor did with him. The order to retreat must have looked like a good idea to everybody—one more proof that Howe's men were pressing Whiting hard.

An old man leaning on a stick came up to Victor. "Look what they've done to our town!" he shouted in a mushy voice that proclaimed he'd lost most of his teeth.

"I'm sorry, sir," Victor said. The old man cupped his left hand behind his ear. Victor said it again, louder this time.

"Sorry? Sorry! Why didn't you stay away from Bredestown, then?" the graybeard said. "They would have, too, and everything would have been fine."

Things didn't work that way, no matter how much Victor wished they did. Explaining as much to the old man struck him as more trouble than it was worth. And he had other things to worry about. He'd picked troops to get his men back over the bridges in good order. The retreating soldiers didn't want to listen to them. Atlanteans seldom wanted to listen to anybody—one more demonstration of the thought that had occurred to him not long before.

He had hoped to have a cannon firing across every bridge to make sure English soldiers couldn't swarm after his own men. Losing some of the guns at the north end of Bredestown ruined that scheme. He posted three- and six-pounders where he could, and squads of musketeers where he had no guns.

The redcoats didn't push toward the bridges with great élan. They might have suspected he had something nasty waiting for them. Again, he'd lost the battle but mauled the enemy while he was doing it. He had, he supposed, met Isaac Fenner's requirements.

Once all the Atlantean soldiers made it to the Brede's south bank, Victor dealt with the bridges. Gunpowder charges blew gaps in a couple of stone spans. His men poured tubs of grease on the wooden bridges and set them afire. Without boats, General Howe's troops wouldn't cross here. The closest ford was another twenty miles upstream. He sent a detachment to hold it for a while.

"Well," he said to no one in particular, "we did what we came here to do." He would have felt happier about things if the moans of the wounded didn't make him wonder if it was all worthwhile.

VI

General Howe's army did not pursue Victor's as the Atlanteans fell back toward New Hastings. The redcoats seemed content—for the moment—with Bredestown. Victor Radcliff was not content to yield it to them. His men had fought well, but, again, not well enough.

A messenger from the Atlantean Assembly rode out to meet him halfway between Bredestown and New Hastings. Victor eyed the man with (he hoped) well-hidden apprehension. What new disaster had the Assemblymen sent him out to report?

"General, I am told to inform you—"

"Yes? Out with it!" Maybe Victor's apprehension wasn't so well hidden after all.

"Several hundred new recruits await your attention on your return, sir. I am also told to let you know that more than a few of them gave as their reason for volunteering the strong opposition the forces under your command have offered against the English tyrant's murderers."

"You are? They do? The Atlantean Assembly sent you to me for *that*?" Victor couldn't hide his surprise. Bad news usually traveled faster than good. And with reason: bad news was the kind you had to do something about right away ... if you could. Most of the time, good news could wait.

But the courier nodded. "That's right, sir. Mr. Fenner and Mr. Cawthorne both told me to tell you they know you are doing the best you can, and the rest of Atlantis seems to know it, too."

"Well, well," Victor said. That didn't seem enough somehow, so he said it again: "Well, well." The splutters bought him a few seconds to think. "Please convey my gratitude to the gentlemen of the Atlantean Assembly, and particularly to Mr. Cawthorne and Mr. Fenner."

"I'll do that, sir," the messenger said.

"Thank you. I'll thank the recruits myself when I get back to the coast," Victor said. "The Assembly has been gracious enough to note that I did not despair of the republic. The same holds true for these volunteers, and in rather greater measure. If I fall, finding a new general will be easy enough. But if no one chooses to fight for Atlantis, our cause is dead, dead beyond any hope of resurrection."

"That's a fact." Now the man who'd come out from New Hastings sounded surprised. "Not a fact you think about every day, though, is it?"

"Maybe not." Victor knew damn well it wasn't. The powers that be didn't want potential fighting men to realize how the shape of the future lay in their hands. If they sat on those hands, no war could go on for long.

The messenger sketched a salute. "Well, then, I'm off. I'll pass things on like you said, and I know your sergeants will whip the new chums into shape pretty damn quick." His chuckle held a certain amount of anticipation. Gloating? That, too, Victor judged.

He felt better the rest of the way back to New Hastings. He wondered why. Nothing had changed. General Howe had still seized Bredestown, the second- or third-oldest city in English Atlantis. The redcoats were still likely to move on New Hastings. A regiment's worth of raw volunteers wouldn't slow them down, much less hold them back.

But the spirit that brought forth a regiment's worth of raw volunteers would . . . eventually. If Atlantis didn't lose the war before England got sick of fighting it. That could happen. It could happen much too easily, as Victor knew much too well.

"I have to make sure it doesn't, that's all," he murmured. Easy enough to say something like that. Keeping the promise might prove rather harder.

Small bands of Atlantean cavalry still roamed north of the Brede. Every so often, they managed to cut off and cut up a column of supply wagons coming down to General Howe. Some of what they took supplied the Atlantean army instead. Some they kept. And some they sold. They thought of it as prize money, as if they were sailors capturing enemy ships.

Prize money, though, was a long-established official custom. Theirs was anything but. Victor didn't complain. He wouldn't complain about anything that made his men fight harder.

They didn't just loot. He *would* have complained if they were nothing but brigands. He'd been back in New Hastings only a few hours when a troop of horsemen brought in a glum-looking prisoner.

"We caught him in civilian clothes, General, like you see," one of the troopers said. No wonder their captive looked glum—the laws of war said you could hang an enemy soldier caught in civilian clothes. What else was he then but a spy?

"How do you know he's a soldier at all?" Victor asked the Atlanteans who'd brought in the captive.

"We found this here on him, sir." One of the men handed him a folded letter.

Radcliff unfolded it and read it. It was a letter from General Howe to the officer in charge of the Royal Navy detachment that was harrying New Hastings. "You were going to give some kind of signal from the shore, and they'd send a boat for you so you could deliver this?" Victor asked the captive.

The man stood mute—for a moment. Then one of the Atlanteans who'd brought him in shook him like a

dog shaking a rat. "Answer the general, you silly bugger, if you want to go on breathing."

"Uh, that's right," the captive said unwillingly.

"Did you men read this?" Victor asked the Atlanteans who'd caught him.

"Enough to see what it was," one of them answered.
"Enough to see that you needed to see it right away."

"And I thank you for that," Victor Radcliff said. "But
I'd like to read you one passage in particular. General
Howe writes, 'As before, the resistance offered by the
Atlanteans in Bredestown was unsettling, even daunt-
ing. They withdrew in good order after inflicting casualties we are barely able to support. This rebellion has
a character different from and altogether more serious
than what we were led to believe before we embarked
upon the task of suppressing it.' " He folded the paper.
"That's you he's talking about, gentlemen!"

"Think he'll pack up and go home, then?" asked the
big man who'd shaken the prisoner. "If he thinks he
can't win, why keep fighting?"

Reluctantly, Victor shook his head. If Howe kept advancing in spite of his losses, Victor wasn't sure he could
keep him out of New Hastings. He didn't tell that to the
Atlanteans, lest they be captured in turn or infect their
comrades with the doubt they'd caught from him. What
he did say was, "No, I think we need to give him a few
more sets of lumps before he's ready to do that."

"Well, we can take care of it," the big Atlantean said.
The others nodded. They knew less than Victor. They
didn't worry about things like why they didn't have
more bayonets or where the gunpowder for the battle
after the battle after next would come from. That made
them more hopeful than he was. Maybe their hope
would infect him.

Plaintively, the Englishman they'd captured asked,
"What will you do to me?"

"Ought to knock you over the head and pitch you
into the Brede. Better than you deserve, too," one of the
Atlanteans said. The prisoner turned pale.

"No, no," Victor said. "Can't have that, or Howe's soldiers will start knocking our men over the head after they catch them. I'll fight that kind of war if I must, but I don't want to. We'll keep him as a prisoner till he's properly exchanged, that's all."

"Thank you kindly, your Honor," the Englishman said. "If you let me go, I'll give my parole not to fight until I'm exchanged."

"Sorry. I think we'd do better to hold you for now," Victor replied. "Let General Howe think his letter's been delivered." He turned to the Atlanteans who'd captured the man. "Keep him with our other prisoners, and keep an eye on him. We don't want him slipping away while our backs are turned."

"Right you are, General," the big man said. He set a hand the size of a ham on the prisoner's shoulder. "Come on, you." The Englishman perforce came. The Atlantean soldiers led him away.

Victor Radcliff slowly read through Howe's letter once more. He nodded to himself. Nice to learn he wasn't the only commander with worries, anyhow.

After taking Bredestown, the redcoats lay quiet for a fortnight. *Licking their wounds*, Victor thought, though he had no idea whether that was the explanation. Then General Howe cautiously began moving skirmishers down the Brede toward New Hastings.

Atlantean skirmishers met them right away. Victor didn't want Howe coming after him. Maybe a show of force would persuade the English that an attack on the oldest town in Atlantis would prove more trouble than it was worth.

On the other hand, maybe it wouldn't. The redcoats kept pushing forward. Victor sent more of his army back toward the west to delay them. He wished he could write General Howe a stiff letter. The continual pressure the Englishman applied to his forces struck him as not the least bit sporting.

Then nature took a hand. It rained buckets, sheets,

hogsheads. The Brede turned into a raging brown torrent that threatened to burst its banks and lay New Hastings waste before Howe could. Every road for miles around became a knee-deep quagmire.

And every firearm became no more than a fancy club or a wet spear. If steel squelched when it struck flint, no spark flew. And keeping powder in the priming pan dry was a separate nightmare. Victor wished for a thousand armored knights all carrying lances. As long as the rain lasted, they might have driven the redcoats from the field.

But it wouldn't last. He knew that all too well. He set his men to work on field fortifications north and south of the Brede. If the English army wanted to try to bull through to New Hastings, he aimed to set as many obstacles in its path as he could.

No matter what a man aimed at, he commonly got less. Victor did here. Earthworks sagged to muddy lumps as soon as they were built. Trenches turned to moats just as fast. And rumbles of mutiny came from the soldiers.

"They think you're trying to drown them," Blaise reported. He eyed the general commanding. "Maybe they're right, too."

"No." Radcliff shook his head. "That is not so. I'm trying to keep them from getting shot when the fighting picks up again. But . . ." The rain drummed down on his tent. He was standing in mud. He had a cot, that being one of the privileges a general enjoyed. So he slept dry— except when the tent leaked. Too many of his men slept in the open if they slept at all. He sighed. "We'll give it up, then. Sooner or later, though, the sky will clear."

After a week and a half, it did. General Howe tried to get his army on the move as soon as he could, which turned out to be too soon. Wagons and guns bogged down in the gluey mud. The redcoats' advance stopped almost before it got started.

"If we could get at 'em, we could slaughter 'em," reported a scout charged with keeping an eye on the enemy. "Some of their oxen are in it up to their bellies."

"So are ours," Victor replied. "And what sort of time did you have coming back to bring your news to me?"

"Well . . ." The cavalryman grimaced. "It wasn't what anybody'd call easy—I will say that."

Victor didn't attack. The sun made everything from the grass to the soldiers' wet clothes steam. Victor wondered how much of their powder was dry. Enough to fight a battle? Enough to shoot at all? He had a few men fire their muskets. Most of the firelocks went off. That was about as much as he could have hoped for. Even in the driest weather, misfires were all too common.

Scouts reported hearing musket fire from the redcoats, too, though they'd thought better for the moment of moving forward. No doubt General Howe was also making sure his soldiers could shoot if they had to.

Sergeants exhorted men to push oily rags through their musket barrels to hold rust at bay. Radcliff could only hope the stubbornly independent Atlanteans would listen. Over in the English army, other underofficers would be telling the men they led the same thing. The redcoats would obey—Victor was mournfully sure of that.

At last, slowly and cautiously, they did edge forward once more. Victor's men skirmished and sniped from behind fences and trees. The Englishmen caught a sniper who was wearing a green coat and cut his throat, leaving his body for his comrades to find.

"We ought to do that to the next redcoat we catch!" a rifleman raged. "If they want to fight filthy, we can fight filthy, too!" His comrades shook their fists and shouted agreement.

Do you intend this to be a war without quarter? Victor wrote to General Howe. *If you do, sir, we shall endeavor to oblige you. But murdering men taken prisoner only adds cruelty to the conflict without in the least changing its likely result.* He added details about the killing and sent off the note under flag of truce.

An English junior officer carrying a white flag brought the enemy general's response the next day. *Please accept my apologies and my assurances that such distasteful in-cidents shall not be repeated,* Howe wrote. *The men responsible have been punished.*

He didn't say how. Victor Radcliff muttered to himself. Was it enough? Victor used a penknife to trim a quill, then dipped the tip of the goose feather in a bottle of ink. *So long as these assurances be respected and observed, we shall not reply in kind,* he wrote. *But if we meet with such barbarities again, you may rely on our ability and intention to avenge ourselves by whatever means seem fitting. Very respectfully, your most obedient servant . . .* He signed his name.

The subaltern who'd brought General Howe's reply waited for Victor's. The young man saluted as he might have done for his own commanding officer. He took Victor's letter, performed a smart about-turn, mounted his horse, and rode off toward his own lines.

War's politesse, as formal as a gavotte's, Victor thought. *It doesn't stop us from killing one another. It doesn't even slow us down much. But it does make sure we do it by the rules.*

His chuckle held a distinctly wry edge. Blaise had never got used to those rules. He thought they were nothing but white men's foolishness. He might have been right. Still and all, though, the whole business might have ended up even worse without them.

A few days later, Victor was wondering how the whole business could end up any worse. The redcoats probed at the lines he'd tried to set up to hold them away from New Hastings. They probed, and they found that the lines weren't nearly so solid as he'd wished they were.

Too many of his men hadn't learned how to stand up under an artillery bombardment. Most cannon balls harmlessly buried themselves in wet earth or went skipping over the landscape, dangerous only if you were rash enough to try to stop one with your foot. Every so often, though, a roundshot would mash a man—or two or three men—into a crimson horror not usually seen outside a slaughterhouse. It was worse when the cannon ball didn't kill right away. Then the luckless soldier's shrieks spread his agony to every man who heard them.

And when the Atlanteans, having seen a few red horrors and heard a few agonized shrieks, streamed out of a length of trench, their opponents, ruthlessly competent, went in and took it away from them. That threatened more Atlantean companies with enfilading fire. Clever enough to see as much, the men from those companies would pull back, too. And so, little by little, Victor's defensive position dissolved like a salt statue in the rain.

He wished for more rain. The sun smiled down from a bright blue sky. The small, puffy clouds drifting across it only mocked his hopes. He had to fall back two or three miles closer to New Hastings and try to set up new positions from which to withstand the English advance.

One of his captains asked, "What's to keep that bastard Howe from doing the same thing all over again?"

Victor Radcliff gave him a bleak look. "Nothing I can see."

He did set his riflemen to sniping at the English artillerists. If the redcoats had trouble serving their guns, they wouldn't be able to hurt his men so much the next time around. He could also hope they wouldn't be able to intimidate the Atlanteans so much.

And he sent a message back to New Hastings, warning the Atlantean Assembly he might not be able to hold the town. *You must prepare yourselves to leave expeditiously*, he wrote. *Much as I regret to state it, I cannot promise New Hastings' security nor your safety in the event the city falls*.

He was watching the redcoats get ready to assault his newest makeshift defensive works when a horseman leaned down and thrust a folded sheet of paper into his hand. "From the Atlantean Assembly, General," he said.

"Thank you," Victor said, though he didn't want his elbow joggled at just that moment.

No matter what he wanted, he unfolded the paper.

He had to hold it a little farther from his eyes than he would have liked; his sight was beginning to lengthen. But Isaac Fenner's hand was large and clear. *Thank you for alerting us to what may come*, Fenner wrote. *If need be, we shall evacuate confident the fight will continue even without this town and expecting you to bloody the tyrannous foe here as you did at Bredestown.*

"Is everything all right, sir?" Blaise asked, and then, a moment later, "Is anything all right?"

"Now that you mention it," Radcliff replied, "no." Isaac Fenner was a very clever man—no doubt about it. No doubt, also, that he would never make a soldier. The Atlanteans had had an easy retreat from Bredestown. If they were driven into New Hastings, where would they go once driven out again? *Yes. Where?* Victor asked himself. He might need an answer soon.

"Anything I can do?" the colored sergeant inquired.

"Can you make the redcoats disappear? Can you give the Atlantean Assembly a dose of common sense?" Victor said.

"Let me have a rifle, sir, and I'll see what I can do about General Howe." Blaise never lacked for confidence.

Marksmen with rifles did their best to pick off enemy officers. Deliberately trying to assassinate the English commander, however, struck Victor as surpassing the limits of decency. Moreover, the redcoats were altogether too likely to try to return the disfavor. He hoped that consideration didn't influence him too much when he replied, "I'm not sure how much point there would be. His second-in-command is said to be a skillful officer."

"Kill him, too." Blaise was ready to be as ruthless as the situation required—or a bit more so.

"If the opportunity arises," Victor said, and not another word. Blaise snorted; he knew Victor wouldn't do anything along those lines.

Victor did send out more snipers to try to discourage the redcoats from advancing. They picked off a few Englishmen. Maybe they slowed the enemy's movements a little. Victor knew too well they didn't slow them much.

General Howe methodically formed his men for the assault on the Atlanteans' positions in front of New Hastings. He put most of his strength on the right. Watching that, Victor realized what it meant: if the English attack succeeded, Howe would try to pin the Atlanteans against the Brede and pound their army to pieces.

It had better not succeed, then, Victor thought. He shifted men to shore up his own left, and moved cannon to cover that part of the field, too. He also posted a couple of companies to try to hold the road east to New Hastings in case his army had to retreat down it. By holding them out of the battle, he made it a little more likely that the army would need to retreat. But he also made it more likely that the force as a whole would survive. To him, that counted for more.

Howe opened with a cannonading like the one that had frightened the Atlanteans out of their lines farther west. This time, to Victor's vast relief, his men seemed less alarmed. Atlantean guns fired back at the English troops. Every so often, a roundshot would knock down a few men. The redcoats stolidly re-formed and held their ground. Victor hated and admired them at the same time. They were too damned hard to beat.

On they came, advancing to the music of fife, drum, and horn. Sunfire flashed from their bayonets. The inexperienced soldiers facing them feared cold steel almost as much as they feared artillery. They had reason to fear it, too: it gave the redcoats the edge in the hand-to-hand.

Atlantean muskets thundered. The volley was sharper than it would have been when the uprising began. Victor's men couldn't match Howe's in drill or discipline, but knew more of the soldier's trade now than they had when the fighting started.

A great cloud of grayish smoke obscured the field ... and Victor's view of the oncoming Englishmen. Not even his spyglass helped. He swore. How could he know what was going on through that man-made fogbank?

Here and there, fresh shots rang out from the Atlantean position. Some musketeers, having fired once, could reload fast enough to send another three-quarter-inch ball against the redcoats before the foe reached them. Most men, unfortunately, weren't so skilled—or so lucky.

For a few seconds, Victor let hope run away with him. Maybe the insurrectionists' fearsome volley had knocked Howe's men back on their heels. Some storms of lead were too much to bear. He'd seen that himself, fighting against the French settlers in the last war and in the fight north of Weymouth only a few weeks before.

Some storms were . . . but not this one. The English soldiers burst through the smoke and began jumping down into the trenches that sheltered the Atlanteans. Not only were the redcoats' muskets bayoneted, they were also all loaded, while too many of Victor's men still struggled with powder charge and wad and ball and ramrod.

The Atlanteans fought hard. Victor had seldom seen his summer soldiers do anything else. If courage and ferocity were all it took to win the day . . . But cold-hearted professional competence also had its place. And the redcoats had more of that than his men did, while they also didn't lack for courage.

Fighting and cursing, the Atlanteans fell back. One well-sited gun loaded with canister shredded half a dozen redcoats. No matter how perfectly disciplined the Englishmen were, that horrific blast slowed down their pursuit. Victor wouldn't have wanted to storm forward when he was all too likely to get blown to cat's meat, either.

Half an hour later, seeing that Howe's infantry would let his battered army escape again, he said the best thing he could: "Well, we're still in the fight, by God."

"Yes, sir," Blaise agreed. "And we still stand between the enemy and New Hastings."

"So we do." *But for how much longer?* Victor wondered. He didn't care for the answer he foresaw. Because he didn't, he called for a messenger.

A young man on horseback rode up and touched two fingers of his right hand to the brim of his shapeless straw hat. It might have been a salute; it was more likely nothing but a friendly wave. "What do you need, General?" the youngster asked.

"Take word to the Atlantean Assembly," Victor said. "Tell them they'd better get out of New Hastings while the going is still good."

By the time Victor's battered force limped into New Hastings, the Atlantean Assembly was already gone. Some people claimed the leaders of the rising against King George had fled north across the Brede and then west, towards Atlantis' sparsely populated interior. Others said they'd gone south, in the direction of Freetown and the formerly French settlements beyond.

Victor had no sure way to judge which report was true. When he rode into New Hastings from the west, men who had reason not to desire the return of English rule were abandoning the city in both directions. Had the Royal Navy not lain offshore, he suspected plenty of people would also have fled by sea.

He wondered which way to take the army. He was tempted to make his best guess about which way the Atlantean Assembly had gone, then head in the opposite direction. That way, he could fight General Howe without the useless advice and even more useless orders the Assembly gave him.

Reluctantly, he decided that wasn't the proper course. This wasn't his solo struggle against the redcoats; it was Atlantis' fight. If anybody represented Atlantis, the Assembly did. And if it was cantankerous and confused . . . it accurately portrayed the people it served.

After some thought, he took his own force north over the Brede once more. In the French settlements, his men might be thought of as invaders no less than General Howe's. They would also be reckoned no less English than the redcoats, at least by the inhabitants who'd dwelt in those parts longer than ten or fifteen years.

He sent messengers to the seaside forts, ordering their garrisons away with the rest of his force. They were precious far beyond their numbers. In Atlantis, skilled artillerists didn't hatch from honkers' eggs. (Or maybe they did, for the big flightless birds and their eggs were regrettably scarce these days, especially in the better-settled eastern regions.)

The artillerists also brought out their lighter guns, the ones that could keep up with the army. They drove spikes into the touch-holes of the heavier cannon and broke up their carriages, doing their best to deny them to the enemy.

Some of his men carried bits of this and that with them as they crossed the bridge over the Brede: loot from New Hastings shops. Victor kept quiet about it. Many of those shops had been abandoned. The proprietors who stayed behind were mostly men who favored King George. Radcliff would lose no sleep to see them plundered.

Fires broke out in the old town even before the Atlantean army finished evacuating it. Victor did hope the ancient redwood church would survive. It had already seen two wars and three centuries. Losing it now would be like losing a piece of what made Atlantis the way it was.

Such considerations didn't keep him from blowing up the stone bridge after his army was over it. The artillerymen from the forts did a first-rate job, dropping part of the elliptical arch into the Brede. General Howe's men would take some time to repair it. With luck, that would mean they'd have a hard time pursuing the battle-weary Atlanteans.

Victor hoped for luck. As far as he could see, his side hadn't had much up till now. He was sure the English commander would laugh at him and complain that the redcoats hadn't caught a break since the fighting started. No general since Sulla had ever thought of himself as a lucky man.

"Come on! Come on!" Victor called. "We can stand

here gawping while New Hastings falls, but we can't stop it. What we can do is get away and keep fighting. We can—and we'd better. So get moving, boys! We'll beat them next time—see if we don't!"

He wondered if they would laugh at him or jeer at him or just ignore him and go their separate ways. If they did, he didn't know what he could do about it. He didn't have much in the way of coercion ready to hand right now. Armies sometimes fell apart, and damn all you could do about it.

To his surprise—no, to his slack-jawed amazement— the soldiers raised a cheer. He doffed his tricorn to them. The cheers got louder. "We'll whip 'em yet, General!" somebody shouted. "You see if we don't!"

"Damned right!" somebody else yelled.

"Huzzah for General Radcliff and the National Assembly!" someone else said. That won him three cheers, each louder than the one that had gone before.

The Assembly had voted him their thanks because he hadn't despaired of the cause after a defeat. The men he led seemed to deserve those praises more than he did. He doffed his hat again, and waved it, and waited for the cheering to subside.

"Thank you, men. Thank you—friends," he said huskily. "Thank you for the faith you show in me, and thank you for the faith you show in Atlantis. As long as Atlantis has faith in you, I know we cannot possibly lose this war. The redcoats have more training, but you are fighting for your country, for your homes. In the end, that will make all the difference in the world."

Over on the other side of the Brede, General Howe's soldiers would be marching into New Hastings. They already held Hanover and Croydon farther north, and most of the smaller towns along the coast in those parts, too. They had to think they were strangling Atlantis' freedom, the way Hercules strangled the serpents in his cradle.

When Victor was down, as he was now, he had to think they were right. But were they? Fighting had hardly touched the southern settlements or the west coast of Atlantis. And, more to the point, it had barely reached into the interior. No English soldier had come within many miles of chasing Margaret off the Radcliff farm.

Maybe I'm not lying to these fellows after all, then, Victor thought. *By God, I hope I'm not. England sees the coast, because that's what she trades with. But Atlantis is bigger than that.*

Atlantis was, when you got right down to it, several times larger than England, Scotland, Wales, and Ireland put together. One of these days, it would grow richer, stronger, and more populous than King George's realm. When you looked at things that way, how outrageous of George's soldiers to try to hold this land down by force!

For the moment, though, England was a man grown, Atlantis only a stripling. No matter how much promise Atlantis held, England was stronger—and better able to use the strength it had—now. Staying in the fight, wearing the enemy down ... that was what Atlantis would have to do.

"Let's go, men," Victor called. "We need to get away. We need to make sure the damned redcoats can't catch us till we're ready for them." He respected Howe's engineers too much to imagine a blown bridge would keep them on the wrong side of the Brede very long. "And we need to get in touch with the Atlantean Assembly again, to find out what they require of us."

Did I just say that? he wondered. But he did, no doubt about it, even if he'd been at least half glad the Assembly wasn't telling him what to do every chance it got. If he had to decide everything on his own, he would turn into something closer to king than to general. The only thing he knew about kings was that he didn't want to be one.

Dark clouds blowing over the Green Ridge Mountains swept in front of the sun. The day got cooler in a hurry. All at once, the air tasted damp. More rain was coming. For that matter, fall was coming. How much longer would either side be able to campaign in any serious way?

One thing rain would do: as it had before, it would turn the roads to mud. The redcoats would have a devil of a time catching up to his army in bad weather. Their force would bog down worse than his, in fact, because they had more artillery and a bigger, more ponderous baggage train.

His horse snorted softly. Its nostrils flared. If that didn't mean it smelled rain, he would have been surprised.

If I have a winter's worth of time away from the English, a winter's worth of time to train my men, to turn them into proper fighters . . . Victor Radcliff nodded to himself. Even now, the Atlanteans proved they could confront hardened professional soldiers from across the sea. With drill, with discipline, wouldn't they be able to rout the redcoats? He hoped so. Sooner or later, Atlantis would likely need victories, not just hard-fought defeats.

•

VII

Victor Radcliff was a much-traveled man. All the same, he didn't think he'd ever been in Horsham before. He wasn't completely sure; if Atlantis had less memorable places than Horsham, he'd long since forgotten about them. A couple of taverns—one of which had a few rooms for benighted travelers and called itself an inn—a few shops, a gristmill, a smithy, a few streets' worth of houses . . . Horsham.

The Atlantean Assembly had come through the town. He heard that at least a dozen times as he ate half a greasy capon at the tavern that didn't put on airs. The men of the Assembly had kept on heading northwest, which only proved they had better sense than Victor had credited them for.

"They could have stayed here. I don't know why they didn't," said the girl who brought him the capon and fried parsnips and beer.

He could have told her. But she'd doubtless lived her whole life here, and so didn't know any better. Besides, she was blue-eyed, snub-nosed, and full-figured. That had more to do with his discretion.

Even with rain pattering down, he preferred his tent to anything Horsham's inn offered. He was about to blow out the candle when a sentry nearby challenged someone. Victor reached for a pistol. He'd told Blaise he didn't want to play the game of assassinations. He had no guarantee General Howe felt the same way.

A voice came out of the darkness. It was a vaguely familiar voice, but Victor couldn't place it, especially through the muffling raindrops. Then the sentry stuck his head into the tent. Despite a broad-brimmed hat, water dripped from the end of his nose. He sneezed before he said, "Your cousin Matthew's here to see you, General."

"Bless you, Jack. And for God's sake tell him to come in before he drowns," Victor said. He and Matthew Radcliffe were cousins, but hardly more than in the sense that all men were brothers. Still, the Atlantean Assemblyman from Avalon wouldn't have come back from wherever the Assembly had gone unless something urgent was going on. Victor hoped he wouldn't have, anyway.

Once inside the tent, Matthew shook himself like a wet dog. He was as soaked as the sentry, or maybe worse. He sneezed, too. Victor produced a flask of barrel-tree brandy. "Here," he said. "A restorative."

"You're a good man, General. Damned if you're not." Matthew Radcliffe took a hearty nip. "Ahh! That'll warm me up, or I hope it will. I hope to Jesus something will."

"Did you see Noah's Ark when you rode back here?" Victor asked gravely after his own pull at the flask.

He didn't faze the man from the west. "See it? The old man dropped me off just outside your camp."

"Generous of him." Victor wasn't about to let anybody out-calm him. But small jests went only so far, especially by the dim light from a candle. "Why did you need to see me in weather like this?"

"Because in Honker's Mill—which is where the Assembly is right now, and may stay a while—I met a man who'd come over the mountains with news from Avalon." Matthew Radcliffe punctuated that with another sneeze.

"God bless you." Victor drank from the flask again. "I don't suppose the news is good. If it were, it could have waited. The bad is what they have to tell you as soon as they can."

"Too right," his distant cousin agreed. "And I have bad news to give you, all right. The English, damn their black hearts, landed a band of copperskin warriors from Terranova south of our town. They've got hatchets and bows and arrows—and muskets and powder and ball the Englishmen gave 'em—and they're robbing and killing and burning and raping as they please. To tell you the truth, they're having a rare old time."

"Good Lord!" Victor had talked about copper-skinned mercenaries with Isaac Fenner, but he'd really expected to have to deal with Germans. Terranova's east coast, across the Hesperian Gulf from Atlantis, was dotted with Dutch and English and Spanish settlements. There had been French settlements there, too, but King Louis lost those along with the ones he'd ruled here in Atlantis.

White men were spreading into the interior of northern Terranova, but more slowly than they were in Atlantis. The barbarous copperskins fought against them—or sometimes, as here, fought for them.

"What can we do, General?" Matthew Radcliffe asked. "Can you spare men to send over the mountains or around the coast by sea? The Avalon militia is trying its best, but a lot of our men have already come east to fight the redcoats."

Traveling across Atlantis' mountainous spine still wasn't easy. Small bands could make it, living off the land as they went. With farms and villages few and far between, a real army was liable to starve on the way west.

Most of the time, sailing would have been a better bet, in merchantmen or in fishing boats. Now ... Now the Royal Navy was much too likely to snap them up like a cat killing mice that tried to sneak past it. "If I send a hundred men, most of them ought to get to Avalon," Victor said slowly. "And most of the ones who do ought to be able to fight. How many copperskins did the English turn loose over there?"

"I don't know exactly," Matthew Radcliffe replied. "I'm not sure anyone does know—except the savages and the damned sea captain who brought 'em, may the Devil fry his soul as black as his heart is already."

"Well, are a hundred soldiers and your militiamen enough to put paid to them?" Victor asked. "If they aren't, I fear you have more trouble than I know what to do with."

"Me, I fear the same thing," Matthew said. "But God bless you, General. I'll take your hundred men, and gladly. They're a hundred more than I reckoned you'd give me."

"We have to hold Avalon. It's our window on Terranova," Victor Radcliff said. "One of these days, travel across Atlantis will be easier. The west will be more settled. Avalon's the best harbor there, far and away—New Marseille doesn't come close. If the Royal Navy ties up in Avalon Bay, if the Union Jack flies on the hills there, they've got us by the ballocks. And they'll squeeze, too. They'll squeeze like anything."

"God bless you," Matthew Radcliffe said again. "Too many easterners can't see any of that. We ought to pay King George back for trying to bugger us this way." That wasn't quite the figure of speech Victor had used, but it got the Atlantean Assemblyman's meaning across. Matthew turned the subject: "Anything left in that flask?"

Slosh. "A little." Victor handed it to him. "Here."

"God bless you one more time." His cousin tilted his head back. His throat worked. He set the flask down. "Not any more, by Christ!" He bared his teeth in something more snarl than smile. "But what the Devil *can* we do to England in Terranova? The settlements there are quiet. Quiet as the grave, if you ask me. Quiet as the tomb. Those bastards don't give a farthing for freedom. If they'd risen with us, King George would have a harder time of it, to hell with me if he wouldn't. Am I right or am I wrong, General?"

"Oh, you're right—no doubt about it. I wish you weren't, but you are." Victor stared sorrowfully at the empty silvered flask, which gave back what candlelight there was. He wished he had another nip of his own. Well, no help for it: not right now, anyway.

"We ought to send missionaries to them, the way the Spaniards send missionaries to the copperskins they've conquered," Matthew Radcliffe said. "If they can turn nasty savages into Papists, can't we turn nasty Englishmen into freedom-lovers?"

"Missionaries." For a moment, Victor chuckled at the other man's conceit. Then his gaze focused and grew more intense, like the sun's rays brought together into a point by a burning glass. "Missionaries," he said again, this time in an altogether different tone of voice.

"You've got some kind of scheme," Matthew said. "Tell me what it is."

Instead of answering him directly, Victor clapped on a hat and stuck his head out into the pouring rain. He spoke with Jack for a minute or two. The sentry let out a resigned sigh. Then he squelched off into the darkness.

"You *have* got some scheme." Matthew Radcliffe sounded half curious, half accusing.

"Who, me?" Victor, by contrast, did his best to seem innocence personified. By the look Matthew sent him, his best came nowhere close to good enough. The Assemblyman kept shooting questions at him. Victor ducked and dodged and finally said, "You'll find out soon, I hope." That also failed to leave Matthew Radcliffe serene.

In due course, Jack returned. Thanks to the rain's steady hiss, he almost got back to the tent by the time Victor made out his soggy footfalls. And he came closer yet before Victor—and Matthew—could hear that he wasn't alone.

"Who's he got with him?" Matthew asked. "Our very own Jesuit, panting to bring the heathen English settlers of Terranova to the true faith of freedom?"

Ignoring the sarcasm, Victor Radcliff nodded. "As a matter of fact, yes."

Right on cue, the tent flap opened. The man who

stumbled inside didn't look like a Jesuit, or any other kind of missionary. He looked like a drowned rat—an angry drowned rat. "Whatever this is, couldn't it wait till the bloody morning?" he asked, his accent strongly English.

Matthew Radcliffe glanced toward Victor. "You have your own pet spy?" he inquired.

The newcomer glared at Matthew. "You have your own pet idiot?" he asked Victor.

"Matthew, let me present to you Master Thomas Paine," Victor said before things went beyond glances and glares. "Master Paine, this is Matthew Radcliffe, member of the Atlantean Assembly from Avalon. He—and all Atlantis—can use your persuasive abilities."

"What persuasive abilities?" Matthew Radcliffe looked unpersuaded.

So did Paine. "What does he need from me that I can't give as a soldier? I did not come to Atlantis for any reason but to seek my own freedom and some way to make a tolerable living—which I could not do in the mother country."

"Tell him what's happened by Avalon, Matthew," Victor said, and his distant cousin did. Victor went on, "If we can stir England's Terranovan towns to rebellion, she won't be able to do things like this to us again, and she will have to divide her attention, fighting two wars at once."

Matthew still seemed dubious. "Meaning no disrespect to Master Paine, but why should he be able to rouse England's settlements on the far side of the Gulf when we've had no luck at it up till now?"

"Because he is the best speaker—and especially the best writer—who backs our cause," Victor answered.

"You give me too much credit," Paine murmured.

"I'd better not," Victor told him.

"Better than Uncle Bobby? Better than Isaac Fenner? Than Custis Cawthorne, for God's sake?" Matthew Radcliffe shook his head. "I don't believe it."

Victor took a rumpled, damp, poorly printed flyer

from New Hastings out of a jacket pocket. " 'Men are born, and always continue, free—in respect of their rights,' " he read. " 'The end of all political associations is the preservation of the natural rights of man, and these are liberty, property, security, and resistance of oppression. The exercise of every man's natural rights has no other limits than those which are necessary to secure to every *other* man the free exercise of the same rights. The law ought to prohibit only actions hurtful to society. What is not prohibited by the law should not be hindered; nor should any one be compelled to that which the law does not require.' " He looked up; reading by candlelight was a trial. "You will have heard that, I am sure. Who do you suppose wrote it?"

"Isn't it from Custis' pen? I always thought so," Matthew said.

Victor set a hand on Thomas Paine's wet shoulder. "Meet the author. If he can't set Terranova alight, no one will make it catch."

"Well . . . maybe," Matthew Radcliffe said.

"You want me to go to Terranova, General?" Paine sounded less than delighted at the prospect. "You want me to put aside everything I have in Atlantis, cross to Avalon and sail over the Hesperian Gulf?"

Matthew Radcliffe started to make apologetic noises. Victor cut him off. "Master Paine, you are at the moment a common soldier in the Atlantean army. What precisely is it you have to give up, pray tell?"

Thomas Paine opened his mouth to answer. Then he closed it again before a single word crossed his lips. He gave Victor a crooked grin instead. "Put it that way, General, and you've got a point."

"Can he really fire the Terranovans?" Matthew asked.

Victor Radcliff nudged Paine. "What was it you said about William the Conqueror, and about how little hereditary monarchy means? Better Matthew should hear it from you than from me—I wouldn't get it right."

"All I said was that a French bastard who landed with armed bandits and established himself as King of

England against the consent of the natives was in plain terms a very paltry and rascally original." Paine quoted himself with obvious relish.

"You see?" Victor said to Matthew. "All they have to do is listen to him even a little, and he's bound to infect them."

"You make me sound like the smallpox," Paine observed.

"No. You inoculate men with freedom—and there's no inoculation against you," Victor said. "As for Terranova, better to inoculate than never, by God."

Paine and Matthew Radcliffe both winced. The latter still seemed to need convincing. "Maybe . . ." he said again.

"Give him something else," Victor told Paine.

"Am I then auditioning for the stage?" Paine asked.

"For the most important stage of all: the stage of the world," Victor Radcliff replied.

That seemed to get home to the wet incendiary from England. His voice grew lower, deeper, and altogether more impressive as he said, "Call to mind the sentiments which nature has engraved in the heart of every citizen, and which take a new force when they are solemnly recognized by all. For a nation to have liberty, it is enough that she knows liberty. And to be free, it is enough that she wills it."

"You see?" Victor said to Matthew once more. "He can do it!"

"And do you propose to command me to make Terranova free?" Thomas Paine asked. "I trust you note the irony involved?"

"I note it, yes," Victor answered. "But, having joined the Atlantean army, you do leave yourself open to command, you know."

"If you command me in any soldierly way, I will obey you," Paine said. "But if you command me to play the politico, do you not agree that that takes me out of the soldier's province?"

"Master Paine, you are a weapon of war, no less than

a six-pounder," Victor Radcliff said. "I hope you can harm the enemy more than any mere cannon might, even one double-shotted with canister. Will you tell me I may not aim you and fire you where you will have the greatest effect?"

"We need you, Master Paine," Matthew Radcliffe added. "The general—and yourself—have persuaded me. If Terranova rises against King George, too, that all but guarantees the safety of Avalon and the rest of western Atlantis. It ensures that the redcoats cannot carry copperskins across the Hesperian Gulf to harry our western settlements."

Thomas Paine sneezed. "Bless you," Victor said.

Paine waved that aside. He rounded on Matthew. "They're carrying savages across the sea to assail us? I had not heard that."

"Nor had I, till he brought me word of it," Victor put in.

"It is the truth, damn them," Matthew Radcliffe said.

"Then I must do—*must* do—everything in my power to oppose them. I had not thought they would stoop so low as to loose the copperskins against their own kith and kin." Thomas Paine turned back to Victor. He sneezed again. Then he said, "If I am your weapon, General, aim me and fire me as you think best. This king's wicked minions must be checked."

"Thank you," Victor said. Not until later did he wonder about the propriety of a commanding general thanking a common soldier. At the moment, he asked Matthew Radcliffe, "Will you undertake, either in your own person or through your fellow westerners, to convey Master Paine to Avalon as expeditiously as may be, and thence to one or another of the English towns of eastern Terranova, whichever may seem most advantageous at the time?"

"I will, General," Matthew replied. To Paine, he added, "Rest assured, you also have my thanks and that of the Atlantean Assembly." Victor also didn't marvel at that till after the fact.

"Let me lay hold of my chattels, such as they are, and I am your man from that time forward," Paine said. "Using barbarians to lay waste to civilization is to me unconscionable. If the king's ministers and admirals fail to find it so, what are they but mad dogs who deserve no better than to be hunted out of this land?"

Without waiting for an answer, he plunged out into the rain. "A fire-eater," Matthew Radcliffe observed, making ready to follow him.

Victor Radcliff shook his head. "Not quite. He is a fire-kindler. Others will eat the flames he sparks—and may they choke on them."

"Amen." Matthew squelched off into the night after Thomas Paine.

General Howe seemed content to enjoy his control of most of the northeastern coast of Atlantis. In his shoes, Victor might have felt the same way. The redcoats held most of the richest parts of the land, and most of the towns that deserved to be styled cities. From London, that might have seemed almost the same as crushing the Atlantean uprising underfoot.

On bad days, it also seemed almost the same as crushing the uprising to Victor Radcliff. But only on bad days, when he looked at all the things he'd failed to do. Holding Hanover and New Hastings topped the melancholy list. Beating the English in a pitched battle anywhere came next. He'd come close several times—which did him less good than he wished it did.

If he could have given the redcoats a black eye in any of their fights along the Brede, New Hastings would still lie in Atlantean hands. The Assembly would send its decisions and requests to the settlements from the oldest town in Atlantis, not from the grand metropolis of Honker's Mill. An edict coming out of New Hastings seemed much more authoritative than one emanating from a backwoods hamlet with a silly name.

Winter gave Victor the chance to drill his troops. New recruits kept coming in, both from the interior and from the coastal regions where King George nominally reigned supreme. That was encouraging. Less so were the Atlanteans who headed for home when their enlistment terms expired. There were at least as many of them as raw replacements.

Victor sent a letter to the Assembly, urging it to enlist troops for longer terms: for the length of the war, if at all possible. The Assembly forwarded the letter to each settlement's parliament. Maybe those august bodies—the ones not under the English boot, anyhow—would do as he asked. Or maybe they wouldn't. Neither he nor the Atlantean Assembly could compel them.

Sometimes he wondered whether the Atlanteans wanted to rule themselves, or whether they wanted no rulers at all. They didn't give their Assembly much to work with. The English Parliament had the power to tax its own folk. It wanted the power to tax the Atlanteans, too. Victor's people didn't aim to put up with that. They didn't aim to put up with taxes from the Atlantean Assembly, either. Anyone who tried to tax Atlanteans did so at his peril.

Victor also wondered how his people expected to pay for the war if they weren't taxed. The Assembly was doing the best it could, issuing paper money it promised to redeem with gold or silver once the war was won. When the uprising began, that paper was almost at par with specie. But it seemed to lose a little value every day.

How long before the Assembly's paper was worthless? Victor feared the time would come sooner than he wished. What would the Assembly do then? He didn't have the slightest idea, and suspected they didn't, either.

In the meantime, the war went on. His drill sergeants did their best to turn the recruits into men who could march and deploy and follow orders without fussing about it too much. Despite his great chest, Tom Knox died of some lung ailment. Victor mourned the English deserter—he might have ended up a major had he lived.

The Atlanteans did get a handful of a new kind of recruits: professional soldiers from Europe who saw a need across the sea and hastened to meet it. Some of them were frankly horrified at what they found.

"A proper soldier," one said in a thick German accent, "you tell him what to do, and by God he does it or he dies trying. You Atlanteans, you always must know why before you do anything. It is of time a waste. It is a—a foolishness!" By the way he said that, he couldn't think of many worse names.

"Well, I'll tell you, Baron von Steuben," Victor said. Steuben was no more a baron than he himself was a king. The German captain also had no right to the aristocratic *von*. But he was far from the first man to improve his past on coming to Atlantis. And the idea of being drilled by a European nobleman appealed to the Atlantean soldiers. Victor went on, "And what I'll tell you is this: officers can be wrong, too. Knowing why they want you to do something isn't so bad. The men do fight hard. They've stood up to the redcoats plenty of times." They hadn't stood up quite well enough, but he didn't dwell on that.

"English regulars is—are—good troops," Steuben admitted. "But maybe your men win if they move faster, if they don't spend time with questions always. Foolishness!" Yes, that did seem to be the nastiest printable word he used.

"Maybe." Victor didn't think so, but he didn't feel like arguing the point. He did want to make sure the German captain knew what he was up against. "No matter how fine a drillmaster you may be, sir, I don't think you'll cure Atlanteans of needing to know why. That would take an act of God, not an order from a mere man."

"I shall petition the Lord with prayer," Steuben said. "If He loves your cause, He will do what is needful."

"They do say the Lord helps those who help themselves," Victor remarked. "We're trying to do that against the English."

He kept sending out little bands to harry the redcoats. Moving small units and keeping them supplied was easier than moving and subsisting his whole army would have been. He gave men who performed well on the practice field the chance to test what they'd learned against some of the sternest instructors in the world. If his raiders won, they came back proud and delighted. And if they lost—which they did sometimes—they didn't lose enough to endanger his main body or to hurt morale much.

One band of horsemen reached the sea near Weymouth. "It's not redcoats everywhere," Habakkuk Biddiscombe reported to Victor. "They're like any other men. They mostly stay where it's warm and cozy. If we broke in amongst 'em with a big enough force, they wouldn't know what the devil to do."

"It's a thought," Victor said. His own soldiers, as he knew full well, wanted to stay warm and cozy, too—and who could blame them? If they got through the winter and started the second year of the war as a force in being, wasn't that a sizable achievement all by itself? It seemed so to him.

The young captain, a born attacker, had different notions. "If it all goes well, we might threaten Hanover. We might even run them out of it. One of the prisoners we took says they haven't got that many men there. They can't garrison and campaign very well, not at the same time."

"Neither can we," Victor said mournfully. A solid company of Croydon men had just marched off to the north. Their enlistments were up, and they didn't intend to stay around one minute longer than they were obliged to. The English occupied the town that gave their settlement its name? If that bothered them, they hid it very well.

"We ought to try," Biddiscombe persisted. What would happen to a junior officer in a European army who kept on arguing with the general commanding? Victor wondered if he ought to ask "Baron" "von" Steuben. He enjoyed watching the German gutturally sputter and fume. Victor was sure a persistent captain like this one would be hanging his career out to dry.

But Habakkuk Biddiscombe didn't have a military career to worry about. When the war ended—in victory or defeat—he would go back to whatever he'd done beforehand. And so he didn't worry about speaking his mind now.

"We could use a win," he told Victor, as if the general didn't know. "And I think we could get one without a great deal of trouble. The redcoats aren't within miles of being ready for us."

They don't think we'd be stupid enough to do any serious campaigning in the wintertime, Victor thought. He hadn't expected the Atlanteans would, either. The younger officer's enthusiasm made him wonder if he was making a mistake by doing what the English looked for. *They look for me to have an ounce of sense—maybe even two ounces.*

Still, if he fought the kind of war General Howe would approve of, wasn't he bound to lose? Howe had the professional soldiers. The Atlanteans, by the nature of things, were amateurs. They had fire and dash to offer, not stolid obedience. Shouldn't he take advantage of that? If he could make the English react to him, instead of his having to respond to Howe's every carefully planned advance . . .

"Do you know," Victor said slowly, "I believe I shall hold an officers' council. If we decide the attack can go forward with some hope of success, I expect we'll put it in."

Captain Biddiscombe stared. "D'you mean that?" He answered his own question: "You *do* mean that! By God, General, I never dreamt I'd convince you, never in a thousand years."

"Life is full of surprises," Victor Radcliff said. "May King George's soldiers not enjoy the one they get soon." Officers' council or not, he'd made up his mind. Now, if he could bring it off . . .

*   *   *

The weather had gone from rain to freezing rain and sleet to snow. Victor hoped it would stay cold. He wanted the roads frozen so his men could make good time on them. If the Atlanteans had to slog through mud to get at the redcoats, they could come to the battle late and worn out.

His first target was a fort on the outskirts of a town named Sudbury. It was farther north than Weymouth, farther south than Hanover, and about thirty miles inland. General Howe had run up several such fortresses to try to keep the Atlantean army away from the prosperous and well-settled seacoast. The intrepid Biddiscombe's raid was one thing. An attack by all the force the Atlantean Assembly could muster would be something else again.

I hope, Victor thought.

He didn't let his men conceive that so much as a single, solitary worry clouded his mind. Much of the art of command consisted of acting unruffled even—or rather, especially—when you weren't. "Press on, lads! Press on!" he called. "Before long, we'll subsist ourselves on good English victuals. We'll wear good English boots on our feet."

Again, he hoped. Quite a few of the Atlanteans weren't wearing anything resembling good boots now. The men who'd served longest and done the most marching suffered worst. Some of them had wrapped cloth around their boots to hold uppers and soles together and to try to keep their feet dry. A few soldiers had only cloths—or nothing at all—on their feet. They tramped along anyhow. If they eagerly looked forward to a little plundering . . . well, who could blame them?

In earlier times, Sudbury had made turpentine from the conifers in the dense Atlantean forests. After some years of settlement, those forests were nowhere near so dense as they had been once upon a time. These days, wheatfields replaced woods. The Atlantean army marched past snow-covered stubble.

More snow swirled around them. Victor blessed it; it

helped cloak them from the garrison inside the works on the western edge of town. The sentries the Atlanteans seized were too astonished to let out more than a couple of yelps that the wind drowned. They seemed almost relieved to be taken: it gave them the chance to go back to the Atlanteans' camp and get out of the cold.

"Forward! As fast as you can!" Victor called. "If we get ladders up against their palisade before they start shooting, the fort's ours."

He almost managed it. His men were throwing fascines into the ditch around the palisade when a redcoat on the wall fired at them and raised the alarm. Victor heard soldiers inside the fort yelling in dismay. He also heard their feet thudding on the wooden stairs leading up to the walkway.

"Hurry!" he shouted. "Hurry for your lives!"

Ladders thudded into place against the wall. Atlanteans swarmed up them. The redcoats tipped one, spilling soldiers into the ditch. An Englishman killed the first greencoat coming up another ladder. But the second Atlantean shot the defender in the face. The English soldier fell back with a howl, clutching at himself. By the time another redcoat neared the ladder, the Atlanteans were already on the walkway.

After that, taking the fort was easy. The attackers badly outnumbered the men who were trying to hold them back. Before long, white flags went up and the redcoats threw down their muskets.

"We never looked for you blokes," a sergeant complained to Victor. "Most of our officers are still in town, like."

"Are they?" Victor said tonelessly, and the underofficer nodded. The English officers probably had lady friends in Sudbury. Once the town was retaken, people who'd favored King George's soldiers were liable to have a thin time of it. Well, that was their lookout. Victor sent men into Sudbury with orders to capture any redcoats they found there. He added, "If you can, keep them all from getting away. With luck, we'll be able to roll up several of these forts. Maybe we *will* push all the way to the sea." The ease with which the fort by Sudbury fell made him think of grander things.

One English officer wearing a shirt and nothing more leaped onto a horse and made his getaway. Victor wouldn't have wanted to try that in warm weather; the Englishman's privates were going to take a beating. Several other officers and other ranks, less intrepid, gave themselves up.

"What are you doing here?" a captured lieutenant asked with what sounded like unfeigned indignation.

"Fighting a war in the name of the Atlantean Assembly and of the Lord Jehovah," Victor told him. "What are *you* doing here, in this land you only oppress by your presence?"

"Obeying the orders of my king and my superiors." The lieutenant had nerve: he added, "He is your king, too, I remind you."

"My king would not send soldiers to invade his country. He would not arrest subjects who had done him no wrong. Neither would he tax subjects who have no say in his governing councils," Victor replied. "If King George stopped doing such things, he might be my king. As it is?" He shook his head. "As it is, you are welcome to him."

The English officer would have argued more. He might have surrendered, but he hadn't changed his mind. But Victor Radcliff took a winner's privilege and walked away from him. He didn't have to listen to nonsense if he didn't feel like it.

His men plundered the fort and their prisoners—and Sudbury, too, for it had lain quiet in enemy hands. They marched away better fed, better shod, better clothed, and better armed than they'd arrived. They marched away with silver and a bit of gold jingling in their pockets, too. After nothing to spend but Atlantean paper of shrinking value, hard money seemed doubly welcome to them.

Two days later, they fell on Halstead, fifteen miles

south of Sudbury. The Englishman unencumbered with trousers had ridden north, so Victor dared hope the redcoats in Halstead didn't know his army was on the march. And so it proved; the fort there, which was weaker than Sudbury's, fell even more easily than the first one had.

And Halstead hadn't stayed quiet while occupied. Only a few days before the Atlanteans arrived, someone had knocked an English corporal over the head. And so the whole garrison there stayed in the fort. Victor thought he swept up every last redcoat in the neighborhood.

"If I can seize one more fort," he told Blaise, "that will open the way for a march to the sea."

"Why not?" the Negro replied.

VIII

*D*ue south of Halstead, only an easy day's march away, lay Pittman's Ferry. The English had a fort there, too, not far from the creek that necessitated the ferry and made the town spring up near it. Town and fort both lay on the north bank of Pittman's Creek. That helped determine Victor to move down and attack it: he wouldn't have to worry about gathering boats to cross in a rush.

He set his men on the southbound road the morning after Halstead fell. They showed more confidence than they had when they were approaching Sudbury. With two English forts behind them, why shouldn't they expect the next one to be easy? They were better fed and clothed and shod and accoutered than they had been then, too. The men who carried bayoneted muskets seemed especially proud of them. The redcoats had used them to fearsome effect. Now Atlanteans could, too.

Pistols boomed, up in the vanguard. "Don't like the sound of that," Blaise remarked.

"Nor do I," Victor Radcliff agreed. "Well, we'll have to see what it was."

A rider eventually came back to tell him. "They had pickets posted on the road, damn them," the man reported. "We went after 'em good, but I think some of 'em got away."

"Damnation!" Victor said, and then something really flavorful. The cavalryman stared at him—did generals talk that way? This one did when he got such news. Taking a fort by surprise was one thing. Taking a fort that was ready and waiting was something else again.

"We can do it," said a soldier who'd heard the news. In an instant, the whole army seemed to be chanting: "We can do it!"

Pulling back would wound their spirits—Victor could see that at a glance. Going on would hurt a lot of their bodies. The general commanding needed to be no prophet to foresee that. What he couldn't see was how to withdraw in the face of their insistent chant. He wished he could.

"Well, we'll have a go," he said at last. The redcoats might have heard the cheers in Pittman's Ferry. In case they hadn't, he added, "Double-time, boys. We'll get there before they expect us."

Drummers and fifers gave the army its new marching rhythm. The men weren't far from Pittman's Ferry. They wouldn't get too worn to fight, even if they double-timed it all the way. Victor hoped they wouldn't, anyhow.

He rode forward himself with the vanguard to reconnoiter the fort. The untrimmed pine logs from which it was built made it a dark blot against the snow and against the painted planks of Pittman's Ferry. Now Victor swore at the swirling snow as he raised the spyglass to his eye to survey the structure. He wanted to see as much as he could, but the weather hindered him.

Frowning, he passed the telescope to the cavalry officer who commanded the vanguard. "Tell me what you think they're up to, Captain Biddiscombe, if you'd be so kind."

"All right, General." Habakkuk Biddiscombe raised the glass, slid the brass tube in ever so slightly, and peered ahead. Puzzlement in his voice, he said, "They don't seem to be up to . . . anything, do they?"

"Well, I didn't think so," Victor answered. "I wanted to know how it looked to you. Maybe they're feigning this, to draw us on. Or maybe—who knows? We'll find out pretty soon, though."

When his foot soldiers came up half an hour later, he pointed them at the fort. They knew what to do. Some would attack two sides. As soon as the defenders rushed to hold them out, the rest would assault the other two.

And the fort at Pittman's Ferry fell as easily as the one at Halstead had—more easily than the one at Sudbury. The Atlanteans dragged the dejected English captain in charge of the place in front of Victor Radcliff. "Didn't you know we were on the way?" Victor demanded.

"No, dammit," the redcoat said sullenly.

"Why not, Captain? Didn't your pickets warn you? Our outriders thought some of them got away."

"They did." The English officer made as if to spit in disgust, whether over himself or Victor the Atlantean didn't know. In any case, a growl from his captors dissuaded him. Angrily, he went on, "They came in, but I didn't believe 'em. Who would? A winter campaign? Pshaw!"

"No wonder we surprised you," Victor murmured. "None so blind as those that will not see."

"The Devil may quote Scripture to his purpose," the captain said.

"I am not the Devil, sir, and neither is that Scripture," Victor said. "It is Reverend Henry's commentary on the Book of Jeremiah, but it is not the prophet speaking in his own person, you might say."

"I don't care what it is, not to the extent of a fart in a thunderstorm," the redcoat said miserably. "You will eventually exchange me or parole me, will you not?"

"That is the custom with prisoners of war, yes." Victor spoke as if to an idiot child. What else were they to do with prisoners? Knock them over the head? It was easier than holding them and feeding them, but otherwise had little to recommend it.

So Victor thought, anyhow. The English captain saw things differently. "General Howe will skin me like an ermine when he finds out how I lost this fort. They'll

cashier me and disgrace my family's name forever."
Sudden hope flared in the man's eyes. "Will you uprisers
take me on?"

"Well . . . no." Victor needed to think about it, but not
for long. True, the Atlantean army was short of trained,
capable officers. But, while this fellow might be trained,
he'd just proved himself incapable.

"A pity," the captain said. "I don't know how I am
to go on. . . . Would you be kind enough to take me to
some small room, lock me in, and lend me a loaded pistol, then?"

"No, I won't do that, either," Victor said. "If you
choose to dispose of yourself, sir, that is between you
and God. If you seek to make me a party to your deed,
however, I must decline."

He made sure the unhappy officer marched off into
captivity with the rest of the English garrison. Once the
campaign ended, and the need for secrecy with it, they
could be properly exchanged.

Victor Radcliff couldn't have been more delighted
with what his ragtag force had done. It wasn't so ragtag
as it had been before the campaign began, either. The
Atlanteans might have had a lean time of it during the
winter, but their enemies were living well. Part of that
came from supplies fetched across the ocean, part from
plundering the countryside. Now the Atlanteans made
some of the enemy's bounty their own.

Still, what had he accomplished if he stopped here
and drew back? Nothing that would last, and nothing
that would more than annoy General Howe. Whereas, if
he struck for the coast . . .

If you do, you may lose your whole army. Normally,
that thought would have been plenty to hold him back.
Not here. Not now. After the series of defeats he'd suffered during the summer, didn't he have to remind the
English that Atlantis remained a going concern? Didn't
they need to see they couldn't march where they pleased
whenever they pleased?

He thought they did, and so he ordered, "Now we move on Weymouth."

One of these days, Victor supposed, Atlantis would be thickly settled north and south, east and west. That day wasn't here yet. He was reminded it wasn't with every mile toward the coast his army gained. General Howe wasn't so foolish in trying to confine the rebels to the interior. Howe skimmed the fat off the rich, populous seaside regions that way, and left his foes with whatever they could gather from the rest.

Farms clustered close together here. Even though the English had occupied these parts for a while, plenty of livestock remained. Victor requisitioned what he needed, paying with the Atlantean Assembly's banknotes.

"What makes you think I want these arsewipes?" a furious farmer howled. "They'll never be worth more than the dingleberries they leave behind."

"Would you rather we gave you the bayonet instead?" Victor asked mildly. The farmer's bravado deflated like a pricked pig's bladder.

The real trouble was, a good many people who dwelt near the ocean were loyal to King George. Some farms the Atlantean army passed were bare of livestock and of people. The men, women, and children had fled their own countrymen's advance. That they should want to do such a thing was demoralizing. It was also dangerous; they would bring word to the redcoats in Weymouth that the Atlanteans were coming.

"No surprises any more," Victor said gloomily. "I wanted to descend on them before they knew I was there."

"Won't happen," Blaise said.

"I know," Victor answered. "When this war ends, we shall have to settle accounts with all the traitors still living amongst us. I fear it will prove neither quick nor easy." His mouth twisted. One way or another, he was bound to be right about that. But if the redcoats prevailed, the hunt would be on for everyone who'd risen against King George. *On for me and mine*, he thought, which made matters unmistakably plain.

On pressed the army, northeast toward Weymouth. They made good time. The roads were frozen hard, and the men better shod than they had been at the start of the campaign. If English captives with rags on their feet came down with chilblains ... too bad. Victor's worst dread was a thaw that would turn the roads to mud. That would slow the army to a crawl.

Scouts reported an English detachment moving into place to block the Atlanteans. "How big a detachment?" Victor asked.

The men looked at one another. Almost in unison, they shrugged. "Don't rightly know, General," one of them answered. "They had horse out in front, so we couldn't push on and take a good gander at the foot."

"A pox," Victor muttered. Was he rushing into a trap? Or were the redcoats trying to bluff him out of a prize he could win? "Well, from which direction do they come? From the northeast? Or from the southeast?" he asked. If the former, the English force likely came out of Weymouth's garrison, which—he thought—was none too big. If the latter, then he might be heading toward the bulk of General Howe's army, sallying from New Hastings. He knew too well how poor his chances were of beating it in the open field.

One or two scouts pointed southeast, the rest northeast. After some shouting and name-calling, the minority swung to northeast like a compass swinging towards a lodestone.

Victor hoped they swung because they were persuaded and not, like the lodestone, because they had no choice. He turned to one of the young messengers who always rode beside him. "Tell the musicians to play *Form line of battle*, if you would be so kind," he said.

"*Form line of battle*. Yes, General." Eyes bright with excitement, the messenger set spurs to his horse and galloped away.

Atlantean evolutions were smoother than they had been the summer before. Compared to the redcoats, though, Victor's men still wasted too much time and motion deploying from column to line. Baron von Steuben's guttural obscenities helped chivvy them into place. With cavalry out in front and off to either flank, they tramped forward across frozen fields.

Horse pistols and carbines boomed up ahead of Victor. So did a field gun—obviously, one that belonged to the English. Snow and scattered trees kept him from seeing what was going on. When his men didn't come pelting back with enemy riders in pursuit, he took that for a good sign.

"Forward!" he ordered. "Double-time! We will support the horse with all the force at our disposal."

Urged on by their musicians, the Atlanteans hurried toward combat. Any sensible man, as a cynic like Custis Cawthorne would have been quick to point out, would have turned around and hustled off in the opposite direction. The most a soldier could hope for was not getting shot. All his other possibilities were much, much worse. When you looked at it like that, war seemed a mighty peculiar way to settle disputes.

And yet the men smiled and joked as they advanced. They'd just overrun three English forts in a row. They thought they could beat redcoats any time, anywhere. The summer's defeats seemed to lie as far behind them as Crécy and Agincourt. Quite a few of the men who'd lost those battles had gone home since. Maybe enthusiasm could make do for experience.

There stood the English line, drawn up at the top of a small swell of ground. "Well, God be praised," Victor murmured. Unless the enemy was hiding some huge force beyond the crest, this *was* only a detachment. And the Atlanteans handily outnumbered it.

The officer commanding the redcoats must have seen the same thing at about the same time. Too late for him—he had little choice now but to accept battle. The Atlanteans had drawn too close to let him pull back.

They would have harried him all the way to Weymouth. His chances here might not be good, but they were better than the ones retreat offered.

"We'll lap round his flanks," Victor said. "If we can get in behind him, the game is up."

To keep the English soldiers from meeting that threat, he also threw in a frontal assault. Most of the greencoats who went straight at the enemy had captured bayonets tipping their flintlocks. The redcoats wouldn't have things all their own way in the hand-to-hand, as they so often did.

They gave the Atlanteans a volley. Victor's men—the majority still standing, at any rate—returned it. The redcoats reloaded with urgent competence. The Atlanteans closed on them, yelling like fiends. If they could turn it into a mêlée before the Englishmen recharged their muskets . . .

They did, or most of them did. Soldiers swore and screamed and stabbed at one another. The Atlanteans were bigger men than their foes. The English still had more experience and know-how. Had that frontal attack been the only string in Victor's bow, it would have failed.

But, with his superior numbers, he could outflank the redcoats to left and right. The foe couldn't stand and fight the Atlanteans directly in front of him, not when men to either side poured enfilading fire into his ranks. If the English held their ground, they might get cut off and surrounded. They wouldn't last long after that.

Common soldiers saw the danger—or simply panicked, depending on one's point of view—before their officers did. They started streaming away from their battle line. Some left by squads, in fair order, and kept firing at the Atlanteans who harried them. More simply tried to save their own skins. They went off every man for himself. When greencoats challenged them, they were quick to throw down their muskets—if they'd held on to them—and raise their hands.

About half the English force fell back toward Weymouth in a compact mass. Victor let them go. Wiping them out or forcing their surrender would have been more expensive than it was worth. He had another victory.

Crows and ravens and vultures spiraled down to feast on the bounty laid out for them. Surgeons did what they could for the wounded from both sides. They gave them bullets or leather straps to bite on as they probed for musket balls and sutured bayonet wounds. For amputations, the surgeons had a little opium and a lot of barrel-tree brandy to dull the torment. All that might have slightly softened the shrieks rising to the uncaring sky. It assuredly did no more. It might not even have done so much.

"Do we press on, General?" Habakkuk Biddiscombe asked.

Victor eyed the twisted bodies and the trampled, blood-splashed snow. He listened for a moment to the cries of the wounded. Then he did what he had to do: like Pharaoh, he hardened his heart and made himself nod. "Yes, Captain Biddiscombe. We press on."

The redcoats in Weymouth were as ready to receive Victor Radcliff's Atlanteans as they could be, given their usual practices and the weather. Their practices meant they were not in the habit of digging entrenchments under any circumstances. The weather, which froze the ground hard, meant they would have had trouble trying it even had it occurred to them.

He sent a messenger into town, calling on the English commander to surrender. "Tell him I am not sure I can answer for my men's behavior if they take Weymouth by storm," he instructed the man. "If he thinks us no better than a pack of bloodthirsty copperskins, it may frighten him into yielding."

"I get you, General." The messenger tipped him a wink. "I'll make us out to be most especially frightful."

He rode in under flag of truce. When he came back that afternoon, he handed Victor a note from the English commanding officer. *I must respectfully decline your offer*, the man wrote, *and I fear I cannot answer for the conduct of my soldiers once they have a pack of rebels in their sights. I am, sir, your most obedient servant, Major Henry Lavery*.

"He won't quit, General," the messenger said.

"So I gather," Victor Radcliff replied. This Major Lavery did not lack for nerve or style. "Well, if they won't do it of their own accord, we shall have to make them."

He wondered if he could, and what the butcher's bill would be. He wondered all the more because a pair of Royal Navy frigates lay just offshore. Bombardment from the sea had hurt him when he held Weymouth. How much more would it hurt him while he was trying to retake the town?

Instead of trying to storm Weymouth, he sent his riflemen forward to take up positions as close to the outskirts as they could. "Whenever you see a redcoat's head, I want you to put a bullet through it," he told them. "Don't let the enemy move in the streets by day."

The riflemen nodded. But one of them asked, "What if they come out after us? We can shoot straighter than they can, but musketeers put a lot of lead in the air."

"If they come out, fall back," Victor answered. "I do not ask you to personate the Spartans at Thermopylae. You are there to make their lives miserable, not to sell your own dear."

That satisfied the marksman and his comrades. They worked their way forward from tree to fence to woodpile. Before long, the rifles' sharp, authoritative reports began to ring out, now singly, now two or three at a time. The men would, Victor supposed, shift their positions after every shot or two. He wondered how the redcoats liked them.

He got his answer when a cannon inside Weymouth boomed. The roundshot smashed a pile of wood. But the sniper who'd fired from behind it had moved on ten minutes earlier. Victor was more than pleased to see the English waste such a good shot.

Atlantean rifles went on barking as long as the light lasted. They would take until the day before forever to wipe out the enemy garrison. But they made the red-coats shun the streets and slink around like weasels. One of the marksmen came back to Victor at sundown and said, "I shot me a major, or maybe even a colonel."

"How can you be so sure?" Victor asked.

"Well, General, if he wasn't a big officer, he must've been one of those what-do-you-call-'ems—peacocks—like, on account of he sure did have some fancy feathers," the Atlantean answered.

"All right. That's good news. Maybe it will stir the English out of their lair come tomorrow." Radcliff listened to himself. Once he said that out loud, it struck him as much too likely. And he hadn't done anything about it. In the fading light, he ordered his musketeers and his fieldpieces forward. If the redcoats did come out, he wanted to be ready to receive them.

They didn't emerge right away. As soon as the eastern sky paled enough, his riflemen started shooting into Weymouth again. A horsefly couldn't do a horse much real damage, but could drive it wild anyhow. Victor hoped for the same effect.

And he got it. The redcoats in Weymouth sallied forth just after the church bells in town rang ten. As soon as they left the cover of houses and shops, the marksmen began to fire at their officers. As the sniper had said the evening before, those splendid uniforms made them stand out. They fell one after another, and so did the common soldiers unlucky enough to be stationed near them.

The English troopers advanced anyhow. Victor might have known they would. They barely needed officers to tell them what wanted doing. They went after the riflemen with professional competence and perhaps unprofessional fury.

Victor's marksmen fired and fell back, fired and fell back. Some of them didn't fall back fast enough. The ones the redcoats caught had a hard time surrendering.

Then the English force came into range of the Atlantean artillery, which lurked just inside an orchard. Cannon balls tore bloody tracks through the enemy's ranks. The attackers swung toward the guns. Victor wanted nothing more than for them to charge. Canister and grape would do worse than roundshot ever could.

But, even if many of their officers had fallen, the redcoats knew better than to expose themselves to that kind of murderous fire. They swung away again, and went back to chasing the riflemen.

"Forward!" Victor shouted, and the main body of the Atlantean army moved up to support the marksmen.

They outnumbered the soldiers who'd sallied from Weymouth. Their lines hadn't been thrown into disarray by a long pursuit. Encouraged by three easy wins and a successful skirmish, they thought they could do anything. That went a long way toward making them right.

The redcoats dressed their ranks faster than Victor would have dreamt possible. They thought they could do anything, too. They'd fought in Europe, in India, in Terranova. Some of them would have fought in Atlantis against the French. They'd also had good luck facing the rebellion from their own kinsmen here. No wonder they thought they could win again.

"Fire!" Victor yelled as the English drew near. Flintlocks clicked. Priming powder around touch-holes hissed. Then the muskets boomed.

Some of the redcoats went down. The rest kept coming. They didn't fire. If they could stand the gaff, if they could get in among their foes, they thought they could win the battle with the bayonet. They'd seen how much the Atlanteans feared cold steel in earlier fights.

Another volley tore into them. More English soldiers fell. By then, the survivors were very close. They were close enough, in fact, to see that most of the Atlanteans also carried bayoneted muskets, as they had in the skirmish on the hillcrest. All that plunder from the English forts was coming in handy.

True, the greencoats weren't masters of the bayonet

the way the English were. But they were most of them big, strong men. Skill counted. But so did reach and ferocity. And so did numbers, and the Atlanteans had the edge there.

As the two lines met in bloody collision, Victor wondered how much weight each factor carried. Before long, one side or the other would give way. Flesh and blood simply couldn't stand going toe to toe like this for very long.

Spirit oozed from the redcoats first. Victor sensed it even before they began to fall back. Part of it, he judged, was their surprise and dismay at not sweeping everything before them. They should have known better. They'd beaten the Atlanteans in the summer, yes, but they'd never routed them—and the Atlanteans had just forced many of them back into Weymouth.

Now they were routed themselves. Some fled back across the snow toward the town. Others raised their hands in surrender. And still others, the stubborn few, went on fighting and made Victor's men pay the price of beating them.

"Give up!" Victor called to the knot of embattled Englishmen. "Some of your friends have got away. What more can you hope to do now?"

They kept fighting. Then the Atlanteans wheeled up a couple of fieldpieces and started firing canister into them. One round from each gun was enough to make the redcoats change their minds. The men still on their feet laid their muskets in the snow and stepped away from them. The ones blown to rags and bloody shreds didn't need to worry about it any more.

Victor's men hurried forward to take wallets and muskets, boots and breeches and bayonets. He told off enough greencoats to ensure that the prisoners wouldn't be able to get away. With the rest of his army, he pressed on toward Weymouth.

Had the remainder of the English garrison wanted to fight it out street by street and house by house, they could have made taking the place devilishly expensive.

Victor might have made that kind of fight. It didn't seem to occur to the redcoats. Perhaps that sniper had killed Major Lavery the day before, and taken the linchpin out of their resistance. Badly beaten in the field, the English survivors must have concluded they couldn't hope to hold Weymouth.

They chose to save the remains of their army instead. They marched off to the south, toward New Hastings, in good order, flags flying and drums beating. They might have been saying that, if Victor wanted to assault them, they remained ready to give him all he wanted.

Later, he wondered whether he should have swooped down on them. Maybe their demeanor intimidated him. Or maybe he focused so completely on taking Weymouth, he forgot about everything else. Whatever the reason, he let them go and rode into Weymouth at the head of his army.

Some people in the seaside town greeted the green-coats with cheers. Here and there, a young woman—or sometimes one not so young—would run out and kiss a soldier. Victor suspected a baby or two would get started tonight, and not by the mothers' husbands.

But some houses and shops stayed closed up tight, shuttered against the new conquerors and against the world. Victor knew what that meant. The people in those places would have been too friendly toward the redcoats. Now they feared they would pay for it. And they were likely right, if not at his hands then at those of their fellow townsfolk.

That was a worry for another time. Victor had plenty to worry him now. The Royal Navy frigates naturally realized Weymouth had changed hands. They started bombarding the town. One of their first shots smashed a house belonging to somebody Victor had tagged as a likely partisan of King George's. The unhappy man, his wife, and two children fled.

"My baby!" the woman screamed. "My baby's still in there!"

The man wouldn't let her go back. "Willie's gone, Joan," he said. "He's—gone." He dissolved in tears. His wife's shrieks redoubled.

That's what you get for backing England. Victor almost said it, but checked himself at the last moment. However true it might be, it was cruel. He would only make these people hate him more—he wouldn't persuade them that they should take up the Atlantean cause. Better silence, then.

He pulled most of his men out of range of the frigates' guns. But he also fired back at the warships with a couple of six-pounders he ran out onto the strand. He'd made that gesture of defiance before, and felt good about doing it again. *Weymouth is ours!* it said.

This time, though, the frigates were waiting for it. They opened a furious fire on the field guns. One roundshot took off an artilleryman's head. Another pulped a man standing on the opposite side of the six-pounder. Yet another wrecked the other fieldpiece's carriage and killed a horse.

Victor got the intact gun out of there right away, and the surviving gunners and horses with it. The other gun lay on the sand till night fell, a monument to the folly of repeating himself.

"We did it! *You* did it!" Blaise didn't let a small failure take away from a larger success.

"So we did." Victor didn't want all the credit. "Now we have to see if we can hold what we've taken."

They couldn't. However much Victor Radcliff wanted to believe otherwise, that soon became plain to him. It wasn't just because the Royal Navy kept sending heavy roundshot crashing into Weymouth. But people friendly to the Atlantean cause sneaked up from New Hastings to warn him that General Howe was getting ready to move against the captured town with most of his army.

Getting a large force ready to march didn't happen

overnight for anyone. And Howe valued thorough preparation over speed. Victor had the time to hold an officers' council and see what the army's leaders thought.

To his amazement, some of them wanted to hold their ground and fight the redcoats. "General Howe purposes bringing a force more than twice the size of ours, with abundant stores of all the accouterments of war," he said. "How do you gentlemen propose to stand against him?"

"We can do it—damned if we can't," Habakkuk Biddiscombe said. "If we lead 'em into a trap, like, we can slaughter 'em like so many beeves."

Victor couldn't tell him he was out of his mind. The French Atlanteans had done that very thing to General Braddock's army of redcoats south of Freetown. Victor counted himself lucky to have escaped that scrape with a whole skin. He did say, "Beeves are rather more likely to amble into a trap, and rather less so to shoot back."

That won him a few chuckles. But intrepid Captain Biddiscombe was not so easily put off. "If we do thrash 'em, General, we throw off the English yoke once for all. They can't treat us like beeves, either."

"I don't intend to let them do any such thing," Victor said.

"*Gut!* Good!" von Steuben boomed. "No point throwing away an army on a fight we don't win."

"Thank you, Baron," Victor said, and then, to Biddiscombe, "How did we learn of Howe's planned movement?"

"Patriots from New Hastings told us," the captain answered at once.

"And do you not believe traitors from Weymouth are even now telling General Howe of our debate?" Victor said. "Only the Englishmen will style them patriots, reckoning our patriots traitors."

The cavalry officer opened his mouth. Then he closed it again. "Well, that could be so," he said, his tone much milder than it had been a moment before.

"We cannot hope to lay a trap where the foe is privy

to our plans," Victor said. "Can we beat him in a stand-up fight?"

"Anything is possible." Habakkuk Biddiscombe didn't want to admit the Atlanteans weren't omnicapable.

"Anything is possible," Victor agreed. "Not everything, however, is likely. I find our chances of success less likely than I wish they were. Since I do, I should prefer to retire rather than fight."

Debate didn't shut off right away. If Atlanteans were anything, they were full of themselves. Everyone had to put in his penny's worth. Baron von Steuben was rolling his eyes and muttering by the time Victor's views carried the day. The greencoats got ready to abandon Weymouth.

Quite a few locals also abandoned the town. They'd given King George's partisans—the ones who hadn't escaped—some rough justice. If General Howe's troops returned, they feared a dose of their own medicine.

"We are not running away," Victor told anyone who would listen. "We won every battle we fought. We returned to the Atlantic after the English thought they had barred us from our own seacoast. We proved that Atlantis remains hostile and inhospitable to the invaders."

He got cheers from the men who marched with him, and more cheers from the families that were leaving Weymouth to go with the greencoats. Not one word he said was a lie. He still wished he could have told his army something else. He wished he could have followed Captain Biddiscombe's advice and fought.

Back in the last war, he might have. No defeat he suffered then would have ruined England's chances and those of the English Atlanteans against the French. Now all of Atlantis' hopes followed his army. He couldn't afford to throw them away.

And now he was older than he'd been then. Did that leave him less inclined to take chances? He supposed it did.

General Howe has to win. He has to beat me, to crush me, he thought. *All I have to do is not to lose. If I can keep from losing for long enough, England will tire of this fight.*

Dear God, I hope she will.

But his doubts were for himself alone. He kept on exuding good cheer for the men around him. Maybe Blaise suspected what his true feelings were. Blaise would never give him away, though. And he'd proved one thing to General Howe, anyway. The Atlantean uprising was not about to fold up and die.

IX

*V*ictor Radcliff admired his splendid new sword. The blade was chased with silver, the hilt wrapped in gold wire. The Atlantean Assembly had given it to him in thanks for his winter campaign that—briefly—brought the rebels back to the sea.

Blaise admired the weapon, too. "You going to fight with that?" he asked.

"I can if I have to," Victor said. "They gave it to me as an honor, though, and because it's worth something."

How much that last would matter was anyone's guess. Yes, if things went wrong he might be able to eat for several months on what he got from selling the sword. But, if things went wrong, odds were the English would catch him, try him for treason, and hang him. What price fancy sword then?

Blaise changed the subject: "Not going to snow any more, is it?"

"I don't think so," Victor answered. "Can't be sure, not here, but I don't think so." The west coast of Atlantis, warmed by the Bay Stream (Custis Cawthorne had christened the current in the Hesperian Gulf), already knew springtime. The lands on the east side of the Green Ridge Mountains had a harsher climate.

"By God, I hope it isn't!" The Negro shivered dramatically. "I never knew there was such a thing as cold weather, not like you get here." He shivered again. "The language I grew up talking, the language I talk with Stella, has no word for snow or ice or hail or sleet or blizzard or anything like that. In Africa, we didn't know there were such things. Frost? Frostbite? No, we never heard of them."

"Spring seems better after winter," Victor said. Blaise, who'd grown up in endless summer, looked unconvinced. Victor tried again: "And winter has its advantages. Do you like apples?" He knew Blaise did.

"What if I should?" Blaise asked cautiously.

"Apple trees will grow where there's no frost. They'll flower, but they won't bear fruit. They need the frost for that. So do pears."

Blaise considered. "If I had to give up apples or give up snow, I would give up snow," he said. "What about you?"

"Well . . . maybe." Victor had seen lands without snow. It rarely fell on Avalon, and never on New Marseille. But he didn't hate cold weather the way Blaise did. "Depends on what you're used to, I suppose. I wouldn't want it hot and sticky all the time—I know that."

"Neither would I. It should be hot and dry sometimes," Blaise said. "One or the other was all I knew till I came here."

"Before long, it will be hot and sticky again," Victor said. The Negro nodded and smiled in anticipation.

They could talk about the weather forever without doing anything about it. One of the reasons to talk about the weather was that you couldn't do anything about it. Before long, Victor would have to decide what he could do about the English invaders. Even now, they might be trying to decide what to do about him.

He stepped out of his tent. Blaise followed. Everything was green, but then everything in Atlantis was green the year around unless covered in snow or imported from Europe or Terranova. Fruit trees and ornamentals did lose their leaves. Along with rhymes and songs, they let Atlanteans imagine what winters were like across the sea.

Greencoats marched and countermarched. They would probably never grow as smooth in their evolutions as the professionals they faced, but they were ever so much better than they had been.

A robin perched in a pine burst into song. Englishmen said Atlantean robins behaved and sang just like the blackbirds they knew back home. Atlantis had birds the people here called blackbirds, but they weren't much like Atlantean robins—or the smaller, redder-breasted birds that went by the same name in England, or even English blackbirds. It could get confusing.

The war could get confusing, too. Both sides had got some unpleasant surprises the first year. Victor hadn't imagined King George's government would send so many men to Atlantis, or that they would secure the coast from Croydon down to New Hastings. And General Howe hadn't looked for the kind of resistance the Atlanteans had put up. So deserters assured Victor, anyhow.

He wondered what Atlantean deserters told the English general. That Atlantean paper money lost value by the day? That morale went up and down for no visible reason? That equipment left a lot to be desired? All true—every word of it.

But if the deserters told Howe the Atlantean army didn't want to fight, he had to know they were liars. They couldn't match the redcoats' skills or their stoicism, but they didn't lack for spirit.

And how were the English soldiers' spirits these days? Victor's best measure of that was also what he learned from deserters. If what the Englishmen who came into the Atlanteans' lines said was true, their countrymen were surprised and unhappy the war had gone on this long. Before they crossed the ocean, their officers told them they would put down the rebellion in weeks if not days.

Radcliff discounted some of what he heard from

them. They had to be discontented, or they wouldn't have deserted in the first place. And they wouldn't have been human if they didn't tell their captors what they thought the Atlanteans wanted to hear.

Still, he did think they were having a harder time than they'd expected. He wanted them to go on having a hard time. If they had a hard enough time for long enough, they would give up and go home.

Or they might decide they weren't doing enough and send in more soldiers. As far as Victor knew, the mother country was fighting nowhere else at the moment. England had more men than Atlantis. She could raise more troops—if she had the will.

And if she stayed untroubled elsewhere. Victor wondered how Thomas Paine was doing among the English settlements of northeastern Terranova. If those towns and their hinterlands also rose in rebellion, King George's ministers wouldn't be able to focus all their attention on—and send all their redcoats to—Atlantis.

If Paine had turned the Terranovan settlements all topsy-turvy, word of it hadn't come back to Atlantis. Victor shook his head after that thought crossed his mind. Word of whatever Paine was doing hadn't reached *him*. That wasn't necessarily the same as the other. News crossed the Green Ridge Mountains only slowly. And, if Terranova did have trouble, word of it might have reached English officers in Croydon or Hanover or New Hastings without spreading any farther. Those officers certainly wouldn't want him to find out.

He pulled a small notebook and pencil from a waistcoat pocket. *More spies in cities—Paine?* he scribbled. One of these days, if and as he found the time, he would do something about that or tell off someone else to do something about it.

He started to put the notebook away, then caught himself. He jotted another line: *Copperskins around Atlantis?* He'd heard next to nothing since sending his hundred men against the Terranovan savages the English had landed south of Avalon to harry the west coast.

If anyone on this side of the mountains knew more about that than he did, it was his distant cousin, Matthew Radcliffe. Victor sent a rider off to the Atlantean Assembly with a letter for him.

The man came back a few days later with a letter from Matthew. *My dear General—I regret to state I can tell you nothing certain*, the Assemblyman wrote. *Only rumor has reached me: or rather, conflicting rumors. I have heard that our men have routed the Terranovan barbarians. Contrariwise, I have also heard that the copperskins have slaughtered every Atlantean soldier sent against them, afterwards denuding the corpses of hair and virile members as souvenirs of their triumph. Where the truth falls will, I doubt not, emerge, but has yet to do so. I remain, very respectfully, your most ob't servant.* His signature followed.

"Drat!" Victor folded the letter as if washing his hands of it.

"Is the news bad, General?" Like any messenger, the fellow who'd brought the letter wanted to be absolved of its contents.

"Bad?" Victor considered. He had to shake his head. "No. The principal news is that there is no sure news, and *that* is bad—or, at least, I wished it to be otherwise."

"What can you do about it?" the man asked.

Victor Radcliff considered again. He could go himself to investigate . . . if he didn't mind entrusting command in the vital eastern regions to someone else. He could send someone he trusted to see what was going on around Avalon . . . if he didn't mind depriving himself of that man's services for some weeks. Or he could simply wait to see which rumors proved true.

Had any of the rumors Matthew Radcliffe cited been that the Royal Navy was about to try to seize Avalon, he would have despatched someone on the instant to investigate. As things were . . . With a sigh and a shrug, he answered, "I believe I shall await developments, both in the west and here. I do not think I'll need to wait long in either case."

*　　*　　*

Salty pork sausage, hard bread, and coffee enlivened with barrel-tree brandy—not the worst breakfast Victor Radcliff had ever had. As far as he remembered, his worst breakfast was some raw pine nuts and a roasted ground katydid. The flightless bugs grew as big as mice. You could eat them if you got hungry enough, and Victor had.

Atlantis hadn't had any rats or mice till they crossed the Atlantic with the first settlers. Now they were as common in towns and in farms as they were back in England. Away from human settlement, the pale green katydids still prevailed.

As he had more than once before, Victor wondered why Atlantis had no native viviparous quadrupeds but bats. England and Europe did; so did Terranova. Yet Atlantis, which lay between them in the middle of the ocean, didn't. It was as if God had arranged a special creation here.

Many of His former productions were far scarcer than they had been when Edward Radcliffe came ashore in 1452. Englishmen who felt unfriendly called Atlanteans honkers. Yet the great flightless birds were extinct in settled country east of the Green Ridge Mountains. They were rare anywhere east of the mountains, and growing scarce in the wilder west, too.

The same held true for the great red-crested eagles that had preyed on them—and that also didn't mind preying on people and sheep. Atlantis used the red-crested eagle to difference its flag from England's, but the bird itself was seldom seen these days.

Oil thrushes, though less drastically reduced than honkers or eagles, were less common than they had been. Few eastern farmers found enough of them to render them down for lamp oil. The first settlers' tales said that had been a common practice.

Along with people, the oil thrushes had to worry about foxes and cats and wild dogs these days. Even in the woods, there were more and more mice. Oak and ash and elm and nut trees grew in the woods, too, while deer roamed where honkers had.

Taken all in all, Atlantis became more like Europe year by year. Victor resolved that it wouldn't come to resemble Europe in one way: it wouldn't supinely submit to rule from a tyrannical king. If General Howe didn't understand that . . .

"General! *Oh*, General!"

When somebody called for him like that, Victor knew the news wouldn't be good. He wished he'd poured more brandy into the coffee. He still could . . . but no. He gulped a last mouthful of sausage. For a second, it didn't want to go down; he felt like a small snake engulfing a large frog.

Then it headed south and he stepped out of his tent. "I'm here," he called. "What is it?"

"Well, General, now we know how come the redcoats ain't come after us even with the weather getting good and everything," the courier replied. He'd dismounted and was rubbing his blowing horse.

"Perhaps you do. If so, you have the advantage of me," Victor said. "If you would be so good as to share your enlightenment . . ."

"Sure will." The man went on rubbing down the horse. "There you go, boy. . . . The redcoats . . . Well, the truth of it is, most of the bastards in New Hastings climbed into ships and sailed away."

"Sailed away where?" Victor demanded. "To Hanover? To Croydon? Back to England?" If it was back to England, they'd won the war . . . hadn't they?

"Nope. None of them places," the courier said. "Word is, the ships they were on sailed south."

"South? To Freetown? To the settlements we took away from France?"

"General, I'm mighty sorry, but I don't know the answer to that," the man replied. "I don't believe anybody does, except the damned Englishmen—and they didn't tell anybody."

"Too bad!" Victor Radcliff said. More often than

not, somebody blabbed to a whore or a saloonkeeper or a friend. Maybe someone had, but the courier hadn't got wind of it. Then something else occurred to Victor: "How big a garrison did they leave behind?"

"Not *too* big," the courier said. "And if we try and take New Hastings away from them, what happens wherever they are heading farther south?"

That question had claws as sharp as those of any red-crested eagle. "Are they taking the war into the old French settlements? If they seize tight hold of those, can they move up against us the way Kersauzon did?" *Do I want to find out?* He knew he didn't.

"General, how in blazes am I supposed to know that?" The man who'd brought the news sounded reproachful.

Victor couldn't blame him. He didn't know the answer himself. He only knew England had widened the war, and he'd have to find some way to respond. He muttered under his breath. One more thing he didn't know was how the still largely French population of the southern settlements would react when English and English Atlantean armies started marching and counter-marching down there.

Many French Atlanteans resented England for taking their settlements away from King Louis and bestowing them on King George. But they also resented English Atlanteans for swarming down into their lands and grabbing with both hands after the conquest. And, of course, settlers from England and France had been rivals here since the long-vanished days of Edward Radcliffe and François Kersauzon.

Other related questions bubbled up in Victor's mind. How much would the whites—French and English alike—in the southern settlements resent the redcoats if General Howe tried to weaken slavery down there? How much help would he get from the enslaved Negroes and copperskins in the south if he did?

And what would France do when a large English army started traipsing through lands that had been French less than a generation before? Maybe nothing, but maybe not, too. Even though France had lost settlements in Atlantis, in Terranova, and in India, she'd recovered from the late war remarkably well. If she wanted to resent English incursions, she could.

Or am I letting hope run away from reality? Victor wondered. He couldn't judge what France was likely to do. He could think of three men from the Atlantean Assembly who knew more about that than he did: Isaac Fenner, Custis Cawthorne, and Michel du Guesclin.

The courier said, "You look like you just had a good idea, General."

"Do I?" Victor Radcliff shrugged. "Well, I can hope so, anyway."

Deliberating in a three-hundred-year-old church in a town of respectable size, the Atlantean Assembly made people who saw it in action think of the English Parliament that had treated Atlantis so shabbily.

Deliberating in a chamber that was half a tavern's common room and half a tent run up alongside to give more space, in a hamlet with the illustrious appellation of Honker's Mill, the Assembly seemed oddly diminished. The men were no less eloquent, the issues they debated no less urgent. But their setting made them seem no more than farmers gathered together to grumble about the way life was treating them.

New Hastings was a city. Honker's Mill would never be anything but a village. The honkers that had helped name it were long gone. The stream that powered the gristmill was too small to float anything more than a rowboat. The road that crossed the stream went from nowhere to nowhere. As far as Victor was concerned, it went through nowhere traversing Honker's Mill.

Isaac Fenner had got word of General Howe's movement south before Victor brought it. That encouraged Victor; the Assembly needed to know what was going on if it was to make sensible decisions. *To have a chance to make sensible decisions, anyhow*, Victor thought cynically. Even knowing what was going on, some Atlantean Assemblymen hadn't the vaguest idea what to do about it.

But Fenner wasn't of that ilk. The clever redhead from Bredestown nodded when Victor told him what was on his mind. "General Howe doesn't expect his move to stir up the French—else he'd not have done it," Fenner said. "Of course, that doesn't necessarily prove he's right."

"What can we do to help make him wrong?" Victor asked. "If we fight with France on our side, we're much better off than we are fighting alone."

"We've already done some of what we need. We've stayed in the field against England," Isaac Fenner answered. "We've shown we're an army, not a rabble that melts away when things turn sour. Your winter raids went a long way toward proving that: we didn't vote you your fancy sword for nothing."

"I'm glad to hear it." Victor touched the gold-wrapped hilt for a moment. "The French will have heard of this, then?"

"Rely on it," Fenner told him. "Even though they no longer have settlements here, they are well informed as to what transpires in these parts. And they will also know of Howe's incursion."

"Capital! This being so, how do we cast the incursion in the worst light possible?" Victor asked.

Isaac Fenner smiled at the way he phrased the question. "I know the very man to do it, provided we can get him to France. You will, I daresay, be better able to judge the likelihood of that than I."

"And this nonpareil would be . . . ?" Victor asked.

"Why, Master Cawthorne, of course." Fenner seemed disappointed he couldn't see that for himself. "Imagine Custis in Paris. A man should not have to enjoy himself so much, even for the sake of his country."

Victor chuckled. "Yes, I can see how he might have a good time there. The other question is, how will the French receive him? If he is but one more English Atlantean to them, I judge him to be of greater value here."

"Oh, no, General, no." Fenner shook his head. "If any of us has a reputation in Paris, Custis is the man, in part for his printing, in part for his dabbling in natural philosophy, and in part because they reckon him a delightful curmudgeon, if you can imagine such an abnormous hybrid."

"Well, then, to Paris with him," Victor said. "He may lose some dignity coming to France in a fishing shallop or a shallow-draught smuggler, but I expect he'll be able to make up for that."

"I should be astounded if you were mistaken." Isaac Fenner smiled again, this time in a distinctly lickerish way. "The pretty women of Paris will greet him with open arms—and, I shouldn't wonder, with open legs as well."

Victor Radcliff sighed. "You remind me how long I've been away from Meg."

"We are all having to do without companionship, or to make do." By the way Fenner said it, he hadn't always slept alone. Since Victor hadn't, either, he couldn't very well reproach the other man. But he *did* miss his wife. Relief was not the same thing as satisfaction. Fenner went on, "If a fourth part of what I hear is true, General Howe has made do quite well. I shouldn't wonder if he's sailing south not least because he's gone through all the willing women of New Hastings."

"He does have that reputation," Victor agreed. "So did General Braddock, and deservedly so. I will say, that had no part in Braddock's failure and death south of Freetown. And General Howe has fought better than I wish he would have, regardless of his lechery."

"A pity," Fenner said, and Victor nodded. The Assemblyman from Bredestown went on, "I have heard he left behind only a very small garrison. Is that also your understanding?"

"Not a large one, certainly," Victor replied. "As we shall move south after him come what may, I assure you I purpose investigating the situation in New Hastings. If we can recapture it, that will mark a heavy blow against

England—far heavier than when we reclaimed Weymouth during the winter."

"New Hastings is and always has been Atlantis' cradle of freedom," Fenner said seriously. "For it to groan no more under the spurred boot of tyranny would be wonderful. I should greatly appreciate anything you can do toward that end, I assure you."

If you help me, I'll help you. Isaac Fenner wasn't so crass as to come straight out and say that. He got the message across all the same.

"I'll do what I can," Victor said. "I understand why you don't care to have the Atlantean Assemblymen continue meeting here in Honker's Mill."

"Oh, my dear fellow, you couldn't possibly! You haven't been here long enough. On brief exposure, this place is merely stifling. Not until you've had to endure it for a while does it become truly stultifying. Boredom dies here . . . of boredom."

"Heh," Victor said, though he didn't think Fenner was joking. "I wonder what Cawthorne and du Guesclin think of Howe's incursion."

"In my opinion," Fenner said sagely, "they'll be against it."

And so they were. Michel du Guesclin couldn't have opposed it more vigorously had he rehearsed for a year. "Bad enough to have English Atlantean settlers on what was French soil," he said. "Worse to have so many English ruffians tramping through as if they owned the countryside."

"Um . . . King George believes he does. He believes he has since the end of the last war," Victor pointed out.

Du Guesclin waved his words aside. "What can you expect from a German?" he said. "A blockhead, a stubborn blockhead—his Majesty the King of England is assuredly nothing more."

"Assuredly, his soldiers will arrest you for treason if they hear you saying such things," Victor reminded him.

"I doubt you shall inform on me," du Guesclin said, which was true.

"You believe, then, that the French settlers are more likely to resist the redcoats than to oppose an army mostly made up of English Atlanteans?" Victor said.

Michel du Guesclin nodded. "I do. I believe this to be especially probable if the soldiers from England show an inclination to interfere with the institution of servitude as it is practiced there."

"I see." That had already crossed Victor's mind. How much would Howe care? How much help would he get from the Negroes and copperskins in the southern settlements if he interfered with slavery? Those were questions easier to ask than to answer. Victor found another one of a similar sort, and asked it anyway: "What about the settlers from English Atlantis who moved south after the last war?"

Du Guesclin's shrug was peculiarly Gallic. "There, I fear, you would be better able to judge than I. Being one yourself, you will naturally have a better notion of the English Atlanteans' desires than I ever could. If I might venture to predict, however—"

"Please do," Victor broke in. "I highly value your opinion."

"Thank you. Very well, then. My guess is that some will favor the German dullard on the English throne while others will oppose him, as seems true here farther north. If General Howe should move against slavery, he will make more enemies than friends among the English Atlanteans. Many of them, after all, moved south in hopes of acquiring a plantation."

Did his lip curl ever so slightly? Victor Radcliff wouldn't have been surprised. The plantations English Atlanteans wanted to acquire would have been made by French Atlanteans who died during the last war, whether in battle or from disease. A lot of them would have left widows but no heirs. Not all those widows were too fussy to look down their noses at vigorous Atlanteans of English blood, either.

"One more question, if I may," Victor said. Du Guesclin regally inclined his head. He looked down *his* nose at English Atlanteans, though he tried not to show it most of the time. Victor went on, "How will France respond to this latest English move?"

"Frenchmen from France are proud they were not born in distant settlements. I must tell you, *Monsieur le Général*, that I am equally proud I was not born in France," du Guesclin replied. "I do not know what goes on there, especially with this new young king. France will do whatever she does. It may prove wise or foolish. It *will* prove to be in what she imagines to be her interest. Custis Cawthorne, I suspect, would make a better—certainly a more dispassionate—judge than I."

"I was going to speak with him anyway," Victor said. "Thanks to your advice, I'll do it now."

It wasn't easy to live well in a place like Honker's Mill. Even the locals had trouble managing it. Oh, they mostly stayed dry and they seldom went hungry, but animals in the forest could match that. So could the inhabitants of backwoods towns all over Atlantis.

Even in Honker's Mill, Custis Cawthorne lived well. He smoked the mildest pipeweed. He ate the finest poultry and beef and mutton. He drank the smoothest barrel-tree rum, the best ale, the finest wine brought up—by whom? at whose large expense? not his, assuredly—from the south. He enjoyed the companionship of not one but two of the prettiest women for miles around.

"How do you do it?" Victor asked when one of those women—the younger, a buxom blonde—admitted him to Cawthorne's presence.

"If you are going to live, you should *live*," Cawthorne declared. "It probably sounds better in Latin, but it's just as true in English. What can I have Betsy bring you? Don't be shy—I've got plenty."

"Ale will do. I want to keep my head clear." Victor didn't say anything about whatever Cawthorne was drinking. He knew from experience that the printer wouldn't have listened to him if he had. Betsy smiled provocatively as she handed him the mug. With some regret, Victor declined to be provoked. He saluted Cawthorne. "Your health."

"And yours. God save the general!" Cawthorne could be provocative, too, even if less enjoyably than Betsy. After drinking, he inquired, "And what is the general's pleasure?"

"One of the things I desire to know is your view of the French view of the English incursion into the former French settlements there." Victor smiled at his own convoluted phrasing.

"I can't imagine that Paris will be delighted," Custis Cawthorne answered. "Nor is it in our interest that Paris should be."

Victor nodded. "Isaac Fenner said the same thing."

"Did he?" Cawthorne sounded less than pleased. "So I am doomed not to be original, then?"

Ignoring that, Victor went on, "He also said you were the right man to ensure that Paris was not delighted, and to incite the French against England if that be at all possible. How would you like to sail east and try your luck along those lines?"

"Fenner said I was the right one to go to France? Not himself?" Cawthorne asked. Victor nodded again. The printer let out a rasping chuckle. "Well, in that case I must beg his forgiveness for the unkind thoughts about him that just now went through my mind. Paris! I would be smuggled there, I suppose, disguised as salt cod or something else as tasty and odorous?"

"It's likely, I fear," Victor admitted. "We are not going to be able to challenge the Royal Navy on the high seas any time soon."

"So long as I make myself into a stench in the nostrils of King George, I shan't complain overmuch," Cawthorne said. "I doubt not that one of my ancestors was a fisherman. Precious few Atlanteans whose families have been here a while and can't claim that."

"I certainly can," Victor said.

"Radcliffs. Radcliffes." Custis Cawthorne pronounced the *e* that should have stayed silent. "If not for you people, we'd probably all be speaking Breton or French or Basque or something else no one in his right mind would care to speak."

"It could be." Victor hadn't much worried about that. "Get ready to leave Honker's Mill. Get ready to sail. I shall make arrangements to take you out of Atlantis by way of some port or another the English aren't watching too closely—maybe even New Hastings."

"New Hastings, eh? Do you think so?" Behind his spectacle lenses, Cawthorne's eyes were keen. "So you will be moving south after General Howe, will you? I thought as much. You can't just let him have the south, or we may never see it again."

"That did occur to me, yes," Victor said. "News travels fast. You and Isaac have both heard of Howe's move, while I wondered if I was bringing word of it here."

"News travels fast," Cawthorne agreed, a touch of smugness in his voice. It traveled fast when it came anywhere near him—not because he'd produced a newspaper but because he was who he was. Draining his mug of ale, he added, "I shall have to give Betsy and Lois something to remember me by."

"They aren't likely to forget you," Victor said.

"True," Cawthorne said, more than a touch of smugness surfacing now. "I hope I shan't forget them. French popsies are enough to make a man forget everything but his last name—and, if he's lucky, his wallet."

"I shall rely on your superior experience there," Victor told him.

"Get your hands on a French popsy, and I guarantee you a superior experience," Custis Cawthorne replied.

"Enough!" Victor said, laughing. He switched to French to ask, "Does your wit work in this language as well?"

"By God, I hope so." Custis Cawthorne had a better accent than Victor did. He actually sounded like a Parisian, where Victor talked like a French Atlantean settler, which would have left him seeming a back-country bumpkin if he ever had to present himself at Versailles.

He smiled at the unlikelihood of that. English Atlanteans sounded like bumpkins to the aristocrats commanding regiments of redcoats, too. Of course, so did most of the aristocrats' own soldiers, so things evened out.

Cawthorne's other . . . friend—Lois, yes: a statuesque brunette—grabbed Victor's sleeve as he was about to leave. "Are you going to take Custis away from us?" she demanded.

"Atlantis needs him," Victor said gravely.

Atlantis was not configured to do what she told it to do. As far as Victor knew, neither was anything else. "Betsy and me, we don't want him to go away," Lois said. "We never had fun like this before he came to Honker's Mill."

How did she mean that? *Do I really want to know?* Victor decided he didn't. "He can help bring France into the war against England," he said.

"So what?" Lois returned. "Why should the likes of us care one way or the other who wins?"

What difference *would* it make to her? Very little Victor could see. "Maybe your children will care," he said, and retreated with her laughter ringing in his ears.

X

*B*redestown fell. The English garrison fired a few shots for honor's sake and then marched away down the Brede toward New Hastings. Exultantly, the Atlanteans pursued. Taking back their first city, the city that still thought of itself as Atlantis' leader (Hanover? New Hastings never had cared a farthing for Hanover) would be a strong blow against King George.

But New Hastings didn't fall. No one could say that the redcoats lacked for clever engineers. They'd worked all winter to fortify the landward approaches to the town. Worse—certainly from Victor's perspective—they'd taken big guns off some of their warships and mounted them in their fieldworks.

Some of those guns seemed to fire roundshot as big as a man's head. One cannon ball sent a column of almost a dozen men to the surgeons—or to the gravediggers. After that, the Atlanteans lost their zeal for approaching the enemy works. The redcoats might not be there in numbers, but they could badly hurt any assault Victor tried.

And so Victor swung south without trying one. He didn't expect the English garrison to come out after him. He hoped—he prayed—it would. But he didn't expect it. The redcoats would have been giving themselves into his hands. Their commander, to Victor's disappointment, saw that for himself.

Blaise laughed at him. "You want the duck to walk into the oven and roast itself," the Negro said.

"Well ... yes," Victor admitted in some embarrassment. "Why should I work hard if the other fellow can make things easy for me?"

"Just because he can doesn't mean he will," Blaise said, which was true even if unpalatable. "How much French do you recall?"

"Un petit peu, j'espère," Victor answered. *"Et tu?"*

"La même chose," Blaise said, and then, in English, "French was the first white people's language I learned after the slavers brought me here. Some of it got beaten into me, and that stuck. The rest ... I use English all the time now, except when I'm with Stella."

His wife came from the same part of Africa he did. Till Victor got to know Blaise, he hadn't thought that Africa might have as many languages as Europe. He wondered why not; he knew Terranovan copperskins spoke many different tongues. Maybe it was because blacks looked more nearly alike to him than copperskins did.

How did whites look to Terranovans and Africans? That was an interesting question. One of these days, maybe he'd ask Blaise about it. For the moment, he had more urgent things to worry about.

First and foremost was keeping Freetown in Atlantean hands—if it still was. Maybe General Howe had sailed for the southernmost good-sized town in English Atlantis rather than heading farther south. And if he had, maybe Freetown had opened up for him. It had always been a royalist center—especially when viewed from the perspective of New Hastings or even Hanover.

"Push it, boys! Push it!" Victor called. "We've got to keep Freetown living up to its name."

The men seemed eager to march. He cherished that, knowing there would be times when they weren't. They also had enough to eat, which wasn't always true. And the roads were good: hard enough to march on, but not summer-dry so that travelers choked in their own dust and advertised their coming from miles away.

Victor breathed a sigh of relief when Freetown welcomed him as warmly as the place ever welcomed anybody who wasn't born there. His own name was in good odor in these parts. He'd helped defend Freetown against an attack from French Atlantis fifteen years earlier. He would have put more credit in that if he hadn't had redcoats as allies then. Freetown also remembered them fondly.

Discovering the place wasn't flying the Union Jack, Victor sent a messenger back to Honker's Mill: "Tell them that if Custis Cawthorne wants to head for France, this may be the best place to leave from."

"I'll do it, General," the man promised, brushing the brim of his tricorn with a forefinger.

Freetown fishermen said they'd seen the Royal Navy sailing south past their home. They said as much after Atlantean soldiers sought them out and grilled them, anyhow. They showed no great desire to come forward on their own and share what they knew.

Talking to one of them, Victor Radcliff said, "We might have walked into trouble if you'd kept your mouth shut."

He got back a shrug. "I just want this war to end, one way or the other," the fisherman said. "Don't much care which."

How many people felt the same way? How many went *A plague on both your houses* when redcoats or greencoats came near them? More than a few, unless Victor missed his guess. Most of the time, that didn't matter. It might have here.

"I think you just helped us take a step toward winning," he told the fisherman.

"Huzzah," the fellow said. "What difference does it make to me? D'you think the cod care one way or the other?"

"You'll have more places to sell them when Atlantis

is free." Victor refused to say, or even to think, *if Atlantis is free*.

"And some nosy bastard seeing how much I caught and how much he can tax me for it." No, the fisherman didn't care for the war or freedom or anything else.

Victor Radcliff raised his right hand, as if taking an oath. "If the day comes when Atlantean officials do such things, pick up a musket and march on them. By God, you'll see me marching on them, too."

He still failed to impress the Freetown man. "You don't catch on, General. I don't want to march on anybody. I don't want anybody marching on me, either. I just want to get left alone and not be bothered. Is that too damned much to ask?"

Yes, Victor thought. "I was going to give you a couple of pounds for what you knew," he said. "If you don't want to be bothered, I'll keep them in my wallet."

The fisherman turned out not to have anything against money going into his pocket, no matter how little he liked paying taxes. He left Victor's presence happier than he'd entered it. That didn't happen every day; Victor supposed he should have cherished it.

He made a quick tour of Freetown's ocean-facing forts. The Royal Navy hadn't cared to test them by landing here. As far as Victor could see, the sailors had missed a chance. They could have put an army of redcoats ashore with little risk from these popguns. Maybe General Howe thought he could win the war farther south.

"Here's hoping he's wrong," Blaise said when Victor mentioned that.

"Yes," Victor said. "Here's hoping."

Howe could land wherever he chose. He had plenty of time to maneuver after landing, too. Ships sailed faster than men marched. And they sailed all through the day and night, while marching men had to rest.

Determined to do what he could, Victor sent riders ahead of his army, urging the former French settlements to call out their militias and resist the redcoats wherever the enemy happened to come ashore. Even if they all obeyed the summons, he wondered whether he was doing them a favor. The English soldiers would likely go through raw militiamen like a dose of salts. He shrugged. If he couldn't stop the enemy, he had to try to slow them down.

Moving south from Freetown took him back in time. When he was a younger man, he'd fought French settlers and French regulars again and again in these parts. The redcoats were his allies then. He'd been glad to lean on their skill and courage. Now he had to beat them . . . if he could.

Coming up from the south, French Atlanteans had named the river that ended up dividing their land from that of the English the Erdre. Coming down from the north at about the same time, English Atlanteans called the same river the Stour. Since the English prevailed in their war, the latter name was heard more often these days.

The bridge over the Stour closest to the sea was fine and new and wide. Roland Kersauzon's French Atlanteans had burned the old one behind them when they crossed back into their own territory after their defeat south of Freetown. The new one, intended as a symbol of unity, was mostly stonework. Fire wouldn't bring it down. Hogsheads of black powder probably would.

Blaise's eyes seemed to get wider after the Atlantean army crossed into what had been French Atlantis. When the men stopped for the night, he took special care to clean his musket. "You are among friends, you know," Victor told him.

"Am I?" The Negro's voice was bleak. "On this side of the river, the law says I can be a slave. On this side of the river, maybe even now, is the master I was running from when we first met." He squinted at the rod he was using to push an oily cloth down the flintlock's barrel.

"No one's going to put chains on you, by God," Victor said.

"Not unless I wander away from the army and somebody knocks me over the head," Blaise answered. "I got no freedom papers. How could I, when I ran off? It could happen—it has with others."

"Well, stay out of dark corners and don't go off by yourself," Victor said. "Past that . . . My guess is, anybody who wanted a slave would be afraid to buy one who'd worn three stripes on his sleeve."

Blaise thought that over. His smile would have made any slaveholder's blood run cold. "You've got something there. Put together an army of blacks and copperskins and all this part of Atlantis runs for its mother."

Victor Radcliff laughed, even if his heart wasn't in it. He hoped Blaise couldn't see that. One of these days, Atlantis would have to face up to slavery and either let it go or decide it was a positive good and cling to it more tightly than ever. He had the bad feeling that that choice would prove rougher and nastier than the one between the Atlantean Assembly and King George—which was proving quite rough enough on its own.

He also had the bad feeling that that struggle shouldn't start till this one was over. *One thing at a time*, he thought. Sometimes accomplishing even one thing at a time seemed much harder than it should have.

"General Radcliff! General Radcliff!" someone shouted.

Blaise's grin reverted to its usual mocking self. "Somebody needs you," he said. "We can talk about this other thing some more later."

"All right," Victor said. Sometimes *not* accomplishing something didn't seem so bad. He waved and raised his voice. "Here I am! What's the trouble?" Something had to be bunged up. People didn't yell for him like that when everything was rosy.

A cavalryman came over to him. "There's Frenchies shooting at us when we try and forage," he said. "They're coming out with all kinds of daft nonsense, like here we are invading them again."

"Oh." Victor swore in English, French, and, for good

measure, Spanish. He wished the Atlantean army included more French settlers. He'd tried to include some of the ones he did have in all of his foraging parties. "Why didn't these Frenchies want to listen to the people who tried to tell them we aren't after them—we're fighting the English?"

Without being in the least Gallic, the cavalryman's shrug was a small masterpiece of its kind. "Why, General? On account of they're French, I reckon."

"Can you tell me more than that?" Victor clung to patience.

"They say we're robbing them again, same as we did before," the horseman answered.

"But we're not. We're paying for what we take." Victor eyed the man who'd brought him the bad news. "You *are* paying for what you take, are you not?"

"Yes, General." Butter wouldn't have melted in the horseman's mouth. "But they don't fancy our money, and that's the Lord's truth."

Radcliff took the Lord's name in vain again. His army couldn't pay gold or silver—or even copper—for what it requisitioned from the countryside. It paid in paper printed by the Atlantean Assembly: possibly printed by Custis Cawthorne in person. If all went well in the war against England, that paper might be redeemable for specie . . . some day. As things were, it was worth what people decided it was worth—at the moment, not so much. With better choices, Victor wouldn't have been delighted to get Atlantean paper himself.

But the French Atlanteans had no better choices. They could take the paper money they were offered, which was worth *something*. Or they could take nothing. Or they could get killed and have their property run off anyway. Victor couldn't see anything else they might do.

"Do you want to go softly, or do you want to crush them?" Blaise asked.

"I was wondering the same thing," Victor answered.

"I'll try to go softly at first—I don't want to make them hate us."

"More than they do already," the cavalryman put in.

"More than that," Victor agreed. "The war is against King George. If we have to fight the French settlers, too, that only makes things harder. If they join General Howe, that also makes things harder. So I want to keep them sweet if I possibly can."

Blaise made a discontented noise deep in his throat. Victor might have known he would. French Atlanteans were enemies to the Negro, and always would be. He had his reasons for that. Victor even sympathized with them, but his own concerns overrode them.

He shouted for a groom to fetch his horse. "Let's see if they'll listen to me," he said.

"What if they don't?" the cavalryman asked.

"They will wish they would have," Victor replied.

He found his cavalrymen just outside musket range of a stone farmhouse and barn. He could see men moving around inside the house. Maybe friends had gathered together to oppose the cavalry, or maybe it was one of the huge families common in Atlantis. He rode forward under flag of truce.

"Is that smart, General?" one of his men asked.

"Even if they fire, chances are they'll miss," Victor answered. He raised his voice and switched to French: "I am General Radcliff! I wish to parley!"

A farmer stuck his head out a window. "You wish to steal, you and all the other English Atlanteans!"

"We will pay you for what we take," Victor answered.

"In worthless paper," the farmer jeered.

"It is not worthless," Victor said, which was technically true. He went on, "Your only other choice is to die fighting. We have no quarrel with you, but we must eat."

"So must we," the farmer said. "And how do you propose to kill us? If you attack, we will shoot you down as you come. We know how to deal with mad dogs, by God. You cannot force us from this house. It is our patrimony."

"We do not want to fight you, but we will if we have to." Victor couldn't let the farmer get away with too much, or he would spend the next five years parleying at every little homestead in French Atlantis. "We will bring up our cannon and knock your patrimony down around your ears."

The farmer disappeared back into the house. Victor could hear argument inside, but couldn't make out what was going on. Some of the defenders seemed to realize they couldn't hold out against field guns. Victor didn't want to slaughter them. But war made you do all kinds of things you didn't want to do.

When the farmer came back to the window, he shook a fist at Victor. "You are a bad chalice!" he shouted, which was anything but an endearment from a French Atlantean. "I will take your paper, and you will redeem it, or I will hunt you down and make you sorry."

"It is agreed," Victor said. If the rebellion won, the Atlantean Assembly's paper would be redeemed—he hoped. And if the uprising failed, more people than this rustic would be on his trail.

He gave the man the paper money as the cavalrymen rounded up livestock. "This looks like a lot," the French Atlantean said. "If it really were a lot, though, you'd give me less." He wasn't wrong. The farmers whose ancestors had sprung from Britanny and Normandy were commonly canny, and he seemed no exception.

"Do please remember—you have one other gift of me," Victor said.

"Oh?" The farmer quirked a bushy eyebrow. "And what may that be?"

"Your life, *Monsieur*. I was not joking about the artillery."

"I know," the farmer said. "If I thought you were, I would have shot you out of the saddle."

"We don't have to love each other. All we have to do is work well enough to keep from shooting," Victor said.

"You have more guns, which makes this easier for you to say," the farmer replied—and, again, he had a point. Since he did, Victor tipped his hat and rode away. No one from the farmhouse or the barn shot him in the back, which was as good a bargain as he could hope for.

General Howe's army landed at Cosquer, the oldest French town on the coast. Victor had expected that. The only other choices the redcoats had were to land at St. Denis, a seaside hamlet south of Cosquer, or to sail around the Spanish-held southern coast of Atlantis and put in at New Marseille or even at Avalon. No one could stand against them in the west, but they would be too far away from the more settled regions to harm the uprising much.

"Nouveau Redon again?" Blaise asked when the news came in.

"I don't think so," Victor answered. Nouveau Redon, up the Blavet from Cosquer, had been French Atlantis' greatest fortress till English soldiers and settlers besieged and took it. The siege involved cutting off the unfailing spring that watered the town. Without it, Nouveau Redon had to rely on the river, and was far more vulnerable than it had been.

"Now we have to see how many people in these parts bend down and kiss King George's boots," Blaise said.

Victor had trouble imagining the King of England in boots. Apart from that, Blaise knew his onions. If the locals flocked to the Union Jack, the war down here would be hard. If they didn't . . . In that case, General Howe would have more work to do.

Blaise also had other things in mind, even if he didn't mention them now. Plenty of people in these parts cared not a farthing for either King George or the Atlantean Assembly. But those people had skins either black or coppery, and people with white skins—people who counted, in other words—cared not a farthing for what they thought.

Most of the time, Victor wouldn't have cared, either. He owned no slaves, and had no great love for men who did. Then again, he also wasn't one of the stubborn hot-heads who thought Negroes and copperskins should all be free. If they made their owners money, he was willing to let them go on doing that.

If they rose up against General Howe and the red-coats, he was willing to let them do that, too. If they rose up against the Atlanteans . . . That was a different story. And they might, because Howe had little to lose in incit-ing them to rebellion. He'd shown farther north that he wasn't afraid to play that card.

"Blaise . . ." Victor said.

"What is it, General?" By the way the colored ser-geant said it, he was a natural-born innocent. Victor smiled; if he believed that, he was dumb as a honker.

"I must make myself clear here, Blaise," he said. "We didn't cross the Stour to free the slaves. We came down here to free ourselves from the English. Once we man-age that, we can look at the other, too. But I fear we can't even look at it till we free ourselves. Do I make myself plain enough?"

The Negro's scowl said he made himself much too plain. "General Howe won't care about any o' that," Blaise said, which paralleled Victor's thoughts of a mo-ment before much too closely.

"Whatever he tries to do, we will set about stopping him," the Atlantean general said. "And we will not do anything or say anything about the way of life in these parts unless we have no choice in the matter. Do I also make myself plain there?"

"I'll say what I please about it," Blaise retorted. "It's filthy. It's wicked. By God, I should know. I wouldn't have run off if it weren't."

Victor wasn't so sure about that. Some people—blacks, whites, copperskins—felt the urge to be free so strongly, they would run from even comfortable surroundings. But Blaise had been a field hand, not a house slave, so he was likely telling the truth.

In the grand scheme of things, it didn't matter much, and Victor Radcliff had to worry about the grand scheme of things. "One of these days, this whole business will sort itself out, Blaise," he said. "You know that's true as well as I do. If you think a little, you'll know this isn't the right day."

"Don't want to think," Blaise said sullenly. "Want to—" He mimed aiming a flintlock and pulling the trigger.

"One thing at a time. I've said as much before." Victor sounded as if he was begging. And he was. "Most of the time, we have enough trouble managing that. When we try to do two things at once, we go to the Devil."

"He can have the bastard who brought me over here, the white-toothed dealer who sold me, and the mangy hound who bought me," Blaise said. "If anything in your religion is true, they're all bound for hell."

"I am a Christian," Victor said. So was Blaise . . . most of the time. But Victor had grown up with and in his faith, and took it as much for granted as the air he breathed. Coming to it first as an adult, Blaise enjoyed tinkering with it and trying to figure out how it worked, much as a watchmaker might enjoy disassembling a complicated clock and then putting it back together.

Blaise looked at him now. "You are a Christian when it suits you. You are a Christian to white Atlanteans— even to white Englishmen. When will you be a Christian to niggers and mudfaces?" Only in southern Atlantis, a region with reddish dirt, would that have stuck as an insulting name for copperskins.

Victor's cheeks heated. "One thing at a time," he said yet again. "Once we drive the English from this land, we can make it what we want it to be for everyone who lives. Everyone."

"How long will you and I be dead before that day comes?" Blaise asked.

Victor wasn't fifty yet, while Blaise wasn't far from his age. He didn't want to claim they'd see the day he'd talked about. Well, he wanted to, but Blaise would only mock him if he tried.

He did say, "I think it will take longer if England wins. General Howe cares more about slaves because he can use them against us than for any other reason."

"And you are proud this is so because . . . ?" Blaise asked.

Try as Victor might, he found no good answer for that. Blaise's smug look said he hadn't thought Victor would.

Victor hadn't seen the Blavet for a long time. The river was at least as important in the history of French Atlantis as the Brede was to English Atlantis. He'd crossed it several times during the war, and more than once before that. And he'd helped besiege and capture Nouveau Redon even though the French thought the fortress impregnable. Custis Cawthorne's judgment on that had been *An impregnable position is one in which you're liable to get screwed*: as usual, pungent and cogent at the same time.

Since taking Nouveau Redon, Radcliff had assumed the French Atlanteans would love him better at a distance. No one from the south had ever told him he was wrong, either. That left him sad but unsurprised.

But among the things war made you do were ones you'd stay away from in peacetime. And so here he was on the river again, peering across to the south bank to see if he could spy any sign of General Howe and the redcoats. No unusual plumes of smoke in the sky, no hanging dust that told of an army marching up a dirt road. Howe's men were somewhere on the far side of the Blavet, but farther off than Victor had feared.

Flapjack turtles swimming in the river stared, only their heads and long, snaky necks above water. They made good eating, but you had to treat them with respect: a big one could bite off a finger. Worse things than flapjack turtles lurked in the rivers down here, too. Spanish Atlanteans called them *lagartos*—lizards.

English Atlanteans mostly used the Biblical word: crocodiles.

Bridges still spanned the Blavet, a sure sign fighting in these parts hadn't been going on for long. "Are we going to cross, General?" Habakkuk Biddiscombe asked.

The cavalry officer sounded dubious, for which Victor could hardly blame him. All the same, he answered, "Yes, I think we are. We came down here to fight the enemy, not just to keep an eye on him."

"Yes, sir. But . . ." Sure enough, even the pugnacious Biddiscombe seemed unhappy. "If they get between us and the river after we go south of it . . ." His voice trailed off again.

"If they get between us and our homes, you mean," Victor said.

Habakkuk Biddiscombe nodded gratefully. "Yes, sir. That *is* what I mean. If they do that, we're in a pile of trouble."

"Then we'd be wise not to let them, don't you agree?" Victor said.

"We would, yes." Biddiscombe nodded again. "But not everything in war happens the way you wish it would, if you know what I mean."

Victor would have been happier if he hadn't had a similar thought not long before. "All we can do is our best," he said. "I am confident every man here will do that. If you are not, I hope you will point out the likely shirkers to me so we can separate them from this force as soon as may be."

"Oh, no, General. I think everyone will fight hard," Biddiscombe said hastily. "I just don't know how much good it will do."

"I see." Victor fought to hide a smile. "Your concern is not for the common soldiers, but for the competence of their commanding general. That is a serious business. I worry about it myself."

Habakkuk Biddiscombe opened his mouth. Then he closed it again without saying anything. And then, sketching a salute, he jerked his horse's head around and retreated in disorder. If beating the enemy proved as easy as routing Atlanteans, everything would go very well indeed.

After crossing the Blavet, Victor thought about leaving a force behind to protect the bridge. In the end, he didn't. No force of reasonable size would be able to stall the redcoats long. He decided the men would be better used with his main body. There, they might keep the English from approaching the bridge to begin with.

He did send cavalrymen riding in all directions. The sooner he learned exactly where General Howe was, the better. If Major Biddiscombe—promoted after his winter heroics—seemed eager to get away, neither he nor Victor had to remark on that.

An English Atlantean and his French-speaking wife—a soldier's widow from the last war?—came into the army's encampment to complain. "Why are you requisitioning from us?" the man asked. "What did we ever do to you?"

"Would you go to General Howe the same way?" Victor asked.

"By thunder, I sure hope so," the prosperous farmer replied.

"I suspect he'd clap you in irons if you tried, but never mind," Radcliff said. "We need supplies. An army does not subsist on air. I wish mine did; it would make the quartermaster's job easier. But until that day comes . . ." Victor spread his hands in apology.

"How do you expect people to rally to the red-crested eagle if you plunder the countryside?" the farmer demanded.

"Plunderers don't commonly pay," Victor said, as he had so often before.

The English Atlantean's wife proved she understood the language by letting out an unladylike snort. "And what is your paper good for?" she asked, before making an even more unladylike gesture to show what it was good for.

"After the war is won, it will be as good as silver and gold," Victor insisted—hopefully.

"And on the twelfth of Never, they'll put a crown on my head and feed me pudding all day long," the farmer said.

"Well, sir, you have got another choice," Victor said.

"Oh? What's that?" The man perked up.

"We could kill you both and burn the farmhouse over your heads," Victor said with no expression in his voice or on his face.

If he'd made it sound more like a threat, he might have frightened the farmer less. The man eyed him to judge whether he was joking. "We'll take your paper," he said quickly. Whatever he saw must have convinced him Victor meant every quiet word. That was wise on his part, for Victor did.

"Should have killed him anyway," Blaise said when Victor told the story back at camp. "Now he will take the Atlantean Assembly's paper and then say bad things to his neighbors even so."

That struck Victor as all too probable. All the same, he said, "Our names would be blacker if we started killing everyone we didn't trust."

After *blacker* came out of his mouth, he wished it hadn't. So many phrases in English weren't made to be used around free Negroes. To his relief, Blaise didn't call him on it, instead saying, "Maybe better to lose reputation than to let some of those people hurt us."

"Maybe," Victor said. Some loyalists would end up getting hurt—he was sure of that. Some had already. He went on, "General Howe doesn't hang people just for being on our side, either. I don't care to give him the excuse to start."

"You white people." Blaise shook his head. "You and your rules for war."

"It's not quite so bad with them as without them," Victor said.

"Half the time, I still think you are crazy, every one of you," Blaise said.

"Why not all the time?" Victor inquired.

"Because I remember you can make ships to sail from Africa to Atlantis. You can make guns. You can make whiskey and rum. You can make books." Blaise named the things that impressed him most. "My people, they cannot do any of these. So if you are crazy, you are crazy in a clever way."

"Crazy like a fox, we'd say," Victor replied.

"Foxes. Little red jackals," Blaise said, and Victor supposed they were. The Negro went on, "I hear tell these foxes don't live naturally in Atlantis. I hear tell people bring them. Is this so?"

Radcliff nodded. "It is. No four-legged beasts with fur but for bats lived in Atlantis before people brought them here."

"Some of your beasts—horses and cows and sheep and pigs—I see why you brought them. But why foxes? They kill chickens and ducks whenever they can."

"In England, hunting them is a sport," Victor answered. "People wanted to do the same here."

"I take it back. You white people *are* crazy," Blaise said. "You bring in beasts that cause so much trouble—to hunt them for sport?"

"Well, I didn't do it myself," Victor said. "And I don't suppose the lizards and snakes and oil thrushes here thank whoever did."

"I believe there were no four-legged furry beasts here before people brought them. They would have eaten up all the oil thrushes like *this*." Blaise snapped his fingers. "We have no stupid birds like them in Africa."

As far as Victor knew, there were no such stupid birds in England or Europe, either—or in Terranova, come to that. "There were—what were they called?—dodos, I think the name was, on little islands between Africa and India."

"Were?" Blaise echoed.

"Were. People ate them and ate them, and now none are left," Victor said with a shrug. "I suppose the oil thrushes and honkers will go that way, too, before too many more years pass."

"All gone. How strange," Blaise said.

Before he could say anything more, a cavalryman rode into camp shouting, "General Radcliff! General Radcliff, sir!"

Victor ducked out of his tent. "I'm here. What's wrong?" The hubbub made him sure something was.

"We found the redcoats, General," the rider answered. He pointed southeast. "They're headin' this way."

XI

"Well, we crossed the river to find them." Victor Radcliff hoped he sounded calmer than he felt. The sun was sinking toward the Green Ridge Mountains. "How close are they? Will they get here before night falls, or can we fight them in the morning?"

"In the morning, I'd say," the rider replied. Then he shook his head. "Or maybe not, if they push their march. Hard to be sure."

"Damnation," Victor muttered under his breath. He couldn't stand people who couldn't make up their minds. And he had to rely on what this fellow said, no matter how indecisive it was.

He did the best he could. He sent out pickets to cover a fan-shaped arc from due south to northeast of his position. If General Howe did try a forced march, the Atlanteans would slow him down and warn the main body of his approach. Victor didn't really anticipate it. Howe made a better strategist than a field commander. On campaign, he'd proved several times that he didn't move as fast as he might have.

Better to send out the pickets without need than to get an ugly surprise, though.

"If we don't fight the redcoats this afternoon, we will fight them on the morrow," he told the men still in camp.

"Clean your muskets. Riflemen, take especial care with your pieces—they foul worse than smoothbores. Cooks, ready supper now. If we do fight today, better to fight on a full stomach."

Thanks to their foragers, they would have enough to eat for the next couple of days. After that, they would need to shift again and take what they could from some other part of formerly French Atlantis.

Victor wondered how the English troops were subsisting themselves. Did they have a wagon train from Cosquer and the ocean? Did boats bring their victuals up the Blavet? Or were they foraging like the Atlanteans?

It didn't matter now. It might if he routed them and fell on their baggage train. He laughed at himself. He was nothing if not ambitious. He had yet to beat the redcoats in a pitched battle, and now he was thinking about what might happen after he routed them? If he wasn't ambitious, he'd slipped a cog somewhere.

No sudden spatters of gunfire disturbed the rest of the afternoon. General Howe hadn't eaten hot Terranovan peppers or anything else that made him break out in a sweat of urgency. More riders came in. Victor got a better notion of the enemy's position.

And an English Atlantean who'd settled south of the Blavet rode into camp just after sunset. He introduced himself as Ulysses Grigsby. "I hear the redcoats aren't so far off," he said.

"I hear the same," Victor agreed gravely.

"You aim to fight 'em?" Grigsby asked.

"The thought had crossed my mind," Victor admitted. "Why do you wish to know?" If this stranger was some loyalist spy, he might imagine he could waltz away with the Atlanteans' battle plans. If he did, he was doomed to a most painful disappointment.

But Ulysses Grigsby said, "On account of if you do, I know a damned good place to do it at." He was between forty and fifty, skinny and weathered: if he hadn't seen a good many out-of-the-way places, Victor would have been surprised. He smelled of sweat and pipeweed.

"Oh, you do?" Victor said. Grigsby nodded. Victor eyed him. "If you try to put us in a bad spot, or in a good one where General Howe knows of some weakness and can use it, I promise you it will be your final mistake."

"And if I tell you nothing but the plain truth?" the other man returned.

"Then Atlantis will have cause to be grateful," Victor said. "We are not in an ideal position to show our appreciation at the moment, things being as they are. But, once we prove to England we are not to be defeated and she leaves off trying to subjugate us, we shan't forget our friends. If that is not enough for you, sir, I will tell you good evening."

"And be damned to me?" Grigsby suggested.

"You said it, not I," Victor answered.

"Heh." Grigsby's chuckle was dry as dust in an August drought. "Well, I'll take you there now, if you like." He chuckled again. "Bring as many guards as you please. You don't need to—it's inside your picket line. But I expect you'll bring 'em anyhow. You've no reason to trust me . . . yet."

"You got past the pickets unnoticed, I gather?" Victor said.

"I sure did. But don't fret yourself." That dry chuckle came out once more. "I expect they'd likely spy an army as tried the same."

"One may hope." Radcliff wasn't about to let anybody he'd just met outdry him. Ulysses Grigsby laughed yet again. Between the two of them, they could probably evaporate the Blavet.

"Well, let's get going," said the English Atlantean who'd settled south of the old dividing line. "Sooner you see I'm not a prevaricating son of a whore, sooner you can commence to ciphering out how to steer General Howe into your jaws."

"Prevaricating," Victor echoed, not without admiration. He would have bet Grigsby was self-taught. He'd known several Atlanteans like that: they would trot out the proofs of their learning whenever they could. Well-built women often wore *décolleté* dresses for similar reasons of display.

He took along half a company's worth of soldiers. If that force couldn't let him get away from an ambush ... then it couldn't, and he and Atlantis would have to lump it. He watched Grigsby out of the corner of his eye. The other man gave no sign of wanting to betray him to the enemy. Of course, if he was worth anything at all in this game, he wouldn't.

As twilight deepened, a poor-bob somewhere under the trees loosed its mournful two-note call. It sang once more, then fell silent as the riders got closer. If redcoats skulked nearby, the night bird likely wouldn't have called at all. More than a few people reckoned hearing a poor-bob unlucky. This once, Victor took it for a good sign.

"Not much farther," Grigsby said a few minutes later. "Still ought to be enough light to let you see what I'm going on about."

"That would be good," Victor said, which got one more chuckle out of his guide.

Grigsby reined in and gestured. "This here is the place. You're the general. Expect you'll see what I've got in mind."

Victor looked east: the direction from which Howe's army would advance. He eyed the ground on which his army would fight if things went well. Slowly, thoughtfully, he nodded. "Promising, Mr. Grigsby. Promising," he said. "But I am going to keep you under guard till after the fighting's over even so."

He waited to see whether the leathery settler got angry. Grigsby only nodded back. "Didn't reckon you'd tell me any different," he replied. "Doesn't look like I'll have to wait real long any which way."

"You're right," Victor said. "It doesn't."

The Atlantean soldiers grumbled when their sergeants and officers routed them from their bedrolls well before sunup the next morning. The sergeants and officers, having been awakened earlier still so they could rouse the men, had already done their own grumbling. Stony-hearted, they ignored the honking from the common soldiers.

Tea and coffee and breakfast helped reconcile the troops to being alive. The eastern sky went gray, then pink, then gold as sunrise neared. Stars faded and dis-appeared; the third-quarter moon went from gleaming mistress of the heavens to a pale gnawed fingernail in the sky.

"Keep moving!" Blaise called to the Atlanteans near him as they marched along. "Every step you take, you have less excuse for tripping over your own big, clumsy feet."

When they got to Ulysses Grigsby's chosen battle-field, a lot of the men murmured appreciatively. As Baron von Steuben had noticed, one difference between Atlanteans and Englishmen was that Atlanteans liked thinking for themselves instead of letting somebody else do it for them. Most of Victor's troopers imagined themselves captains if not generals. They could see—or believed they could see—what would happen if the red-coats came up that road through the meadow.

As Victor made his dispositions, his soldiers' disposi-tions grew cheerier by the minute. "Might even've been worth booting us out of bed so bloody early," a rifleman called to Radcliff.

"So glad you approve," Victor said.

"You won't get higher praise than that," Grigsby remarked.

Victor nodded. "Don't I know it!"

Spatters of musketry started up, off to the east. Victor had sent reinforcements to his pickets during the night. He wanted his men to harass the redcoats if they chose the wrong roads and to leave them alone if they came along the ones he wanted. This was the tricky part. If the Atlanteans guided too openly, Howe would wonder why . . . wouldn't he?

Little by little, the gunfire faded away. Ulysses

Grigsby sketched a salute. "Damn me if I don't believe you've brung it off.".

"Well, we can hope so," Victor answered. He had his men and fieldpieces deployed the way he wanted them. He needed to make General Howe think he was ready to fight here, but not that he was excessively eager about it.

For that matter, he needed to make himself feel the same way. The spot Ulysses Grigsby had suggested looked good, but he wouldn't know it was till the fighting ended. And, if Grigsby had somehow contrived to play him false, it would prove to be not so good as it seemed. In that case, the English Atlantean's fate would prove less pleasant than Grigsby wished.

"Skirmishers forward!" Victor commanded. He had to look as if he'd just stumbled upon this position and chosen to fight here more or less on a whim. Soldiers sniping at the redcoats and trying to slow down and disrupt their advance would add a convincing touch.

Cavalrymen rode back through the advancing skirmishers. "They're coming!" the riders shouted, and some added obscene embellishments on the theme.

Victor Radcliff surveyed the field. "I do believe we're ready to greet them properly," he said, and then, to Ulysses Grigsby's guards, "Take the gentleman back and keep him out of the way till we see how things develop. After that, we'll know whether he stabbed us in the back or we should pat him on his."

"Come along, you," growled the sergeant in charge of the guards.

"You're an endearing chap, aren't you?" Grigsby said.

The sergeant looked at him as if flies buzzed around him in an open field. "No. Come on, I said."

"You certainly did." Grigsby came.

Victor eyed his men behind a stone wall. They shouldn't disconcert the redcoats. General Howe knew the Atlanteans liked to fight from cover when they could. Sometimes, they'd made English troops sorry.

Others, the redcoats had managed to storm their positions in spite of everything. When the redcoats came to close quarters, their skill—and viciousness—with the bayonet gave them the edge.

More gunfire erupted up ahead. That had to be the skirmishers fighting a delaying action against the English. Yes, here they came, firing and falling back. The musketeers, who could shoot more quickly, helped keep the redcoats off the riflemen, who could hit from longer range.

"Come on! Come on!" Victor Radcliff waved his hat. "You can do it! The line's just ahead now!"

Most of the skirmishers took their place behind the stone fence. Some went off to the surgeon, either under their own power or helped by their friends. Brave banners from the Atlantean regiments fluttered in the morning sun.

And more brave banners appeared from out of the sun. It didn't seem that an English squad could march into battle without drums thumping and flags flying, much less a company or a regiment. Had trees sprouted flags in place of leaves, Victor would have thought Birnam Wood was out looking for Dunsinane.

When General Howe and his officers spotted the flags marking the Atlantean position, they paused well out of rifle range and methodically dressed their lines. Very faint in the distance, sergeants' angry shouts reached Victor's ears. He smiled. Underofficers seemed much the same regardless of army or uniform.

With his spyglass, he found General Howe. A slightly less gorgeously clad officer was talking to the English commander. The lower-ranking man pointed to the woods ahead and to either side of the stone fence the Atlanteans defended. Victor idly wondered if that was Richard Cornwallis or some other English officer who'd fought the French Atlanteans the last time around.

Whoever the Englishman was, General Howe didn't want to listen to him. Howe pointed to the Atlantean banners, then waved his hand. The spyglass didn't let

Victor recognize expressions, but he had no doubt what that dismissive gesture meant. The English commander did it so well, he might have used it on the stage.

The other officer tried once more. This time, Howe's gesture seemed more imperious than dismissive. *Stop bothering me and carry out your orders*—that was what he had to mean. The junior officer saluted and rode away. Whatever he was thinking, he perforce kept it to himself.

Howe's field artillery deployed. The men performed their evolutions with admirable speed and precision. Victor would have found them even more admirable if they weren't aimed at his men.

One after another, the English cannon boomed. A roundshot roared over the Atlanteans. Another smacked the fence they sheltered behind. Flying chunks of stone wounded several men.

Atlantean cannon posted by the fence thundered a reply. A lucky shot from one of them knocked a wheel off an English gun carriage. The enemy fieldpiece pointed at an odd angle, as if trying to stand up straight while drunk. Artillerymen rushed to repair the wounded cannon.

Another Atlantean roundshot plowed through several ranks of redcoats before finally losing its momentum. Victor heard those distant soldiers shriek. Their comrades dragged badly hurt men off to the surgeons and took their places without any fuss. The slaughter machine that was an English army tramped forward to the beat of the drum and the wail of the fife.

"Don't shoot too soon, you damnfool musketeers!" That had to be an Atlantean sergeant: no officer would have shown common soldiers so much scorn. The man went on, "You just waste powder and lead if you do! We can get more lead out of your thick skulls, but we really are low on powder."

A cannon tore another furrow in the English ranks. The redcoats closed up and kept coming. Riflemen opened fire on them. Those men could have won the war single-handed if only they reloaded faster. Since they didn't . . .

"Musketeers—be ready!" Victor shouted. That command wasn't in the manual of arms. The men knew what it meant all the same. Victor hoped they did, anyhow. He'd yelled himself hoarse instructing them as they marched from their encampment to this position. Now . . . had they listened? Would soldiers pay attention when you tried to get them to do something they weren't used to doing?

"Musketeers—*fire!*" That wasn't Victor: several sergeants and officers yelled the same thing at the same time.

The muskets roared. Darts of flame spat toward the oncoming redcoats. A young fogbank of fireworks-smelling smoke rose above the stone fence in back of which the Atlanteans sheltered.

Surprisingly few Englishmen fell. The ones who didn't let out a cheer full of as much relief as ferocity. The fifes and drums picked up their rhythm. The redcoats double-timed toward the fence. At a shouted command, their bayoneted muskets lowered in a glittering wave of sharp steel.

Victor tensed. If things went wrong now, it would be embarrassing. Fatally embarrassing, most likely. And things went wrong all the time in war. Anyone who'd done any fighting knew that.

Why didn't the rest of the Atlanteans . . . ? And then, all of a sudden, they did. He'd posted men and field guns in the trees in front of and to either side of the stone fence. All the banners stayed in plain view behind the fence. A well-disciplined Englishman like Howe might conclude from that that all the Atlanteans also stood behind the fence.

Such a conclusion was reasonable. It was logical. Unfortunately for the redcoats, it was also wrong. Dead wrong.

Musketry and canister tore into the English soldiers from both flanks. The soldiers in back of the wall abruptly stopped shooting high on purpose. Muskets weren't very accurate under any circumstances, but they could hit more often than they had been.

How the redcoats howled! Victor whooped and flung his hat in the air and danced an ungainly dance—his side of it, at least—with Blaise. "They haven't learned one damned thing since General Braddock's day!" he shouted to anyone who'd listen. "Not one damned thing!"

"How do they ever win battles, let alone wars?" Blaise asked.

"Because they're brave," Victor answered. "Because other people are just as stupid as they are. But not today, by God!"

"No, not today," Blaise agreed. "They can't get through, and they can't get away, either."

The redcoats tried charging the stone fence. If they could smash the Atlanteans there, they would fight on their own terms once more, not on Victor Radcliff's. Several scorching volleys showed them they couldn't. Dead and wounded men lay drifted in front of the fence. And the galling fire from right and left kept costing them more casualties, and they were altogether unable to answer it.

"General Howe's down!" somebody shouted. The news blazed up and down the Atlantean line, fast as a quick-burning fuse.

"It *is* like Braddock's battle!" Blaise exclaimed. Marching blithely into a trap, General Braddock had nearly killed English hopes in Atlantis along with most of his own soldiers. Victor and the English Atlanteans he led were the ones who'd got the redcoats' remnants away from the French Atlanteans. Who would extricate this batch of redcoats? Anyone at all?

"Punish them, boys!" Victor shouted. "Make them pay for all they've done to us!"

Whooping with delight, the greencoats did. They'd won skirmishes over the winter, but never before a pitched battle against the English. Considering all the close fights they'd lost the year before, they had a lot to pay back. They did their best to settle the debt all at once.

English trumpets blared. The foot soldiers stopped trying to force their way over the stone fence. That was plainly impossible, which hadn't kept them from going on with the attack. Only the trumpeted order to pull back ended the self-inflicted torment. Victor admired the redcoats' discipline more than their common sense.

They sullenly re-formed their ranks and began to march away. "Do we pursue, sir?" Habakkuk Biddiscombe asked.

Victor's first impulse was to say no. He didn't want to throw away the fine victory his men had already gained. But the English soldiers had to be more rattled than they seemed ... didn't they? If he pushed them, they'd go to pieces ... wouldn't they?

He decided he had to find out. The only thing better than a fine victory was a great victory. If you were going to get one, you had to take a chance now and then. "Yes, by God, we do pursue!" he exclaimed.

"Thank you, sir!" the cavalry officer exclaimed, a broad grin spreading across his face. "I was afraid I'd have to ... do something insubordinate to get that order out of you."

To thwack you with a big stick, was what he had to mean. Victor grinned back. "Well, you've got it. Now make the most of it."

"We'll do that very thing, General." Biddiscombe started shouting orders of his own. Victor Radcliff realized he knew exactly what he intended to do. How long had he been working that out? Since the moment he first saw this position, chances were. Well, good. Officers needed to think ahead.

And that reminded Victor of something. He called for a runner. When the young man appeared before him, he said, "My compliments to Mr. Grigsby's guards, James, and they may release him. It seems plain enough that he didn't purpose betraying us to General Howe."

"Right you are, sir." James sketched a salute and

darted away. Victor wished for that much energy himself.

Horsemen and field guns went after the retreating redcoats. So did the foot soldiers who'd pummeled them from the trees. And—Victor watched in amazed delight—damned if the redcoats didn't fall to pieces right before his eyes. In the space of a few minutes, an army turned into a panic-stricken mob. Men threw away packs and muskets to flee the faster.

"Will you look at that?" Victor said to Blaise. "Will you *look* at that? We've whipped them! They've never been beaten like this, not in Atlantis. I don't know when they last got beaten like this back in Europe."

"What do we do now?" Blaise asked.

"I'll tell you what," Victor answered. "Custis Cawthorne must be in France by this time. We make sure he knows about it. And we make sure he lets the French hear about it. If they help us, our chances go up. France's navy has got better, a lot better, since the last time she fought England."

Blaise was more immediately practical. "No, no. I mean, what do we do with all the prisoners we are taking? What do we do with all the muskets and things the redcoats throw out?"

"Oh." Victor felt foolish. Yes, what he'd talked about also needed doing. But what Blaise talked about needed doing right away. "We especially need to round up bayonets. With a little luck, we'll never run short of them again. And we need to see if we've captured any supply wagons. The ones they make in England are better than any we have here."

"I will give those orders." Blaise hurried away.

Victor whistled softly. The whole war had just changed. He hadn't yet proved that, generalship being equal, Atlanteans could match Englishmen in the open field. But, if the Atlanteans had even slightly better generalship, they could not only match the redcoats but beat them.

"I told you so."

For a moment, Victor thought the words came straight

from his own spirit. Then he realized Ulysses Grigsby had come up beside him. He nodded. "Yes, Mr. Grigsby, as a matter of fact, you did."

That took the wind out of Grigsby's sails. With a wry chuckle, he said, "How am I supposed to stay sore at you when you go and admit something like that?"

"Plenty of people would think it was easy," Victor assured him.

"I hope I know what gratitude's worth." Ulysses Grigsby hesitated, then plunged: "And speaking of which, your Excellency, any chance you might reward me in specie instead of paper? You didn't get something small from me, you know."

"I do indeed, and I would be glad to give you specie if only I had any to give." That wasn't the full truth, but Victor didn't think the other man needed to know everything about how the Atlanteans financed their war. He went on, "I will put the question to the Atlantean Assembly. If the Conscript Fathers choose to reward you in the fashion you request, no man will be happier than I."

"Oh, one man will, I reckon." Grigsby jabbed a thumb at his own chest. "Gold and silver, they last. Who knows what Atlantean paper will be worth ten years from now? Meaning no disrespect, General, but who knows if it'll be worth anything ten years from now?"

"Our best chance to have it at par with specie is to win this war against England," Victor said. "Thanks to you, Mr. Grigsby, we're far closer to that goal than we were at this hour yesterday."

"Damn right we are. That's why I want specie." Grigsby had the simple rapacity of a red-crested eagle. Victor didn't care why the other man had warned the Atlantean army. As long as he had, nothing else mattered.

The sun was going down in crimson glory over the Green Ridge Mountains when several grinning Atlanteans led an English subaltern carrying a flag of truce into Victor Radcliff's presence. "What can I do for you, Lieutenant . . . ?" Victor asked, though he supposed he already knew the answer.

"My name is Fleming, General—John Fleming," the young Englishman said. "I have the honor to convey General Cornwallis' compliments to you, and to ask if your side, having prevailed today, would be gracious enough to return General Howe's body for proper interment."

"Do you suppose we would bury him improperly?" Victor asked with some asperity. "We are not barbarians, sir—unlike the Terranovan savages England loosed against our western settlements."

"Please excuse me. That is not what I meant. It is not what General Cornwallis meant, either," Lieutenant Fleming said quickly.

"Well, I am pleased to have General Cornwallis' compliments. In days gone by, as you may know, we fought on the same side," Victor said. "So perhaps you will be so kind as to explain to me what he did mean."

"Certainly, sir," Fleming said. "If a fight went badly for you, would you not sooner be buried by your friends than by your foes?"

"I would sooner not have to make such an unhappy choice, but I do see what you mean," Victor answered. "We have captured more than a few of your wagons in the pursuit. I shall return one of them to you with General Howe's body—which, I assure you, has not been badly plundered."

"What does *that* mean?" Lieutenant Fleming could also sound sharp.

"He is fully accoutered," Victor said. "When I first saw his body, his purse was empty. Whether he went into the battle with it empty, I fear I cannot say." He spread his hands. "War is what it is."

"True enough." The English officer sighed, but he nodded. "I accept your assurances on that score."

"If you would like to take back as many other bodies as the wagon will carry, you may do so." Having won,

Victor could afford to be generous about trifles. He did believe the redcoats would have returned the favor had things gone the other way.

"Very good of you, sir." John Fleming sketched a salute. "If I may look at the bodies, since you make this offer . . ." A grimace got past the correct mask he'd worn. "I fear my older brother, Captain James Fleming, is among the fallen. Several men saw him go down in front of that damned stone fence you defended so stoutly."

"Oh, my dear fellow! My deepest sympathies! You should have spoken sooner!" Victor exclaimed. "May I give you brandy or rum? As with an amputation, they will dull the worst pain a bit."

"No, thank you. I can in good conscience transact military business with you, but, meaning no disrespect, I would rather not drink with you."

"I understand. I *am* sorry." Victor raised his voice and waved. When a messenger came up, he said, "Fetch a torch and lend Lieutenant Fleming here every assistance in examining the English dead. He believes his brother lies among them. If he should prove correct, Captain Fleming's body will go back through the lines with him along with General Howe's and as many others as a wagon may hold."

"Yes, sir." The messenger nodded to the English officer. "That's mighty hard. You come with me. We'll do what we can for you."

"Very well. I am . . . as grateful as one can be under the circumstances." Lieutenant Fleming followed the messenger toward the redcoats' tumbled corpses.

"More he takes, more we don't have to bury," Blaise remarked.

"I don't think one wagonload will make much difference." Victor paused. "But I must admit I won't be on the business end of a shovel, either."

"Worth remembering," Blaise said. No doubt he'd been on the business end of a shovel during his days as a slave. But slaves worked as slowly as their overseers would let them get away with. Free men had a different rhythm. Victor had used a shovel often enough on his farm, in building fieldworks, and in burying his children when they died too young.

After a while, the wagon rattled off toward the east. Victor didn't ask whether Lieutenant Fleming had found his brother. It might matter to the redcoat, but it didn't to him. He did what he had to do next: without waiting for morning, he sent a messenger off to the Atlantean Assembly with word of the victory. He also recommended that the Assembly get the news to France as soon as it could. When the French learned the locals had beaten English regulars in a pitched battle, they might have a higher regard for this uprising. Then again, they might not. But the Atlanteans had to find out.

"If Custis Cawthorne can't talk King Louis into coming in on our side, nobody can," Major Biddiscombe said when Victor told his officers' council what he'd done.

"Just so," Victor said. Of course, given how badly the French had lost in their last fight with England, the painful possibility that no one could persuade them to try again was very real.

"We ought to chase the redcoats all the way back to Cosquer," Biddiscombe added. "We ought to take the place away from them again."

"If we can. If they have no fieldworks in place around it, which I confess to finding unlikely. If the Royal Navy does not lie close offshore," Victor said. "I am anything but eager to face bombardment from big guns I cannot hope to answer. I had enough of that up in Weymouth, enough and to spare."

Habakkuk Biddiscombe looked discontented. He sounded more than discontented: "Nobody ever won a fight by reckoning up all the things that might go wrong before he started."

"Perhaps not," Victor said. "But plenty of officers—the late General Howe being only the most recent example—have lost battles by *failing* to reckon up what might go wrong. I trust you take the point, sir?"

Biddiscombe didn't like it. No matter how intrepid he

was, though, he wasn't blindly intrepid. He could smell something if you rubbed his nose in it. Reluctantly, he nodded. "I think I do, General."

"Good." As Victor had with the English lieutenant, he threw his own subordinate a sop: "I also trust you will pursue vigorously. The more English stragglers we scoop up, the more muskets and wagons and, God willing, cannon we capture, the better our cause will look: here and up in Honker's Mill and, in due course, in France."

Blaise said, "It would seem strange, fighting on the same side as France after going against her in the last war."

"The redcoats were on our side last time," Victor reminded him. "War and politics are like that. When Lieutenant Fleming came in to ask for Howe's body, he gave me General Cornwallis' compliments. Our old friend—and I *did* count him a friend—now commands the enemy. Could something like that not happen in Africa, or do your tribes never change alliances?"

"I suppose it could," Blaise said. "But I think you white men are more changeable than we."

"It could be so," Victor said. "Still, you've also talked about the things we know how to do that your people don't. Learning such things comes with being changeable, too. I think it comes *from* being changeable. Don't you?"

"I suppose it could," Blaise said again.

"Well, it's an argument for another time, not for a council of war," Victor said: he could see that some of his officers would have said the same thing if he hadn't. Better to beat them to the punch. He went on, "The argument for this council is how best to exploit our victory—the victory that you won, gentlemen!"

They raised three cheers. They'd chewed over too many narrow but undeniable defeats. Victory tasted so much better!

XII

*C*osquer didn't fall easily. Victor had hoped it might, but hadn't really expected it to. He remembered how well Cornwallis, then a lieutenant-colonel, had fortified Freetown after General Braddock fell. The new English commander was no less diligent now, his engineers no less clever.

And the redcoats in the works remained ready to fight. Maybe they weren't quite so eager to face the Atlanteans in the open field as they had been. But they didn't mind letting Victor's soldiers come to them. Why should they, when they hoped to bloody the locals on the cheap?

But Victor didn't oblige them. Attacking fieldworks was a fool's game, or a desperate man's. He wasn't desperate, and he hoped he wasn't that kind of fool, anyhow.

Even if he had been tempted to assault Cornwallis' entrenchments, knowing Royal Navy frigates and ships of the line lay offshore would have made him think twice. Their firepower didn't reach far inland, but within its reach he had nothing that could reply to it. Heavy guns on land sat in forts. They moved slowly, if they moved at all. Ships carried them faster than unencumbered men could march, as fast as cavalry scouts could ride.

"Can we starve them out?" Blaise asked.

Unhappily, Victor shook his head. "Not as long as they rule the sea. They can bring in food from other parts of Atlantis, or even all the way from England."

"What are we doing here, then?" Blaise asked, a much more than reasonable question.

"Holding them in," Victor answered. "They can't do anything much as long as we pen them there."

Blaise grunted. "Neither can we."

"Yes, we can." Victor said it again: "We can. They have to beat us, to make us quit fighting. All we have to do is show them they can't do that. As long as we stay in the field, as long as we prove to them they can't do whatever they please in Atlantis, they will lose. I'm not sure they understand that yet. I'm not sure how long they will need to understand it. But we have to keep fighting till they do, however long it takes."

The Negro grunted again, but on a different note. "Anyone who knows you knows how pigheaded you are—"

Victor assumed a pained expression. "Stubborn, please. People you don't like are pigheaded. Your friends are stubborn, or hold to their purpose."

"Stubborn, then," Blaise said . . . after a pause to show he was thinking it over. "You are, yes, but can you keep your army stubborn?"

He knew how to get to the bottom of things, all right. He always had. Victor said the only thing he could: "I aim to try, anyhow."

He wondered whether Cornwallis would get reinforcements from farther north. If the English officer did, Victor feared he had a decent chance of breaking out of Cosquer. What would he do then? What *could* he do? Fight more battles like the ones the redcoats and Atlanteans had tried the year before? What would that prove? That the redcoats were better than the settlers in the open field if they didn't get careless? It might not even prove that. The Atlanteans were improving with every fight they had. They might not match Cornwallis' veterans yet, but they were getting close.

Green-coated riflemen sniped at the English soldiers in the trenches. That wouldn't decide anything; Victor knew it, and Cornwallis had to know it, too. But it did sting the redcoats, and they seemed to be without riflemen of their own to reply in kind. Maybe it could sting them into doing something foolish.

Victor also had to keep his own men from doing something foolish. Habakkuk Biddiscombe wanted to storm Cosquer. "We can beat them, General!" the cavalry officer insisted. "By God, we can! And then everything below the Stour is ours for good!"

"If I order an attack, we will make one," Victor said. "Until I order one, we won't. I don't think we can succeed."

"I do!" Biddiscombe said.

"When you wear a general's sash, you may use your men as you can find best," Victor said, as patiently as he could. "For now, though, the responsibility still rests on my shoulders—and there are times when I think Atlas had it easy holding up the heavens, believe me."

"There are times when I think . . ." The cavalry officer left it there, which was bound to be lucky for both of them.

Then General Cornwallis solved the Atlanteans' problem, withdrawing from his fieldworks. He did it with his usual skill. He left fires burning in the works all night long to fool the Atlanteans into thinking his men still occupied them. By the time the sun came up to show they had gone, they were already back in Cosquer.

And they, and the rest of the redcoats with them, were climbing into boats and going out to the warships anchored offshore. It was as if Cornwallis were saying, *Well, if you want Cosquer so much, here it is, and be damned to you.*

Victor did want Cosquer, but not at the price of bringing his soldiers under the Royal Navy's guns. If the redcoats were pulling out, he'd let them go. He unlimbered his field guns and fired at them from long range. He probably knocked over a few of them, but they had to know, as he did, it was only more harassment. It didn't change their evacuation a farthing's worth.

Once the English army had boarded the warships, sails blossomed on their masts. Slowly at first but then building momentum, the ships sailed off . . . toward the south.

"Where do they think they're going?" Habakkuk Biddiscombe sounded angry, as if he suspected Victor had been listening in on Cornwallis' deliberations and hadn't told him. "Do they think they can land in Spanish Atlantis and then come back up and go on with the war that way?"

"I wouldn't be surprised if they do," Victor answered. "Have you ever had anything to do with the dons?"

"Not me." The prospect seemed to affront the major. English and French Atlanteans both looked down their noses at the Spaniards farther south. Spain had a rich empire in Terranova, but her Atlantean dominions were an afterthought, and had been for many years. Most Spanish settlers here were men who'd failed or hadn't dared try in the broader lands beyond the Hesperian Gulf. The dons also had a reputation for being uncommonly cruel to their slaves: one reason uprisings always bubbled just below the surface.

"For my sins, I have," Victor told Biddiscombe. "They are the touchiest human beings God ever made. If Cornwallis landed at Gernika, say, without their leave, they would drop all their private feuds—of which they have a great plenty, believe me—to do him all the harm they could."

"I'm sure he loses sleep over that." Scorn filled Habakkuk Biddiscombe's voice. Spain had, and had earned, an unenviable military reputation. The only reason England hadn't seized Spanish Atlantis at the end of the last war was that she hadn't thought it worth seizing.

But Victor said, "Rile a Spaniard and he'll try to kill you without caring for his own life. A Spanish army is nothing much. Spanish bushwhackers ... It's no accident that 'guerrilla' is a Spanish word."

Biddiscombe said a few Spanish words Victor hadn't thought he knew. When he ran out of foreign incendiaries, he added, "You can bet Cornwallis feels the same way about them."

"No doubt," Victor said. "But the question is how they feel about Cornwallis—and about whether he purposes landing there at all."

"Where else would he go? Down to the islands?" Biddiscombe answered his own question with a shake of the head. "Not likely! That'd take him clean out of the war. He has to head for Spanish Atlantis."

"No one *has* to do anything." Victor spoke with great conviction. By the way Habakkuk Biddiscombe eyed him, he might suddenly have started spouting Blaise's language.

Cosquer greeted the incoming Atlantean army the same way it had probably greeted the incoming English army: with indifference. New Hastings was a trifle older, but Cosquer's founder, François Kersauzon, had stumbled upon Atlantis even before the Radcliffes. People in Cosquer remembered, even if hardly anyone else in these modern times did. They looked down their noses at all latecomers.

Some of them still spoke buzzing Breton instead of French or English. Victor didn't think all the strange names he heard riding into Cosquer were compliments. As long as no one did more than mutter in a half-forgotten tongue, he didn't care.

He went on to the quays, hoping some longshoreman or tapman or even doxy had heard where Cornwallis planned to sail. No one who might have seemed to want to tell an English Atlantean, though. The tapmen and doxies were willing enough to take his men's silver. As for the longshoremen ...

"How soon will you get out of here?" asked one of the few who condescended to speak to Victor at all.

"When we're ready," Victor said. "How soon will you learn some manners?"

"When *I'm* ready," the local answered cheekily. "Don't hold your breath—manners are for friends."

"I am not your enemy. You should be glad of that," Victor said.

"Stinking *Saoz*," the longshoreman said, and turned away.

That one Victor did know: the fellow'd called him an Englishman. "Save that name for Cornwallis," he said. "I'm an Atlantean, by God."

"A *Saoz* is a *Saoz* no matter where he's whelped," the longshoreman answered. "God may care about the details, but I don't."

"God has better sense than you do." Victor rode away to see if he could find answers anywhere else.

But no one in Cosquer seemed to know anything. No one who did seemed inclined to tell it to a *Saoz*, anyhow. To Victor, they amounted to the same thing. Then he got a rush of brains to the head. He hunted up Blaise and handed him some money. "What's this in aid of?" the Negro asked.

"Take off your uniform. Put on some ordinary clothes, none too fancy," Victor answered. "Wander through the taverns. Buy yourself a few drinks. See what you can hear about where the English went."

"Maybe I won't hear anything," Blaise said.

"Maybe you won't," Victor agreed. "But maybe you will, too. Make them think you're a slave on a toot. White people talk too much in front of slaves. They think the slaves aren't listening or can't understand."

Blaise raised an eyebrow. "I know things like that." He brushed two fingers of his right hand against the back of his left to show off his black skin and to remind Victor how he knew. "Why do you know them?"

Radcliff used the same gesture the Negro had. "Because I'm a white man myself, and I know how white men think. I would have thought the same way—I did think the same way—before I met you. I hope I know better now."

"Ah," Blaise said, and then, "Well, maybe you do." With that faint praise Victor had to be content.

Off the Negro went on his mission of espionage. Victor fell asleep before he came back from it. Lamps weren't bright enough to tempt the general to stay up long after the sun went down. He did wonder whether Blaise would remember what he'd heard come morning.

And when he got a look at Blaise the next morning, he wondered even more. "Oh, my," he said sympathetically. "Oh, dear."

With trembling hand, Blaise reached for a tin mug of coffee. He was badly the worse for wear, the whites of his eyes yellowish and tracked with red. "Don't know why you brew that hellwater you call rum," he said. "People feel mighty bad after they drink it. Mighty bad." He gulped the steaming coffee, then gulped again, hoping it would stay down.

"Most folks don't worry about the day after while they're drinking," Victor observed. "That goes for blacks and copperskins and whites alike. I expect it goes for Chinamen, too, but I can't prove it—I don't know any."

After one more gulp, Blaise seemed to decide things would stay where he wanted them to. "Well," he said, "no one will ever tell me I did not earn the money you gave me last night."

"No one is trying to," Victor said. "Did you learn anything except that a hard night leads to a harder morning?"

"Oh, doesn't it just!" Blaise agreed with the fervor of a reformed sinner. Or perhaps not completely reformed: he held out the tin cup, saying, "Have you got any brandy to help me take the edge off?"

Not many Atlanteans with pretensions to being gentlemen failed to carry a flask. Victor had one. You never could tell when you might need a nip against the cold or simply want one. Victor poured a careful dose into Blaise's coffee.

"Obliged, sir." The Negro drank. He nodded. "Oh, yes. Much obliged."

"Better now?" Victor inquired.

"Some." Blaise nodded. He didn't seem to fear that his head would fall off any more, or even to hope it would. Having been through some long drunken nights himself, Victor knew progress when he saw it.

He tried again: "How much of what you heard in your tavern crawl do you recollect? Anything interesting?"

"Maybe." Blaise took another sip of the improved—no, here in French Atlantis, they would call it corrected—coffee. "People seem to think Cornwallis will come up on the west coast. One of them called it buggering a sheep."

"Heh," Victor Radcliff said uneasily. The redcoats could steal a march on him over there, sure enough. Atlantean forces, even counting the men sent west to fight the copperskins the English had imported, were thin on the ground. But, having landed there, what could Cornwallis do next? Cross the Green Ridge Mountains and return to the more settled parts of the country? Maybe, if he landed at New Marseille or one of the smaller towns south of Avalon. Hunting was still supposed to be very easy in the southwest. Even so ... "How sure are these, ah, people? Did they hear his plans from some English officer? Or are they guessing, the way you will when you don't know?"

"Some of them sounded pretty sure," Blaise answered. "I don't think I heard one of them say an Englishman told him what the redcoats were doing, but they thought they had a good notion."

"All right." Victor paused. Eyeing the Negro's decrepit condition, he decided something more than that was called for. "I thank you, Blaise. You did everything you could, and you did Atlantis a good turn."

"I hope so." Blaise seemed to have gone through the mill, all right. "What are you going to do now?"

Even more than *To be or not to be*, that was the question. Victor had even more trouble than Hamlet had coming up with a good answer. Unhappily, he said, "I don't know. Getting our army across to New Marseille . . . We might do it. Or we might lose two men out of three, sick or starving, if we try. Taking a lot of men across Atlantis has never been easy."

"You were going to do it when we were down in the Spaniards' country, till the Royal Navy came and took us back to Freetown," Blaise said.

Still unhappily, Victor nodded. "We were in trouble, then—and we'd've been in worse trouble if we'd had to try it. And we had a lot fewer men then than we do now."

"More settlers in the back country now than there used to be," Blaise observed.

"That's so." Victor admitted what he couldn't very well deny. But he went on, "Are there enough to subsist us on the way? I think not. Whatever we need, we'll have to fetch with us."

"Or kill along the way," Blaise said.

"Honkers. Oil thrushes. Deer that run wild through the woods. Rabbits, too, I suppose. I hope we aren't down to eating turtles and frogs and snakes by the time we get to the Hesperian Gulf. And we can't very well kill cannon along the way. Somehow or other, we'll have to get our field guns over the mountains. I don't look forward to that."

"Mountains down here are lower than they are farther north. Some tracks through them, too," Blaise said. "I was thinking about running off that way, but I decided to go north instead. I hear there are villages of runaway blacks and copperskins across the mountains."

"I've heard it, too," Victor said. "I don't know if it's true."

"Oh, I think so." Blaise sounded more certain than he had when he was talking about what the English in-

tended. How much did he know? How much of what he
knew would he tell a white man? A good deal and not
very much, respectively—that was Victor's judgment.
And, all things considered, who could blame him for
that?

Marching west had all the appeal of grabbing a snake
by the tail to find out if it was venomous. *Not* marching west struck Victor as even worse, though—that was
waiting for the snake to bite you. And so, without enthusiasm but without shirking, he got ready to leave Cosquer behind.

He left a garrison in the town. He didn't want the
Royal Navy simply sailing in and retaking it as soon as
he marched away. That also gave him an excuse to take
fewer men over the Green Ridge Mountains. He gratefully seized on any excuse he could get.

He and the army hadn't gone more than a few miles
up the south bank of the Blavet when a rider from out
of the west came up to them. Victor eyed the fellow in
bemusement. Cornwallis couldn't have got to New Marseille yet, could he? And, even if by some miracle of
perfect winds and wild sailing he had, news that he had
couldn't have come back across the mountains.

And it hadn't. Brandishing a rolled and sealed sheet
of paper, the horseman said, "General, I bring you this
from the Atlantean Assembly at Honker's Mill." He
managed to invest the little town's silly name with a dignity it certainly hadn't earned.

This turned out to be the floridly official Thanks of
the Atlantean Assembly, written in magnificent calligra-
phy by some secretary who probably had no other talent
he could sell. Victor held it out for his soldiers to see, fin-
ishing, "They sent it to me, but it belongs to all of you."
The men cheered.

The courier handed him another, smaller, rolled and
sealed sheet. "Isaac Fenner gave me this to give to you
just before I set out."

"Did he?" What Fenner said privately might be more interesting than the public proclamation it accompanied. Victor popped off the seal with his thumbnail and unrolled the letter. Fenner's hand was legible enough, but small and cramped: nothing much beside the secretary's splendid script.

Well done, the redhead from Bredestown wrote. *You've given England one in the slats she'll be a long time forgetting. And something more may come of it. Not quite certain yet, but the chances look better by the day. You'll know when it happens—I promise you that. The whole world will know.* His scribbled signature followed.

"What does Fenner say?" Habakkuk Biddiscombe asked with the air of a man entitled to know.

Since he was no such thing, he only succeeded in putting Victor's back up. "That something important will be coming out of Honker's Mill soon," he answered, which had the virtue of being true and the larger virtue—in his mind, at least—of not being informative.

"Fenner is full of moonshine promises," Biddiscombe said. "No wonder his hair is red—it shows he's descended from a fox, and not descended very far, either."

"If you feel that way, I'm surprised you're not riding alongside King George's men," Victor remarked.

"Oh, I hope I'm a loyal Atlantean, which I hope I've proved by now, too," the cavalry officer said. "But I also hope I know a rogue when I see one, and may I be damned if I don't see one whenever I look towards Isaac Fenner."

Victor Radcliff shrugged. "Maybe he is a rogue. But so what? If he is, he's our rogue."

"England has a great plenty of them. A few of our own may prove useful, as the mild dose of smallpox in inoculation commonly holds the stronger sickness at bay," Major Biddiscombe allowed. "Still and all, I doubt I'll be much impressed after Honker's Mill labors to bring forth a ridiculous mouse."

"Good to know you remember your Horace," Victor

murmured. "All we can do is wait to see what happens there while we do our best down here. Have you ever crossed the mountains before?"

"No, sir," Biddiscombe said. "I like the comforts of civilization. I can live without them when I must, but I prefer not to."

"Not the worst attitude. You seem to cope in the field well enough."

"Your servant, sir." Habakkuk Biddiscombe doffed his tricorn at the praise.

But Radcliff hadn't finished: "We'll need your talents as we travel, and those of the ruffians you lead. You'll be widely spread out in front of the army, to find trouble before it finds us and to forage for the main body."

"We'll do all we can—you may rely on that," Biddiscombe said. "And we'll slaughter every honker and oil thrush we come upon."

"Up in Hanover and New Hastings, I've heard people who style themselves natural philosophers say we should try to preserve the honkers and other unique natural productions of Atlantis, to let forthcoming generations see and study them alive rather than from specimens and stories," Victor said.

"General, meaning no disrespect to such people, but talk is cheap," Biddiscombe said. "I'd like to hear them babble about not shooting honkers after they try to cross the mountains and get to New Marseille overland. If they didn't declare that there ought to be a bounty on the big, stupid birds, I'd be astonished."

"Well, now that you mention it, so would I," Victor admitted. "An empty belly makes a stern taskmaster."

Habakkuk Biddiscombe nodded. "I should say so! And how many 'natural philosophers,' so called, have ever known its pinch?"

"Why ask me? The next time you keep company with one, enquire of him," Victor said. "And in the meanwhile, why don't you go keep some order among your horsemen?" *I've had enough of you*, he meant, but he didn't say it.

He would have if Biddiscombe had argued with him. But the cavalry officer, for a wonder, too, took the hint. "Just as you say, sir," he replied, sketching a salute, and rode away.

"What *does* Fenner have in mind?" Blaise asked quietly.

As quietly, Victor answered, "I truly don't know. He's being coy. Whatever it turns out to be, I hope it proves as important as he thinks, that's all."

Nouveau Redon again, this time traveling from east to west. The town wasn't what it had been. It never would be again, not unless someone found a way to resurrect the spring that had watered it. Several ingenious engineers and charlatans—the difference between the two wasn't always easy to see in advance—had tried, but none with any success.

These days, Nouveau Redon drew its water out of the river that lay below the heights it commanded. That made it easy to besiege despite its still-formidable works. People said it was a sicklier place now than it had been when the spring gurgled up through the living rock. Victor didn't know for a fact that that was true, but he'd heard it more than once.

He didn't stop at the town, skirting it to the south. His foot soldiers didn't seem sorry not to have to climb up to it. The cavalry, whose horses would have had to do the work, might have had a different view. Victor didn't ask them. He was starting to find dealing with Habakkuk Biddiscombe as wearing as the intrepid horseman probably found dealing with him.

He wanted to force the march. If the redcoats got there before him . . . *Then they do, that's all*, he told himself sternly. If he confronted them with a few hundred starving skeletons, he wouldn't do Atlantis' cause any good. And that would happen if he pushed too hard. He'd leave men behind all the way to the mountains, and all the way across them as well.

The quartermasters at Nouveau Redon were unenthusiastic about turning loose of what they held in their storehouses. That was, as Victor had seen before, an occupational disease of quartermasters. These fellows had a worse case than most.

Only a direct order made a couple of them condescend to come down and talk to him. "We're here to protect these stores, General, and to preserve them," one of the men said importantly.

"Why?" Victor Radcliff asked.

"Why?" the quartermaster echoed. He and his comrade looked at each other. That didn't seem to have occurred to either of them.

"Why?" Victor repeated. "What's the point of protecting and preserving the supplies in Nouveau Redon?"

Again, he'd taken the officers by surprise. At last, the fellow who'd spoken before ventured a reply: "I suppose, to keep them in readiness in case they were to be required by some military situation."

"Aha!" Victor struck like a lancehead or some other southern viper. The quartermaster officers flinched as if he really did have fangs. He wished he did—he would have bitten both of them. In lieu of that, he said, "Do your Excellencies suppose a march west from here in the direction of the Hesperian Gulf might possibly be a military situation requiring the release of stores from Nouveau Redon?"

"It . . . might," said the quartermaster who talked more. He wasn't about to admit anything he didn't have to—oh, no, not him.

"Let me ask the question another way, gentlemen," Victor said in his iciest tones. "Do you suppose that, if you don't turn loose of what I need, I won't cashier the lot of you and clap you in irons?"

"You can't do that!" the quartermaster gasped.

"Watch me," Victor said. "I took Nouveau Redon back in the days when it didn't need to haul water up from the Blavet. I can damn well take it again if I have to. Cornwallis and I were on the same side then. I didn't think you were on his side now. Perhaps I was wrong."

"General, that is an insult," the man from Nouveau Redon said stiffly. His colleague nodded.

"Not by the way you act, it isn't," Victor told them. "This *is* a military necessity. You have the supplies I need. You can release them to me in accordance with the orders I am lawfully entitled to give by virtue of my appointment at the hands of the Atlantean Assembly— or you can declare yourselves the foes of Atlantis' freedom. Which will it be, gentlemen?"

He drew his sword. The quartermasters, as befitted their unmilitary soldiering, were unarmed. But Victor didn't assail them ... directly. Instead, he drew a circle in the ground around their feet.

"Be so kind as to answer me before you step out of that," he said, not sheathing the blade.

The quartermaster who'd been quiet up till then spluttered, "We are not Antiochus' officers, General!" He'd had some classical education, too, then.

Victor grinned savagely. "That's true. You're *my* subordinates. Can you imagine what a Roman general would have done with a set of insubordinate officers? Lucky for both of you that we don't crucify these days, or you'd have more in common with our Savior than you ever wanted."

When the men from Nouveau Redon tried to retreat, he held them in place with the sword—they hadn't answered him. "You'll get what you want," the talkier one said. With a sudden access of spirit, he added, "We commonly find it wiser to humor madmen."

"If you drive me mad with excuses, who's to blame?" Victor slid the sword back into its sheath. "Go on, both of you. And remember one thing: Atlantis isn't big enough for you to hide in if you play me false once you get back inside those walls."

They hurried away. Supplies started coming out of Nouveau Redon. Victor nodded to himself. He hadn't expected anything else.

Blaise was of less sanguine temperament. Where Victor saw things going well, the Negro saw things that might go wrong. "What happens if, once we get farther away, they stop sending wagons after us?" he asked.

"Simple," Victor answered. "I send back a detachment, and I start hanging quartermasters. *Pour encourager les autres*." He quoted Custis Cawthorne quoting Voltaire.

Since French was the first white men's language Blaise had learned, he followed with no trouble. He smiled like a crocodile—like a wolf, an English-speaker in a land where there were wolves would have said. "Yes, that will work," he said. "Those people, they put on uniforms, but they would piss themselves if they had to fight."

Victor nodded. "I shouldn't wonder," he said. "But have you seen how many soldiers do piss themselves or shit themselves when they almost get killed? You can't always help it. I don't think I've ever done it, but I know I've come close. What about you?"

"I've seen it," Blaise replied. "I never quite did it myself. I wouldn't admit I was close if you didn't say the same thing first."

"I'm the general. People will think I'm brave till I do something to show them I'm not," Victor said.

"I wish they felt that way about me." Blaise shrugged. "Won't happen, not the color I am. Folks see a black man, they think, *He's a nigger. He's a coward.* Makes it easier for them to keep slaves, I reckon. They do the same damn thing with copperskins, too."

"Wouldn't be surprised," Victor said. He'd heard Africans were made house slaves more often than Terranovan natives were. They were reckoned less likely to stab their owners in the middle of the night and abscond after setting the house afire. But anyone who thought Blaise and a lot of blacks like him were docile would make his last mistake.

Nouveau Redon fell well behind. The Green Ridge Mountains rose higher in the west. Supply wagons kept coming. Blaise nodded in somber approval. "You did put the fear of God in them," he said.

"Here's hoping. The real worry is, what happens once

we cross the mountains?" Victor said. "Wagons won't be able to follow us then."

"We manage. One way or another, we manage," Blaise said, which left Victor wondering which of them was the sanguine one after all.

He also wondered what Isaac Fenner had been talking about in his last note. Usually, Victor grimaced whenever a courier from Honker's Mill came up. The Atlantean Assembly couldn't run his army from a distance, which didn't always keep it from trying. That left him with the unwelcome choice between idiotic obedience and mutinous disobedience. If they told him what they wanted and then let him try to do it . . .

If he expected that to happen, he was sanguine, all right. Or possibly stark raving mad.

Now, though, he would have welcomed news from the backwoods capital. And, no doubt because he would have welcomed it, none came. He wondered whether couriers could follow over the mountains, too. He'd soon find out.

A rider caught up with the army just before it started heading up into the foothills. The man was brandishing a big sheet of paper even before he came up to Victor. "Proclamation!" he shouted. "The Atlantean Assembly's proclamation!"

"Well, let's see it," Victor said gruffly. He sometimes thought the Assembly's proclamations came three for a farthing. Two of the Conscript Fathers couldn't blow their noses at the same time without convening a meeting to issue a solemn proclamation commemorating the occasion.

He quickly read through this one. "What does it say?" someone asked.

"It's a—a proclamation of liberty," he answered. "It says that King George has mistreated the settlements so badly, no one here can stand to live under him any more. It says the settlements are free, independent states from now on. And it says they come together of their own free will to form what it calls the United States of Atlantis. It says we're as much of a country of our own as England or France or Spain or Holland. And it says we'll fight to the death to hold the rights God gave us." He waved the Proclamation of Liberty himself. "God bless the United States of Atlantis!"

"The United States of Atlantis!" the soldiers shouted, and, "Down with King George!" and as many other things in those veins as they could come up with. This time, Isaac Fenner was right. The Assembly hadn't done anything small.

XIII

*F*og drifted in front of Victor Radcliff like a harem girl's veil in a spicy story about the life of the Ottoman sultan. Here and there, he could see fifty yards ahead, maybe even a hundred. But the men to either side of him were indistinct to the point of ghostliness.

One of those ghosts was Blaise. "Are we still going west?" he asked.

"I think so." Victor had a peer at a compass to be sure. He nodded in some relief. "Yes. We are."

"You could have fooled me," Blaise said. "Come to that, you could be fooling me now. I'd never know the difference."

"We may not keep on going west for long," Victor said. The pass through the Green Ridge Mountains twisted and doubled back on itself like a snake with a bellyache. A path of sorts ran through it, but only of sorts. Travelers had passed this way, bound for New Marseille. An army? Never.

Because the pass climbed, the weather here reminded Victor of that farther north. Not only was it moist, it was also surprisingly cool. Ferns and mushrooms grew lush. One horse had eaten something that killed it in a matter of hours. Seeds? A toadstool? Victor didn't know. Neither did anyone else. That discouraged the men from plucking up mushrooms, which they eagerly would have done otherwise.

Pines and towering redwoods grew on the slopes above the pass. They hadn't been logged off here, as they had so many places farther east. Strange birds called from the trees. Blaise pointed at one when the fog thinned. "Is that a green woodpecker?"

"I think it may be," Victor answered.

The bird drilled on a branch, proving what it was. "Never seen one like that before," Blaise said.

"Neither have I." Victor wondered whether some wandering naturalist had ever shot a specimen. Did a preserved skin sit in a cabinet in the museum in occupied Hanover, or perhaps across the sea in one in London? Or was the woodpecker nondescript—new to science?

He shrugged. He had more urgent things to worry about. Getting through the pass came first. Getting to New Marseille with his army more or less intact ran a close second. Then came beating General Cornwallis and driving him away. Next to those, Victor couldn't get excited—he couldn't let himself get excited—about a green woodpecker.

A man slipped on a wet fern or on some muddy moss or a rotten mushroom and landed hard on his backside. He took the name of the Lord in vain as he got to his feet. "You don't want to say such things, Eb," chided one of his comrades. "God, He punishes blasphemy."

"Well, I expect He must," Eb responded. "If He didn't, why would He afflict me with idiots for friends? You come down the way I did, you're just naturally going to let out with something with a bit of spice to it."

"But you shouldn't. You mustn't," his friend said earnestly. "For all you know, God made you fall just then so He could test you. If He did, things don't look so good for you."

Eb had one hand clapped to his bruised fundament. He clapped the other to his forehead. "God knows everything that was or is or will be, ain't that right?"

"I should hope it is," his friend answered.

"All right, then. In that case, He knew ahead of time I'd call on Him, like, when I slipped there. So how can He get angry at me for doing something He knew I was going to do anyhow?"

"That isn't how predestination works, Ebenezer Sanders, and you know it blamed well." Now Eb's friend sounded shocked.

"You sound like a parrot, giving back what the preachers say," Eb replied. "The only one who *knows* is God. Preachers are nothing but damn fools, same as you and me."

His friend spluttered. No more words seemed to want to come out, though. Blaise showed Victor he wasn't the only one who'd listened with interest to the argument, asking, "Do you think God knows everything ahead of time? Do you think we do things because He wills it?"

Victor shrugged. "I'm a Christian man—you know that. But I'm with Eb on one thing: the only One who knows God *is* God. He's the only One Who can know. People do the best they can, but they're only guessing."

"I suppose so." Blaise pursed his thick lips. "Gods in Africa don't pretend to be so strong. Well, except the Muslims' God. Is He the same One you worship?"

To Victor, what Blaise called Muslims were Mahometans. He'd also discovered Blaise knew more about them than he did. He shrugged again. "I can't tell you."

A little to his surprise, the answer made Blaise smile. "One thing I have to say—you're an honest man. When you don't know something, you say so. You don't try and talk around it, the way so many people do."

"Do they do that in Africa, too?" Victor asked.

Instead of smiling, Blaise laughed. "Oh, yes. Ohhh, yes. Doesn't matter what color you are, not for that. Black or white or copper-skinned, lots of folks won't even tell themselves they don't know something."

"I know it's true of white men," Radcliff said. "I shouldn't wonder if you're right for the others."

"You'd best believe I am ... sir." Blaise sounded absolutely certain. "And if your fancy ships find an island full of green men, or maybe blue, some of them will talk bigger than they know, too."

That set Victor laughing. "Right again—no doubt about it. Green men!" He chuckled at the conceit.

"You never can tell," the Negro said. "I wouldn't have believed there were white men till I saw one—and till our enemies sold me to them. I wouldn't have believed a lot of the things that happened to me after that, either."

"It hasn't been all bad, has it? You wouldn't have met Stella if you'd stayed behind in Africa," Victor said.

"No. But she was taken and sold, too." Blaise's face clouded. "And what white men do with—do to—their slave women . . . It isn't good. It's maybe the very worst thing about keeping slaves. *The* worst."

"Do you tell me black men don't treat slave women the same way?" Victor asked. "Or copperskins? Or the green and blue men on that mysterious island out in the Pacific?"

"Oh, no, sir. We keep slaves, too, some of us, and our men futter the women," Blaise answered. "But that doesn't make it right. Not for us, not for you, not for nobody. Do you say I'm wrong?" Before Victor could say anything, Blaise added, "So the settlements of Atlantis are the liberated United States of Atlantis? How can they be, really, when so many folk in them aren't liberated at all?"

Victor discovered he had no answer for that.

"On the downhill slope, General," one of the scouts told Victor. "No doubt about it—not a bit."

"Good," Victor said. *If it's true*, he appended—but only to himself. Aloud, he asked, "Have you come this way before?"

"Not me," the scout said, and Victor discounted the report almost as steeply as Atlantean paper money was discounted against specie. But the fellow went on, "The Frenchie I'm riding with has, and he says the same thing."

"Well, good." The report's value jumped again. Victor wished Atlantean paper would do the same. Maybe the Proclamation of Liberty—and his victory outside Nouveau Redon—would help it rise.

Here in the wilderness, money didn't need to be the first thing on his mind. He and his men couldn't get their hands on any they hadn't brought with them, and couldn't buy anything they hadn't likewise brought along. Life would have been simpler—but less interesting—were that more widely true.

He sucked in a lungful of hot, humid air. He wouldn't breathe any other kind this far south in the lowlands on the west side of the Green Ridge Mountains. The Bay Stream brought warmth up from the seas to the southwest, and western Atlantis got its share before the current went on towards Europe.

Victor had heard Custis Cawthorne and other savants speculate that, absent the Bay Stream, Europe would be as chilly as was the land at corresponding latitudes of northern Terranova. He didn't know enough to form an opinion pro or con there. From everything he could see, neither did the savants. That didn't stop them from speculating, or even slow them much.

Beards of moss hung from horizontal branches. He'd seen that farther south on the other side of the mountains: mostly down in Spanish Atlantis. Some people called the stuff Spaniards' moss, in fact. When you found it at all in the east at these latitudes, it was more like the down beginning to sprout on a youth's face than a proper beard.

Hunting parties brought back plenty of oil thrushes. Their flesh, though greasy, was quite good. The southwestern quadrant of Atlantis was most thinly settled, and oil thrushes were still common, for which he was grateful. They made good eating, and one bird was a meal for anywhere from two to four soldiers, depending on how hungry they were. He looked forward to gnawing meat off a leg bone himself. The wings weren't big enough to be worth bothering with.

He'd just finished supper when a commotion at the

edge of the camp made him hurry over to see what was going on. A soldier clutched his leg. Another man pointed to the beaten corpse of a colorful little snake. "It bit him!" the pointer said. "He stepped on it, and it went and bit him."

The snake had been minding its own business. What was it supposed to do when somebody trod on it? Victor eyed the remains. Stripes of red and black and yellow . . . "Get him to the surgeons," Victor said. "Let's hope they can do him some good."

"It hurts," the bitten man said. "Am I going to die?"

"I don't think so." Victor lied without compunction. If that was a coral snake, as he feared, the Atlantean might very well. Coral snakes lurked in undergrowth. They hid beneath chunks of bark. They didn't go out of their way to strike people. But when they did . . . He tried to stay cheerful: "The surgeons will give you plenty of whiskey, to keep your heart strong."

"Well, hot damn!" the sufferer exclaimed. "Take me to 'em, by Jesus!"

He died the next morning, unable to breathe, his heartbeat fading to nothingness. "Sorry, General," one of the surgeons told Victor. "We did everything we knew how to do, but. . . ." His shoulders wearily slid up and down. If a poisonous serpent bit you, you were in God's hands, not any surgeon's.

"I'm sure you did," Victor said. "We'll bury him and we'll go on. Nothing else we can do."

On they went. Some supplies did come over the Green Ridge Mountains after them—some, but not enough. Victor would have been more disappointed had he expected anything more. The path west to Avalon was far and away the best on this side of the mountains. He'd never thought he could keep an army of this size supplied from the far side of the mountains even on that track. This route to New Marseille didn't compare.

Well, the hunting was better down here. He'd told himself that before. He did once more, hoping he was right.

Red-crested eagles screeched from cypresses. Seeing and hearing them raised Victor's hopes. The eagles were dangerous—men reminded them of honkers, their proper prey. But in this part of Atlantis, red-crested eagles could more readily find that proper prey.

And if they could, people could, too. So Victor hoped, anyhow. And Habakkuk Biddiscombe's horsemen did. They brought back more than a dozen of the enormous birds on the backs of packhorses. Each honker carcass would feed a lot more than two to four soldiers.

Victor imagined his many-times-great-grandfather gaping at a salted honker leg in some low tavern in Brittany. That was how the story of Atlantis started, with François Kersauzon telling Edward Radcliffe about the new land far out in the sea. The English had always put more into this land and got more out of it. So Victor thought, anyhow. Any French Atlantean ever born would have called him a liar to his face.

His horse splashed across a stream. A frog as big as his fist hopped off a rock and churned away. He hoped there were no crocodiles or so-called lizards in the water. They'd come far enough south to make it anything but impossible, especially on this side of the mountains.

Blaise took the notion of crocodiles in stride. "They have bigger ones back in Africa," he said.

"Well, they're damned well welcome to them, too," Victor said.

"Maybe one of these is big enough to eat up General Cornwallis when he gets off the boat by New Marseille," Blaise said. "How much does he know about crocodiles?"

"Only what he learned the last time he was in Atlantis—if he learned anything at all," Victor answered. "They haven't got any in England. It's colder there than it is by Hanover."

"No wonder people from England want to come here!" Blaise said. He came from a land with weather worse than Spanish Atlantis'. Weather like that surely came from Satan, not from God. Good Christians denied the Devil any creative power. Such weather was the best argument he could think of for turning Manichee.

"It's not always sticky. Dry half the year. But always warm. All what you're used to," Blaise said. "The first time I found out what winter was like, I thought the world had gone mad. I was afraid it would stay cold like that forever. I wondered what I'd done to deserve such a thing."

"But now that you know better, aren't you glad you're not in a bake oven all the time?" Victor asked.

Blaise shrugged. "This right here, this is not so bad." By the way he said it, he was giving the local weather the benefit of the doubt.

To Victor, *this right here* was an alarmingly authentic approximation of a steam bath. "A wise man who lived a long time ago said custom was king of all—a fancier way to say 'All what you're used to,' I suppose. Me, I'd prefer something cooler."

"Even here, it will get cooler in the wintertime." Blaise made that sound like a damned shame. To Victor, it sounded wonderful. Sure enough, they bowed to different kings of custom.

But neither one of them bowed to the King of England. With a little luck—and with good fortune in war—they never would again.

Victor had heard that runaway Negroes and copperskins lived in villages of their own on the far side of the Green Ridge Mountains. Stories said they tried to duplicate the life they'd led before they were uprooted and brought to Atlantis. He'd never known whether to believe those stories. They sounded plausible, but anyone above the age of about fourteen needed to understand the difference between plausible and true.

The stories turned out to be true. Habakkuk Biddiscombe's men led him to what was plainly a copperskin village. The huts, which looked like upside-down pots made of bark over a framework of branches, were like none he'd ever seen before. Near them grew fields of maize.

Everything was deserted when he rode up to look the place over. "Some of the savages are bound to be watching us from the woods," Biddiscombe said, gesturing toward the tall trees surrounding the village. "But even if they are, we won't get a glimpse of them unless they want us to."

"Or unless they make a mistake," Victor said. "That does happen every now and again."

"Not often enough," the cavalry officer said, and Victor couldn't disagree with him. Biddiscombe continued, "Now that we've found this place, I suppose you'll want us to tear it down? If the weather were even a little wetter, I'd say burn it, but too easy for the fire to run wild the way things are."

The weather was wet enough to suit Victor and then some. "Why would we want to wreck the village?" he asked in genuine surprise. "These copperskins have done nothing to us."

His surprise surprised Habakkuk Biddiscombe. "They're runaways, General," Biddiscombe said, as if that should have been obvious to the veriest simpleton.

And so it was. But its consequences weren't, at least to Victor. "Well, yes," he replied. "They seem to be happy enough here, though. If we rob them of their homes, they may try to hunt us through the woods. They aren't our enemies now, and I'd sooner try not to make them hate us unless we have some reason for doing so."

"They're nothing but runaways," Biddiscombe repeated. "Copperskin runaways, at that."

"Leave them alone. Leave this place alone. That is an order," Victor said, so the cavalry officer could be in no possible doubt. "If they harry us, we shall make them regret it. Until they do, I prefer to concentrate on the English, who truly are the enemy. Do I make myself clear?"

"Abundantly." Biddiscombe might have accused Victor of picking his nose and then sticking his finger in his mouth.

"Carry out your orders, then—and no 'accidental' destruction for the sport of it, either." Victor did his best to leave no loopholes in the orders. By Habakkuk Biddiscombe's expression, he'd just closed one the horseman had thought about using.

He wondered if he would have been so firm about protecting a village built by Negro runaways. Somehow, whites had an easier time looking down their noses at blacks than at copperskins. Blaise wouldn't have approved of that, which made it no less true.

Before long, Victor became pretty sure his men would be able to keep themselves fed on the road to New Marseille. He must have put the fear of God in the quartermasters at Nouveau Redon: supplies did keep coming over the Green Ridge Mountains. They weren't enough by themselves to victual the soldiers, but they were ever so much better than nothing. With oil thrushes and honkers, with fish and turtles taken from the streams (and with snails almost the size of roundshot and big, fat frogs taken by the French Atlanteans in the army), the men got enough to eat.

Marseille, Victor knew, lay in the south of France. Maybe that was why the French Atlanteans had named their western town after the older city. The weather here certainly was southern in nature. It was hot and humid. The army could have marched faster in a cooler climate. Too much haste here, and you were much too likely to fall over dead. A handful of soldiers did. They got hasty, lonely graves, like the one for the man bitten by the coral snake. The rest of the army pushed west.

Victor waited for someone to come over the mountains and tell him General Cornwallis had pulled a fast one, landing his army somewhere on the east coast of Atlantis. If the English commander had, Radcliff didn't know what he could do about it, not right away. Local militias would have to try to keep the redcoats in play till he shifted his men back to the east. And how obedient his army would stay after getting marched and countermarched like that was anyone's guess.

But Habakkuk Biddiscombe brought a couple of French Atlanteans before him. "I found them fleeing from the west," Biddiscombe said. "I don't talk much of their lingo, but I know you do." By his tone, speaking French lay somewhere between affectation and perversion.

Ignoring that, Victor asked the strangers, "Why were you running through the woods?"

"Because swarms of soldiers have landed in New Marseille," one of the men answered. "When soldiers come out of nowhere, it is not good for ordinary people." He eyed Victor and the troops he led as if they proved the point. Very likely, in his eyes, they did.

"Are their warships still in the harbor?" Victor asked.

"They were when we left," the French Atlantean said. His comrade nodded. After a moment, so did Victor. The Royal Navy wouldn't drop Cornwallis on this half-settled shore and then sail off to do something else far away. It would support him and, if need be, take him somewhere else.

Victor tried a different question: "Did anyone try to fight to hold the redcoats out of New Marseille?"

Both French Atlanteans looked at him as if they had trouble believing their ears. The one who'd spoken before said, "Suicide is a mortal sin, *Monsieur*." He didn't add, *and you are an idiot*, but he might as well have. His manner would have offended Victor more if he hadn't had a point.

"Have you heard of the Proclamation of Liberty?" Victor asked. "It announces that Atlantis is to be free of the King of England forevermore."

"Has anyone given this news to the English soldiers in New Marseille?" the refugee enquired in return.

"We are on the way now to deliver the message," Victor said.

"When the hammer hits the anvil, the little piece of

metal in the middle gets flattened," the French Atlantean said. Was he a blacksmith? His scarred and callused hands made that a pretty good guess. Whether he was or not, his figure of speech seemed apt enough.

Victor had to pretend he didn't understand it. "Will you guide us to New Marseille and help us take your town back from the invaders?"

The local and his friend looked anything but delighted. "Do we have another choice?" he asked bleakly.

"In a word, no," Victor said. "This is a matter of military necessity for the United States of Atlantis." *Les États-Unis d'Atlantis*: he thought it sounded quite fine in French.

If the refugees thought so, too, they hid it well. The one who did the talking for them said, "How generous you are, *Monsieur*. You offer us the opportunity of returning to the danger we just escaped."

"You escaped it alone. You return to New Marseille with the Army of the Atlantean Assembly at your back," Victor said.

"And where is your navy, to drive away the English ships?" the French Atlantean asked.

Victor would rather have heard almost any other question in the world. "One way or another, we'll manage," he said gruffly.

The French Atlantean had no trouble understanding what that meant. "There is no Navy of the Atlantean Assembly," he said.

Since he was right, Victor could only glare at him. "Nevertheless, we shall prove victorious in the end," he declared.

"But the end, *Monsieur*, is a long way away," the other man said. "In the meanwhile, much as I regret to say it, I fear I prefer the chances of the Englishmen. Good day." He wanted nothing to do with the Proclamation of Liberty or any other idealistic project. He wanted nothing more than to be left alone. But King George's forces and the Atlantean rebels seemed unlikely to pay the least attention to what he wanted.

An eagle screeched overhead. Victor looked up. As he'd thought, it wasn't the red-crested eagle that stood for the uprising, but the smaller, less ferocious white-headed bird. Instead of boldly attacking honkers—and livestock, and men—white-headed eagles ate fish and carrion. One of their favorite ploys was to wait till an osprey caught a fish and then assail the other bird till it gave up its prize. As far as Victor was concerned, the white-headed eagle made a fine symbol for England.

He laughed at himself. He might have become a fair general, but he knew himself to be the world's most indifferent poet. And he would never get better if he couldn't come up with imagery more interesting than that.

Victor stood on a rise a couple of miles east of New Marseille, peering down into the town and its harbor through his brass telescope. He muttered under his breath. The redcoats were there in force, all right. They had already ringed New Marseille with field fortifications. They'd gone to some effort to conceal their cannon, but he could still pick out the ugly iron and brass snouts.

And General Cornwallis couldn't hide the Royal Navy ships that had brought him here and still supported him. They filled the harbor of New Marseille. More anchored offshore. Avalon Bay farther north could have held them all with ease. Because New Marseille's harbor was so much less commodious, it had neither the checkered past nor the bright future of Avalon.

A little warbler with a green head hopped about in the tree that shaded Victor. The tree itself, a ginkgo, was curious not only for its bilobed leaves but also for its existence. Others like it grew only in China. Scholars had expended gallons of ink trying to explain why that should be so. Custis Cawthorne—Victor's touchstone in such matters—was of the opinion that none of them had the slightest idea, but that they were unwilling to admit as much.

Thinking about the ginkgo and about Custis made

him wonder how the printer was doing in France. He also wondered how news of his victory over General Howe and the subsequent Proclamation of Liberty would go over there. All he could do was wonder and wait and see.

He didn't think he could do much more about New Marseille. If he hurled his army against those works, the redcoats and the Royal Navy would tear it to shreds. If he didn't ... Sooner or later, Cornwallis would come after him. The English could bring in supplies by sea. He was proud of keeping his army fed in its overland march across Atlantis. If it had to stay where it was for very long, though, it would start running out of edibles.

He contemplated the prospect of retreating across Atlantis. After a moment, he shuddered and did his best to think about something else. He almost wished he hadn't crossed the Green Ridge Mountains—but if he hadn't, he would have tamely yielded western Atlantis to the enemy. Sometimes your choices weren't between bad and good but between bad and worse.

Blaise came up beside him. "What do we do now, General?" the Negro asked: one more question Victor didn't want to hear.

He parried it with one of his own: "What would you do in my place?"

Blaise eyed the redcoats' fieldworks. He didn't need the spyglass and the details it revealed to come up with a reasonable answer. "Wait for whatever happens next," he said. "That is a strong position. Mighty strong."

"It is, isn't it?" Victor said mournfully. "I wish our engineers were as good as theirs."

"Why aren't they?" Blaise asked.

"Because we never needed professional soldiers till this war started," Victor said. "I suppose the United States of Atlantis will from this time forward—and it will have them, too. But we don't have them yet, worse luck."

That made Blaise grunt thoughtfully. "Too peaceful

for our own good, were we? You wouldn't think such a thing could be so."

"I fear it is," Victor said in mournful tones.

Blaise grunted again. "Well, if my tribe had more warriors, and better warriors, I never would have crossed the sea. I'd still be back there, still talking my own language." He spoke several incomprehensible syllables full of longing.

"Your life might have been—would have been, I suppose—easier had you stayed in Africa. But I would have missed a friend." Victor set a hand on the Negro's shoulder.

"Too late to worry about it now," Blaise said. "You *are* a friend, but this is not my land. It never will be."

"The United States of Atlantis should be any free man's land," Victor said, more stiffly than he'd intended to.

"Should be, yes." Blaise used that gesture Victor had seen before from him, brushing two fingers of his right hand against the dark back of his left. "Easier to talk about *should be* than *is*."

"Mmm, maybe so. We do what we can—nothing more to do," Victor said. "We aren't perfect, nor shall we ever be. But we keep heading down the road, and we'll see how far we fare."

He got one more grunt from Blaise. "Heading down the road on the backs of blacks and copperskins."

"Not on the backs of freemen, regardless of their color," Victor said uncomfortably.

This time, Blaise didn't answer at all. That might have been just as well. The United States of Atlantis might be heading down the road towards a place where a man of one color was reckoned as good as a man of another. Victor wasn't sure the land was heading toward that place, but it might be. He was sure it hadn't come close to getting there.

All of which brought him not a hairsbreadth nearer to deciding what to do about New Marseille. Attacking those works looked like something only a man who craved death would try. Going back the way he'd come yielded Atlantis west of the mountains to England, and God only knew what it would do to the army's morale. Unfortunately, things being as they were, he couldn't simply stay where he was for very long, either.

He ordered his men to start digging works of their own. If the redcoats came after them, they had to be able to hold their ground if they could. As far as he could see, General Cornwallis would have to be a fool to attack him, but maybe Cornwallis *was* a fool, or at least would turn out to be one this time. Victor could hope so, anyhow. He realized he wasn't in the best of positions when hoping for a foe's mistake was the best he could do.

A couple of days went by. Not much came from the far side of the Green Ridge Mountains. The hunters shot less than he'd wished they would, too. Before long, the army would get hungry. It might get very hungry.

He began planning an attack. It wasn't one he wanted to make, but when all his choices looked bad he had to pick the one that wasn't worst. He'd thought about that not long before, and now it stared him in the face again. Still, if he could take New Marseille from the English, he'd redeem this campaign.

If he could . . .

And then, to his amazement, the redcoats abandoned the town. They did it with their usual competence, leaving fires burning in their outworks to fool his men into thinking they remained there through the night. When the sun rose, the last few Englishmen were rowing out to the Royal Navy ships. The warships' sails filled with wind, and they glided off to the south.

Victor's first thought was that smallpox or the yellow jack had broken out in Cornwallis' army. But the English commodore would scarcely have let soldiers onto his ships in that case. Knowing only his own ignorance, Victor rode into New Marseille.

If the locals were glad to see him, their faces didn't know it. They seemed more French—and more superciliously French—than most southern folk on the other side of the mountains. Englishmen? English-speaking Atlanteans? If they recognized the difference, they didn't let on.

And they seemed proud of themselves for their Frenchness. "Don't you know why this Cornwallis individual absconded?" one of them demanded.

"No," Victor replied, "and I wish I did."

"Well, it's all because of King Louis, of course," the local told him.

"Perhaps you would be good enough to explain that to me?" Victor said. The King of France hadn't done much lately, not that he knew about.

But he knew less than the local did. "Word came here that France has declared war against the rascally English," the fellow said. "And . . . oh, yes . . ."

"What?" Victor asked, now eagerly.

"And recognized your United States of Atlantis," the man told him.

XIV

*H*abakkuk Biddiscombe rode back to Victor Radcliff with a self-satisfied smirk on his face. Radcliff eyed the cavalry officer a trifle apprehensively. Biddiscombe wore that smirk when things were going very well—and when they were going anything but. Which would it be this time? *Do I really want to know?* Victor wondered.

"I have news, General," Biddiscombe said portentously.

"I thought you might," Victor said. "Otherwise—I do hope—you would have stayed in your assigned position, with the men you lead." That failed to quash the bumptious cavalryman. Biddiscombe also failed to disgorge whatever he'd brought back. Sighing, Victor prompted him: "And that news is ... ?"

"Without question, General, my men have reached the eastern slope of the Green Ridge Mountains." From the pride in his voice, Habakkuk Biddiscombe had only a little less to do with that eastern slope than the Almighty Who'd created it in the first place.

"Well, I am glad to hear that." Victor meant it. His men wore lean and hungry looks, and did not wear them gladly. "We'll be much better able to subsist the soldiers once we return to civilization."

"Civilization?" Biddiscombe flared a nostril and

curled his lip. "Nothing but Frenchies, and not a devil of a lot of them."

"Some English Atlanteans, too," Victor said mildly. "And don't be too quick to sneer at the French. We stand a much better chance to make the Proclamation of Liberty good with France fighting England at our side."

"England licked France the last time they quarreled," Biddiscombe said. "You ought to know about that, eh, sir? You helped England do it."

"England and English Atlantis together beat France and French Atlantis." Victor was stretching a point. He did tell the truth . . . for this part of the world. In Terranova, in India, on the Continent, England had done fine against France with no help from Atlantis. But France, shorn of much of her former empire, would be fighting a smaller war this time. Victor went on, "Add France's weight to ours and the pan swings down."

"Till the Frenchies jump out of it and run away. They can afford to do that. We can't." No, Habakkuk Biddiscombe wasn't convinced.

Victor tried a different tack: "News that France was in the war made Cornwallis pull out of New Marseille as fast as he could go. He must think it means something. So must his commodore."

"More likely, they're a couple of little old ladies." Biddiscombe didn't bother hiding his scorn.

"General Cornwallis isn't, I assure you. As you said a moment ago, I ought to know about that. And the Royal Navy isn't in the habit of giving little old ladies command of a flotilla." Victor wanted to shake sense into the younger man. The main thing holding him back was the near-certainty it would do no good. He did say, "Having a real navy on our side is bound to help. The French have worked hard to build up their fleet since the last war."

"They're still French, so how much good will all that work do?" Yes, Biddiscombe's opinions were strong—and fixed.

Victor shrugged. "If they make England pull ships

away from Atlantis, that will let us get back some of our strangled commerce. It may let us build warships of our own, or at least get more privateers out on the sea."

"Fleabites." The cavalry major scratched melodramatically.

"We aren't going to land greencoats outside of London. It isn't in the cards." Victor held tight to his patience. "Enough fleabites, and George's ministers will decide we make England itch more than we're worth. That's the best hope we have." As far as Victor could see, it was Atlantis' only hope. He didn't say that. It would be just his luck to dent Biddiscombe's confidence when he didn't mean to.

"Fleabites," Biddiscombe repeated. Then he made hand-washing motions; he would have been a natural up onstage. "Well, General, now that I've given you the news, I *will* return to my men. Good day, sir." His salute was one more piece of overacting. He booted his horse off toward the east.

Riding after him to give him a proper boot in the backside was a temptation Victor had to fight hard to resist. One of the messengers who habitually accompanied him said, "That man is nothing but trouble."

Not without regret, Victor shook his head. "If he were nothing but trouble, I could dismiss him in good conscience. But he's more dangerous to the English than he is to us."

"Are you sure, sir?" the youngster asked.

"Sure enough," Victor said. "Nobody else could have done what he did last winter."

"All right." The messenger didn't seem to think it was.

"And his men did a great deal to keep us fed while we were on this side of the mountains," Victor added. "My biggest worry was that we'd get so hungry, we'd come to pieces. That didn't happen, and our cavalry are the largest reason it didn't."

"Yes, General," the messenger said resignedly. He

sounded more interested as he asked, "What will we do once we get back to the east?"

"First thing we must do is find out where Cornwallis has landed," Victor replied. "After that ... After that, we'll do whatever looks best."

The messenger looked dissatisfied. Victor would have, too, getting an answer like that. He would have thought the person who gave it didn't trust him. That wasn't true here; he wouldn't have kept the young man in his service without thinking him reliable. But he had nothing better to say. Maybe Alexander the Great or Julius Caesar knew what he would do months before he finally did it. Maybe ... but Victor had trouble believing it. He would have bet General Cornwallis felt the same way. In that, at least, the two of them were well matched.

After a spell marching through the wilderness, even scattered farms and occasional villages seemed downright urban to Victor. Unfamiliar faces, some of them belonging to women ... Taverns ... Shops ... For a little while, till he got used to them again, they almost overwhelmed him.

He sent a rider to the Atlantean Assembly, announcing that New Marseille was in Atlantean hands once more. He also sent messengers to the coast, to pass on that same news and to see what he could learn of Cornwallis' movements.

Even on this side of the Green Ridge Mountains, keeping his army fed was harder than he would have liked. The locals, whether of French blood or English, resented having to part with their grain and livestock. One of them bluntly asked, "What have you done for me, that I should cough up my hard-won substance for your ragamuffins here?"

"We hope to free you from the King of England and his greedy, lawless officials," Victor said. "Is that such a small thing?"

"King George never bothered me his own self, and

I never saw any of his officials way the devil out here. That's why I dwell in these parts," the man replied. "But you, now, General, you're the one hauling off my wheat and my cattle. Why shouldn't I get my firelock and go after you?"

"You may do that, if you like," Victor said politely. "If you do, and if we catch you, I shall regret giving the order for your hanging."

"Which doesn't mean you won't do it." The farmer's voice was bleak.

"That is correct, sir. It doesn't mean I won't do it," Victor agreed. "Were you in my place, you would act the same way, I assure you."

"It could be so," the farmer said. "But if you were in my place . . . Well, you'd think about getting out your firelock and doing something about it."

Out of slightly more than idle curiosity, Victor asked, "Have you Radcliff blood?"

"On my mother's side," the man answered. "But there's a devil of a lot of Atlanteans who can claim it one way or another. Even a lot of the Frenchies, if you listen to them. If the whole mob took up arms against you, you'd lose."

He was bound to be right about that. But they wouldn't. Victor had quite a few cousins he knew about in the army, and doubtless many more of whom he knew nothing. He said, "Most of them would sooner fight for Atlantis than against her."

"That's a fancy way to say you aren't robbing most of them right this minute." The farmer certainly had his share of Radcliff directness—and then some.

"I am not robbing you, sir," Victor said stiffly. "You are being repaid with paper the Atlantean Assembly will make good come victory."

"Preachers talk about heaven, but they don't cobble the road for you," the farmer said. "I expect it's the same way with your precious paper. And it looks like it'd be scratchy if I used it on my backside."

"I am doing the best I can to compensate you. Had I

gold or silver enough, I assure you I would spend them," Victor said.

The rustic eyed him. "I may even believe you, odd as it seems. But you *haven't* got 'em, which is the point of it, eh?"

Victor wondered whether he ought to post a guard to keep an eye on this farm after he rode away from it. If the farmer came after him with a musket—or, more likely, with a rifle—odds were he stood a good chance of hitting what he aimed at. In the end, Victor didn't. No one tried to assassinate him, so he supposed he'd judged the local's temper correctly. He'd also judged that not trusting the fellow would more probably set him off than acknowledging that he had reason to complain but there was nothing to be done about it.

A rider came back, reporting that, wherever General Cornwallis was, he wasn't at Cosquer. "Somewhere in the north, then," Victor Radcliff murmured. "Unless he's gone to Gernika, that is."

"To Spanish Atlantis? I wouldn't think so," Blaise said. "But he might have had the fleet turn around and head for Avalon once it got out of sight."

Victor shook his head. "I would believe that at some different time in the war, but not now."

"I don't follow you," Blaise said.

"All the reasons he left New Marseille are reasons he wouldn't go to Avalon," Victor said. "He needs to put his ships between the French fleet and our east coast. France could break into Croydon or New Hastings or maybe even Hanover without the Royal Navy to hold her at bay. Cornwallis' redcoats are less important right this minute. But he has to have those ships in place."

He waited while Blaise thought it over. After a moment, the Negro nodded. "Now that you point it out to me, I see it," he said. "I don't think I would have on my own. In my head, I can picture how war works on land. But out on the ocean—" He broke off, grimacing. "All I know about the ocean is, I don't want to go out on it any more."

"It's rather different when—" Now Victor was the one who stopped in sudden embarrassment.

Blaise grinned crookedly. "When you are not chained belowdecks, with niggers packed in tight as so many hams?" he suggested.

"That's ... not exactly what I was going to say." Victor heard the stiffness in his own voice.

"Why not? It's the truth." Blaise looked down at his wrists. "I used to have scars from the chains, but they are gone now. I wonder when they went away." He shrugged. "Ah, well, what difference does it make? The scars on my heart, the ones on my spirit, those never heal up."

"You have not got a bad life here." Victor still sounded stiff, even to himself.

"No, I have not. I have a good wife—herself brought hither against her will, but good even so—and I have a good friend," Blaise said. "But it is not the life I would have chosen for myself, and that makes a difference, too."

Imagining himself making the best of things in a jungle full of lions and elephants and black men speaking peculiar languages, Victor could only nod.

Hanover. General Cornwallis was at Hanover. In Cornwallis' place, Victor supposed he would have gone to Hanover, too. It was the biggest city in Atlantis, and the best port on the east coast. Though less centrally placed than New Hastings or Freetown, it did let the redcoats strike to north or south.

He set his own men moving north and east, back toward the settlements of English Atlantis from which most of them had sprung. They grumbled, as he'd known they would. They would have grumbled more had he pushed them harder. He would have, too, were he more confident of supplies. He was still close to the Green Ridge Mountains, and settlements still sparse.

Some of his men were willing enough to march toward the settlements from which they'd sprung. They weren't exactly the ones Victor would have had in mind, though: they were soldiers whose terms had expired. When they came back to the farms and towns in which they'd grown up, they weren't going to fight. They'd just head for home.

"Sorry, General," one of them said, and he even sounded as if he meant it. "I signed up for a year, and that's all I aim to give." He produced a dirty, much-creased-and-folded sheet of paper that showed he had indeed met his promised commitment.

It only irked Victor more. "God damn it to hell," he ground out. "I begged the Atlantean Assembly that henceforward all terms of enlistment were to be for the war's duration."

"Don't reckon they listened to you." Yes, the soldier *did* sound sympathetic, which was the last thing Victor Radcliff needed. With a whimsical shrug, the insufficiently embattled farmer added, "And what else is new?"

"Not a thing," Victor said heavily. "Not a . . . stinking thing. Well, that's one letter I shall have to write over again."

He did, too, when the army stopped for the night. When he sanded the sheet to blot up excess ink, he was amazed smoke didn't rise from the paper. He'd put heart and soul into the missive—and spleen as well. He glanced down at his midsection. Yes, if his spleen wasn't well vented by now, it never would be.

He stepped out of his tent and shouted for a messenger. The youngster who came up to him looked alarmed—he was usually a quieter man. Right this minute, Victor cared nothing for what he usually was. He thrust the letter at the youth. "Get this to the Conscript Fathers in Honker's Mill quick as you can."

"I'll do it, General," the young man said. "But how come you're so all-fired angried up all of a sudden?"

"Because, as near I can tell, the Assembly and the settlements' parliaments are doing their level best to lose us the war," Victor answered. "You wouldn't think the gentlemen there assembled could be such dunderheads, would you? Especially not after France has come into the war on our side, I mean. But they are. By God, a thundermug's got more sense in it than half the heads at Honker's Mill."

That won him a chuckle from the messenger, who asked, "What have they gone and done now, sir?"

"They keep recruiting short-term soldiers, that's what. Why would I want men who can go home just when I'm likely to need them the most? Answer me that, if you please."

"Beats me." The messenger sounded much too cheerful. But then, why shouldn't he? Recruiting soldiers and retaining them wasn't his worry. It was Victor Radcliff's. And it was supposed to be the Atlantean Assembly's. Expecting the Assembly and the parliaments with which it had to dicker to remember as much was evidently too much to hope for.

The messenger rode away. Victor stood outside the tent listening till the horse's hoofbeats got too distant to make out, and then a little longer besides. When he finally went back inside and lay down on his cot, he wondered whether he'd sleep. He tossed and turned for some time. Just when he was sure the Atlantean Assembly's idiocy would cost him a night's rest, he dozed off. Next thing he knew, the army's buglers were blowing morning assembly.

Instead of tea or coffee, he drank a brew of roasted native roots and leaves. He made a point of eating and drinking no better than the men he led. Even well-sugared—that, the Atlanteans could do—the brew tasted nasty. Worse, it was less invigorating than the ones that had to be imported. But it was what the cooks had left, so Radcliff drank it.

"Enjoy your coffee, General," said the man in the dirty apron who filled his tin mug.

It was no more coffee than Victor was Czar of all the Russias. And enjoying it stretched the bounds of probability if it didn't break them. A man could learn to tolerate it, and Victor had.

None of that showed on his face or in his voice. "Much obliged, Innes. I expect I shall," he said, and smiled when he said it. Sometimes you had to deceive your own men as well as the enemy.

More soldiers whose terms had expired marched away from the Atlantean army. To Victor's well-concealed surprise, fresh companies joined him. Some of them had enlisted for six months or a year. He gave their men a choice: they could fight the English till the war ended, or they could go home at once.

"Do whichever suits you," he told them. "I am better off without you than I would be to have you for a short term. If I must plan my campaigns around your enlistments, I would do better to pray General Cornwallis' mercy now."

He exaggerated; most of the time, short-term soldiers were better than no soldiers at all. To his relief, most of the new recruits agreed to serve for the duration. "Ha!" Blaise said. "Only shows the dumb strawfeet don't know what the devil they're getting into."

"I shouldn't be amazed if you were right," Victor agreed. Then he chuckled. "Strawfeet, is it?"

"Oh, they are, General. You can tell by looking at them," Blaise said.

Atlantean drillmasters often despaired of teaching country bumpkins the evolutions they needed to learn if they were to move from column to line of battle or do any of the other things soldiers had to do. Baron von Steuben frequently ran out of English when he tried to show them what they needed to do. They couldn't understand his German, but it sounded as if it ought to be worth remembering.

Among the worst complaints the drillmasters had was that raw recruits couldn't reliably tell their right feet from their left. They did know the difference between hay and straw, though. Drill sergeants tied a wisp of hay to their left feet and straw to their right. "Hayfoot!" a drillmaster would call. "Strawfoot! Hayfoot! Strawfoot!" It was an awkward makeshift, but it worked. And, more and more often, Atlantean veterans called new men strawfeet. (Von Steuben called them everything he could in English, and worse than that *auf Deutsch*.)

Naturally, the new men were inclined to resent the name. Just as naturally, the veterans didn't care. There had already been several scraps about it. Victor expected more to come. As long as veterans and recruits didn't squabble with the redcoats in front of them, he wouldn't worry.

A courier rode up. "I have a letter for you, General, from the Atlantean Assembly," he said importantly.

"Oh, you do, do you?" Victor growled. He took the letter, broke the seal, and unfolded the paper.

It was, to his utter lack of surprise, a missive censuring him for what the Assembly characterized as his "ill-bred, ill-tempered, intemperate, and altogether ill-advised communication of the twenty-seventh *ultimo*."

Had they recalled him from his command, he would have gone home without a backwards glance. If they didn't care for the way he was carrying on the fight, they could go ahead without him.

But they didn't do that. Several of his officers were convinced they could command Atlantis' forces better than he. The Atlantean Assembly and he might snap at each other, but the Assembly wasn't minded to give any of those ambitious officers a chance to show what they could do.

A small force of foot soldiers skirmished with the Atlantean army after it crossed the Stour. Victor's men took a few prisoners as the enemy fell back. They brought them to the commanding general. "Shall we hang these traitor bastards from a branch, sir?" one of the guards growled.

The prisoners looked frightened. Except for wearing brown coats rather than green, they also looked just like their captors. "You can't do that! We fought fair!" one of them said. His accent was the same as that of the man who wanted to hang him. And well it might have been:

they were both Atlanteans, probably from the same settlement.

Victor Radcliff glowered at him. "So you'll spill your blood for a king who won't lift a finger for you?" he said.

"He is my king. England is my country." The prisoner set his chin. "He's your king, too, by God, and England's your country."

"Atlantis is my country. I have no king," Victor said. His men cheered. Some of their captives looked defiant, others alarmed. Victor turned to his troops. "Did they fight like soldiers?"

"We *are* soldiers," another prisoner said. "Third company of King George's Atlantean Rangers, that's me."

"Shame!" one of Victor's men said. Several others hissed.

They might have started hanging the Atlantean Rangers then, but Victor held up a hand. "No, we shan't do that," he said, "not if they didn't play the savage against us. It's easier to start hanging people than to stop."

"They've got it coming!" one of his men said hotly. "God-damned traitors!"

"Traitor yourself!" a captive yelled, and almost won himself a hempen cravat in spite of everything Victor could do.

He had to draw his fancy sword (which he supposed balanced out the letter of censure) to keep his Atlanteans from lynching the bold prisoner. "No!" he shouted. "What will they do if they take some of our men next time? Do you want a war like that?"

Some of his men nodded, which scared him. But more looked worried. A war like that could keep on poisoning Atlantis long after it ended. How many feuds, how many barn burnings and stock killings and murders from ambush for revenge, would spring from it? Too many. Victor might have had to point that out, but his soldiers could see it once he did. The men from King George's Atlantean Rangers remained prisoners of war.

After the excitement was over, Blaise said, "None of those scuts even thanked you. Not a single one."

"I didn't expect it of them," Victor answered.

"Why not?" the Negro exclaimed. "If not for you, they'd be dead." He laid his head on his shoulder and stuck out his tongue as if hanged. "If that isn't worth some thanks, what is?"

Patiently, Victor said, "If they thanked me, they would have to own to themselves that I'm not such a bad fellow. Then they might have to own that my cause isn't so bad. And then they might have to wonder about the one they chose. How many people care to do that? Here, not many. Is it different in Africa?"

"Everything here has more gears turning round. Everything." Blaise did not sound as if he were complimenting Atlantis.

Victor shrugged. "It is what we have. Changing from belonging to the king to belonging to ourselves is hard enough—the Rangers show as much. But if you want to change human nature at the same time ..." He shook his head. "Good luck to you, that's all. I don't believe it can be done."

"And you expect men to live without a chief or a king or whatever you call him?" Blaise shook his head, too, laughing at the silly notion.

He was no political philosopher, but he had a keen feel for what was real. "No," Victor said, "only without a leader who can do as he pleases no matter what the laws say."

"Only?" Blaise threw his own words in his face: "Good luck to you, that's all."

Habakkuk Biddiscombe thought each of his schemes was finer than the one that had gone before it. "We can spirit Cornwallis out of Hanover and strike off the enemy's head!" he told Victor.

Did he mean that as a figure of speech or literally? However he meant it, Victor shook his head. "I don't think that's a good notion."

"Why not?" Biddiscombe swelled and turned purple. Victor wondered if he'd explode. No man was ever so enamored of his own schemes as the cavalry officer.

But Victor ticked off points on his fingers: "Item—chances of success strike me as slim. Item—any men captured whilst making such an attempt would assuredly wear a noose soon thereafter. And, item—even if your plan should be accomplished in every particular, so what?"

Habakkuk Biddiscombe gaped. "What d'you mean . . . uh, General? I told you what would happen then."

"Indeed. You did. But, I say again, so what? Someone might well capture me. If that unpleasantness came to pass, this army would continue the struggle under our second-in-command. We might do as well with him as we have with me. For all I know, we might do better, though I dare hope not. Why do you suppose the redcoats to be in a different situation?"

"Well . . ." Biddiscombe faltered. "Isn't the best man commonly placed in command?"

"Again, in our case, I dare hope so. Yes, that may be true. But it is also possible that the general commanding is but the most senior officer present. General Cornwallis is not elderly and *is* clever, but I doubt he will ever be spoken of in the same breath with Gustavus Adolphus or Turenne. Another man, thrust suddenly into his place, might well match his accomplishments."

"Only reason you don't want to try it is on account of I'm the one who came up with it." Anger clotted Biddiscombe's voice. "If you or your nigger thought it up, you'd be all for it." He turned on his heel and stormed away.

Blaise appeared as if by magic. "Did I hear somebody call me nigger?" He could hear that word where he might miss others. Well, who could blame him? What man with the faintest hope of being a gentleman wasn't sensitive to slights?

"He did. You did," Victor said wearily. "He meant nothing by it, though. He was in a temper at me, not at you."

"Huh," Blaise said: a wordless sound packed with disbelief. "Anybody says *nigger*, he means something by it, all right." He spoke like a man very sure of what he was talking about. Chances were he had every right to be.

Even so, Victor said, "I showed him how and why his harebrained scheme was harebrained, and he responded with all the gratitude you might expect."

"What scheme is this?" Blaise asked. Victor explained. The Negro grunted. "Well, you told him true. That scheme is harebrained from mouth to arsehole."

Victor would have said *from top to bottom*, which didn't mean he disagreed with the more pungent phrase. "Sometimes Habakkuk simply needs to get things out of his system," he said.

Blaise grunted again. "If he's costive, let him take one of those little pills. That'll shift him." He rolled his eyes. "Those little pills'll shift anything."

"No doubt." Victor knew the ones Blaise was talking about. They were made from antimony. If you had trouble moving your bowels, you would swallow one. A few hours later, you would think a barrel of black powder had gone off in your gut. They weren't cheap, but they did the trick, all right. You could, if you were so inclined, rescue the little devil from the chamber pot, wash it off, and save it for the next time you needed it.

"Ought to knock him over the head." Blaise returned to the subject at hand. "That will get things out of his system, too. And it will save you trouble. You see if it don't—doesn't." He corrected himself before Victor could.

"He'll be all right," Victor said. Blaise rolled his eyes once more. He was as stubborn as Habakkuk Biddiscombe, if in a different way. He would have been highly offended had Victor said so, so Victor didn't. He did remember the conversation for a long time afterwards.

Every so often, a loyalist would take a potshot at Victor's soldiers from behind a roadside tree, then try to get away. Rebellious Atlanteans who fired at redcoats marching past were heroes, at least to other rebellious Atlanteans. When Victor's men captured the loyalist snipers, they hanged them without ceremony.

Cornwallis' soldiers did the same thing to the insurrectionist marksmen they caught. Every printer who favored the Atlantean Assembly damned them to Satan's fiery furnace as murderers on account of it. Victor Radcliff noticed the irony, which didn't mean he intended to stop hanging loyalist *francs-tireurs*.

One of them put on a brave show, saying, "I am proud to die for my king."

"You won't be once the rope goes around your neck," Victor predicted. "And you aren't dying for your king. You could have been as loyal to George as you pleased, so long as you didn't fire at my men from ambush."

"I should prove myself a traitor to my sovereign did I not take up arms against those treacherously in arms against him." Yes, the loyalist had pride.

It did him no good. "You and your friends should have joined a properly enrolled company, then," Victor said coldly. The man was hanged with the three or four other bushwhackers Victor's soldiers had flushed out of the woods. They died hard, strangling from the nooses instead of getting their necks broken as a proper hangman's knot might have done. Or it might not have, when they were hanged from branches instead of getting a long drop from the gallows.

Blaise eyed the limp bodies and discolored faces with cold dispassion. All he said was, "They had it coming."

"I think so, too," Victor said. "But if you listen to the likes of them, we're the ones who deserve to dance on air."

"Dance on air." The Negro tasted the words. "I like that."

"It's not mine, I fear," Victor told him. "I don't know where I first heard it. Use it as you please. People will understand you when you do."

"All right." Blaise glanced toward the corpses again. "They don't dance."

They'd had their feet tied together and hands bound behind them. "I've seen livelier jobs, with the legs free," Victor said, gnawing on the inside of his lower lip at the memory. "Only a cruel man could enjoy the spectacle, believe me."

"They are enemies," Blaise said. "Why should I be sorry to watch enemies die?"

"I have nothing against enemies dying," Victor replied. "But rejoicing in suffering, even in an enemy's suffering, strikes me as unchristian."

"Maybe I don't make such a good Christian, then," Blaise said.

He and his wife had gone to church with Victor and Margaret most Sundays since the fighting in French Atlantis ended. He attended divine services with the other soldiers in Victor's army. Radcliff suddenly wondered how much he really believed. How much of his piety was no more than fitting in where he had to live, and how much of his savage creed from Africa still lurked below?

No matter what he wondered, he didn't ask. Papists and Protestants of all sects and even Jews joined together in the Atlantean Assembly and in its army. If there was room for all of them, wasn't there also room for one perhaps unregenerate African?

Despite the snipers—most of whom, being as woodswise as Victor's men, escaped instead of getting captured—the army pressed on toward Hanover. More loyalists, not daring or caring to meet it in arms, fled before it with nothing but what they could carry. Men who preferred the Atlantean Assembly's cause gleefully swooped down on the homes and fields and livestock they abandoned. "Buggers made us sweat while they was in the saddle," one man told Victor. "Now let's see if they ever set eyes on what used to be theirs again."

Strict justice might have made Victor speak of courts and due process of law. "We'll use them as they deserve," he said, and the local nodded.

A few days later, the army was camped near a village

called Brandenburg. A cavalryman rode up to Victor. After a sketched salute, the man asked, "General, have you seen Major Biddiscombe? I needed to ask something of him, but he's nowhere about."

"I haven't got him," Victor answered.

He thought no more about it till the army was getting ready to move out the next morning. There was still no sign of Habakkuk Biddiscombe. A man who'd been on sentry duty said, "He rode out past me not long after we stopped here. He said he was going to reconnoiter what lay ahead."

"By himself?" Victor's eyebrows leaped toward his hairline.

The sentry only shrugged. "You know how he is."

Victor Radcliff did, much too well. "Even for Major Biddiscombe, that's excessive," he said. "When he comes in, I'll give him a talking-to he'll remember for a month of Wednesdays." The sentry laughed, but Victor wasn't joking.

Only Habakkuk Biddiscombe didn't come in. Victor feared he'd fallen into the hands of English scouts or local loyalists. The only trouble was, his own scouts turned up no signs that the enemy was operating anywhere close by.

Another fear began to grow in him—and not in him alone. "How bad was that last quarrel you had with him, sir?" Blaise asked.

"Well, it wasn't good." No one would accuse Victor of exaggerating, anyhow.

"Uh-*huh*," Blaise said thoughtfully. Then he asked, "How much harm could he do us if he went over to Cornwallis?"

"He wouldn't do that!" Victor squawked, and he could hear himself protesting too much. After a moment, he added, "I hope he wouldn't do that," which was nothing but the truth.

XV

*H*abakkuk Biddiscombe not only went over to General Cornwallis and King George, he reveled in his treason. To him, of course, it seemed anything but. What man ever acted for any save the highest motives? None: not if you asked the actor himself.

A scout brought back a broadsheet from a village still under the redcoats' control. It was called "The True Relation of Colonel Habakkuk Biddiscombe, Formerly of the Rebel Cavalry."

"Huh," Blaise said when he saw that. "He won himself a promotion for running off, he did."

"Thirty pieces of silver," Victor said bitterly. "I wonder if he would have stayed had I granted him higher rank." He sighed. "We'll never know now."

Biddiscombe—or, more likely, some pro-English hack purporting to be Biddiscombe—characterized the Atlantean Assembly as "a witches' Sabbat of betrayal." He called the army that fought on behalf of the Assembly "a pack of starveling hounds, remarkable alike for savagery and cowardice." And he described Victor Radcliff as "the blackest traitor since Judas" (a man likely to be mentioned when anyone turned his coat) and "an oaf masquerading as a general: a leader utterly incapable of recognizing and acknowledging a clever stratagem."

Remembering the cavalry officer's scheme he'd turned down, Victor suspected that, at least, came straight from Biddiscombe.

"What do you aim to do about this—this arsewipe, General?" the scout inquired.

Victor felt of the paper. "I think I'd sooner use a handful of leaves," he said. The scout and Blaise both laughed. Victor went on, "What *can* I do about it? If the famous Colonel Biddiscombe should dare lead enemy horse against us, we shall try to shoot him out of the saddle. Of that I have no doubt—he betrayed the soldiers he formerly commanded more foully than any others here, for he enjoyed more of their trust. Other than killing him first chance we find, I know not what course to take."

"Me, I'd sooner catch him alive," Blaise said. "Then I could roast him over a slow fire and turn him on a spit so he got done on all sides." He grinned evilly. "Easy enough to tell with a white man, eh? And that would give the dirty scut plenty of time to think on his mistakes before he gave up the ghost."

"Devil take me if I don't fancy the sound of that myself," the scout exclaimed.

"So long as we kill him, that will suffice," Victor said.

Blaise was born a savage, of course. But men who favored the Atlantean Assembly and those who remained loyal to King George were roasting each other over slow fires: oh, not where the main armies marched and countermarched, but in the countless little ambushes and affrays that would never make the history books or change the war's result by one iota but went on nonetheless. And those men on both sides gleefully played the savage without Blaise's excuse.

"We'll go on," Victor said, as he had so many times. "If we can winkle them out of Hanover, that will be a great triumph for us and a great disaster to them. And if Habakkuk Biddiscombe has to sail off to England—on which he has never in his life set eyes—even that will be enough."

"Devil it will," Blaise muttered, but not loud enough for Victor to call him on it.

Victor was anything but sure they could squeeze Cornwallis out of Hanover. Even if they didn't, they might reach the sea and cut the English coastal holdings in half. That would be worth doing in and of itself.

Go on they did. Loyalists skirmished with them. Like King George's Atlantean Rangers, these men fought as soldiers, not in ambuscades. Sometimes redcoats stiffened their ranks; sometimes they managed well enough on their own. Victor ordered his own men to treat them as prisoners of war when they were taken. "If they meet us fairly, we must return the favor," he insisted.

And his troops obeyed him ... more often than not. Even so, an unfortunate number of such captives were shot "trying to escape." He wondered whether he should issue harsher orders. In the end, he decided not to. Issuing orders that weren't likely to be obeyed only damaged the force of other commands.

Before long, a scout carried another broadsheet back into his encampment. This one announced the creation of something called "Biddiscombe's Horsed Legion." Volunteers in the Legion would "root out, eradicate, extirpate, and utterly exterminate the verminous rebels opposing in arms his brilliant Majesty, good King George."

Most printers worked in the coastal towns the English held. Victor found one back in Brandenburg who was loyal to the Atlantean Assembly. He had the man crank out a counterblast, one warning men who leaned toward King George that "no individual from the cavalry formation styled Biddiscombe's Horsed Legion who may be captured by the armies of the Atlantean Assembly shall under any circumstances hope for quarter."

No Horsed Legion appeared. Victor wondered whether Cornwallis had had second thoughts—and, if he had, whether Habakkuk Biddiscombe was contemplating desertion from the English cause. Probably not, Victor decided—the cavalry officer had to know

Atlantis would never take him back. Biddiscombe had made his bed. Now he had to lie in it, even if it proved uncomfortable.

Victor also wondered when the French declaration of war would produce soldiers on the ground in Atlantis. Indeed, he wondered if it ever would. In the last war, the French managed to convey one small army across the Atlantic, all their later efforts failing. Their navy was stronger now. Was it enough stronger? *It had better be*, he thought. His own men made vastly better soldiers than they had when they first enlisted. All the same, he could use some cynical, hard-bitten professionals to show them by example how the job was done.

Meanwhile, he used what he had. Redcoats and loyalists skirmished with his forces before falling back toward Hanover. Cornwallis seemed less interested in fighting big battles than General Howe had been before him. Maybe he was clever. Howe had tried to crush the Atlantean uprising. The only thing he'd proved was that he couldn't. Cornwallis, by contrast, seemed to want to force the Atlanteans to crush him. As long as he held the towns on the eastern coast, the United States of Atlantis were only wind and air. They weren't a nation, any more than a man deprived of his head was a man.

And then, to Victor's surprise, he got word that some of Cornwallis' garrison in Hanover was putting to sea and sailing away. When he heard the rumor the first time, he had trouble believing it. But it came to him again the next day, brought by a man who didn't know anyone else had carried word ahead of him.

"Why would he do that, when we're pressing him toward Hanover?" Victor asked. "I know the Englishmen make good soldiers, and I know Hanover has good outworks. All the same, if too many forts are empty of men, the place will fall."

"Well . . ." His second informant was a plump merchant named Gustavus Vasa Rand, who plainly enjoyed knowing things the commanding general didn't. The man steepled his fingers, then tugged at his ear before going on, "I hear tell the redcoats have themselves trouble somewheres else."

"Where?" Radcliff exploded. If it was anywhere in Atlantis, he thought he would have known about it. If the English had trouble anywhere in Atlantis, he hoped he would have helped foment it.

But Gustavus Vasa Rand replied, "Over in Terranova, is what folks say. Some of the settlements there, they've decided they don't fancy King George any more'n we do."

"Have they?" Victor breathed. "Well, well, well. Has anyone reported why they chose this moment to rise up?"

"Don't you know?" Yes, Gustavus Vasa Rand exuded the amiable scorn the man who's heard things feels for the poor, ignorant twit he aims to enlighten. "Why, this past year or so a demon pamphleteer's appeared amongst 'em. He's tossed so much red pepper into the stew, even the boring old Terranovans can't help breathing fire after they go and eat of it."

"I dare say he's caused King George's men in those parts a good deal of, ah, pain," Victor remarked with malice aforethought.

"Why, so he has." One of Rand's bristly eyebrows rose. "Funny you should put it so, General, for Paine's his family name."

"And Thomas his Christian name," Victor agreed. "I am acquainted with the gentleman, and with his qualities. Indeed, I sent him west across the Hesperian Gulf, hoping he would do exactly as he has done."

"Well, good on you, then," the merchant told him. "The more toes England has on the griddle, the more hopping she needs must do." Now the look he sent Victor was more speculative than pitying. A general who could work out a plot and have it come off the way he wanted wasn't some harmless bumpkin, but a man who might need some serious watching.

"I am grateful for the news, believe me," Victor said.

"It will surely influence the way I conduct my campaign from this time forward."

"Ah? Influence it how, pray?" Gustavus Vasa Rand leaned forward, eager to be even more in the know than he was already.

But Victor Radcliff only laid a finger by the side of his nose. "By your leave, sir, I'll say no more. What you have not heard, no red-hot pokers or thumbscrews may tear from you should the redcoats decide they must learn all the secrets you carry under your hat."

"They wouldn't do that." Rand's voice lacked conviction. Victor refrained from mentioning one other possibility: that the trader from Hanover might tell the English what he knew under no compulsion whatsoever. Some men tried to work both sides at once, or pretended to serve one while actually on the other. He had spies in Hanover; he had to assume Cornwallis played the same game.

"Whilst the Hesperians make England divide her forces, you may be sure I shall do my best to keep the occupiers, ah, occupied here in Atlantis," Victor said. "And, sir, you may publish that abroad as widely as you please."

"I'll do it, General. You can count on me," Rand said.

Victor Radcliff smiled and nodded. Maybe the man from Hanover would. Then again, maybe he wouldn't. If he didn't, the world wouldn't end; nor would the Atlantean uprising.

And if he did, Victor hadn't said a word about strategy. Of course Cornwallis would expect him to try to take advantage of what England had to do to try to put down the new rebellion far to the west. Cornwallis would be right, too. But how Victor would try to exploit the new situation . . .

Cornwallis won't know, Victor thought. *He can't possibly, for I haven't the faintest idea myself*. He didn't believe that was what the military manuals meant when they talked about "the advantage of surprise," but it was what he had. Now he needed to figure out how to make the most of it.

Several rivers met at or near Hanover, which helped make it Atlantis' most important harbor. (Some of the people who argued about such things argued that Avalon had a better site. They might well have been right. But Hanover faced towards Europe, Avalon toward Terranova. When it came to ships and cargoes heading in and out, that made all the difference in the world.)

These days, cargoes heading in and out of Hanover did so for England's benefit, not Atlantis'. Oh, dribs and drabs of what came into Hanover got smuggled out to the lands that owed the Atlantean Assembly allegiance, but only dribs and drabs. As General Howe had before him, General Cornwallis hoped that keeping his opponents poor would detach them from the United States of Atlantis and make them take another look at King George.

What worried Victor Radcliff was that Cornwallis might be right. A patriot without a ha'penny in his pocket was only one long step—sometimes not such a long step—from discovering he was really a loyalist after all.

The most important river that flowed into Hanover, the Severn, ran down from the north. Victor led his own army along the north bank of a smaller stream, the Blackwater, that approached from the west.

"Why did they name it the Blackwater?" Blaise asked. "What's in there looks like any other water to me."

"To me, too—now," Victor answered. "But when we get a little closer to Hanover . . . Well, you'll see."

Before they came that close to Hanover, they had to deal with a hastily run-up English stockade that blocked their approach to the city. One of the popguns inside the stockade boomed defiance at the Atlantean army. The roundshot it fired fell far short of Victor's men. After the ball stopped rolling, one of his gunners picked it up.

If it fit an Atlantean gun—and it probably would—it would fly back toward some redcoats one of these days.

Instead of assaulting the little fortress right away, Victor marched his troops past it before halting. Maybe the soldiers inside hadn't sent anyone east toward Hanover to warn Cornwallis of his advent. But if they had, the redcoats in the seaside city might sally forth to see if they could smash the Atlantean army between themselves and the garrison.

"They may think they can get away with that, but I don't aim to let them," Victor told his assembled officers—and, inevitably, Blaise, whom everyone took for granted by now.

"How will you stop 'em, General?" one of his captains asked.

"I'll tell you how, in the name of the Lord God Jehovah," Victor said. "We shall attack the stockade at midnight tonight—that's how. Once it has fallen, all their hopes of playing hammer and anvil against us fall with it."

The officers buzzed like bees. "Can we do it?" one of them asked.

He might not have meant for Victor Radcliff to hear him, but Victor did. "We can, sir, and we shall," he declared. "The idea *may* surprise you, but I intend that it *shall* flabbergast the poor foolish Englishmen mured up behind those pine and redwood logs. Flabbergast 'em, I say!"

To that end, the Atlanteans encamped as they would have done at the end of any ordinary day's march. They pitched tents. They built up cook fires. They ambled back and forth in front of and around those fires. Victor had learned his lessons watching the redcoats abandon positions they could hold no longer. If the enemy commander inside the stockade was watching the encampment through a spyglass, he would notice nothing peculiar.

He wouldn't be able to see, for instance, that the men silhouetted in front of the fires were always the *same* men: a group left behind to make the camp appear normal from a distance, even when it wasn't.

Meanwhile, the rest of the Atlanteans took care to stay out of the firelight. Victor Radcliff led them against the English works. The night was moonless and cloudy and dark. "Move as quietly as you can," he called—quietly. "If you fall, pick yourself up with no loud, profane swearing."

"Indeed, for such vileness offends against God," said a voice out of the blackness.

"Well, so it does," Victor agreed. "But it's also liable to mark our advance against the foe. Unless you have such a clean conscience that you can meet your Maker sooner than you might have had in mind, keep your lips buttoned."

The Atlanteans did ... for the most part. No cries of alarm rang out from the stockade ahead. The redcoats inside the log palisade kept big bonfires blazing. The red-gold light shone through chinks between one log and another, and also lit up the buildings inside the stockade: barracks that could double as a redoubt in time of need.

Motte and bailey, Victor thought. *The Normans used that scheme in England, and it's still a good one.* Would it be good enough to hold up against complete surprise? He had to hope not. He also had to hope he could bring off a complete surprise. That, at the moment, remained what barristers called a Scotch verdict: not proven.

Those bonfires made advancing against the enemy position easier than it would have been otherwise. On a night this dark, Victor might have had trouble finding an unilluminated fort—and tramping past it would have been embarrassing, to say the least. No risk of that, not now.

With so much light behind them, with their eyes not accustomed to gloom, the redcoat sentries up on the walls might also have a harder time spotting the Atlanteans moving up on them. Again, Victor dared hope so.

No one raised the alarm as his men drew near. "Scaling ladders forward!" he hissed urgently. Forward they came. He pointed toward the fortress. "Do you see where to place them?"

"We do that, General," replied a soldier who'd surely been born in Ireland.

"Then advance against the palisade—slowly till you're discovered, and after that quick as you can."

Off went the ladders, one by one. Storming parties—he hoped they weren't forlorn hopes—followed them. If everything went well, the fort would fall to the Atlanteans almost before the enemy inside realized it was under attack. But how often did everything go well? Not often enough, as Victor had seen . . . too often.

Tonight, though, the scaling ladders were about to thud into place against the palisade before a redcoat up there let out a startled yelp: "Bloody 'ell! It's the bleedin' Atlanteans!"

A moment later, a rifle barked. The sentry yelped again, this time in pain. He had been a dark blotch against the lighter background of the barracks hall. Now that blotch disappeared.

"Atlantis!" Victor's men cried as they swarmed up the ladders, and "The Proclamation of Liberty!" and "Down with King George!"

Down with King George it was, at least in that one spot. So many men in green jackets got up onto the palisade and dropped down into the courtyard behind it, the defenders never had a chance. Only a few shots were fired before the gates swung open. Someone sang out in an Atlantean accent: "All yours, General!"

"Well done," Victor said as he walked into the little fortress. "Very well done indeed, boys!"

The English captain who'd commanded the garrison didn't think so. "A night attack? Not sporting," he said sourly.

"If you show me where Hoyle's rules state I'm not allowed to make one, perhaps I'll march away," Victor said. "Or perhaps I won't."

His men jeered. The captain glared, and then tried

a different tack: "Another thing—one of your blighters lifted my pocket watch."

"Can you tell me which one?" Victor asked.

"No, dammit." The English officer shook his head. "He was tall. He was skinny. He had an evil leer and foul breath."

"Well, sir, as a matter of fact, so do you," Victor said, which won him another glare. Taking no notice of it, he continued, "You do realize you're describing more than half of my army?" He wasn't exaggerating; most Atlanteans seemed tall to their shorter English cousins.

"I shouldn't wonder if more than half your army consists of thieves." The captain didn't lack for nerve.

But Victor only laughed. "And you think yours doesn't? By God, sir, I've served with redcoats before. I know better."

"We may be thieves, but we aren't foul rebels," the captain said.

"Not yet, perhaps. You would be surprised, though, at how many in the Atlantean army took the King's shilling first," Victor responded.

He couldn't down the English officer, who said, "And what of Habakkuk Biddiscombe? Will you tell me he is the only Atlantean who at last came to see where his true loyalty should lie?"

"All I'll tell you of Biddiscombe is that sooner or later—likely sooner—he'll quarrel with his English superiors, as he quarreled with me," Victor said tightly. "And I wish them joy of him when he does."

That actually made the captain thoughtful. "Mm . . . I've met the man, and I must say I shouldn't be astonished if you prove right. But, having antagonized both sides in this struggle, where can he go next?"

"He can go to the Devil, for all of me," Victor said. "I'll tell you where *I'm* going next, though. I'm going to Hanover."

More often than not, the wind blew down from the Green Ridge Mountains toward the sea. When it did, it carried the spicy, resinous scents of Atlantis' vast evergreen forests with it. Victor took that odor for granted. He noticed it only when it changed.

As his army neared Hanover, it did. The breeze swung around to come off the Atlantic for a while. The ocean's salt tang seemed to quicken Victor's pulse. Was that because all Radcliffs and Radcliffes sprang from fishermen, and so naturally responded to the smell of the sea? Or did Victor's excitement grow because the oceanic odor reminded him how near his goal he was? Some of each, he guessed; a man's reasons were rarely all of one piece.

Blaise pointed to the river beside which the army marched. "It did turn black, General, like you said. Why?"

"Because it flows through peat beds under the meadows," Victor answered. "You know peat?"

"You can burn it," Blaise said. "Like God was trying to make coal but didn't know how yet."

Victor laughed in surprise. He wouldn't have come out with anything so blasphemous, but he probably wouldn't have come out with anything so apt, either.

Before long, the breeze from the east brought more than the odor of the Atlantic to his nostrils. It carried the smell of smoke with it—and also, less attractively, the reek of sewage. That combination always proclaimed a large settlement not far away.

"Cities stink," Blaise complained.

"Well, so they do," Victor said. "Do your African villages smell any sweeter?"

Blaise clicked his tongue between his teeth. "Er—no."

"I didn't think so," Victor said. "When I use the privy, it's not angels that come out. No reason your folk should differ there."

The colored sergeant changed the subject, from which Victor concluded that he'd made his point: "How do you propose to take Hanover away from Cornwallis?"

"I can't answer that yet. I shall have to see just where

the English have placed their lines and their forts, and how many men they can put into them now that they're dealing with trouble in Terranova, too," Victor said.

"Ah," Blaise said. "You do make fighting more complicated than it needs to be."

More complicated than you were used to in Africa, Victor translated. But anyone—black, white, or, he supposed, copper-skinned—took what he'd grown up with as the touchstone for what was right and proper the rest of his days.

Before long, Victor had a pretty good notion of the lie of the English works outside Hanover, and of how many redcoats Cornwallis had in them. The enemy commander did his best to keep the locals inside his lines. Cornwallis didn't want them bringing Victor such news.

Cornwallis' best wasn't good enough. His lines leaked. The English captain at the fort had been right: there were plenty of loyalists and royalists in land held by the forces following the Atlantean Assembly. Sometimes they did go over to King George's army, as Habakkuk Biddiscombe had done.

But that coin had two sides. Hanover was a fair-sized city by anybody's standards—not London, not Paris, but a fair-sized city. Of course it had its share of people who cheered behind closed doors when the United States of Atlantis were proclaimed. And of course some of those men, seeing liberation as one of Victor Radcliff's outriders, would leave the city to tell him what they knew of its defenses and the soldiers who manned them.

He made a point of separating his informants one from another. He interviewed them one at a time, and made a sketch map of what each described. If one of them told a tale different from the others' . . . He wouldn't put it past Cornwallis to try to lead him into a trap. He knew he would have done the same thing to the English general had he found the chance.

Adding all the sketch maps together . . . By the time he called a council of war, he had a pretty good notion of what wanted doing. "We will feint *here*," he told his assembled officers—and Blaise—pointing with the fancy-hilted sword the Atlantean Assembly had presented to him. "A good portion of our field artillery will accompany the feint, to make it seem the more persuasive. Having drawn Cornwallis' notice thither, we strike *here*." He pointed again, farther south this time.

Blaise held up his right index finger. Victor nodded to him. "What do we do if Cornwallis hears of this plan?" the Negro asked.

He did come up with cogent questions. "Well, that depends," Victor said. "If I find out ahead of time that he's heard of it, the real thrust becomes the feint and the feint the real thrust."

"What if you don't find out, General?" a colonel inquired.

Victor spread his hands. "In that case, we walk into a snare." He waited for the startled laughter to die down, then added, "I shall endeavor to extricate the army from it with losses as small as possible."

At the beginning of this fight, the mere thought of losing a battle would have filled his officers with a curious blend of rage and panic. Now they took the possibility in stride. They would do everything they could to win. If that turned out not to be enough, they would pull back and try something else later.

What did the Bard say about such coarsening? Victor tried to remember his *Hamlet*. And he did—the line was *Custom hath made it in him a property of easiness*. Shakespeare was talking about gravedigging, but he might as well have meant war, the proximate cause of so much gravedigging. The Atlantean officers had that property of easiness now. They were veterans.

The redcoats had worked the transformation. And now—Victor hoped—they would pay for it.

General Cornwallis warded Hanover with a ring of forts. These weren't timber palisades, like the one that had tried to bar the way down the Blackwater. Their outwalls were of thick earth. A roundshot wouldn't de-

molish them, as it would smacking into wood or stone.
Instead, it would sink deep and disappear without doing
any harm.

Trenches and covered ways let English soldiers move
from one fort to another without exposing themselves
to Atlantean riflemen and cannoneers. The enemy was
as ready as anyone could reasonably be.

So was Victor Radcliff. He thought he was, anyhow. In Europe, mortars—guns firing explosive shells
at steep angles so they topped the walls of a fort and
came down inside—had given attackers at least a fighting chance when assaulting works. The Atlanteans had
a few iron and brass mortars smuggled in despite the
English blockade. They had a few more their smiths had
made, imitating the European models. And they had
quite a few improvised from hollowed-out tree trunks
bound with iron bands. Because a mortar's barrel was
so short, it didn't have to withstand anything like the
pressure an ordinary cannon did. The wooden mortars
seemed to perform about as well as their stubby metal
counterparts.

No one came out to warn Victor the English had
learned of his plans. He suddenly wished he would have
established a homing-pigeon connection with Hanover.
More than a century before, back in the days when Avalon was the wickedest city in the world, one of the pi-
ratical Radcliffes had done something like that. Victor
consoled himself by remembering that the pirate—not a
close kinsman of his—had gone down to defeat despite
his pigeons.

All the same ... Finding a scrap of paper, Victor
scribbled *Croydon* and *Pigeons* on it. Would he find
that scrap again? Would he remember what the cryptic
note meant if he did find it? Even if he did come across
it and did recall, would it matter? He couldn't know
now. All he could do was give later the best chance he
could.

Off went the detachment that would make the noisy

demonstration against the northern part of Cornwallis' fieldworks. Most of the ordinary guns went with it. It was also brave with banners, to fool the redcoats into thinking it held all the units whose standards waved above it.

Before long, the thunder of cannon fire and the fierce clatter of musketry—a sound much like rocks falling on sheets of iron—told him the demonstration was well under way. Some of those volleys from the muskets could only have come from perfectly trained and disciplined English regiments. If the redcoats hadn't taken the feint, they never would.

If they hadn't, a lot of his men would get shot soon. He was liable to get shot himself. He made himself shrug. He'd done the best he could.

"Come on, boys!" he called. "Hanover's got the prettiest women in Atlantis, people say. You'll see 'em for yourselves before long."

That won him a cheer, which he hushed as fast as he could. Fortunately, all the gunfire up ahead meant the redcoats weren't likely to notice it. He led the rest of the Atlantean army—including most of the mortar crews—south at a quick march. Their comrades had to keep the English troops in front of them busy for an hour, maybe a little longer. . . .

Several of his men had grown up in these parts. They pointed out paths that ran east toward the weak spot in the works he thought he'd found. He sent mounted scouts ahead of his main force. With luck, they would scoop up any redcoat pickets or loyalist Atlanteans who might dash east and warn the main English force the Atlantean Assembly's army was on the way.

Without luck . . . Victor refused to dwell on that. *We will be lucky*, he told himself, as if telling himself something like that would make it come true.

No horse pistols boomed ahead of the advancing Atlanteans. Victor took that for a good sign. His scouts hadn't found a reason to shoot at anyone. Nor had they run into English cavalry—or into Biddiscombe's Horsed Legion, if it was real and not a figment of some Englishman with a quill pen and an overactive imagination.

"Almost to the enemy's line, General," said one of the men who'd come out from Hanover to give Victor Radcliff what news he had.

"So we are," Victor agreed. One more swell of ground, maybe two, and they'd be able to see what awaited them. Just as much to the point, the English soldiers in Cornwallis' fieldworks would be able to see them. Victor raised his voice: "Form line of battle!"

The Atlanteans deployed as if they'd been doing it for years. Well, a lot of them had. Baron von Steuben would have been proud. At the last council of war, Victor had realized his officers were veterans. So were many of the troopers. He was surprised to hear them cheer as they swung from column to line. They hadn't done that since the early days of the war. He'd assumed they knew better. Maybe they had, too. But they also knew what taking Hanover back would be worth. It was worth a cheer, evidently.

"There!" The man from Hanover pointed.

"I see," Victor said quietly. The forts and trenches scarred what had been fields of wheat and barley. They were well sited; Victor had never known English military engineers not to take what advantage of the countryside they could. His men would have to charge up a gentle slope to reach the English positions. If those positions were packed with redcoats . . . Well, in that case this wouldn't be one of those lucky days—not for his side, anyhow.

A musket thundered in the trenches. He watched the cloud of gunpowder smoke rise. That was a signal shot, warning the Englishmen up and down the line that the Atlanteans were *here*.

"Mortarmen!" Victor shouted. Then he drew his fancy sword and flourished it over his head. "Come on!" he cried to the Atlanteans whose bayonets glittered in the sun. "Hanover is *ours*!"

Not if the redcoats had anything to say about it. They started shooting from the trench. Cannon boomed from a redoubt. Several Atlanteans went down as a round-shot plowed through their ranks.

The men who served the mortars did what they could. They dropped mortar bombs on the soldiers in the trenches and on the enemy artillerists. They didn't take long to find the range. Hurting the foe was a different story. Mortar bombs had to be the most irksome weapons artificers had ever almost perfected. Their fuses proved much more art than science. Some dropped harmlessly to the ground without exploding. Some burst high in the air, which was frightening and distracting but not even slightly dangerous. A few, and only a few, actually did what they were supposed to do.

One of the English cannon abruptly fell silent. That was good, for Victor's troopers were scrambling through the stakes and felled trees set out in front of the enemy trench line. Then another well-placed mortar bomb blew several English soldiers to bloody rags, right in front of the gap the Atlanteans had cleared. Whooping, Victor's men rushed forward.

Clearing trenches could be nasty, expensive work. Not this time—the redcoats here really were thin on the ground. Only a few of them fought when Victor's troopers bore down on them. More threw away their muskets and surrendered or ran from the Atlanteans.

"Keep moving!" Victor shouted. "On to Hanover!"

"On to Hanover!" his men roared.

English officers shouted, too, trying to get their men to form up in the open country behind their lines to slow the Atlantean advance. The redcoats were nothing if not game. But then Victor's mortar crews dropped several bombs on their lines. Stolid as the English soldiers were, they weren't used to that kind of bombardment. Along with sharp volleys from the Atlantean infantry, it disrupted them and kept them from putting up the kind of fight they might have.

Bit by bit, the Englishmen decided they'd had enough.

They retreated to the north and south, toward Croydon and New Hastings. Church bells chimed in Hanover. People streamed out into the streets to welcome the Atlantean army. Tears stung Victor's eyes. If he could hold the city, he'd done one of the things he had to do to win the war.

XVI

$\mathscr{H}$anover. Not the oldest city in Atlantis, but the largest and the richest. And now in Atlantean hands again! How Cornwallis had to be gnashing his teeth! How Thomas Paine would rejoice when word came to distant Terranova ... if the redcoats hadn't caught him and jailed him or hanged him by now.

Cornwallis, of course, wasn't the only one gnashing his teeth as the Army of the Atlantean Assembly got ready to winter in Hanover. Quite a few Atlanteans who lived in Hanover felt the same way. Some of them were loyalists down to their toes. Others had made a lot of money providing the redcoats with food and drink and complaisant women.

One of the locals, a fat taverner named Absalom Hogarth, looked apprehensively at Victor Radcliff. Victor sat in the study that had once belonged to his great-grandfather and was now owned by his merchant cousin, Erasmus. A dusty honker's skull stared at him with empty eye sockets. Along with the antique brass sextant and leather-bound folios, it had sat in that study for a long, long time.

Absalom Hogarth didn't seem to see any of them, or the inquiring mind that had accumulated them. Hogarth's gimlet-eyed gaze was focused on Victor as sharply as the sun's rays brought together in a point by a burning glass.

Victor had already talked to a lot of people like the tavern-keeper. They depressed him, but he had to do the job. Steepling his fingers, he spoke in tones as neutral as he could make them: "You look to have done pretty well for yourself while the English ruled the roost here."

"Well, General, as a matter of fact I did," Hogarth said.

That was a response out of the ordinary. "Tell me more," Victor urged, still neutral.

The taverner shrugged broad shoulders. Chins bobbed up and down. "Not much to tell. The redcoats were here. I saw to their wants. I would've done the same for you and yours. By God, General, I *will* do the same for you and yours."

He looked as if he expected Victor to pin a medal on him for his selfless patriotism. Maybe he did. More likely, years of dealing with—and, no doubt, bilking when he saw the chance—other people had made him a better than tolerable actor. "Let me make sure I understand you," Victor said slowly.

"Please." Absalom Hogarth all but radiated candor.

"You say you will treat us the same way as you treated the English."

"So I do. So I shall." The taverner sounded proud of himself.

"You say you would have treated us as well as you treated them had we held Hanover in their place."

"I not only say it, General, I mean it."

"Then you must be saying that who rules Atlantis, whether she be free in the hands of her own folk or groaning under the yoke of English tyranny, is a matter of complete and utter indifference to you."

"I do say that.... Wait!" Too late, Hogarth realized the trap had just dropped out from under him. He sent Victor an accusing stare. "You're trying to confuse me. Of course I'm an Atlantean patriot."

"Why 'of course,' Mr. Hogarth? Plenty of Atlanteans aren't. Plenty of Atlanteans in this very city aren't," Victor said. "I know for a fact that the so-called loyalists had little trouble recruiting their rabble here." Too many of the Atlanteans who fought for King George were anything but a rabble, and Victor knew it, however much he wished they were.

"None of them could recruit me," Hogarth said virtuously.

Victor eyed his bulk. "There, sir, I believe you. You are not made for marching, and every horse in Atlantis must also know relief that you did not choose the cavalryman's life."

"Heh," Hogarth said. Were his position stronger, he might have added a good deal more. He tried a jolly fat man's chuckle instead. It came off well, but perhaps not quite well enough. He must have sensed as much, for he sounded nervous when he asked, "Ah, what do you aim to do with me?"

"I've been wondering the same thing, Mr. Hogarth," Victor replied. "If I treated you as you deserve, you—or your heirs—would have scant cause to love me thereafter." He waited for that to sink in. By the way Hogarth gulped, it did. "On the other hand, you cannot expect me to love you for playing the weather vane."

"You have a way with words, you do." The taverner kept trying.

"Here is what I will do," Victor Radcliff said after more thought. "I will fine you a hundred pounds, payable in sterling, for giving aid and comfort—chiefly comfort, or it would go harder for you—to the enemy."

"A hundred pounds!" This time, Hogarth's yelp of anguish seemed altogether unrehearsed.

"A hundred pounds," Victor repeated. "Be thankful it's not more, for I doubt not you have it. After that, you shall do as you offered, and serve us in the fashion to which the redcoats became accustomed. And if I hear any complaints of cheating or gouging . . . But I won't . . . will I?"

"No, indeed, General. I am an honest man—not a, a political man, but an honest man," Hogarth said.

Victor Radcliff didn't laugh in his face, judging him humiliated enough. A world that held such oddities as cucumber slugs and flapjack turtles might also hold an honest taverner or two. It might, but Victor didn't think he'd ever set eyes on one before. He didn't think he was looking at one now, either.

"Just pay your assessment," he said wearily. "Pay your assessment, and try to remember you're an Atlantean, not a damned Englishman."

"I'll do it," Absalom Hogarth declared. And maybe he would, and maybe he wouldn't. Chances were he didn't know yet himself, or care.

There were plenty more in Hanover like Hogarth: men who were loyal, or at least obedient, to whoever'd paid them last. And there were others who'd unquestionably leaned toward King George and who didn't care to lean away. Some were silent; others spat defiance at him. They called themselves patriots. He hated the word in their mouths, but had trouble denying the justice of their using it.

Justice . . . The worst offenders (no, the worst enemies, for they thought they were doing the Lord's work, and in no way offending) had fled with Cornwallis' men, knowing what was likely to await them if they found themselves in Atlantean hands. Victor didn't hang anyone who remained behind. He did send a handful of men out of his lines with no more than the clothes on their backs. Whatever they held in Hanover he confiscated in the name of the Atlantean Assembly.

"I reckoned your horde a pack of thieves before you broke in," one of the men who was to be expelled told him. "You do nothing to make me believe myself mistaken."

"You love us not," Victor said. "If you war against us, do you doubt we shall love you not in return?"

"A Christian man loves his enemies," the loyalist returned.

"Well, then, we show our love as you showed yours," Victor said. He pointed north, in the direction of Croydon and, much closer, the nearest English lines. "Now get you gone."

"Maybe you should have been rougher," Blaise said after the last of the expulsions and confiscations. "Our men would like to see some of those scoundrels go to the gallows."

"Scoundrels, is it?" Victor managed a twisted smile. "Sometimes the words you know surprise me. Sometimes it's the ones you don't know."

"Did I go wrong? Is scoundrels not what they are?" Blaise asked seriously.

"Scoundrels is what they are," Victor assured him. "It's a fancy word for what they are, but not a wrong one."

"Scoundrels." Blaise said it again, with relish. "I like the sound. It makes them seem like dogs."

"Like dogs?" Victor was briefly puzzled. Then he realized what the Negro had to mean. "Oh, I see. Like spaniels."

"Those dogs, yes. With the floppy ears," Blaise said. Maybe he told the joke to a printer, or maybe someone else had the same idea, for a few days later a newspaper had a front-page woodcut of several prominent men leaving the city with sorrowful expressions and big spaniel ears. LET THE DOGS GO! it said beneath the cartoon. Custis Cawthorne showed more wit—and hired more talented engravers—but Custis was in Paris these days. Artistic or not, the woodcut struck Victor as effective. That would do.

As soon as spring came, the redcoats would try to recapture Hanover. Victor was as sure of that as he was of the Resurrection and the Second Coming, and it struck him as rather more immediately urgent than either of those. He set his men to digging trenches and throwing up earthworks to keep the enemy from getting past them.

His soldiers concealed their enthusiasm for all that cold-weather pick-and-shovel work very well. The most he ever heard any of them say in its favor was a remark from one tired Atlantean to his comrade as they both piled up an earthen rampart: "Maybe all this slaving means we ain't so likely to get shot."

"Maybe." The man's friend seemed unimpressed. "But it's near as bad as if we were, eh?"

"Well . . ." The first soldier weighed that. Then he nodded. "Afraid so," he agreed mournfully.

But neither of them stopped working. Victor didn't mind grumbling. William the Conqueror's soldiers must have grumbled, and Augustus Caesar's, and King David's as well. As long as they did what wanted doing, they could grumble all they pleased. Grumbling only turned dangerous when it started swallowing work.

English scouts rode down to see what Victor's men were up to. Atlantean riflemen fired at the scouts to make them keep their distance. Every so often, a rifleman would knock a scout out of the saddle. Then the others would stay farther away for a while.

Sometimes patriotic Atlanteans would sneak down from the north to tell Victor what Cornwallis' men were up to. Sometimes Victor wasn't so sure whether the Atlanteans who sneaked down from the north were patriotic or not. But he had soldiers from all over the northern settlements. *States*, he reminded himself. *They're states now. We're states now.* More often than not, he could find somebody who knew his would-be informants, either by name or by reputation.

He didn't seize the men he reckoned untrustworthy. No: he thanked them for what they told him, and then threw it on the mental rubbish heap. He sent them back to the north with as much misinformation as he could feed them. Maybe Cornwallis would realize Victor realized he was being fooled, or maybe not. The chance to confuse King George's commander seemed worth taking.

As spring approached, Victor wondered whether the enemy would let him hold Hanover undisturbed till summer. He wouldn't have done that himself, but Howe and Cornwallis had already tried several things he wouldn't have done himself. Some of them had worked, too, worse luck.

But then three reliable men in quick succession came down to warn him the redcoats were moving at last. He put men into his north-facing works. He also sent horsemen out beyond those works to shadow the English army.

Cornwallis, naturally, had his own spies. Just as patriots hurried south to warn the Atlantean army, so loyalists galloped north to tell the English what Victor Radcliff was up to. They must have given him a good report of Victor's field fortifications. Instead of trying to bull through them, Cornwallis slid around them to the west.

"He wants to fight it out in the open," Victor told a council of war. "He thinks his regulars will smash our Atlantean farmers."

The officers almost exploded with fury. He'd never heard so many variations on "We'll show him!" in his life. He got a stronger reaction than he really wanted, for he retained a solid respect for the men who filled the ranks of the English army. They were miserably paid, they were trained and handled harshly enough to make a hound turn and snap, but they were deadly dangerous with musket and bayonet to hand.

If he marched out of Hanover and lost a battle in the open field, he wasn't sure he could fall back into the city and hold on to it. And he wanted to keep Hanover—no, he had to. An Atlantean presence on the east coast was visible proof the United States of Atlantis were a going concern. Not only that: the harbor gave France a perfect place to land troops—if France ever got around to sending them.

And so Victor temporized: "First, let's see how mad we can drive him. Most of you remember how bad the mosquitoes were down in the south." He waited till the other officers nodded. Anyone who'd forgotten what the mosquitoes were like had to have an iron hide. Victor said, "I aim to make us into mosquitoes, the way we were when the war began."

"Sounds pretty, General," a captain said. "What's it mean?"

What would Cornwallis have done after a question like that? Had the luckless questioner flogged? Cornwallis was a good-natured man, as Victor had cause to know, but.... Most likely, the question would never be asked in an English council. Unlike rude colonials, English junior officers knew their place.

Being a rude colonial himself, Victor didn't drag the captain off to the whipping post. "I want to put riflemen or musketeers behind every tree and bush along the enemy's line of march. I want to capture every man of his who goes off into the bushes to answer nature's call. I want to shoot the animals hauling his cannon and supplies. Let's see how much he enjoys an enemy with whom he cannot close. Does that satisfy you, sir?"

"Reckon so," the captain answered. "But if that's how you aim to fight, seems a shame we wasted all that time on close-order drill."

"Wasted!" Baron von Steuben roared—actually, "Vasted!"

" 'Bout the size of it," the captain said—he didn't seem to care whom he antagonized. "*Form square!* and *By the right flank march!* and *Deploy from column to line!* and I don't know what all else. This here coming up sounds like a lot more fun."

Before the German officer could murder the man, Victor said, "We need both styles. And our men are better soldiers because they can fight like regulars as well as *guerrilleros*. Close-order drill improves discipline generally. Will you tell me I'm wrong?"

"Hayfoot! Strawfoot!" the captain said reminiscently. He spread his hands. "All right, General. You've got me there."

"Good." Victor smiled. "Now let's go get the damned redcoats."

The portly English sergeant was almost beside himself with rage when three grinning Atlanteans marched him into Victor Radcliff's presence. "Hello, Sergeant," Victor said. "What seems to be your trouble? Are you not relieved to be captured rather than killed?"

"Relieved, sir?" The word only infuriated the sergeant more. "I was taken with my trousers down! Is that any way to fight a war?"

"Evidently," Victor answered.

The Atlanteans went from grinning to laughing out loud. "You should've seen him jump when old Isaiah here went and yelled, 'Hands up or we'll blow your arsehole off!'" one of them said.

Another—Isaiah, by the way he made as if to bow—added, "He didn't just jump, neither. He went and shat them fancy breeches. Had to try and clean 'em off with some leaves he tore off a bush."

"General!" the English sergeant cried piteously. For how many years had he made his living tormenting the redcoats luckless enough to serve under him? And a good living it had been, too, judging by that bulging belly. But now others were giving it to him, and he was finding he didn't like it so well.

"If you sniff, General, you can still smell him," Isaiah said. "He let go, all right—damned if he didn't."

"That will be enough of that," Victor said. "Had his men taken you, you wouldn't want them gloating afterwards."

"God bless you, sir," the sergeant said, knuckling his forelock. "You're a gentleman, sir, you are, a merciful gentleman."

"Huh." The third Atlantean spoke up. "A great tun like him don't deserve nobody's mercy. He's the kind who loots and murders and takes the women upstairs whether they want to go or not."

Victor thought the soldier had made a shrewd guess. The sergeant turned the color of paste, which said a lot about how shrewd it was. "I don't know anything about any of that," he said, but he didn't sound persuasive.

"Maybe so. Then again, maybe not," Victor said. The Englishman went paler yet; Victor hadn't thought he could. But if he was sweating like that, why not sweat something out of him? "I'm sure the sergeant does know where General Cornwallis is going and what he intends doing once he gets there."

Not only did the sergeant know, he was pathetically eager to tell. He sang like a nightingale. Victor had heard the birds in England; while European creatures like the wild hog and the rat flourished in Atlantis, all efforts to naturalize the nightingale had failed.

After the Englishman spewed out everything he knew, the Atlantean troopers took him away. "He runs on at both ends, seems like," Isaiah remarked.

By then, more confident he wouldn't be murdered out of hand, the sergeant had regained some of his spirit. "If you were my man, I'd cane you for speaking of me so," he said gruffly.

Isaiah gave him a look as cold as the blocks of ice that sometimes drifted down near North Cape in winter. "Any man lays a finger on me without my leave—a finger, mind you, let alone a cane—I'll gutshoot him. And you, your God-damned Sergeantship, sir, you've got a devil of a lot of gut to shoot."

Victor smiled as the sergeant, suddenly silenced again, trudged away with his captors. Anyone who thought he could use an Atlantean as he used an Englishman was liable to get a rude surprise. This underofficer had got a whole string of them.

And yet, quite a few Englishmen found they liked Atlantean ways once they got used to them. Maybe the sergeant would be one of those. He'd make a good drill-master . . . as long as he left his cane behind.

Redwood Hill must have held the name for a long time. No redwoods grew on it now, or for miles around. It was crowned by a rank tangle of second growth. Ferns and bushes and saplings, some Atlantis' native productions and others imported from Europe or Terranova, warred for space and sunlight.

Redwood Hill was also crowned by an English observation post. An alert man with a spyglass up there could see for a long way. He could easily keep an army under observation.

He might have much more trouble spotting greencoats armed with rifles as one by one they slipped through the second growth toward him. Victor hoped that would be so, and set about finding out empirically. Rifles banged, up near the hilltop. Before long, the greencoats sent a messenger down to Victor to report that Redwood Hill now lay in Atlantean hands. "We've even got the bugger's spyglass," the man reported.

"Capital!" Victor said. The art of grinding lenses was further advanced in England than in Atlantis. "Now we shall spy upon Cornwallis, not conversely."

Cornwallis must have foreseen that possibility, too. It pleased him less than it did Victor Radcliff. He promptly despatched a good-sized force of English regulars to dislodge the Atlanteans from the hilltop. He also sent a small troop of loyalist riflemen to match wits and weapons with the sharpshooters in green.

When the Atlanteans found themselves hard-pressed to hold the crest of Redwood Hill, Victor sent more men forward. They drove the redcoats down the western slope of the hill ... until Cornwallis fed more Englishmen into the fight.

That meant Victor had to reinforce again or yield the crest. After he'd already done so much fighting for it, he wasn't willing to let that happen. And, plainly, the English commander wasn't willing to let him keep it.

"I did not purpose fighting our battle here," he told Blaise. "Nor do I believe Cornwallis purposed any such thing. But this fight has taken on a life of its own."

"It is war. It has its own purposes." The Negro spoke as if war were a live thing, and one at least as much in control of its own destiny as either of the opposing generals. Well, maybe he wasn't so far wrong. He finished, "If it wants a fight at Redwood Hill, a fight at Redwood Hill there shall be."

Victor couldn't contradict him. A fight at Redwood

Hill there was: a most cursed irregular fight, mostly because of the terrain. The Atlanteans were used to fighting from cover whenever they got the chance. They'd harried the redcoats' looping march down from the north in just that way.

On overgrown Redwood Hill, not even the English regulars or their officers could dream of advancing in neatly dressed ranks. They made their way forward as best they could. Some came up the narrow paths that led to the top of the hill. They could move quickly, but they also exposed themselves to a galling fire from the Atlanteans lurking in the undergrowth. Others pushed through the bushes, fighting Atlantean-style themselves. That might not have been what they were used to, but they managed. Or maybe they just had a strong disinclination to retreat. It amounted to the same thing either way: a harder fight than Victor would have looked for.

He also would have guessed that the Englishmen's red uniform jackets made them better targets. But when he inquired of a man who came back from the crest with a minor wound, the Atlantean shook his head. "Don't hardly seem to matter. What with the ferns and the shrubs and suchlike, and what with the powder smoke, them bastards spy us about as quick as we set eyes on them." He held up his right hand, which was missing the last joint of the fourth finger. "I never did see the English son of a bitch who done gave me this."

"Go get it bandaged up," Victor said, and then, to one of his artillerists, "Can we get our guns up to the top of the hill?"

"Well, General, we can try," that worthy answered. "I'm not so sure how much good it'll do, though. Doesn't seem like anybody's all drawn up in rows for us to shoot at, does it?"

"No," Victor answered. "But send a fieldpiece up there anyhow, if you'd be so kind. Try to command the biggest path coming up from the west. If Cornwallis does seek to rush our position, that's how he'll essay it."

The artillerist sketched a salute. "If that's what you

want, General, that's what you'll get. Warm work, it's liable to be, but what can you do?" He gave his own orders to his crew. They limbered up their four-pounder and started for the crest.

Victor hoped he hadn't sent them off to be killed. When a soldier talked about warm work, he commonly meant he didn't think he'd come back from it. But even one gun at the top of Redwood Hill might mean the difference between victory and defeat. Sometimes a general had to move the pieces across the board knowing they might be taken.

But the analogy with chess broke down too soon. A taken chess piece went into the box to wait for the next game, where it would start out fine. A dead soldier sprawled in the dirt, waiting for a raven to flutter down and peck out his eyes. A wounded soldier, especially one hurt worse than the fellow with whom he'd talked not long before, went screaming back to the surgeons, who might spare him a swallow of whiskey and a leather strap to bite on before they started carving. He might fight again if he was lucky (unlucky?), but he would never be the same afterwards.

And yet you would assuredly lose if you didn't place your men where some of them would get hurt or killed. If you didn't care for that unhappy certainty ... you should never have tried the general's trade in the first place.

"Rather too late to worry about that," Victor muttered.

"Worry about what?" Blaise asked—the mutter hadn't been low enough.

"About whether this cup will pass from me," Victor said. "It won't."

"Cup?" Blaise briefly looked blank. Then his face cleared. "Oh. The Bible." He was Christian enough to observe the forms of the majority's religion. How much he truly believed, Victor often wondered. But that was between Blaise and his God, if any—not for anybody else.

He had more urgent things to worry about than Blaise's relationship to his God, too. The rattle of musketry from the top of Redwood Hill grew fiercer and fiercer. That alarmed Victor, for he knew the redcoats could load and fire faster than his men. And then his little four-pounder boomed: once, twice. After the second shot, it fell silent.

Why? Victor wondered—and worried. Were all the gunners dead on the field? The fight went on. It sounded as ferocious as ever. Had the fieldpiece knocked in the head of an enemy column advancing up that path from the west? Or had something else, something incalculable from back here, happened instead?

Victor decided he had to know. He swung up onto his horse. "I'm riding up to the hilltop," he told Blaise.

"You don't want to stop a bullet," the Negro observed.

"Who does?" Victor said.

Blaise exhaled sharply. "Not what I meant. Atlantis don't—doesn't—want you to stop a bullet."

"Atlantis doesn't want me to lose this battle, either, not when I might win it by giving orders without delay from messengers rushing back and forth," Victor replied. He started to trot off toward the hill.

"Wait!" Blaise called. Victor reined in. His not-quite-aide never sounded so imperious without good cause. Blaise mounted and came after him. "If you're going to play the fool, you should have some other fool beside you."

"Honored." Victor tipped his tricorn.

"Honor," Blaise said. "White men's madness." They'd gone round that barn before. Instead of starting around it again, Victor urged his horse forward with the reins and the pressure of his knees. Blaise followed. His elbows flapped as he rode. He bobbed up and down far more than a smooth horseman would have. All that might—and probably did—make better riders look down their noses at him. It didn't stop him getting from hither to yon, or even slow him much.

Wounded men staggered and limped down the east side of Redwood Hill, bound for the surgeons. Litter-bearers carried moaning soldiers too badly hurt to get down by themselves. One of the walking wounded waved to Victor. "You should've seen 'em, General!" he called.

"Seen whom? Seen them doing what?" Victor asked. But by then his horse had carried him past the injured Atlantean. He didn't want to slow down, even to find out more about *them*, whoever *they* were.

Blaise understood, as Blaise commonly did. "You'll know soon enough, one way or the other," he said. Victor nodded.

Redwood Hill didn't look like much till you rode up it. Atlantean soldiers trudging up the path toward the crest didn't seem sorry to stop for a moment and wave to their general as he went by. "Will we lick 'em?" a man asked.

"Of course we will," Victor answered, hoping he was right. But a general who let his men see he had doubts didn't deserve his epaulets. If a general doubted, how could ordinary soldiers do anything else? And soldiers who doubted weren't men who would stand fast when a general most needed them to. A general had to seem confident, even—especially—when he wasn't.

"We still hold the crest." Blaise pointed to the line of greencoats ahead. They reloaded and fired at the enemy as fast as they could.

"We do." Victor fought to keep surprise from his voice, too. He wanted the words to convey that he'd been sure of it all along.

He dismounted before reaching the crest. After tying his horse to a sapling on the reverse slope, he finished the climb on foot. No point to giving the enemy a large target that shouted *Here's the Atlantean general!* His gaudy officer's uniform would take care of that well enough, or maybe too well.

The field gun stood ready and waiting. Most of its crew still stood, too. It had done what Victor hoped, not

what he feared. Those two rounds he'd heard, loaded
with canister, had torn the heart out of an English rush
toward the crest. Dead and wounded redcoats lay in
heaps in front of the gun, but they'd never reached it.

"Right warm work it was, General," said the artilleryman in charge of the piece.

"I see," Victor said. He heard, too. Few sounds raised
more sorrow and pity than the cries of men who'd been
hurt. Aristotle called sorrow and pity the essence of
tragedy. He must have seen his share of battlefields, too.
Even in the days before villainous saltpeter, they were
no place for the faint of heart.

A musket ball cracked past his head. He and the gun-
ner both gave it an automatic genuflection. They grinned
sheepishly at each other as they straightened. Even the
bravest man's flesh was less heroic than he might wish it.

Not many unwounded Englishmen and loyalists were
visible. If nothing else did, their failed charge taught
them not to show themselves, not on this field. And
black-powder smoke and the dust both sides had kicked
up helped mask everyone's movements.

A lieutenant held a rifle that, with its bayonet, was
almost as long as he was tall. He sketched a salute. Victor returned it. At least half the time, nobody gave him
proper military courtesy. A sketched salute seemed ever
so much better than none. "How do we fare?" Victor
enquired.

"Well, General, we're still here on the crest. With a
spot of luck, the redcoats won't be able to take it away
from us."

"Luck?" Victor didn't like the word. "We need to
hold, come what may."

"Sure enough. But I won't turn luck down, either," the
rifleman said. "That field gun got to the top just at the
right time, fry me for an oil thrush if it didn't. Knocked
the redcoats' charge clear down to the bottom of the
hill again. If it ran late, we might be down at the bottom
ourselves, over on the other side." He jerked a thumb
back toward the east.

"So we might," Victor said uncomfortably. And if they were, Cornwallis would hurl the English regulars at them again, driving them in the direction of Hanover—or maybe driving them away from Atlantis' leading city so the Union Jack could fly there once more. Amazing to think how much a couple of rounds of canister could do.

One of these days, historians would write blow-by-blow accounts of the grand and furious Battle of Redwood Hill. Would the learned scholars and soldiers give the canister its due? Or would it fade into the general chaos of battle? Victor had been through several battles against the French Atlanteans and the French that the historians had got their hands on afterwards. The descriptions of the fights he'd read bore precious little resemblance to the fights he thought he remembered.

Which meant . . . what, exactly? Even now, Victor wasn't sure. Maybe the men who'd done their best to rival Thucydides and Tacitus knew better than he did. They'd questioned men from both sides; some of them had got access to French and English and even Atlantean officers' papers—including his own. But if what they wrote differed from his memories, he didn't have to take them seriously. He didn't intend to, either.

Three British fieldpieces unlimbered near the base of Redwood Hill. The gunners aimed them with fussy precision. Victor had never seen a muzzle pointed up so high, not even at the siege of Nouveau Redon. What he would have done for some mortars in his baggage train then! English and Atlantean long guns had tried to reach the French fortress, and hadn't had much luck. Now . . . "They're going to try to blow us off the crest," the lieutenant of riflemen said.

"So they are," Victor agreed. "The next interesting question is, can they do it?" He eyed the cannon apprehensively. Somehow, a gun's bore always seemed two or three times as wide when it pointed straight at you. "They don't look to have any mortars close by, anyhow, for which I'm duly grateful. I was just thinking about that."

"Mm—yes," the younger officer said. "I wouldn't want those nasty bursting shells coming down on my head, and that's a fact." He paused thoughtfully. "Of course, like as not the fusing'd leave somewhat to be desired."

Victor Radcliff only grunted in response to that. Atlantis' mortars, improvised and otherwise, had done yeoman duty in breaking the English lines outside of Hanover. But, as the lieutenant said, they would have done even more had the gunners been better able to control when the shells detonated. Artillerymen all over the world wrestled with the problem, none with much success.

The field guns thundered. Victor watched roundshot speed toward him. Then he watched the cannon balls fall short, smashing through the undergrowth atop Redwood Hill till they came to rest. He hoped they smashed through some redcoats, too.

One of the gunners harangued his comrades. They limbered up; their teams started hauling the guns up the path toward the crest. "Oh, no, they don't!" the lieutenant of riflemen exclaimed. "We'll murder the lot of them if they get much closer." He sketched another salute and hurried off to instruct his sharpshooters.

Even before the riflemen opened up on the English fieldpieces, that Atlantean four-pounder started throwing roundshot at them. An iron ball smashed the wheel of a field gun's carriage. *That* one wouldn't move up any farther.

Then the riflemen did go to work. They couldn't fire nearly so fast as musketeers. But, unlike musketeers, they had some hope of hitting what they aimed at out to three or four hundred yards. Several English gunners went down, one after another. Their friends dove into the bushes to keep from meeting the same fate. None of the field guns got close enough to pound the crest of Redwood Hill.

As the sun sank behind his troopers, Cornwallis gave

up the assault. He sent a man to Victor under flag of truce, asking leave to gather his wounded and withdraw. Victor gave it. Glumly, the Englishman went back down the hill. He could see as well as Victor that the Atlanteans would hold on to Hanover.

XVII

St. Denis was a small coastal town south of Cosquer, in what had been French Atlantis. Cosquer was an important place, and had been for three hundred years. St. Denis wasn't, and never had been. A few fishing boats went in and out. Every once in a while, a merchantman would put in at its rickety quays—as often as not, a badly navigated merchantman that had been bound for somewhere else.

Victor didn't know what made some towns thrive and others falter. Down in Spanish Atlantis, farther south yet, Gernika flourished ... as much as any town in lackadaisical Spanish Atlantis flourished, anyhow. Not far away, tiny St. Augustine, also on the coast, drowsed under the semitropical sun. Yes, Gernika was older, but so what? New Hastings was older than Hanover, too, but Hanover had been the biggest, most bustling town in English Atlantis—in all of Atlantis—for a long time.

Now St. Denis was about to reappear in the history books, or at least in the footnotes. Victor looked down at the note on his desk (well, Erasmus Radcliff's desk, but Victor was using it these days).

That note still said the same thing it had when he first opened it a few minutes earlier. He read it again, just to make sure. French men-of-war and transports had evaded the Royal Navy and disgorged an army at St. Denis. He'd hoped that army would come to Hanover. It was in Atlantis, but....

It was now moving north up the Atlantean coast. Its commander hoped to effect a meeting with the Atlanteans in the not too indefinite future.

"I will be damned," Victor murmured, reading the missive from St. Denis yet again. It still hadn't changed—not a single word of it.

The last time French troops landed in Atlantis, Victor and Cornwallis (then major and lieutenant-colonel, respectively, neither having yet acquired the exalted rank of general) beat them in a series of alarmingly close battles and forced the surrender of those who survived. Now Radcliff would be working with the French commander, whatever sort of officer this Marquis de la Fayette turned out to be, against the man who'd been his friend and ally in the last war.

Which proved ... what, exactly? Only that life could turn bloody peculiar sometimes.

"Oh, yes," Victor muttered. "As if I didn't already know that."

He got to his feet and stretched. Something in his back made a noise like the cork exploding from a bottle of sparkling wine. He blinked, then slowly smiled; whatever'd happened in there, he felt better because of it.

He walked over and picked up the big honker skull William Radcliff had acquired back in the last century. "Alas, poor Yorick ..." he began, holding it in the palm of his left hand.

Blaise came in. Confronted with the spectacle of the commander of the Atlantean army spouting Shakespeare at the cranium of a long-defunct bird, the Negro could hardly have been blamed for beating a hasty retreat. But Blaise was a tough fellow. Giving the honker skull no more than a raised eyebrow, he addressed Victor as if the latter had never heard of *Hamlet*: "Are the Frenchmen really and truly throwing in with us?"

"They are," Victor answered automatically. Only then did he set down the skull and send Blaise a startled stare. "How did you know about that, by God? The letter telling me of it only came just now." He pointed to the paper still sitting on the desk.

"No doubt." Blaise might have been innocence personified, if innocence came with slightly bloodshot eyes. He explained them, and himself: "But you see, General, I've been drinking with the lads who brought it to you, and they blabbed somewhat—or maybe a bit more than somewhat."

"Oh." Victor could see what would spring from that. "You're telling me all of Hanover will know of it by this o'clock tomorrow, and Cornwallis will know of it by this o'clock day after tomorrow."

"Not me." Blaise shook his head. "I don't need to tell you any such thing, since you already know it as well as I do."

Victor sighed. He wanted to start talking to the honker skull again. There was at least some hope it wouldn't turn around and repeat gossip as fast as it got it. Instead, he looked up toward the heavens and the God he hopefully believed in. "Dear Lord, will we ever be able to do anything or even plan anything without letting our foes learn of it almost before we do?"

"If ever you want to get ahead of the English," Blaise said, "go tell all and sundry you're about to do this, make as if you're about to do this, but then at the last moment, without telling anyone but the few who needs must know, turn about and do *that* instead. It will be their ruination. Ruination." He smiled as he repeated the word. "I do fancy the sound of it."

"Ruination." Victor also savored the word. And he savored the conception that had led up to it. "Maybe I should give you my epaulets. Or maybe I should just remember never to let the fox guard the chicken coop."

"You mean people need to remember things like that?" Blaise said.

"Well, remembering them is better than forgetting them, wouldn't you say?" Victor replied.

"It might be," Blaise allowed. "Yes, as a matter of fact it just might be."

The French army's rapid progress up the coast stopped just north of Cosquer. Cornwallis' regulars in Freetown—and the depressingly large number of loyalist troops the redcoats recruited in those parts—skirmished with the Frenchmen, fell back a mile or so, and then skirmished again.

They do not fight as regulars properly should fight, the brash young nobleman commanding the French force complained in his next letter to Victor. *It is to be expected that regular troops should form line of battle in open country and volley at one another until one side establishes its superiority, which the bayonet charge will then enforce. But the enemy forces shoot from behind trees and stones and fences, as if they were so many cowardly savages.*

"Oh, dear," Victor said on reading that: a comment which worked on several levels. The redcoats had learned too much from fighting his Atlanteans, and they and their loyalists were now giving the previously uninstructed French some unpleasant lessons. And France, by all appearances, had learned very little. She'd sent another brave young seigneur across the Atlantic to lead her army during the last war. Marquis Montcalm-Gozon ended up dead despite his dash and courage. Victor had to hope the same wouldn't happen to this fellow.

He also had to flog his faltering French to respond in writing. As well wish for the moon as expect a French nobleman to read English. His pen scratched across the sheet of rather coarse paper: coarse, yes, but made in Atlantis. *My dear Marquis de la Fayette: I regret that the redcoats' tactics have disconcerted you. Perhaps the arrival of an Atlantean officer of suitable rank to instruct your soldiers might improve the situation. Yours faithfully—Victor Radcliff, general commanding.*

Off his response went, by the fastest fishing schooner then in Hanover harbor. He wished he could send it by semaphore or heliograph tower. Unfortunately, the enemy controlled most of the territory that lay between himself and the French. He had to entrust the communication to wind and wave.

In due course, and not a great deal later than he'd hoped, he got his reply. It was, if nothing else, short and to the point. *My dear General Radcliff*, de la Fayette wrote, *I look forward to your joining us at your earliest convenience. Your most obedient servant . . .*

Staring, Victor said, "Where the devil did he get that notion?"

"What is the trouble now?" Blaise asked.

"I told the French general some officer of—I think I said something like 'the right rank'—would come and show his regulars how to fight in Atlantis," Victor answered. "And he thinks I meant I'd go myself!" He laughed at the absurdity.

To his surprise, Blaise didn't. "Maybe you should. If the French know the man they fight beside, it could be that they will fight better because of it. I mean truly know, you understand."

"But—" Victor found himself spluttering. "But—" He finally managed to put his main objection into words: "What if Cornwallis tries to take Hanover away from us again?"

"Not likely, not after he turned away when we beat him at Redwood Hill," Blaise answered calmly. "And even if he does, do you think the army can fight only if it has you to tell it how to go about things?"

Part of Victor thought exactly that. He knew better than to admit it, though. If the cause of liberty had an indispensable man, was liberty what the Atlantean Assembly was really fighting for? Or would the settlements—now styled states—merely be exchanging one master for another?

Slowly, Victor said, "When you put it that way . . ."

"I do," Blaise said. "Besides, don't you want to see

with your own eyes what these French are like, what they can do?"

"I saw too much of that in the last war. This time, at least, whatever they can do, they won't be trying to do it to me." Victor wagged a finger at Blaise. "I think you're telling me I should go because you want to get down that way yourself."

"Who? Me?" Butter would have stayed solid forever in the Negro's mouth. "I don't know what you're talking about, General."

"Like fun you don't," Victor said. "But all right. We'll see what we can do to get this de la Fayette's soldiers moving again, you and I."

"Good," Blaise said equably. Victor hoped it would be.

A brisk breeze from the north wafted the *Rosebud* out of Hanover harbor, bound for Cosquer or somewhere not far north. The schooner had been a big fishing boat before war came to Atlantis. Now she mounted a dozen eight-pounders: plenty for taking unarmed merchantmen, but not nearly enough to stand against even a small English frigate.

Victor Radcliff knew he came from a line that had gone to sea for generation after generation. He himself, however, made a most indifferent sailor. But he outdid Blaise. He'd seen before that the Negro was unhappy aboard ship. Setting a hand on Blaise's shoulder, he said, "Cheer up, friend. You won't end up on the auction block after we disembark."

Blaise gave back a sheepish smile. "You pinned it down, General; that you did. I know *here* that this is no slaver." He tapped his forehead. But then, touching his belly and his crotch in turn, he added, "*Here* and *here*, though, I'm not so sure. I doubt that that'd make sense to someone who's never lain in chains, but there it is."

"No, I've never done that," Victor admitted. He said nothing about the profit various offshoots of the Radcliff and Radcliffe clans had made from the slave trade.

Blaise was bound to know already; still, casting it in his face would be rude. Instead, Victor said, "Maybe I can imagine a little of what you went through."

"Maybe." By the way Blaise said it, he thought Victor was talking through his hat. Since he had the experience and Victor didn't, he might well have been right.

Instead of arguing with him, Victor waited upon the *Rosebud*'s skipper, a potbellied Hanover man named Randolph Welles. "What do we do if the Royal Navy calls on us to stop and be boarded?"

"Well, now, General, that depends." Welles' pipe sent up smoke signals. "If we can run, why, run we shall—I promise you that. But if the choice is between letting them board and getting blown out of the water ... All things considered, I'd sooner go on living." He spread his hands, as if to say there was no accounting for taste.

"I see," Victor said. "And who decides whether we shall run or yield?"

"I do," Randolph Welles snapped. Till that moment, Victor had thought him mild-mannered. Now he discovered he'd labored under a misapprehension. Welles went on, "On land you may do as you please, sir—that is your province. But I am captain of the *Rosebud*, General, no one else—she assuredly is *my* province. Let there be no misunderstandings on that score. They could cause unpleasantness: perhaps even worse."

"All right." Victor wasn't sure it was. If Welles wanted to surrender when that didn't look like a good idea to him ... But what could he do about it? If the *Rosebud*'s sailors seemed inclined to obey their skipper, precious little. Victor's best hope then might be diving over the rail and hoping he could swim to shore. He wasn't much of a swimmer. He could barely see the shore. If he didn't want the English to hang him, though, what other choice had he?

Generals borrowed a lot of trouble. Any commander worth having needed to worry about how he'd respond if the enemy did this, that, or the other thing. Many of the things a general could come up with were wildly unlikely. *Most* of the things a general could come up with never happened. But the day he didn't worry about them would be the day one came true.

So it proved aboard the *Rosebud*. Victor worried about what might happen if Royal Navy vessels came after the schooner. She saw never a one as she sailed south past New Hastings and Freetown. She did see a few fishing boats, all of them smaller and slower than she was. She had favorable winds and a mild sea. A day sooner than Victor expected her to, she slid into the harbor at Cosquer.

Even Blaise said, "Well, that wasn't *too* bad." Knowing how he felt about ships, Victor didn't think he could come out with higher praise than that. From his lips, even so much seemed extravagant.

Cosquer had started as a specifically Breton town. You could still hear Breton in these parts if you knew which fishermen's taverns, which sailmakers' shops, which salt-sellers' establishments, to visit. You could also hear English; that had been true long before France lost its Atlantean possessions. But you were most likely to hear French.

And so Victor was not surprised to find himself hailed in that language: *"Monsieur le Général?"*

"I am General Radcliff, yes," he replied, also in French.

"Excellent," said the tall, lean man standing on the pier. "I have the honor to be Captain Luc Froissart, aide-de-camp to the Marquis de la Fayette. Horses await you and your own aide, who would be . . . ?"

Victor gestured. "Here is Sergeant Blaise Black, who has been my man of affairs since long before this war began."

Captain Froissart had bushy eyebrows. They jumped when he got a good look at Blaise's dark, impassive face. "How most extremely interesting!" he said. "I am sure the marquis will be delighted to acquaint himself with both of you. Is it that the sergeant speaks and comprehends French?"

"Me? Not a word of your language do I speak or comprehend," Blaise replied—in French.

Froissart blinked, then threw back his head and laughed. "*Eh bien*, Sergeant, it seems you are one on whom we shall have to keep an eye."

"You white people have been saying that for as long as I was able to understand your speech," Blaise said. "Nevertheless, saying is easier than doing, or I should never have escaped from slavery." He eyed Froissart with a raised eyebrow. "The fellow who bought me when I first came to Atlantis was a Frenchman."

Victor waited to see how Froissart would take that. "This fellow, he was not me," the French officer said. "He was not the marquis, either, or any of the soldiers who have come to Atlantis from *la belle France*. Please bear it in mind, Sergeant."

It was Blaise's turn to measure, to consider. "Well, I can probably do that," he said at last.

He might have angered or affronted Froissart if not for his earlier gibe. As things were, de la Fayette's aide-de-camp nodded judiciously. "Good enough. And can you also ride a horse?"

"How much you demand of me." Blaise sounded as petulant as a seventeen-year-old girl dreamt of being.

"You?" Victor exclaimed in mock dudgeon. "He doesn't even ask if I can ride."

Captain Froissart made a small production of charging his pipe and flicking at a flint-and-steel lighter till it gave forth with enough sparks to ignite the pipe-weed in the bowl. After puffing a couple of times and ensuring that the pipe would stay lit, the Frenchman spoke in philosophical tones: "They warned me At-lanteans were . . . different. I see they knew what they were talking about."

Who were *they*? Victor almost asked. In the end, though, he decided he'd rather not know. All that mattered was that the French were on Atlantean soil, and on Atlantis' side. As long as he kept that firmly in mind, he could worry about everything else later.

* * *

When camped, French regulars pitched their tents with geometrical exactitude. The perfect rows of canvas might have been part of a formal garden: the effect was pleasing and formidable at the same time.

The effect the Marquis de la Fayette had on Victor Radcliff was almost the same. De la Fayette was both younger and better trained than Victor had expected. He also manifested far more enthusiasm for the Atlantean cause than Victor had looked for.

"It is not just a matter of giving England a finger in the eye, pleasant though that may be," de la Fayette declared. "But the Proclamation of Liberty? Oh, my dear sir!" He bunched the fingertips of his right hand together and kissed them—he was a Frenchman, all right. "This document . . . How shall I say it? This document shall live on as a milestone in the history of the world."

The praise sounded even more impressive in French, perhaps, than it would have in English. The marquis did speak English after a fashion, but both Victor and Blaise were more fluent in French. And, since several of the French officers had only their native tongue, they were happy not to have to try to learn Atlantis' dominant language on the fly.

"You gentlemen certainly have, ah, made yourselves at home here," Victor remarked.

"My dear sir!" de la Fayette said again. "It is from time to time necessary to fight a war. No denying that, however great a pity it may be. Still, it is *not* necessary to make oneself unduly uncomfortable while fighting it, eh?"

"So it would seem," Victor said, and left it there.

His allies lived under canvas: they were, as de la Fayette said, at war. But they'd brought over a variety of light, ingenious folding furniture—not just chairs, tables, and writing desks, but also bed frames and wickerwork chests of drawers—that let them feel as if they were back in their estates on the Loire or the Seine.

And they'd brought over some vintages finer than any

Victor had ever tasted, and some brandies that taught him what brandy ought to be. They supplemented those with beer and ale and spirits taken from the countryside. And their chef . . . Blaise put it best when he said, "It's a wonder you gentlemen don't all weigh four hundred pounds. You've got some of the best victuals I ever tasted."

"You do," Victor agreed; he was thinking about letting his belt out a notch.

"*Merci,*" the marquis said, smiling—he was an affable young man, no doubt about it. "I shall pass your praise on to Henri, who will be grateful for it." Henri was the genius who did things to poultry and beef the likes of which no Atlantean cook had ever imagined.

Captain Froissart said, "You will remember, my friends, that we get our exercise come what may." His colleagues grinned and leered and nodded.

Victor managed a smile himself. Most of the exercise the French officers got was of the horizontal variety. They hadn't been in Atlantis long, but they'd acquired mistresses or companions or whatever the word was. The girls were all uncommonly pretty. Quite a few of them, whatever they were to be called, had dark skins.

Victor wondered what Blaise would have to say about that. Blaise took it better than he'd expected. "If you sleep with an officer, you get presents you don't see from anybody else," he observed. "You hear things you don't hear from other folk, too. You do all right for yourself afterwards, I bet."

"I wouldn't be surprised," Victor said, and left it there.

Knowing the country between Cosquer and Freetown better than the newly come French—he'd fought against Montcalm-Gozon and Roland Kersauzon hereabouts in the last war—Victor accompanied the Marquis de la Fayette on reconnaissance rides to probe the English positions.

And, more than once, he accompanied the marquis

on very rapid returns to the French army's positions. The redcoats also seemed to know the countryside quite well. Some of the Atlanteans who fought on King George's side knew it even better. Radcliff and de la Fayette barely escaped a couple of ambuscades.

"Nothing like being shot at when they miss, *n'est-ce pas?*" de la Fayette said after some English musket balls missed by not nearly enough.

"It is an improvement on getting hit," Victor agreed. "Past that, I don't think it has a great deal to recommend it."

By then, they were almost back to the French commander's tent. "Come in and take some brandy with me," de la Fayette said. "You will see how much better it tastes now than it would have on an ordinary day when nothing interesting happened."

"I don't know about that, your Excellency, but I'll gladly make the experiment," Victor said.

One tumbler of brandy became two, and then three. Victor wasn't sure whether the bottled lightning tasted better than it would have on an ordinary day. He wasn't sure it got him any more drunk than it would have on an ordinary day, either. Well before he finished that third tumblerful, he was sure it didn't get him any *less* drunk.

The marquis seemed convinced he'd proved his point. As he refilled his own tumbler, he solemnly declared, "There is also something else that improves after one is fired upon to no effect."

"Oh?" Victor responded with a certain intensity of his own. "And what might that be?"

De la Fayette got a fit of the giggles. "It might be any number of things, my friend. But what it is . . . If you will excuse me for a few seconds . . ." He hurried out of the tent without waiting to find out whether Victor would excuse him or not. That affronted Victor, which only went to show he'd had a good deal to drink himself—not that he thought of it in those terms at that moment.

The marquis took longer to return than he'd promised. That didn't bother Victor Radcliff, who applied himself to the brandy with a dedication suited to—he supposed—celebrating a narrow escape.

Then de la Fayette did return—with his companion, a charming and intelligent (and Victor had seen that she was both) young mulatto woman named Marie. And with the two of them came another pretty girl, perhaps two shades darker than Marie. The marquis introduced her as Louise.

"Enchanted, *Mademoiselle*," Victor said, bowing over her hand with slow, exaggerated—well, drunken—courtesy.

Louise started giggling then. So did Marie. As far as Victor knew, neither one of them had been into the brandy bottle. The Marquis de la Fayette, who had, laughed so hard he almost fell over. Victor stared at him in owlish indignation. Slowly, de la Fayette straightened. Even more slowly, his laughter faded. He was as sober as an inebriated judge when he pointed to Louise and said, "Does she suit you, Victor?"

"Eh? What's that you say?" Victor wondered if his ears were working the way they were supposed to.

"Does she suit you?" De la Fayette spoke slowly and distinctly, as if to an idiot child. But he was not talking about childish things at all. "I would not make you sleep alone, not after you came all this way to show us the tricks of fighting in Atlantis—and certainly not after you almost got shot a little while ago. If you would rather lie down with someone else, though, that can be arranged."

Victor choked. No matter how much brandy he'd taken aboard, he couldn't very well misunderstand that. He wasn't always perfectly faithful when he was away from Margaret for a long stretch. On the other hand, he'd never acquired a mistress before.

He looked at Louise. She was more than enjoyable enough to the eye. "Is this what you want to do?" he asked her.

Her skin might be dark brown, but her shrug was purely Gallic. "Why not?" she replied.

That question had a large number of possible answers. Victor could see at least some of them. Seeing them and caring about them proved two very different things. He'd drunk a great deal of the Marquis de la Fayette's excellent brandy. He'd been shot at without result, as the French nobleman reminded him. He'd been away from Margaret for much too long. And Louise *was* sweet to the eye. Would she be sweet to the touch as well? He couldn't imagine any reason why she wouldn't be—and he wanted to find out for himself.

"Well, then," he said, as if that were a complete sentence.

As he and Louise were heading out of de la Fayette's tent and off to his own, the French marquis said, "I hope you have a pleasant evening, *Monsieur le Général*. I should also let you know that your man of affairs will not envy your good fortune, for I have arranged companionship for him."

"Have you?" Victor said foolishly. But why not? Blaise had been away from Stella as long as Victor had been away from Margaret. Victor nodded. "Good. That's good."

Louise tugged at his sleeve. "Are you coming?"

"I am, my dear. So I am," Victor said. The guards outside the Marquis de la Fayette's tent presented arms as he and Louise left. The guards outside his own tent presented arms as he and Louise went in. They knew what he'd be doing in there, all right. But they were Frenchmen, too. They might envy him, but he didn't think they'd blab. And if they did—well, so what? The brandy he'd diligently got outside of told him it wouldn't matter a bit.

The camp bed with which de la Fayette had equipped the tent was a masterpiece of compact lightness. It promised one person a fine night's sleep. Victor wasn't so sure it would bear the weight of two, and it was decidedly narrow for entertaining. He shrugged. Nothing ventured, nothing gained.

Louise was every bit as enjoyable as he'd hoped she

would be. Whether she also enjoyed herself... Well, that wasn't a question you wanted to ask a woman who wasn't there because she loved you. Victor approached the issue by saps and parallels, as it were: "Is this but for an evening, or will you join me again?"

In the gloom inside the tent, her face was unreadable. "I am to be yours for as long as you wish me to be yours, *Monsieur le Général*," she answered, which didn't tell him what he wanted to know.

"Does that suit you?" he asked, much as he had in de la Fayette's tent.

And she said, "Why not?," just as she had then. Then she asked a question of her own: "Twice, do you think?"

"I don't know," Victor said in surprise. Twice? So soon? He wasn't such a young man any more. He wasn't an old man yet, though. "Well, let's find out."

Along with potent brandy, the Marquis de la Fayette had brought strong coffee from France. Victor found himself drinking more of it than he was usually in the habit of doing. Without it, he might have found himself nodding off at any hour of the day or night. War had its exertions, but so did ... peace.

He noticed Blaise was also drinking more than his share of that dark-roasted coffee. "A man must keep his strength up," Blaise said seriously.

"Yes," Victor agreed, deadpan. "He must."

Blaise's companion was called Roxane. If not for the shape of her nose and mouth, she might almost have passed for white. The French in Atlantis had mingled with their slaves for as long as they'd brought Africans to this land. Victor wondered whether dark Blaise knew some special sense of conquest, lying with a woman so fair. Wonder or not, he didn't ask. If Blaise wanted to talk about that, he would. If he didn't, anything Victor asked would be prying.

De la Fayette's regulars skirmished with the red-coats and loyalists who blocked their way north. They made little progress. After a while, Victor said, "It might be better to pull away from the coast and try to slide around them. Doesn't look as though you're going to break through."

"But will they not pull away with us, to keep us from sliding around?" By the way the marquis echoed Victor's technical terms, he found them picturesque.

Patiently, Victor answered, "You can use a screening force to harass the enemy and hold them in place while the rest of your army steals a march on them. Then your screeners follow along, leaving the foe facing a fait accompli."

"What an interesting notion! What a brave notion!" de la Fayette exclaimed. He hesitated once more. "I am not sure how many of the local women will wish to accompany us on this journey, or how many of their owners will allow them to do so."

"C'est la guerre," Victor said gravely.

"True." De la Fayette sounded mournful, but only for a moment. "It could be, could it not, that there will be other women in the interior of Atlantis?"

"Well, so it could." Victor carefully didn't smile.

"Good! We shall proceed, then," de la Fayette declared.

Proceed they did. Not only did they proceed—they thrived. Victor had seen enthusiastic foragers before. His own Atlanteans, because of their sadly anemic supply train, did a fine job of living off the countryside: and that regardless of whether the countryside cared to be lived on.

But he soon had to own that his own countrymen couldn't match the French regulars for the thoroughness with which they stripped the landscape of everything even remotely edible. *"Nom d'un nom,"* Blaise said, perhaps surprised out of English at what the Frenchmen could do. "Not even locusts could empty things the way these men do."

"They have locusts in the country you come from?" Victor asked. Atlantis had a profusion of different kinds of grasshoppers. Great swarms of locusts, such as those that devastated Egypt in the Bible when Pharaoh hardened his heart, were fortunately rare.

"Oh, yes," Blaise replied. "They eat our crops, and we roast them and eat them. But they do more damage than avenging ourselves so makes up for."

Victor's stomach didn't turn over, though plenty of Atlanteans' might have. Out in the woods, he'd sometimes got hungry enough to skewer Atlantis' big flightless katydids on a branch and toast them over a small fire. They weren't even bad, so long as you didn't think about what you were eating. He suspected more than a few of his soldiers had done the same on the march to New Marseille. The only trouble here was, those big katydids were getting scarce in settled country. Dogs and cats devoured them without finicky human qualms, while mice outbred them and outran them and scurried through the undergrowth in their place.

The Marquis de la Fayette's troops were relentless foragers of another sort, too. Victor had never seen so many outraged fathers and husbands as congregated outside the marquis' tent. De la Fayette at first seemed inclined to make light of it. "I lead soldiers, not eunuchs," he observed. "They are men. It is war. These things happen. These things will always happen, so long as men go to war."

Were he merely defending a philosophical position, he would have had a point. Rather more than abstract philosophy was at stake, however. "Nothing obliges folk here to remain on the Atlantean Assembly's side," Victor pointed out. "If your army makes people hate our cause, they will turn to King George and England instead. We don't want that. You aren't campaigning in enemy country, you know."

"What would you have me do, *Monsieur*?" De la Fayette seemed genuinely perplexed.

"Next time you find someone who can point out a woman's ravishers with certainty, hang them," Victor said.

"You're joking!" the marquis exclaimed.

"Not a bit of it," Radcliff answered. "I hanged a few of my men for crimes like that, and I rarely have to worry about them any more."

"But these are soldiers," de la Fayette said again.

"Let them find willing women," Victor said. "There are plenty. If the people here decide your men act worse than the redcoats, they'll shoot at us from behind trees and fences. If your soldiers go behind some ferns to answer nature's call, they'll get knocked over the head. They'll have their throats slit. I shouldn't wonder if they don't get their ballocks cut off, too."

"Barbarous," de la Fayette muttered.

"Well, so it is. But what would you call holding a woman down and forcing yourself on her?" Victor returned.

"Half the ones who screech rape afterwards were happy enough while it was going on," the French nobleman said.

"It could be, but so what? That still leaves the other half," Victor said stubbornly. "Your Grace, you have a problem here, and you don't want to look at it. But if you don't, you'll have a worse problem soon. And so will the United States of Atlantis. I don't intend to let that happen."

"Do you presume to give me orders?" the Marquis de la Fayette inquired. "You travel with my army, if you recall."

Victor looked through him. "You travel in my country, your Grace, if *you* recall." De la Fayette turned red—and turned away. Victor wondered if he'd pushed too hard. He couldn't *make* the Frenchman do anything, no matter how much he wished he could.

Three days later, a girl was able to point out the four men who'd taken turns with her. "What will you do about them?" she asked de la Fayette. The smirking soldiers hardly bothered to deny it. Their bravado turned to horror and disbelief when he ordered them hanged.

"To encourage the others," he said after the deed was done, so he knew his Voltaire, too. Then he asked Victor, "Are you now satisfied?"

"That you are serious? Yes, and your men will be, too," Victor said. And so it proved.

XVIII

*B*laise looked around. So did Victor Radcliff. There wasn't much to see: ferns and evergreen trees and occasional bits of grass, a landscape more nearly Atlantean than European. "Where the devil are we?" Blaise asked, and proceeded to answer his own question: "In the middle of nowhere, that's where."

"More like the edge of nowhere, I'd say," Victor answered judiciously.

"Honh!" Blaise's voice might have served as an illustration for skepticism, could voices only have been illustrated. "I wouldn't be surprised if we saw one of those honker birds, like we caught over on the west side of the Green Ridge. If they don't live in the middle of nowhere, I don't know what does."

"*I* should be surprised if we saw one," Victor said. "You're always surprised to see them on this side of the mountains. I'm not sure how many are left here, or if any are."

"If any are, they'd live in a place like this," Blaise insisted. He paused, struck by a new thought: "Lot of meat on a honker bird."

"That there is," Victor said. "As much as on a deer, say. I wouldn't mind seeing a deer in these parts, either."

As if to underscore that, his stomach rumbled. The

Marquis de la Fayette's Frenchmen had indeed left the redcoats behind by marching into the interior of Atlantis. They'd also come perilously close to leaving human habitation behind. As a result, they were living off the countryside, and the countryside had less to offer than Victor would have wished.

Things would have been worse were they Englishmen, or even troops from English Atlantis. Being French, they cheerfully gathered the fist-sized snails in the woods, and made tasty stews of the frogs and turtles they took from the streams they crossed and the ponds they skirted. Blaise ate such fare without complaint if with no great enthusiasm. So did Victor, who'd fed himself on similar victuals in his journeys through the Atlantean wilderness. But plenty of his countrymen would have turned up their noses ... till they got hungrier than this, anyhow.

Victor might have thought the Marquis de la Fayette would turn up his nose at a large snail broiled on a stick over a fire. The French nobleman ate it with every sign of relish. He also failed to falter at flapjack-turtle stew. To see what he would say, Victor remarked, "You can also eat the big green katydids that scurry through the leaves and rubbish on the ground."

"Is that a fact?" Rather than disgusted, the marquis sounded fascinated. "You will have done this for yourself?"

"I will have indeed," Victor answered. "If you're hungry enough, you'll eat anything you can get your hands on."

Whereupon de la Fayette caught a katydid and toasted it over the flames. He chewed meditatively. "You have reason, *Monsieur le Général,*" he said when he'd finished. "They may be eaten. And, as you say, hunger likely makes the best sauce."

"No doubt," Victor answered, eyeing the young Frenchman—was he even twenty?—with new respect.

"Well, well," Blaise said that night as he and Victor

lay side by side rolled in blankets. "More to him than meets the eye."

"There is," Victor agreed. That *well, well* secretly amused him: his factotum was borrowing the phrase from his own way of speaking. "Pretty soon, we'll have to see how well the Frenchmen can fight. If they do it as well as they march, no reason to worry about them."

"I think they will do all right," Blaise said. "French people used me for a slave, so I don't love them. But in the last war, no one ever said the soldiers from France couldn't fight. They fought as well as the redcoats did, but there were not enough of them to win."

"True, every word of it. Besides, they would be embarrassed to fight badly when this bug-eating marquis is watching them, eh?" Victor said.

Blaise didn't answer. A moment later, a soft snore passed his lips. A moment after that, Victor was snoring, too.

Naturally, the Marquis de la Fayette called the river that divided what had been French and English Atlantis the Erdre. That name had gone into French atlases since the fifteenth century. Coming from the other side of the border, Victor just as naturally thought of it as the Stour. Thanks to the way the political winds blew, the English name waxed while the French one waned.

Not all the bridges over the river had been destroyed. Not all of them were even guarded. The French army crossed into English Atlantis without getting its feet wet and hurried northeast.

"You see?" Victor said to Blaise a few days later. "We'd gone farther west than this when we came north with those two copperskins all those years ago. I wonder what ever happened to them. I suppose they went west over sea to Terranova, the way they wanted to. *That* was the middle of nowhere."

Blaise would quibble with anyone. "No, that was the end of nowhere—and the wrong end, too."

"Well, maybe you've got something there," Victor admitted, remembering the swamps they'd splashed through on the way up to the Stour. He changed the subject and lowered his voice at the same time: "What do you think of our French general now?"

Also quietly, Blaise answered, "I wonder what he'll be like when he grows up."

Victor laughed loud enough to make de la Fayette glance his way with a raised eyebrow. Victor looked back as imperturbably as he could. Eventually, seeing that he wouldn't get an explanation, de la Fayette gave it up as a bad job. Victor wasn't sure just how fluent in English he was, but suspected he understood more than he let on. "You are a rascal," he said to Blaise.

"Me?" The Negro shook his head. "You must be thinking of someone else, General." Victor laughed again, not so raucously this time. The marquis eyed him once more, but soon shrugged and went back to talking with his own officers.

"I wonder what Baron von Steuben will make of him." By now, Victor took the German soldier's pretensions to nobility for granted.

So did Blaise, who asked, "Which is higher, a baron or a marquis?"

"A baron. No—a marquis. I think. I'm not sure." Victor scowled. "No one has much use for fancy titles of nobility in Atlantis. There are a few knights here—men you're supposed to call *Sir*—and maybe a baron or two, but not many. If we win the war, if we cast off King George's rule, I don't believe we shall have any nobles left at all. Everyone will be the same, at least in law."

"Everyone white," Blaise said pointedly.

"Everyone free," Victor corrected. "Or what would you be doing with those stripes on your sleeve?"

Blaise grunted, acknowledging the point without wholly conceding it. "Can this work, with everyone the same? Even in my tribe back in Africa—other tribes, too—we have the chief, and other men you have to respect because of who they are.... How do you say that in English?"

"Nobles?" Victor suggested.

"Maybe." Blaise didn't seem happy with the way the word tasted. "Not the same, I don't think. But we have those folk, and then we have the ordinary people, too. Law not the same for chief and respectable people"—no, he didn't like *nobles*—"and ordinary folk. Chief *makes* law. How can it stick on him?"

"Well, King Louis of France would say the same thing," Victor answered. "So would King George, even if Parliament told him he didn't know what he was talking about. How will it work without a king or nobles? I don't know. It seemed to go all right in Athens in ancient days, and in Rome."

"Ancient days," Blaise muttered to himself. "Idea seems silly to me. You win this war against England, you should be King of Atlantis."

That thought had crossed Victor's mind once or twice. Who could stop him if he decided to put a crown on his head after he won this war? Who would *want* to stop him? Not many people. He could, in fact, think of only one. "I don't want to be King of Atlantis, Blaise."

"Why not?" The Negro eyed him in honest perplexity. "What could be better? Then I would be one of the king's—what do you say?—the king's ministers, that's it. You would be very rich, and I would be rich enough. Margaret would be Queen of Atlantis, and Stella her, uh, lady-in-waiting."

"Why fight to take down one king if all you do is set up another one in his place?" Victor returned. "Why—?"

Before he could go on, one of the few French horsemen galloped back toward the head of the Marquis de la Fayette's column. "Soldiers! English soldiers!" he shouted. "English soldiers at the bridge over the Brede!"

What the devil are they doing there? Victor wondered. But the question answered itself. If the redcoats knew the French army was on its way, of course they would do what they could to slow it down.

"Shall we dislodge them?" de la Fayette asked gaily.

"We'd better, if we aim to get up toward Hanover," Victor answered.

"Then let us be about it." The marquis started shouting orders. Like the English, like the Atlanteans, the French used bugles and fifes and drums to maneuver their soldiers. Their calls were different, though, and more musical, at least to Victor's ears. The troopers in their blue jackets moved into line of battle as smoothly as redcoats might have done.

No more than a platoon of English soldiers guarded the bridge. They had one field gun: a little three-pounder. "Surrender!" Victor shouted to them. "You haven't a prayer of holding us off!"

"Be damned to you, sir!" the youngster in charge of them shouted back—he had to be around de la Fayette's age. "Come and get us!"

"Be careful what you ask for, son," Victor said, not unkindly. "Someone may give it to you."

"I am no son of a rebel dog, nor son of a foul Frenchman, neither." The redcoat shook his fist at Victor, at the Marquis de la Fayette, and at the soldiers deploying behind the marquis. "Come on, then, if you've got the stomach for it!"

"What does he say?" de la Fayette asked as Victor rode back to the French army.

"He defies us." Victor whistled sourly; that didn't seem strong enough. "He casts his defiance in our teeth."

"He is brave." The marquis paused for a moment. "It could be that he is also a fool. He seems quite young." Of his own age de la Fayette said not a word.

Methodically, the French troops advanced to the attack. The Englishmen's fieldpiece boomed. Its ball—a plaything to look at—knocked over four Frenchmen. One got up again. One never would. The cries from the other two filled the air.

Just before the French opened up on them, the redcoats fired a volley. More men in blue fell. The French returned fire. Several Englishmen went down. The others retreated to the north bank of the Brede, hauling their popgun after them.

"Rush the bridge," Victor urged. "They're going to burn it or blow it up."

De la Fayette shouted the order. The Frenchmen broke ranks and surged forward at a run. A couple of them were on the bridge when the powder charge under it went off. Timbers flew every which way. One of them speared the leading French soldier. He screamed like a damned soul as he toppled. The blast flung the other Frenchman on the bridge into the Brede. He half swam, half splashed back to the south bank of the river. The charge blew a fifteen-foot hole in the bridge: too far for any soldier to hope to jump.

With a mocking salute, the junior English officer led his surviving men off to the east. "*Damn* him," Blaise said quietly.

Victor Radcliff nodded. "He did everything a man in his place could hope to do—and rather more besides, I should say."

"He shall not delay us long, despite his arrogance," de la Fayette said. Sure enough, French military engineers—pioneers, they called them—were making for the nearest trees. They would have the bridge repaired soon enough: a few hours, a day at the most. All the same, the redcoats *were* costing them that time. A platoon facing an army couldn't do much better.

"Hello, General." The Atlantean courier touched a finger to his hat in a not very military salute. "Good to see you again, damned if it ain't."

"How did you find me? There've been times lately when I wasn't sure Old Scratch knew where I was, let alone anybody else," Victor said.

"You ask me, it ain't so bad if the Devil don't know where you're at," the courier replied, and Victor could hardly disagree. The leathery horseman went on, "Devil or not, General, there's ways." He laid a finger by the side of his nose and didn't elaborate.

Not quite idle curiosity prompted Victor to ask, "Have any of those ways got to do with a foul-mouthed little head louse of an English lieutenant?"

The courier's mouth fell open, displaying discolored teeth and a cud of pipeweed. The man spat brown before asking, "How in blazes did you know that?"

"Blazes or not, there's ways," Victor answered blandly.

"Well, he's been bragging to all and sundry in Bredestown how he slaughtered ten thousand Frenchies single-handed out in the wilderness—something like that, anyways," the courier said. "Figures there'd be some Frenchies left over, don't it? Figures you'd be with 'em if there was, don't it? Tracked them down, tracked you down." He let fly with another brown stream.

Had he seemed even a little more impressed with himself, Victor Radcliff would have felt the urge to take him down a peg. As things were, Victor only said, "Tell me at once—do we yet hold Hanover?"

"That we do. I've got letters telling you this and that, but there's the nub: that we do." The courier shifted his quid from one cheek to the other. As if reminded of something, he added, "Oh, and I've got letters for you from Honker's Mill, too."

"Do you, now?" Victor could hear how toneless his voice went. "And what's the latest from the Atlantean Assembly?" He wondered whether he really wanted to know.

"Some old Jew gave 'em a nice stack of coin, so they aren't quite so flat as they have been lately," the man said.

"Would that be Master Benveniste? He has always been generous in supporting the cause of freedom," Victor said.

"Some old Jew," the courier repeated. *His* voice reflected absolute indifference to the Jew's identity. "They're all a stack of Christ-killers anyways. Ought to chase 'em out of Atlantis for good once we win."

"But take their money in the meantime?" Victor enquired dryly.

"Well, sure. Got to squeeze *some* use out of 'em."

"Your charity does you credit." Radcliff hadn't thought he could get drier yet, but he managed.

"Much obliged, General." The courier recognized no irony. He handed Victor the letters, gave him a smarter salute than he had on first coming up, and then rode away.

"What is one to do with such a fellow!" Victor cried, throwing his hands in the air. "The United States of Atlantis shall have freedom for those who confess any religion—even for those who confess none, by God!"

"So long as their skins be not too dark," Blaise remarked.

"It is not the same thing," Victor said.

"I am not surprised a white man would say it was not," the Negro answered. "If copperskins ruled the seas and held your folk in bondage to grow their sugar and dyestuffs, you would sing a different tune. And if black men did—! Well, you would not fancy that very much, either, I think."

"Settlements make those arrangements for themselves—states, I should say," Victor replied. "If you tell me you are one whit less free than I, I shall call you a liar to your face."

"But you did not have to run away to make yourself free, whilst I did. You did not have to abscond with yourself, so to speak," Blaise said. "Down in the French settlements, I am still a wanted man—for stealing me."

"We are both wanted men all over Atlantis, and for a crime worse than theft." Victor knew he was deliberately trying to turn the subject. He'd gone round the barn with Blaise a great many times on this, but he'd seldom felt the Negro chasing him quite so closely.

Blaise, unfortunately, also knew he was turning the subject. "So the United States of Atlantis can decide that anyone gets to pray to God any which way, but each settlement gets to pick who is free and who gets sold. Well, well."

Slaveowners from the settlements in southern Atlantis

might be persuaded to put up with Papists (for those who were Protestant) or Protestants (for those who followed Rome) or possibly even Jews (and some Jews owned slaves, too). They might even tolerate freethinkers, so long as the men who thought freely didn't publish in the same way (and maybe sending Thomas Paine to Terranova would end up helping him stay safe). That slaveowners who made money from their two-legged chattels would ever tolerate equality with Negroes or copperskins struck Victor as most unlikely.

Blaise tried a different gibe: "You don't hate Negroes enough to keep from lying down with a slave wench. Suppose you got her with child. Would you sell your son for profit? Some men who own slaves do that, you know."

"It isn't likely," Victor said uneasily. "But the issue of my issue does not arise. Louise is not my slave. I have no slaves. You know that, too."

He thought Blaise would yield that point, but his factotum did not. "Is it not so that every white Atlantean has slaves if any white Atlantean has slaves? You go along with it. . . ." He shook his head. "There is a better word."

After a moment's thought, Victor suggested, "Condone?"

"Yes. Thank you. That is what I wanted. You condone it."

"Why do you say 'every white Atlantean'? I did not see you too proud to lie down with a slave, either. Maybe you made her belly bulge."

"I hope not. I shot my seed on it whenever I could." But Blaise looked embarrassed. "Not 'every white Atlantean,' then. 'Every free Atlantean.' Every free Atlantean condones having slaves if any free Atlantean has slaves. And this for the Proclamation of Liberty." He snapped his fingers.

"We do what we can. We are not perfect. I did not say we were, nor would I ever," Victor said. "But we are, or we try to be, on the side of the angels."

"We have a ways to go."

"We are men. I don't shit ambrosia, as I have reason to know." Victor wrinkled his nose. "Let us first get free of England—"

"And we can start to see how to get free of one another," Blaise finished for him.

"That is not what I was going to say."

"Well, it had better be true anyhow. If we do not get free of one another, what point to it that we got free of England? King George should not be my master, maybe. But I do not see that any other man should be, either."

Victor Radcliff laughed. Blaise glared at him till he explained: "Tan my hide for shoe leather if you do not sound like every other free Atlantean ever born, be he white or black or coppery—or green, come to that."

"Mm ... It could be." But, after a moment, Blaise shook his head. "No—say I sound like every other man ever born. Do you think ever a man came into the world looking for a master?"

"I do not know the answer to that, nor do you," Victor said. "Had you no slaves in your African jungles across the sea?"

"We had them," Blaise admitted. "But what we call slavery and what you call slavery are not the same thing, even if they carry the same name. In our land, all the slaves are like what you call house slaves here. No field hands—no work out there under the lash if you slack off. And the other difference is, here you can mostly tell a slave by looking at him. Not so in my land."

Victor thought about that. He found himself nodding. South of the Stour, a black man or a copperskin was far more likely than not to belong to a white man. In a country where all the faces were black ... "That must make runaways harder to catch," he remarked.

"Not so many of them there," Blaise said. "Maybe it is harder for a man who is a master to be rough on a slave who looks like him. Even your Jesus looks like you. He does not look like me."

When you got right down to it, Jesus probably looked

like some modern Mahometan. He came from Palestine, after all, and He was a Jew. But European painters portrayed Him as looking like themselves. They passed that image on to the Negro slaves they converted to Christianity. Victor hadn't thought about what a potent spiritual weapon a white Christ might be.

But that wasn't the point. "So you have masters there, too?" he asked. That *was*.

Reluctantly, Blaise nodded. "We have them."

"You never thought it was wrong and unnatural?"

"I never was a slave before. You see—if someone buys and sells you, won't you think it wrong and unnatural?"

"I daresay I should. But suppose you never got caught and sold. Suppose you grew to be a rich man in your own country. Would you not have slaves of your own now? Would you not be as contented a slaveowner as any white man in the old French settlements or down in Spanish Atlantis?"

This time, Blaise did not answer for some little while. At last, his face troubled, he nodded again. "Maybe I would. You ask nasty questions—do you know that?"

No doubt people had said the same thing about Socrates in Athens long ago. He'd ended up drinking hemlock because of it, too—something modern gadflies sometimes tried to forget. "I will tell you something, Blaise," Victor said. "So do you."

The French regulars showed no more love for the interior of Atlantis than the redcoats ever had. "It is unfairly difficult to subsist an army here in such an empty land," the Marquis de la Fayette complained.

"Not always easy, true," Victor Radcliff answered: a honker-sized understatement if ever there was one.

As he had a while before, he thanked heaven the French soldiers ate anything that didn't eat them first. That helped keep them fed. But you could gather up only so many frogs and turtles and snails and wingless katydids (the French regulars found them better than tolerable, especially with a dash of garlic). And there wasn't any bread to gather up away from farms, nor even fruits and nuts. Some Atlantean ferns had parts you could eat—fiddleheads, country folk called them. Even so . . .

"We need to get into more settled country," Victor added.

"I should say we do." The marquis' crooked grin seemed all the more surprising on the face of a man so young. "Otherwise, we shall be no more than wraiths by the time we have to fight the English. In one way, that might aid us, eh? It could be that bullets pass through wraiths without doing harm. But I do not believe our soldiers would appreciate the diminution of their corporeal frames even so."

"Er—yes." Victor didn't know how to take that. He realized it was a joke, and chuckled to show he did: he didn't want de la Fayette to think him nothing but an ignorant backwoodsman. But it was perhaps the most elaborately phrased joke he'd ever heard. It might have seemed much funnier in a Paris drawing room than it did in this sparsely settled stretch of Atlantis.

That very afternoon, one of the handful of French mounted scouts rode back to the main body of de la Fayette's troops in high excitement. "Beeves!" he cried. "Wonderful beeves!"

They weren't wonderful beeves, or they wouldn't have been to men not staring hunger in the face. They were ordinary cattle: distinctly on the scrawny side, in fact, and of no particular breeding. The same description applied to the two men who kept an eye on them as they grazed in the meadow.

No wolves in Atlantis. No bears. No lions. But French regulars could be even more ravenous. The herdsmen stared at them in bleak dismay. "Is it that they hope to be paid?" de la Fayette asked Victor.

"I don't know how happy even that will make them," Radcliff replied. "Atlantean paper's gone up some since France came in on our side, but we'd have to give them a bushel basket full of it before they got their money's worth."

"Paper?" The marquis sniffed. Then he shouted for the army paymaster. That worthy repaired to one of his wagons. De la Fayette waved to the herdsmen, summoning them into his presence. They came, apprehensively. The paymaster, a sour look on his face, gave them three small gold coins each. The herdsmen stared as if they could hardly believe their eyes. Victor knew he could hardly believe his. "It is good?" de la Fayette asked in accented but understandable English.

"It's mighty goddamn good, your Honor!" one of the herdsmen blurted. The other man, startled past speech, nodded dumbly.

"Haven't seen so much specie in a devil of a long time," Blaise said in a low voice.

"Nor have I," Victor whispered back. He had to gather himself before he could speak to de la Fayette: "Your king provided for you lavishly."

"I will have need to pay the soldiers. I will have need to purchase victuals, as now," the French commander said, shrugging. "And so his Majesty has made it possible for me to do these things."

"So he has," Victor Radcliff agreed tonelessly. The Atlantean Assembly had made it possible for *him* to do those things, too. The only trouble was, the Assembly hadn't made it possible for him to do those things very well. France was rich, populous, and efficiently—many would say, tyrannically—taxed. The United States of Atlantis were none of those things. Here in this meadow, Victor got his nose rubbed in the difference.

French army cooks proved to roast beef in much the same fashion as their Atlantean counterparts. It was charred black on the outside, as near raw as made no difference on the inside. Along with garlic—which Victor didn't much fancy—the French cooks had salt to add to the meat's savor, which Atlanteans might well not have.

"Is this from the salt pans of Brittany?" Victor asked.

De la Fayette looked at him as if he'd started using

Blaise's language. "I have no idea." He asked some of the cooks. When they told him it was, he sent Victor a curious look. "Now how would you have guessed that?"

"Well, my ancestor, Edward Radcliffe, was in Brittany buying salt when François Kersauzon sold him the secret of the way to Atlantis for a third of his catch," Victor said. "Kersauzon found it first, but Radcliffe settled first."

"Atlantis, sold for salt fish." The Marquis de la Fayette sighed gustily. "France has had many long years to repent of that bargain."

"If you'd asked Kersauzon, he would have told you he was a Breton, not a Frenchman," Victor said. "Still a few—not many any more, but a few—in French Atlantis who remember the difference even now."

"I saw as much in Cosquer. They are fools. But England has those, too, *n'est-ce pas?* Welshmen who cling to Wales and the like," de la Fayette said. "Have they no settlements of their own in Atlantis?"

"A few small ones. No big ones I know of," Victor said. The marquis raised an eyebrow at the qualification. Victor explained: "West of the mountains, plenty goes on that people on our side, on the long-settled side, don't find out about till later, if we ever find out at all."

"How charming!" de la Fayette exclaimed, which was hardly the word Victor would have used. Something in his expression must have given him away, for the young Frenchman quickly went on, "In my country, there is no room for villages full of mystery, villages of which the king and his servants know nothing."

"I see," Victor said, and he supposed he did. "In Atlantis, there is still room for people who want to be left alone, yes." He wasn't so sure that was charming. Some of the people who wanted to be left alone weren't far removed from maniacs. Others were just robbers and runaways who had excellent reasons to want to remain undiscovered.

But de la Fayette said, "This is the liberty I am proud to assist: the liberty to be oneself."

That night, Blaise softly asked, "Well, who else can you be but yourself?"

"I don't know," Victor replied. "You have to admit, though, it sounds a lot better in French."

As they came up from the southwest, Victor realized they weren't more than a couple of days' travel from Hooville. He shook his head in bemused wonder. He'd stopped in the little town on his way to Hanover when the fight against England was just on the point of breaking loose. And, if they were only a couple of days away from Hooville, they were only three days from his own farm.

He said not a word about that. He didn't ride away to visit Meg. Blaise didn't go off to see Stella, either. The French might have followed them. A visit from the allies' officers would have been tolerable. A visit from the whole French army? No. Victor knew too well what happened to countryside with soldiers on it. He'd ordered his men to subsist themselves on the countryside often enough. He didn't want to watch his own land stripped bare by locusts in blue jackets.

Instead, the French troops foraged south of Hooville. That was unfortunate. Victor had spent a lot of years building up his own land. Having it plundered, even by friends, would have felt catastrophic.

"Somewhere east of Hooville," Victor told the Marquis de la Fayette, "the English will wait for us in force."

"So I should think, yes," the nobleman said. "That is also the direction in which Hanover lies, is it not so? Hanover and the main Atlantean army?"

"It is," Victor said. "We ought to join forces with them if we can. And even if we can't, I ought to go back and take charge of them again. I've been away longer than I thought I would."

De la Fayette thought for a moment. "And you would perhaps wish my force to make a demonstration to allow you to slip past the English lines?"

"That would be excellent. *Merci beaucoup*," Victor said. The Frenchman might or might not be able to lead men in the field. On that, Victor as yet held no strong opinion either way. But de la Fayette was not without strategic insight. Maybe he really would make an officer.

English cavalrymen—actually, riders from a loyalist troop, perhaps even Habakkuk Biddiscombe's Horsed Legion—collided with the French scouts about halfway between Hooville and Hanover ("Between Noplace and Someplace," as Blaise elegantly put it). They pushed the outnumbered French horsemen back on de la Fayette's main body. French field guns boomed. A roundshot felled an enemy rider's mount as if it were a redwood. From several hundred yards away, Victor couldn't make out what happened to the man whose nag so abruptly departed this world.

French foot soldiers in loose order—skirmishers—advanced on the enemy cavalry. The loyalists with carbines banged away at the Frenchmen. They had their own field gun. It unlimbered and fired a couple of shots. Then, sedately, as if to say they had a luncheon appointment somewhere else and weren't withdrawing in the face of superior forces, the loyalists wheeled their horses and rode away.

"They performed tolerably well. No great discipline, perhaps, but they are well mounted and brave." De la Fayette spoke in the clinical tones of a doctor assessing a case of smallpox.

"Oh, no denying they're brave," Victor said. "I only wish they weren't, or that they were brave in a better cause."

"No doubt they feel the same about your men," de la Fayette observed.

"No doubt," Victor said. "Or they had better, at any rate. If the English weren't worried about us, they wouldn't have to recruit these *salauds*." That wasn't fair, and he knew it. The loyalists weren't—or most of them weren't—men who deserved to be sworn at. They were only men who had different notions of how Atlantis should be ruled. Not men who deserved to be sworn at, no: just men who needed to be killed.

Well, one or two of them had died here, along with one or two Frenchmen. The foot soldiers came up to the horse the cannon ball had killed. They butchered it with as much enthusiasm as if it had been a cow. Victor had eaten all sorts of strange meats, but he didn't remember ever eating horse before.

It wasn't bad. A little chewy—a little gluey, as a matter of fact—and a little gamy, but not bad. The Frenchmen seemed to find it delicious. Victor wouldn't have gone that far. Neither would Blaise, but he said, "A bellyful of horse is a lot better than a bellyful of nothing."

"Isn't it just!" Victor replied.

The French went on skirmishing with loyalists. After the cavalrymen reported their position, loyalist foot soldiers harried them from behind trees and rocks, as Victor's men had harried the redcoats. But the French were less rigid than the English, and quick to fight back the same way. The loyalists melted away before them.

Victor waited for General Cornwallis to commit his own troops against the French. When the English commander did, Victor took his leave of de la Fayette, saying, "I hope we shall meet again. I expect we shall, and with luck the meeting will not be long delayed."

"May it be so," de la Fayette said. "We will keep them busy here. They will never think to look for you as you fare east. Good fortune go with you."

To help good fortune along, Victor and Blaise split up, as they'd done more than once before. They were known to travel together, so each of them headed toward Hanover alone.

XIX

"Halt!" the sentry shouted. "Who comes?"

Victor Radcliff reined in. Answering that question was always interesting—and sometimes much too interesting. He thought the man had an Atlantean accent. Even if he turned out to be right, it might not do him any good. Loyalist positions weren't likely so close to Hanover, but they weren't impossible, either.

"I am a friend," he answered carefully.

"No doubt, but whose?" the sentry said, advancing with purposeful strides. "Are you the Atlantean Assembly's friend, or King George's? In times like these, you cannot be friend to both."

How right he was! And, damn him, he gave no clue as to whose friend *he* was. An answer he misliked, and he would shoot. And he was too close to be likely to miss, even with a smoothbore musket.

"I am the Atlantean Assembly's friend." Victor's hand moved stealthily toward his pistol. If he had to fight for his life, he would.

But the sentry—whose clothes, rough homespun of linen and wool, also refused to declare his allegiance—didn't fire right away. "And *which* friend of the Atlantean Assembly are you?" he demanded.

Had the English or the loyalists captured Blaise? Had

fire and sharp metal torn from him word that Victor was also bound for Hanover? If they had, the sentry was just waiting to be sure before he killed. Sometimes a man had to roll the dice. "I am Victor Radcliff," Victor said. He could—he hoped he could—make sure the enemy didn't take him alive.

"You are?" the sentry said. "Well, how do I know you're him, and not some braggart with more mouth than brains?"

"Take me into Hanover," Victor replied. "If they decide I am an impostor there, they will assuredly hang me for my presumption, and you may have the pleasure of watching me dance on air."

After thinking that through, the sentry nodded. "I'd have to be dumb as a honker to tell you no," he said.

"That would not stop, nor even slow, a great many men I have met," Victor said.

"I do believe it." The sentry raised his voice: "Abraham! Calvin! One of you come down! I got to go into town, I do."

A man did appear from an ambush position. Victor decided he was lucky they were on his side. He would not have had much luck assailing the one fellow who showed himself, not when the sentry had friends.

The soldier—he called himself Jeremiah—did not have a horse. He walked toward Hanover beside Victor, and didn't complain about it. "Got to make these boots fit my feet a little better anyways," he said.

"Very fine boots," Victor said—and so they were. But they weren't perfectly new, so he added, "How did you come by them?"

"Bushwhacked a redcoat," Jeremiah said matter-of-factly. "He was a bigger fellow than I am. I reckoned I could stuff the boots with rags if I had to. But it turned out our feet were just about the same size."

"Good for you," Victor said.

A couple of miles farther east, another sentry challenged Victor and Jeremiah. This one stood by an earthwork not far from the Union-Jack-and-red-crested-eagle flag the United States of Atlantis were using. Victor proclaimed himself with more confidence this time. The new sentry said, "Well, hatch me from a honker's egg if you ain't. Welcome back, General!"

That satisfied Jeremiah's curiosity once and for all. "Since you are who you say you are, I'm back to my friends." Away he went, never once thinking he ought to wait for a general's permission. He was an Atlantean, all right.

Hanover looked much the same as it had when Victor left it. More shops stood empty than he would have liked. Forts made the Royal Navy think twice about drawing near enough to bombard the city, but the English warships stifled seagoing commerce. Even salt cod was in short supply, and expensive in specie—far worse in Atlantean paper. And when the coast of English Atlantis ran low on salt cod, the end of the world or something even worse lay around the next corner.

Victor found that Blaise had got into town a day ahead of him. That usually happened when they didn't travel together. Victor had to be circumspect and careful. Blaise didn't, as long as he wasn't in a land where he had to worry about being reenslaved. Not many people paid much attention to a shabby Negro riding along by himself.

"Oh, yes. The redcoats stopped me once," he said. "I played dumb. They let me go after a while. Some of them tried scrubbing my arm to see if the color came off." He laughed at their ignorance.

"Now we have to see how we go about smashing Cornwallis between our men and de la Fayette's," Victor said.

"That will be good—if we can do it," Blaise said. "Yes, that will be very fine—if we can bring it off." His mixture of hope and doubt seemed almost Biblical in its cadences.

Victor was glad he'd found a certain scrap of paper in his pocket. "What we ought to do next," he said, "is to get some pigeons into de la Fayette's hands."

"He has plenty of food for now." Blaise caught himself, and also caught Victor's drift. "Oh—you mean the messenger birds."

"That's just what I mean," Victor agreed. "Then we can speak back and forth with him without risking human messengers. The English are also less likely to learn what we say to each other if we use pigeons in place of men."

"I do like the idea," Blaise said. "To set words on the wings of the wind ... We use drums in Africa to pass news from one village to another, but anyone can hear a drum and know what it means. The birds are a better answer." Then admiration seemed to curdle into anger, for he added, "One more thing you white men thought of that we did not."

"Well, we're going to use it against other white men," Victor said.

Blaise might not even have heard him. "When I saw the ship that would bring me here ... It was so big, and had all the sails and all the ropes—the rigging—and it was like nothing my folk could have built. And then they chained me in the hold, and now I know what hell and damnation are like."

Victor had never gone aboard a blackbirder—an innocent-sounding name for a slave ship if ever there was one. But he had been in Cosquer harbor when one tied up there. The stink coming from the slaver was enough to knock a man off his feet even a furlong or two downwind. To cross the ocean in the middle of that stench, in chains, on short rations ... Victor was glad he'd been born a white man, and an Atlantean.

But Blaise hadn't finished. "When I came on shore at last, all wobbly and thin and sick, almost the first thing I saw was a horse pulling a man in a two-wheeled carriage. And the first thing that went through my head was, *What a good idea! Why didn't we think of that?*"

"Have you horses?" Victor asked.

"No. They sicken and die," the Negro answered.

"White men try to use them in my country now and then, but they never last long."

"Have you wheeled carriages?"

"For children's toys. Not for carts and carriages and wagons—and guns. Without horses, without oxen, we have no beasts to pull them." Blaise grinned crookedly. "And I know your next question. We also have not the proper roads, only tracks for people on foot. So what good would the fine carriage be in Africa? But it was so clever!"

"One of these days, I hope the world will say the same about the United States of Atlantis," Victor said. "And I hope that what we do in Atlantis will speak even in Africa."

"Maybe so—if it speaks of freeing slaves instead of buying and selling them," Blaise said. And the old argument began again.

In days gone by, Avalon's pirates had pioneered the practice of posting by pigeon. Red Rodney Radcliffe and the other freebooters lost regardless. But the lesson of what they'd done, unlike so many, did not go to waste. Atlantis had been a pigeon fancier's paradise ever since.

Finding out where de la Fayette and the French were came first. The Atlanteans needed pigeons that homed for some nearby village. They also needed to provide the marquis with birds that would return to Hanover. Once those things were done, the two separated forces could easily and quickly talk back and forth.

All that proved harder than Victor Radcliff had dreamt it would. The English, unfortunately, had understood Atlantean predilections. While they held Hanover, they'd harassed and hunted anyone who raised homing pigeons. They'd taken birds, and they'd killed birds, too. Several breeders passed more time than they'd wanted in close confinement.

"Didn't *anyone* keep a flock intact?" Victor cried in dismay—no, in something not far from despair.

One of the pigeon fanciers said, "Wasn't easy, General. By my hope of heaven, it wasn't possible—never mind easy. Too many folk loyal to King George in town. Someone who knew you had birds would run to the redcoats, and then it'd be all up with you. Out in the countryside, there are still birds that will home for Hanover. Hardly any left here to the little towns."

To a Hanover man, any town but his own was a little town. Some Hanover men would likely call London a little town. But that was the least of Victor's worries. He let out a heartfelt sigh. "Well, not every plan works the way you wish it would when you put it together."

"Runners, then?" Blaise asked.

"Runners," Victor agreed, and wished he didn't have to.

He also wished he would have arranged a code with the Marquis de la Fayette before separating from him. Then they would have had a chance to communicate without letting the English understand what they intended even if Cornwallis' soldiers captured a messenger. It would have been a good idea had he thought of it sooner. Of course, many things would have been good ideas had one thought of them sooner.

He had to explain the idea of codes to Blaise. Then he had to explain the explanation. Blaise could read and write, but he'd come late to both arts. The vagaries of English spelling still bemused him—when they didn't enrage him. "You scramble up the words even worse than they are already? Nobody never read them after that," he said in dismay. Grammar deserted him, but not sincerity.

"We scramble them in a fashion upon which we have agreed in advance," Victor said. "That way, they easily may be unscrambled once more."

"Easily? I think not," Blaise said, and maybe he wasn't so far wrong.

Victor's men did everything they could to strengthen the works protecting Hanover's harbors. He didn't know where the Royal Navy had gone—into Terranovan waters, to fight the new uprising there? or off into the eastern Atlantic, to find and fight the French fleet?—but he didn't want ships of the line unexpectedly returning and cannonading the city. He had to be able to give them the warmest reception he could.

In due course, one of his messengers returned with a letter from the Marquis de la Fayette. The fellow also displayed a tricorn with a bullet hole clean through the crown. "Good thing it's a trifle small, and sits high on my head," he told Victor. "Otherwise, you'd be a long time waiting for that there paper."

"Well, Micah, I am glad you came back imperforate," Victor replied. "Easier to get a new hat than a new messenger any day of the week, and that is a fact."

"Prices what they are nowadays, though, I reckon you can get yourself a messenger cheaper," Micah said. "Unless you've got specie in your pocket, anyway. A man with specie"—he sighed wistfully—"he can do anything, near enough. Sure ain't got *my* hands on any for a long time."

Victor maintained what he hoped was a prudent silence. The merchants and shopkeepers and taverners of Hanover discounted the Atlantean Assembly's paper no less steeply than anyone else. If anything, the Assembly's paper was worth less here than elsewhere in Atlantis. Having lain under English occupation for so long, Hanover was used to the sweet clink of silver and gold. Men with nothing but paper to spend had to spend a lot of it.

"Maybe you could do something about it," Micah said hopefully. "Shoot people who won't take paper at face—something like that, anyhow. You're the general, after all."

"Maybe." Victor knew the messenger sadly overestimated his power. The first merchant he shot for not overvaluing the Atlantean Assembly's paper would hurl all the others headlong into the loyalist camp. If that didn't lose the Assembly the war, nothing would. You simply could not ask a man to cheat himself, not even in the cause of liberty.

"What does the Frenchie say?" Micah asked, seeing he wouldn't get Victor to start executing tradesmen.

With a practiced thumb, Victor popped the wax seal off the letter. With his other thumb, just as practiced, he ordered Micah from the room. The messenger muttered as he left, but leave he did. He must have had a pretty good notion that Victor wouldn't tell him what de la Fayette had written. Still, even if the general command-ing hadn't, he might have. How were you worse off for trying?

The marquis spoke in a straightforward fashion. He wrote a much more flowery French, one that showed off his learning. Victor could make sense of it, which was all that mattered. And, having read through the let-ter, he found that de la Fayette made good sense, even if the nobleman used twice as many words to make it as he might have.

De la Fayette proposed a joint attack against Corn-wallis' men two weeks hence, the aim being to push the redcoats away from Hanover and up toward Croydon. *If the foe can be trapped in Croydon and defeated there, the whole of the coastal region from Hanover northwards shall be cleansed*, he wrote. *Should this be accomplished, how shall England continue to maintain that she governs Atlantis? Surely it would be the veriest impossibility.*

"Surely," Victor said aloud. Did that mean England wouldn't keep trying to maintain it? Could the enemy be pinned in Croydon and . . . cleansed, to use the young Frenchman's word? Another good question. Victor read the letter again. Slowly, he nodded to himself. "Worth a try."

He spent a pile of paper and even some precious specie readying the army to move. As he'd thought, the sight of silver spurred Hanover's merchants and artisans to far greater exertions than did the Atlantean Assembly's notes. "Pretty soon you'll need to bring me a wheelbar-rowful of paper to get yourself a wheelbarrowful of hardtack," a prominent baker told Victor.

"Things aren't so bad as that," protested Victor, who knew exactly how bad things were—he watched the exchange rate like a red-crested eagle.

"Didn't saw 'now.' Said 'pretty soon,' " the baker replied. "Nowadays, your barrow of paper'll buy you three barrows of biscuit, easy." He still stretched things, but by less than Victor wished he would have.

Atlantean cavalry patrols ranged north and south of Hanover. They brought back several men—and one woman—who'd tried to abscond with word for General Cornwallis. One of the men had a better written summary of the Atlantean army's plans than Victor had prepared for himself. "Where did you come by this?" Victor demanded, wondering if his officers included another budding Biddiscombe.

"Made it up myself," the captured spy said, not without pride. "Asked around a little here, a little there, put the pieces together, and that there was what I got."

"You do know what you'll get now?" Victor asked.

"Reckon I do." The man shrugged. He was giving a good game show of not showing fear. "Chance you take, isn't it?"

"It is," Victor agreed. "You took it, and you lost."

He watched the spy hanged the next day. The fellow went up the stairs to the top of the gallows under his own power. More than a few men about to die needed help on their last journey. Jeering patriots cursed him as he climbed. His face was pale, but he had the spirit to nod back to them. The hangman tied his legs together, hooded him, and put the rope around his neck. The trap dropped. A snap said the noose broke the spy's neck. He got a quick death, then, and an easy one, as such things went.

Victor wondered how much that meant, and whether it meant anything. Had the riders caught all the loyalists slipping out of Hanover? Was some other man even now giving an English officer word as detailed as this dead spy would have brought? Or were several others passing on smaller pieces of the puzzle, pieces an intelligent enemy could fit together into a pattern that showed the truth?

It struck the commanding general as only too likely. He'd done what he could do, though. He had to hope it would prove enough.

One way to make it enough would have been to move out sooner than he'd planned and catch the English by surprise. Had he been operating alone, he would have done just that. But he had to take his allies into account. Moving out before the date agreed to with de la Fayette would also have caught the French by surprise. Since the whole point of this scheme was to catch the redcoats between the two armies, he couldn't afford to strike precipitately.

A fishing smack coming up the coast from Cosquer brought him a letter. As far as he knew, he'd never heard of *Monsieur* Marcel Freycinet, who inscribed his name on the outside of the letter. Puzzled, Victor broke the seal and unfolded the sheet of paper.

Monsieur Freycinet, it turned out, was grateful to him. As Victor read on, he decided he would much rather not have had the other man's gratitude. If he did have to have it, he would much rather not have known he had it. Freycinet turned out to be the planter who owned Louise, whose embraces Victor had so enjoyed when he was first making the Marquis de la Fayette's acquaintance.

And not only had he enjoyed them, it seemed. Louise was with child, and confidently asserted that Victor was the father. Victor could hardly call her a liar. If he hadn't fathered a child on her, it wasn't for lack of effort. Here was Blaise's query, come back to haunt him.

The situation was impossible. It was impossible, in fact, in several different ways. One reason Freycinet was grateful was that the baby, which would of course be a slave like its mother, would provide pure profit for him. Imagining a son of his on the auction block made Victor feel he was bathing in hellfire.

He couldn't very well claim the baby for his own, though. The mere thought of the scandal made him flinch. And the scandal wasn't the worst—far from it. How would Meg feel if he did such a thing? He thought of the three young children they'd buried together. If he produced an heir of his flesh, but produced that heir from a comely Negress . . . The humiliation wouldn't kill his wife, but it would kill everything the two of them had together.

When Louise opened her legs for him, he'd never dreamt there might be issue from their joining. He wondered why not. He didn't wonder long: he'd cared about his own pleasure, his own satiation, and very little else. But a woman who lay down with a man could get up with child. It happened all the time. If it didn't, there would be no more men and women.

It happened all the time, yes. Why did it have to happen this time in particular? In spite of everything, Victor laughed at himself. How many men had said that before him? Any man who'd ever had it happen when he lay down with a woman not his wife—and that was just for starters.

What was he going to do? "What am I going to do?" he asked out loud. No answer came to him from the empty air. The only folk who found answers there were prophets and madmen. If he was going to come up with any answers, he'd have to find them inside himself.

He couldn't even go talk with *Monsieur* Freycinet and see if they could hash out something. No, he'd have to do it by letter. Travel back and forth would make the conversation long and slow. And, if Freycinet proved no gentleman, he could publish Victor's letters to the world. That would embarrass not only Victor personally but also the Atlantean cause.

Well, no help for it. Even more reluctantly than if he were visiting a dentist, Victor inked a pen. He did the best he could, offering to buy Louise and set her free in whichever northern state she preferred. After a little more thought, he added in the price the child— *his* child!—would likely bring. He could afford it. He thought he could, anyhow. Meg would surely notice the hole this price made in their accounts . . . but what could you do? He'd worry about that when it happened. This had already happened.

He'd never sealed a letter with such care. The last thing he wanted was for anyone, even Blaise, to find out about this. The sealed sheet headed south aboard the first ship bound from Hanover to Cosquer.

Long before Victor could hope for a response—long before that ship could possibly have got to Cosquer—he had to lead the Atlantean army out against the redcoats. The chance of dying in battle had never looked so attractive before.

Redwood Hill remained in Atlantean hands. Victor took the Atlanteans out into open country just south of it, then swung northwest toward the closest English positions. After the first couple of days in the field, thoughts of Louise—and of Marcel Freycinet—didn't fill his every waking moment. He had other things to worry about.

Messengers from the Marquis de la Fayette told him the French regulars were moving, too. Maybe Cornwallis captured some of the marquis' messengers. Maybe his loyalist auxiliaries kept him well informed about what his opponents were up to. Or maybe he simply had a good sense of what he would have done were he commanding them. He maneuvered skillfully, doing everything he could to keep them from joining forces.

De la Fayette pressed hard from the west. Victor pressed . . . not quite so hard from the east. Victor still worried about protecting Hanover in case things went wrong. De la Fayette didn't care about such things so much: even more than Cornwallis, he enjoyed the advantage of fighting on territory not his own. He could afford to be more aggressive than either his foe or his ally. And, of course, he was so very young—headlong attack came naturally to him.

It worked, too. As the French and Atlanteans pushed towards each other, Cornwallis finally had to draw back toward the north to keep from getting pounded between them. Victor's soldiers finally got to meet the men who'd crossed the Atlantic to aid them against King George. And de la Fayette's soldiers got their first look at the army of the Atlantean Assembly.

After hard marching and fighting, the French weren't so elegant as they had been when they first landed in Atlantis. Their uniforms were patched and torn and faded. But they still marched like men who owned the world— and, even if they hadn't, like men who'd invented close-order drill.

"These—these iss *soldiers*!" Baron von Steuben cried as de la Fayette's men approached. He might not be grammatical, but he meant every bit of it.

Looking at the ranks of his own army, Victor knew them for soldiers, too. They weren't so perfect on the parade ground as the French regulars, but they marched well. Their accouterments were far more uniform than they had been when the fight against England commenced. Bayonets tipped most Atlantean muskets. And the men had the look of veterans. They *were* veterans. They eyed their French allies with undoubted respect, but with nothing resembling awe. By now, they had the redcoats' measure. And if they could stand against English regulars, why shouldn't they be able to stand alongside the men from France?

The Marquis de la Fayette rode forward to greet Victor. As he drew near, the Atlanteans smartly presented arms. He did the best thing he might have done: he saluted them. "Three cheers for the Frenchie!" a delighted sergeant cried, and the cheers rang out one after another.

De la Fayette doffed his hat. He saluted Victor Radcliff, who gravely returned the courtesy. "These men are more, ah, presentable than I was led to expect," the nobleman said.

"This is not Terranova. We are not savages in breechclouts and feathers. We do not carry bows and arrows, or hatchets with stone heads," Victor replied with as much dignity as he could muster. "Our troops can give a good account of themselves against a like number of European soldiers. We have given a good account of ourselves against like numbers of English redcoats."

"I beg you to accept my apology, *Monsieur le Général*. If I offended, I assure you it was unintentional," de la Fayette said. "I knew your men could fight before I sailed from France."

He and Victor had been speaking French; Victor was far more fluent in it than de la Fayette was in English. Now Victor loudly translated the French nobleman's comment for the benefit of the Atlantean soldiers. They cheered de la Fayette again.

Grinning in pleasure unashamed, the marquis said, "I had not finished. I knew they could fight, yes, but I had not expected them to present so pleasing an aspect to the eye. More than one European monarch would be delighted to have troops of such an excellent appearance under his command."

Victor translated for his men once more. The Marquis de la Fayette won yet another cheer. Victor Radcliff wagged a finger at him. "I think you're trying to seduce these good fellows away from the Proclamation of Liberty and make them love kings and nobles again."

He was joking. De la Fayette had to know it. All the same, the young Frenchman made as if to push away his words. "Never would I do such a thing! Never!" he exclaimed. "I told you my view of this soon after we met. The Proclamation of Liberty is a shining beacon in the history of the world. And I think its flame will—and should—spread far and wide from Atlantis."

"It's already spread across the Hesperian Gulf to the English settlements in Terranova," Victor said. Truly Thomas Paine was worth his weight in gold—no small praise in the specie-starved United States of Atlantis.

"I understand that, yes. But these settlements are only a small thing," de la Fayette said. They—and their importance to Atlantis—didn't seem small to Victor. Before he could say so, the marquis went on, "I expect the ideals of the Proclamation of Liberty to kindle the kingdoms of Europe before many years go by, *Monsieur le Général*. And not Europe alone, it could be. Like our Lord, the Proclamation of Liberty speaks to all mankind in a voice that cannot be ignored. One day, its words will be heard by the Ottoman Turks, by the Persians, by the Chinese, and even by the hermit kingdom of Japan."

"Well!" Victor said in astonishment. Not even Paine had ever made such claims. Victor bowed in the saddle to de la Fayette. "You are the most . . . republican noble I ever imagined."

"You do me great honor by saying so," the marquis answered. "That is, perhaps, one reason his Majesty chose me to command this army. He knew me to be more than sympathetic to your cause. And he may have judged it safer for the monarchy in France to send me across the ocean."

"I see," Victor said slowly. So King Louis was trying to solve his own problems as well as Atlantis', was he? From things Victor had heard, he wouldn't have judged the King of France to be so clever. Maybe Louis wasn't. So long as one of his ministers was, what difference did it make?

De la Fayette perfectly understood his hesitation. "Have no fear, my friend," the Frenchman said. "My country will not stint nor scant my soldiers because I am not in the best of odors at Versailles."

Remembering how lavishly the French had already provided for their overseas army, Victor Radcliff decided he believed de la Fayette. "Good," he said. "Now that we've joined forces, let's work together until we root out the English from Atlantis once for all."

"Until victory, you mean," de la Fayette said. Victor nodded; he meant that very thing. The marquis cupped his hands in front of his mouth and shouted it in English: "Until victory!"

This time, the cheers from the Atlantean army seemed loud enough to scare Cornwallis and the redcoats all the way to Croydon. De la Fayette made a good friend. He might also make a bad enemy—Victor judged it very likely. Whoever had decided to let the marquis exercise his considerable talents far away from France must have known what he was doing.

However loud the Atlanteans' cheers, they didn't scare the redcoats away. Victor judged that a great pity. Cornwallis hung on north and a little east of Hanover. If anyone was going to drive him out of Atlantis, or even back to Croydon, it would have to be done with bayonet and musket and cannon, and, no doubt, with a formidable butcher's bill. Mere noise would not suffice.

Frenchmen and Atlanteans exercised together. They tried to, anyhow. The Atlanteans could have fit in fine with the redcoats. Atlantean drum and horn and fife calls were the same as the ones the English used. How could it be otherwise, when the Atlanteans had borrowed theirs from the mother country? But confusion ran rampant because the French used different calls and cues. Much polylingual profanity followed.

Victor wanted to place the steady French professionals in the center of the combined army's line of battle. His own men, more mobile and more woodswise, seemed likely to do better on the wings. Or they would have fared well with that arrangement, if only wings and center could each have been sure what the other would do.

"If we do not learn enough to fight together, we will fight our first engagement separately," the Marquis de la Fayette said. "We shall defeat the perfidious Englishmen even so."

"We have a better chance together," Victor said fretfully. "Your men didn't cross the ocean to stand apart from ours."

"We came here to win," the marquis said. "As for how—" He snapped his fingers.

"All right." Victor smiled in spite of himself. "I've been in a few fights like that. Sometimes you can't figure out afterwards how you won."

De la Fayette snapped his fingers again. "I tell you

again, this for how! So long as you take the slave wench to bed and swive her good and hard, what difference does it make who climbs on top? . . . Are you well, *Monsieur le Général*? Did I say something wrong? I have heard that English folk sometimes don't care to speak of matters that have to do with the boudoir. I never heard, though, that English folk don't care to do them!"

"I'm all right," Victor mumbled. Had he turned red? Or white? Or green? He would have bet on green. He and Blaise had joked about green men. But whenever he thought about Louise and about the child she carried—about his own child!—green seemed the only color he could go.

But, in law, the child he'd fathered on Louise wasn't his. In law, that child belonged to Marcel Freycinet. Throughout his arguments with Blaise, Victor hadn't felt slavery's injustice. How should he, when that injustice hadn't bitten him? Well, the trap had closed on his leg now, or perhaps on an even more sensitive appendage.

By this time, his letter should have reached *Monsieur* Freycinet . . . shouldn't it? No sure accounting for wind and wave, but Victor thought so. And the French Atlantean planter's reply ought to be on its way north . . . oughtn't it? Again, no way to be certain, but . . .

"You seem perhaps *un petit peu* distracted, *Monsieur*, if it does not offend you that I should speak so," de la Fayette observed. "If whatever troubles you can be washed away with brandy or rum, I should be honored to lend whatever assistance in the cleansing I may."

Victor Radcliff had never heard—had never dreamt of—a fancier way to propose that the two of them get drunk together. Most of the time, he would have liked nothing better. But if he started pouring it down now, his sad story might pour out of him. He was readier to trust de la Fayette with his life than with his reputation. He was, in short, a man.

"Once we've beaten the English, we'll have something worth celebrating," he said. "Till then, I'd rather not."

"A renunciation! Crusading zeal! Almost a Lenten vow!" the marquis exclaimed. "Meaning no disrespect, but I did not look for such a spirit from an English Protestant."

"We don't always find what we look for, or look for what we find," Victor said. And wasn't *that* the sad and sorry truth!

His force and de la Fayette's kept working together. What choice had they? But Victor feared they would have to fight as separate contingents, not as parts of a single army. He wished he had the French nobleman's confidence. He wished . . . for all kinds of things.

A few days later, a courier thrust a sheet of paper into his hand, saying, "This here just got to Hanover, General."

"Thank you," Victor replied, breaking the seal on Marcel Freycinet's letter. One of his wishes, and not the smallest, had just come true. Now he had to discover how big a fool he'd been in wishing for it.

My dear General, Freycinet wrote, *I am in receipt of your letter of the nineteenth* ultimo. *I regret that I cannot see my way clear to agree to your undoubtedly generous proposal. While I was pleased—indeed, privileged—to have Louise serve you for a time, I do not wish to be permanently deprived of her, nor of the child she is to bear. She is being treated with all consideration, I assure you, and is in excellent health. She sends you her regards, as I send mine. I have the honor to remain your most obedient servant. . . .* He signed his name.

Although Victor hadn't cared to get drunk with the Marquis de la Fayette, he hadn't said a word about crawling into a bottle alone. And he proceeded to do exactly that.

XX

$\mathcal{L}$istening to gunfire while hungover wasn't something Victor would have recommended. However much he wished it would, his head didn't fall off. He disguised what the Spaniards called a pain in the hair with a stoic expression and a few surreptitious nips from a flask of barrel-tree rum.

Maybe those nips weren't surreptitious enough. Both Blaise and the Marquis de la Fayette sent him thoughtful glances. Neither presumed to ask him anything about his sore head, though. That was the only thing that really mattered.

No—that and the advance of the Atlantean and French armies. If not for their advance, musketry and cannon fire wouldn't have lacerated his tender ears. *The things I endure for my country*, he thought. But the rum, even if it did make his factotum and the French commander wonder, also took the edge off his headache. By evening, he was more or less himself again.

"Anything I can do for whatever's troubling you, General?" Blaise asked, adding, "I know *something* is, but damned if I know what."

"It's my own worry, Blaise," Victor said, and not another word. He couldn't very well claim it had nothing to do with the Negro. Knowing what it was, Blaise would have called him a liar—and he would have had a point, too. He didn't know, though. Victor hadn't been too drunk to burn Marcel Freycinet's latest letter the night before. He supposed things would come out sooner or later; things had an unfortunate way of doing that. As far as he was concerned, later was ever so much better than sooner.

By Blaise's expression, he had a different opinion. "If I knew what it was, maybe I could give you a hand with it," he said.

"I don't think so." Victor heard the slammed door in his own voice.

Blaise must have, too. "Well, I bet you'll change your mind one of these days," he said. "Won't be this one, though." And he stopped probing at Victor. Even Meg might have kept at it.

So might the Marquis de la Fayette, but another brisk skirmish with the redcoats the next morning gave him something else to think about. He sent some of the French regulars on a looping march to the north to try to drive in the enemy's right wing. Cornwallis' soldiers, or the loyalists serving beside them, must have sniffed out the maneuver: the enemy fell back half a mile or so rather than waiting to withstand an attack in a disadvantageous position.

Half a mile closer to Croydon, then. If the Atlanteans and the French kept moving forward at that rate, they'd get to the northeastern city . . . some time toward the end of next winter. Victor repented of making such calculations. Then he repented of repenting, for he knew he couldn't help making them.

"I wish the English would stay to be netted," de la Fayette said. "It would make the whole undertaking so much easier."

"Well, yes," Victor agreed, deadpan. "And if a beefsteak cut itself up and hopped into your mouth bite by bite after you cooked it, that would make eating easier, too."

The French noble raised an eyebrow. "It could be that you take me less seriously than you might."

From a man of a certain temper, such a statement could be the first step on the path that led to a duel. Did de la Fayette have that kind of temper? Victor Radcliff didn't care to find out. He'd never fought a duel, nor did he want to fight his first one now. "I was trying to make a joke," he said. "If I offended you, I did not mean to, and I am sorry for it."

"Then I shall say no more about it," de la Fayette replied. And, to his credit, he didn't.

North of Hanover, more fields were planted in rye and oats and barley than in wheat. That was partly because the folk of Croydon brewed a lot of beer. Oh, some Germans brewed beer from wheat, but most folk preferred barley. Victor knew he did. But the main reason the other grains gradually supplanted wheat was that the growing season got short up here. When the weather stayed good, or even reasonable, wheat ripened well enough. But, if you were going to lose your crop about one year in four, you had to own a certain boldness of character to put it in the ground in the first place. Farmers of the more stolid sort chose grains that grew faster.

"Barley and rye, in France, are for peasants," the Marquis de la Fayette said. "And oats . . . Oats are for horses."

"Englishmen say the same thing about Scots and their oatmeal," Victor answered. "But more than one Scot has seen that English farmers eat oats, too."

"Do you?" the nobleman asked.

"If I eat katydids, I'm not likely to stick at oats, *Monsieur*. And I don't—I like oatmeal myself. Nor should you. I've already seen that your French soldiers don't turn up their noses at horsemeat. If you eat the beasts that eat the oats, you may as well eat the oats, too."

"It could be. But then again, it could also be otherwise," de la Fayette replied. "The delicate woodcock feasts on earthworms, while I should be less eager to do the same."

"A point." As Victor Radcliff thought about it, a slow smile spread across his face. "As a matter of fact, the same thing occurred to me not so very long ago, although in aid of our native oil thrushes rather than woodcocks."

"There you are, then." The marquis looked around. "And here we are. If we keep pressing forward, very soon we shall force General Cornwallis and his Englishmen back into Croydon."

"Let's hope we do," Victor said. If de la Fayette had made the same calculation he had himself, the Frenchman would have realized they wouldn't make the redcoats hole up in Croydon all that soon. Plainly, de la Fayette hadn't. Which meant . . . what? Most likely that de la Fayette was of a more optimistic, less calculating temperament. Victor laughed at himself. *As if I didn't already know that.*

Most of the people who lived north of Hanover sprang from one or another of the sterner Protestant sects that had sprung up in England and Scotland in the sixteenth and seventeenth centuries. Their descendants still looked as if they disapproved of everything under the sun. If soldiers in the Atlantean army argued about God's nature or will, chances were at least one of them came from the state of Croydon.

Fortunately, the locals' grim disapproval extended to Cornwallis and his followers. "That man is assuredly hellbound," one farmer told Victor, sounding as certain as if he'd checked St. Peter's registry and discovered the English general's name wasn't there. (A joke Victor refrained from making: the Croydonite would have discovered Papist pretensions in him if he had, regardless of whether they were really there.)

Instead of joking, Victor asked, "How do you know that . . . ah . . . ?"

"My name is Eubanks, General—Barnabas Eubanks,"

the local said. "As for how I know, did I not see him with my own eyes take a drink of spirituous liquor? 'Wine is a mocker, strong drink is raging,' the Good Book says, which makes it true. And did I not hear him most profanely take the name of the Lord in vain, that also being prohibited by Holy Scripture?"

He could as easily have seen Victor drink rum or heard him blaspheme. The profession of arms lent itself to such pastimes, perhaps more than any other. If this Barnabas Eubanks didn't understand that ... But a glance at Eubanks' stern, pinched features told Victor he did understand. He simply wasn't prepared to make any allowances. Yes, he was a Croydon man, all right.

"While I should be glad to see General Cornwallis in the infernal regions, I find myself more immediately concerned with his earthly whereabouts," Victor said. "What did you hear from him besides his blasphemy?"

"He and one of his lackeys were speaking of how they purposed making a stand in Pomphret Landing." Eubanks' mouth tightened further; Victor hadn't believed it could. "The place suits them, being a den of iniquity," Eubanks added.

All Victor knew about Pomphret Landing was that it lay between Hanover and Croydon. Until this moment, he'd never heard that it was as one with Sodom and Gomorrah. "How is it so wicked?" he inquired.

"I am surprised you do not know. I am surprised its vileness is not a stench in the nostrils of all Atlantis," Barnabas Eubanks replied. "Learn, then, that Pomphret Landing supports no fewer than three horrid taverns, that it has a theater presenting so-called dramas, and"— he lowered his voice in pious horror—"there is within its bounds a house of assignation in which women sell their bodies for silver!"

You silly twit! What do you expect sailors coming off the sea to do but drink and screw? No, Victor didn't shout it, which only proved he was learning restraint as he grew older. He also wondered where the wanton women's partners came by silver in these hard times.

He didn't ask that, either. All he said was, "The theater doesn't sound so bad."

"Oh, but it is," Eubanks said earnestly. "The plays presented encourage adultery, freethinking, and all manner of other such sinful pastimes."

"I see," Victor murmured. *If we can drive the redcoats out of Pomphret Landing without smashing the theater or burning it down, I may watch a play there myself.* One more thing he didn't tell his narrow-minded, if patriotic, informant.

Forcing Cornwallis to pull back from Pomphret Landing wouldn't be so simple. The town sat on the east bank of the Pomphret. Cornwallis' engineers had burnt or blown up the bridges over the river. Locals told Victor there was no ford for some miles inland. English artillerists fired their field guns across the Pomphret at his mounted scouts. Most of those shots missed, as such harassing fire commonly did. But de la Fayette's Frenchmen butchered two horses that met cannon balls. And the Atlanteans buried a man who also made one's sudden and intimate acquaintance.

French engineers assured Victor they could bridge the Pomphret. "Fast enough to keep the redcoats from gathering while you do it?" he asked them.

They didn't answer right away. The way they eyed him said he'd passed a test, one he hadn't even known he was taking. At last, cautiously, the most senior man replied, "That could be, *Monsieur*. It is one of the hazards of the trade, you might say."

"No doubt," Victor said. "That doesn't mean we should invite it if we don't have to, *n'est-ce pas?*"

The engineers put their heads together. When they broke apart, their grizzled spokesman said, "Perhaps if we began at night . . ."

"You would be working by torchlight then, is it not so?"

"We are not owls. We cannot see in pitch blackness, you know," the senior engineer said regretfully.

"Do you not believe the Englishmen might notice what you are about?" Victor asked.

"This too is a hazard of the trade, I fear," the engineer answered. "Having commanded for some little while, *Monsieur le Général*, I daresay you will have observed it yourself by now."

Shut up and quit bothering us, he meant. An Atlantean would have come right out and said so. The Frenchman knew how to get his meaning across without being ostentatiously rude. Either way, the result was frustrating. Victor looked up into the heavens. The moon rode low in the east. It would be full soon; against the daylight sky, it looked like a silver shilling with one edge chewed away. The pale-faced man in the moon didn't wink at him—that had to be his imagination.

And if his imagination was working hard enough to see such things . . . If it was, maybe he could make it work hard other ways as well. "Do you think you could bridge the Pomphret by the light of the full moon?"

He made the engineers huddle again, anyhow. That was as much as he'd hoped for—he'd feared they would kill his scheme with genteel scorn. The graying senior man replied, "That is possible, *Monsieur*. Possible, I repeat. It is by no means assured."

"I understand," Victor said. "Here is what I have in mind. . . ." He spoke for some little while.

This time, the French engineers didn't need to confer. Almost identical, slightly bemused, smiles spread across all their faces as near simultaneously as made no difference. "You have come up with something out of the ordinary, *Monsieur le Général*. No one could deny it for a moment," their grizzled spokesman said. "Truly, I admire your original tenor of thought."

"And here I believed myself a baritone," Victor said. The engineers flinched, as if at musket fire. Ignoring that, Victor went on, "Do you think the plan is worth trying, then?"

"Why not?" the engineer said gaily. "After all, what is

the worst that can happen?" He answered his own question: "We can get shot, fall into the river, and feed the fish and turtles and crayfish. Not so very much, eh?"

"One hopes not," Victor said dryly.

"One always hopes," the engineer agreed. "The fish, the turtles, the crayfish—they get fat regardless."

Against the dark blue velvet of the night, the moon glowed like a new-minted sovereign. Torches and bonfires blazed, turning night into day on this stretch of the Pomphret. Engineers shouted orders. Atlantean and French soldiers, most of them stripped to the waist, fetched and carried at the direction of the technically trained officers.

Bridging a river was not quiet work. Bridging a river by firelight at night was not inconspicuous work. It drew English scouts the way those soldiers' bare torsos drew mosquitoes. Some of the scouts fired horse pistols and carbines at the Frenchmen and Atlanteans out of the night. Others galloped away to bring back reinforcements. Victor heard their horses' hoofbeats fade in the distance despite the din of axes and saws and hammers and despite the Pomphret's gentler murmuring. He thought he heard those hoofbeats, anyhow. Maybe that was only his imagination again. He could hope so.

Hope or not, though, he placed some field guns near the Pomphret's west bank. If those reinforcements got here: no, dammit: when they did—they would have cannon with them. He wanted to be able to respond in kind.

But Cornwallis' artillerists would have every advantage in the world. His own guns had to try to wreck the carriages and limbers of enemy cannon hiding in the dark. The English gunners wouldn't even care about his, not unless his men got very lucky. A growing bridge, all lit up by flames and by the brilliant moon, made the easiest target any fool could think of. Sometimes there was just no help for a situation, worse luck.

Crash! A cannon ball tumbled six feet of bridge into

the Pomphret. "Good thing nobody was standing on that stretch," Blaise said.

"So it was," Victor agreed. "But I'm afraid we can't play these games without losses." Hardly had he spoken before another cannon ball jellied a French engineer's leg. The man was carried off shrieking and bleeding to the surgeons. One quick, dismayed glance at the wound—even that was too much, because it made anyone who saw it want to look away—told Victor they would have to amputate to have any chance of saving the fellow's life. A couple of minutes later, the engineer screamed again, even louder.

"Poor devil," Blaise muttered.

Victor nodded; he was thinking the same thing himself. Then he rode out into the firelight to let the redcoats know he was there. It was important that they should understand he was personally supervising this operation.

They didn't need long to realize as much. Bullets cracked past his head. His horse sidestepped nervously. He didn't draw back into the darkness till after a roundshot skipped past, much too close for comfort. And, thanks to the full moon, the darkness was less dark than it might have been. Enemy fire pursued him far longer than he would have wanted.

"That was foolish," Blaise told him after the English finally stopped trying to ventilate his spleen.

"It could be," Victor said. "But it was also necessary. Now they are certain this bridge has the utmost importance to our cause. They will be so very proud of themselves for thwarting its construction."

The Negro clucked reproachfully. "They would have been mighty damn proud of themselves for killing you. Oh, yes, that they would."

"True enough, but they didn't." Victor Radcliff made himself shrug. "You have to take chances sometimes, that's all."

"We could have dragged you off to the surgeons, too," Blaise said. "They would have shot the horse, and then carved it into steaks and ribs and whatnot. They would not do the same for you, even if it would have been a mercy."

"It happens," Victor said. Horribly wounded men sometimes begged to die. If their wounds were dreadful enough, kind friends or appalled strangers would put them out of their torment. As Blaise said, what was mercy for a horse could also be a mercy for a man.

He eyed the moon. It was starting the long, slow slide down toward the Green Ridge Mountains. After midnight, then. An English sniper shot an Atlantean running out to lay more wood on a bonfire. The wounded greencoat hopped away from the blaze. By the way he swore, he wasn't too badly hurt. If blood poisoning or lockjaw didn't carry him off, he'd probably be back in the fight in two or three weeks.

Time dragged on. Try as the French engineers would, they seemed unable to push a bridge very far across the Pomphret. The redcoats mocked them from the far side of the river. Most of the mockery was in English, which few of the Frenchmen understood. They were the lucky ones.

"Any man called me even a quarter of that, I'd kill him," Blaise said.

"We'll have our chance before long," Victor answered. "So I hope, at any rate."

At last, dawn began painting the eastern horizon gray and then pink. The engineers gave up. The redcoats jeered louder and more foully than ever. But now they were more visible to the French and Atlantean artillerists. The gunners answered with balls of iron.

Having made sure their foes wouldn't span the Pomphret here, Cornwallis' men drew back out of range. They left a few soldiers near the river, where the men could keep an eye on their opponents and make sure the French and Atlanteans wouldn't keep trying to bridge this stretch of the river.

Which didn't mean the French and Atlanteans wouldn't

try to bridge the Pomphret somewhere else. It only meant the redcoats wouldn't expect them to bridge it anywhere else. Cornwallis' troops made that unpleasant discovery a couple of hours after sunup.

Pistol shots and carbines announced cavalry coming down from the north. The bigger booms from field guns announced that artillery accompanied the horsemen. Before long, crashing volleys announced that solid blocks of infantry accompanied the cavalry and field guns.

General Cornwallis hadn't sent his whole army north from Pomphret Landing: nowhere near. He'd sent enough men to keep the engineers from bridging the Pomphret where his scouts discovered them making the effort. He'd succeeded in that. Meanwhile, a few miles farther north, more French engineers quietly did bridge the river . . . and the English had no idea they were doing it till after it was done.

Taken in the flank by the troops who'd unexpectedly crossed to the east side of the Pomphret, the redcoats fled south. Victor Radcliff crossed the river in a rowboat.

He shook the hand of the Marquis de la Fayette, who'd led the larger detachment of Frenchmen and Atlanteans over the Pomphret to the north. "My compliments to your engineers," Victor said. "They performed bravely here and splendidly in your position."

"My chief engineer, Major Flamel, extends his compliments to you, *Monsieur le Général*," de la Fayette replied. "He assures me it was by your clever ruse alone that we gained passage over the river."

"Having an idea is easy. Turning it into something useful is anything but," Victor said. "Major Flamel gets the credit for doing that."

"As I have seen before, you are a generous man," the French noble said. "I presume you now intend to drive the Englishmen out of Pomphret Landing?"

"That's what I have in mind, yes. I don't know what

kind of works they've built north of town—it doesn't do to underestimate Cornwallis' engineers, either," Victor said.

"Sadly, I have also seen this for myself," de la Fayette agreed. "But even if their fieldworks prove strong, what prevents us from marching past them to the sea and trapping the redcoats between our lines to the east and the Pomphret to the west?"

"I'd like nothing better than to trap them inside Pomphret Landing," Victor said. "If we do that, we win the war. So it seems to me, anyhow. And if it seems the same to General Cornwallis, he won't let us do it. He'll fall back on Croydon before we can cut him off. Croydon has the best harbor north of Hanover, and it sits on a peninsula easy to fortify. I would much rather stand siege there than in Pomphret Landing, especially with the Royal Navy easily able to supply the garrison by sea."

"With Cornwallis having so much of his force here, the enemy will not easily be able to bring in foodstuffs from elsewhere in Atlantis," de la Fayette said. "Most of the land is under the control of the United States of Atlantis in your person." He bowed.

"There is some truth in that," Victor said. "Some, but less than I would wish. True, most of the redcoats are here. But England could still land more Terranovan savages near Avalon, or a force of German mercenaries down by New Hastings. And forces loyal to King George—native Atlantean forces, I mean—still hold too much of the countryside."

"Custis Cawthorne and your other representatives in Paris spoke little of that," de la Fayette observed. "They talked always of the war against oppressive England, not of the civil war against your own folk."

"Should that surprise you?" Victor said. "Don't French diplomatists also paint the best picture they can of your kingdom's situation and needs?"

De la Fayette bowed again, this time in amusement mingled with rue. "No doubt they do. But one does not expect the vices of civilization from the folk of a land so new and vital. *Eh bien*, perhaps one should."

You aren't such bumpkins as we thought. The marquis couldn't very well mean anything else. Now Victor bowed to him. "Serving one's country to the best of one's ability is surely no vice, your Grace."

"Well, no." De la Fayette seemed faintly embarrassed. "But so many of us were charmed by your seeming rusticity. *Monsieur* Cawthorne gives a masterly portrayal."

Victor had all he could do not to laugh himself silly over that. Could any man be compelled to enjoy himself more than Custis Cawthorne enjoyed playing such a role? While that might be possible, Victor found it most unlikely. "And how many pretty little French girls has *Monsieur* Cawthorne sweet-talked into his bed by playing the poor chap who needs to be instructed in such arts? And how many of them ended up astonished that he turned out to know so much already?"

The Marquis de la Fayette looked astonished himself. "How could you know that?"

This time, Victor did laugh; if he hadn't, he would have exploded. "I've known *Monsieur* Cawthorne many years. I have some notion of how his beady little mind works. Does he ask people to teach him card games, too, and take away their money with what he calls beginner's luck?"

"Nom d'un nom!" de la Fayette said, and not another word on that score, from which Victor concluded that Custis had some of the nobleman's money in his pocket. *Well, good for Custis*, Victor thought. It was high time the United States of Atlantis turned a profit on something.

The field fortifications north of Pomphret Landing were as strong as the talented English engineers could make them. All the same, Cornwallis used them to shield his withdrawal to the east, not to try to hold the town. "It turned out as you foretold," de la Fayette said. "It could be that I should ask you to read my palm."

"I'm sure we both have better things to do with our

time," Victor said. After the Atlanteans and French rode into Pomphret Landing, he found one of those things: he sent a letter to General Cornwallis, urging him to surrender. *Surely you can see your force is reduced to no more than a red-coated carbuncle on the fair face of Atlantis*, he wrote.

Before sending the letter to Croydon under a flag of truce, he showed it to de la Fayette. "A carbuncle on the face of Atlantis?" the Frenchman said after working his way through the English. "You prove yourself to be possessed of a noble heart, *Monsieur le Général*. Me, I would call him a boil on Atlantis' arse."

Victor smiled. "That is what I was thinking, as a matter of fact. Whether I have a noble heart or not, I would not presume to say. But I am sure General Cornwallis has one. This being so, I am confident he will divine my meaning even if I state it obliquely."

"Obliquely?" The marquis savored that. "Not a word I would have used, which does not keep me from understanding you. As you speak English with me more often, I discover in it subtleties of which I would not previously have suspected it was capable."

"You are generous, your Grace," Victor Radcliff said, more sincerely than not. For anyone from France to allow that English might be subtle was no small concession.

Having received de la Fayette's approbation, the letter did go off to Croydon. Victor didn't think he would have to wait long for Cornwallis' reply, and he didn't. The courier who'd taken Victor's missive also brought back the English commander's response. "I didn't get to read it, General, on account of it was upsy-down to me while he was a-writing it, and he sealed it up as soon as it was done, but I don't reckon he's ready to chuck in the sponge," the courier said.

"The worst he can tell me is no," Victor said, breaking the seal. "Even if he should, how am I worse off than I would have been without making the attempt?"

He unfolded the letter. Sure enough, the missive was in Cornwallis' own hand, with which Victor had been familiar since the last war, when they fought on the same side. *Always a pleasure to receive even the smallest communication from you, my dear General Radcliff,* Cornwallis wrote. If he was not a man with a noble heart, he certainly was one who flaunted his urbanity.

Because this pleasure is so great, it pains me doubly to find myself compelled by circumstance to refuse you in anything, the English general continued. *None the less, I am so compelled on this occasion. I do not believe our situation hopeless: very much the reverse, in fact. Whilst we do at present find ourselves occupying only Croydon, this may change at any moment, as you must be aware. The Royal Navy may come with orders for our embarkation, in which case we should land at some spot not well prepared to resist us. Or, contrariwise, ships may bring us reinforcements from across the sea. Should that come to pass, you and your foreign allies would soon have reason to look to your laurels. These things being so, continued struggle seems far preferable to craven surrender. I have the honor to remain your most obedient servant....* Cornwallis appended his signature, complete with a fancy flourish below his name.

The courier had been watching Victor's face. "He says no, eh?"

"He does indeed. He has reasons he finds good for going on with the fight."

"*Are* they good reasons?" the courier asked.

"They ... may be." Victor didn't like to admit even so much. He imagined the Royal Navy taking Cornwallis' redcoats down to Freetown or Cosquer. Their arrival would indeed come as a complete and most unwelcome surprise in those parts. And if transports brought five or ten thousand more English soldiers—or even mercenaries from Brunswick or Hesse—to Croydon, Cornwallis could sally forth against the Atlanteans and French with every hope of success.

"What do we do, then?" the courier inquired.

"I'm still ciphering that out," Victor said slowly. It seemed a better answer than *Damned if I know*, even if they meant about the same thing. What really bothered him was that he would have trouble laying proper siege to Croydon. The Royal Navy didn't have to take the redcoats down the coast or reinforce them to aid them against his army and the Frenchmen. As long as food and powder and shot came into Croydon, Cornwallis' army was and would remain a going concern. And the Atlanteans could do very little to stop the Royal Navy from supplying the enemy.

Victor Radcliff took Cornwallis' reply to de la Fayette. The marquis read it with grave attention. "What he says is very much what I should say if I found myself in his position."

"And I," Victor agreed. "Is there any chance the French navy might interpose itself between Croydon and the ships of the Royal Navy? Prevent Cornwallis from revictualing himself and he becomes vulnerable to all the usual hazards of a siege. That failing, he is in almost as enviable a position as the defenders of Nouveau Redon before the spring was put out of commission."

"I could wish you had chosen a different comparison," de la Fayette said.

"My apologies," Victor said, "but you will, I trust, understand why it sprang to mind. Not only was I there, but so was General Cornwallis—Lieutenant-Colonel Cornwallis, as he was then."

"Indeed." De la Fayette's tone showed him to be imperfectly appeased. With an effort, he brought his wits back to the matter at hand. "As for our navy ... I must confess, I know not whether that may be within its capacity."

"We should find out." Victor's enthusiasm spurred him on. "We truly should, your Grace. If we can cork up the Englishmen in Croydon, the war is ours, and the United States of Atlantis indisputably free. For what other purpose did you and your brave men leave France?"

"For no other purpose," the marquis admitted ... reluctantly? He also found a notable difficulty with Victor's scheme, and proceeded to note it: "How do you propose to inform the French navy that its services in these parts are desired? I have not the faintest idea where in the broad Atlantic—or even the not so broad Mediterranean—its ships of the line and frigates may be."

Enthusiasm or no, Victor Radcliff found himself compelled to contemplate the cogent question. Having contemplated, he delivered his verdict: "Damnation!"

"Just so," de la Fayette agreed.

But, where he seemed to think the heartfelt curse settled things, Victor was less inclined to give in or give up. "We have as yet no Atlantean navy to speak of—" he began.

"Indeed not, or you would give your own vessels the task of interdicting Croydon," de la Fayette said, and then, "Interdicting? It is the right word, *n'est-ce pas?*"

"Yes, it is, but I hadn't finished yet," Victor said. "We have no navy to speak of, but we have a good many merchantmen and a great plenty of fishing boats. If we send them forth in search of your warships, they should be able to find them before long, and to lead them back here to render our cause such aid as may prove within their power."

The Marquis de la Fayette blinked. "God has blessed you with an adventurous spirit—this is not to be denied. Have you any notion how very wide the ocean is, however?"

"I do, sir," Victor replied. "I have crossed it myself, and my ancestors made their living from it for centuries." He didn't mention that he was no sailor himself. De la Fayette might already know that, but what point to reminding him if he did? Victor went on, "With enough boats searching, the enterprise is bound to succeed in time—and, chances are, in not such a long time, too."

"Well, it could be." De la Fayette didn't seem altogether convinced. Victor wasn't altogether convinced, either, but he was convinced it was worth a try. And the French nobleman seemed to admit that much, for he asked, "And what will our land forces be doing whilst awaiting the navy's arrival—which may not prove altogether timely?"

"I expect we will be doing what we would be doing if there were no such thing as the French navy," Victor replied. "That is to say, we will be doing everything in our power to defeat Cornwallis' army in and around Croydon. Had you anything else in mind for us?"

"By no means, *Monsieur le Général*. I merely wished to make certain you did not intend to rest on our laurels, so to speak. The war still wants aggressive prosecution, and will fail without it."

"D'accord," Victor said. De la Fayette smiled at the very French agreement. Victor continued, "My first target for prosecuting the war would be the English works defending the hamlet of Wilton Wells. If we drive them away from the village, we dent their lines in a way Cornwallis won't care for."

"Splendid!" the marquis said gaily. "Let us proceed, then."

Proceed they did. But Cornwallis' fieldworks bristled with cannon. Ditches and abatis kept the Atlanteans from getting close. The forlorn hopes that broke through the interlaced tree trunks and branches proved exactly that. The English guns sprayed them with canister. The men who could staggered back through the gaps they'd made in the abatis. The rest lay where they'd fallen, some writhing and moaning, others ominously still.

Some of the forlorn hopes were French, others Atlantean. Neither commander had any excuse to blame the other's soldiers, for they'd failed together. All de la Fayette said was, "It could be that we will find an easier way toward Croydon than the one that goes through Wilton Wells."

"It could be, yes," Victor said, admiring de la Fayette's *sangfroid*. "I had not thought this one would prove so well defended."

"Not everything works," de la Fayette said. "One

of the tricks of the game is to keep trying even after a failure."

"True enough." Victor had been a good deal older than the Frenchman was now when he'd learned that— which made it no less true.

XXI

The Atlanteans planned to feint at Wilton Wells again and strike a little farther east, just past Garnet Pond. Woods let them closely approach the redcoats' line there, and it didn't seem strongly held. If they could break through, Cornwallis' men would have to fall back toward Croydon in a hurry. Victor and de la Fayette could concentrate their force and attack where they pleased. The redcoats, trying to hold a line well outside of Croydon, had to try to stay reasonably strong all along it. Reasonably strong, with luck, would prove not to be strong enough.

With luck. Victor Radcliff had much too much reason to remember those two little, seemingly innocent, words after the thrust past Garnet Pond came to grief. The worst of it was, he couldn't think of anything he should have done differently.

It was sunny when the attacking column set out for Garnet Pond early in the morning. Sunny—he remembered that very well. Oh, the wind came down from the northwest, but what of it? Summer was over, and chilly winds were nothing out of the ordinary, especially in a northern settlement—a northern state—like Croydon.

De la Fayette seemed as happy with the arrangement as Victor was himself. "This is a well-conceived plan," he declared. Even if he was very young, his praise warmed Victor. "The false attack at the place we struck before will hold the English in place, or even, it could be, draw men from Garnet Pond to the position that seems more threatened."

"I hope so, yes." Victor did his best to keep his smile sheepish and modest rather than, say, full of gloating and anticipation.

"And we have deployed a full complement of sharp-shooters and skirmishers to ensure that the true attack is not detected prematurely," de la Fayette went on. "*Nom d'un nom, Monsieur le Général*, I cannot imagine what could possibly go wrong."

Maybe that was what did it. Had Victor been more pious, he might also have been more nearly certain it was. The Frenchman didn't *precisely* take the Lord's name in vain. He didn't use the Lord's name at all—not directly, anyhow. But wasn't trotting out a euphemism just as bad, really? Assuming the Lord was listening, wouldn't He know what was on your mind, what was in your heart, regardless of whether His name actually passed your lips? Victor wondered about it afterwards. But afterwards was too late, as afterwards commonly is.

"Clouding up," Blaise remarked not ten minutes after the attacking column set out.

"Well, so it is," Victor agreed. "What of it?" He tried to look on the bright side, even if that bright side was rapidly vanishing from the sky. The clouds were thick and roiling and dark. It hadn't been warm before they swept across the sky; it got noticeably colder as soon as they did. The air seemed damper, too, although Victor tried his best to tell himself that was only his imagination.

He might have managed to persuade himself. But Blaise's broad nostrils flared. "Smells like rain," he said.

"I hope not!" Victor exclaimed. But he knew that wet-dust odor as soon as Blaise pointed it out. As a matter of fact, he'd known it before, even if he hadn't wanted to admit it was there.

No matter what he'd managed to talk himself into, he

wouldn't have stayed deluded much longer. When rain started coming down, it was impossible to believe the weather remained fine. And this wasn't a light shower of the kind some of the people farther south called liquid sunshine. This was a downpour, a gullywasher, a cloudburst. . . . The ground under his feet turned to mud, and then to something a good deal more liquid than the stuff commonly known by that name.

"What does the Bible talk about?" Blaise said—shouted, really, to make himself heard over, or through, that roaring rain. "Forty days and forty nights?"

It hadn't even been raining forty minutes then. All the same, Victor understood why the Negro asked the question. It had gone from cloudburst to deluge. Had Noah's Ark floated by, Victor wouldn't have been amazed (but why didn't the Ark seem to contain any Atlantean productions?).

"Maybe I should recall them," Victor said. The Atlanteans would have a devil of a time shooting once they got past Garnet Pond—wet weather turned flintlocks into nothing more than clumsy spears and clubs.

"Redcoats won't be able to shoot at them, either," Blaise replied, understanding what he was worried about.

"Well, no," Victor said. "But not all our men have bayonets." At the beginning of the war, very few Atlanteans had them, giving the redcoats a great advantage when the fighting came to close quarters. These days, thanks to captured weapons and hard work at smithies all over Atlantis, most greencoats were as well armed as their English counterparts. "Or maybe I worry overmuch."

A few gunshots marked the moment when the feint went in. Victor admired the men on either side who'd managed to keep their powder dry. The shots rang out distinctly, even through the rain. But there were only a few. And no one had the slightest hope of reloading. After the scattered opening volley, both Atlanteans and Englishmen might have fallen back through time a thousand years, back to days long before the first clever artificer made a batch of gunpowder without blowing himself up in the doing.

Instead of musketry, a few shouts and screams pierced the curtain of sound the downpour spread over the scene. They were enough to let Victor picture it in his mind. He imagined dripping, muddy men stabbing with bayonets and swinging clubbed muskets as if they were cricket bats. He imagined rain and blood rilling down their faces and rain trying to wash away spreading patches of red on their tunics. And, knowing soldiers as he did, he imagined them all swearing at the weather at least as much as they swore at one another.

Off to the east, the main attacking party should have been able to gauge when to hit the English lines by the noise the men in the feint made. They probably couldn't hear the men in the feint at all, though. The major commanding them had to use his best judgment about when to go on—or whether to go in at all.

Victor Radcliff wouldn't have blamed him for aborting the attack. But he didn't. His men—and the redcoats facing them—also managed to get off a few shots. One cannon boomed. Hearing it go off truly amazed Victor. He had to hope it didn't harm his men too much.

And then he had to wait ... and wait ... and wait. No messenger came back from the main attack to tell him how it was going. Maybe the officer in charge forgot to send anyone. Maybe the messenger got killed or wounded before he went very far. Or maybe he just sank into the ooze and drowned.

If the attackers weren't going to tell Victor what had happened, he had to find out for himself—if he could. He rode toward the woods through which the Atlanteans should have gone. He rode ever more slowly, too, for the rain rapidly turned the road to a river of mud. The horse looked back at him reproachfully, as if wondering whether it would sink out of sight. Not much farther on, Victor began to wonder the same thing.

Where he had trouble going forward, he soon found out the Atlantean soldiers were managing to go back.

"It's no use, General!" one of them bawled through the rain.

"What happened?" Victor asked.

"We damn near drowned, that's what," the soldier answered.

"That cannon ball blew Major Hall's head off," another man added, which went a long way towards explaining why the poor major hadn't sent back any messengers. Losing your head metaphorically could distract you. Losing it literally ... got everything over with in a hurry, at any rate. And whoever'd taken over for Hall must not have thought to send word back, either.

"We got in amongst the redcoats," a sergeant said, "but we couldn't get through 'em. Nobody could do anything much, not in this slop." His wave took in rain and mud and bedraggled men.

"Damnation!" Victor Radcliff shook his fist at the black clouds overhead. They took not the slightest notice of him.

The storm lasted almost a week. By the time it finally blew out to sea, half the English earthworks had collapsed. Entrenchments on both sides were more than half full of water. Since the redcoats had so much trouble using their field fortifications, the Atlanteans might have walked into Croydon. They might have, that is, had walking anywhere not involved sinking thigh-deep in clinging muck.

Victor thanked heaven his own quartermasters had managed to keep most of the army's grain dry. That meant the troops could go on eating till the roads dried enough to bring in more wheat and barley and rye. *Even oats*, Victor thought. No one in these parts would have any trouble finding plenty of water for stewing up oatmeal.

If Cornwallis chose this moment to try to drive the Atlanteans away from Croydon, Victor didn't know how he would be able to hold back the redcoats. But the Englishmen, while working feverishly to repair their lines, didn't try to come out of them. Before long, Victor realized he'd worried over nothing. Had the redcoats attacked, they would have bogged down the same way his own men did.

"Are such storms common in these parts?" de la Fayette inquired, his manner plainly saying Atlantis wasn't worth living in if they were.

But Victor shook his head. "Down in the south, hurricanes are known," he answered. "Rainstorms like this up here ..." He shook his head again. "Bad luck—I know not what else to call this one."

"Bad indeed," the French noble said. "And are we to expect blizzards next?"

"God forbid!" Victor exclaimed, knowing too well that God was liable to do no such thing. But then, trying his best to look on the bright side of things, he added, "If we should have a hard freeze, the ground won't try to swallow us up, anyhow."

"Well, no." If that prospect pleased de la Fayette, he hid it very well. "But I find the climate in this country imperfectly equable. The southern regions suffer from excessive heat, while these parts seem to have a superabundance of both rain and snow. A more moderate regimen would be preferable—a regimen more like that of, *exempli gratia, la belle France*."

His reaching that particular conclusion amused Victor without much surprising him. The Atlantean general spread his hands. "I fear I cannot help it, your Grace. As I said a moment before, the weather is under the good Lord's command, not mine."

De la Fayette crossed himself. "You have reason, certainly. I shall pray that He might extend to your country the blessings He has generously granted mine."

If God hadn't changed Atlantis' climate at least since the days when Edward Radcliffe founded New Hastings—and probably not for centuries before that—he was unlikely to alter it at the marquis' request. De la Fayette had to know that as well as Victor did. All he meant was that he didn't care for the way things were.

Victor didn't, either, not the way they were up here. He liked the weather around his farm much better. Which only proved he, like de la Fayette, liked what he was used to and disliked any departure from it. Blaise felt the same way, though his African norm was far different from either white man's.

"Leaving the power of prayer out of the question, we should discuss what we might best attempt now," Victor said.

"So we should." The marquis sighed. "Such a pretty plan we had before. We would assuredly have surprised the redcoats with it." He paused, considering. "I don't suppose we could simply try it again."

That made Victor pause to consider, too. His first response was to call the suggestion ridiculous. The redcoats would be waiting for it. Or would they? The more he thought, the less sure he grew. He started to laugh. "Our stupidity in repeating ourselves would surprise them, at the least."

"Just so. Just so!" De la Fayette seemed to catch fire at the idea. "However insolent they are themselves, they would never believe we have the insolence to make the second stroke the same as the first."

Victor thought out loud: "Perhaps we should make the previous stroke the feint, and the previous feint the stroke."

"No. But no. Certainly not." De la Fayette shook his head so vigorously, he had to grab his tricorn to keep from losing it. "That, they would anticipate. It is precisely the ploy an ordinary man, a man without imagination, might try, thinking himself clever beyond compare."

"I see," Victor muttered, his ears burning. Well, he'd never thought himself anything but an ordinary man. De la Fayette seemed to agree with him.

Unaware that he might have given offense, the Frenchman went on, "If we try something altogether different from our previous ploy, we may find success. If, contrariwise, we surprise them by our stupidity, we may also hope to triumph. The flaw lies in the middle way, as it commonly does."

And so it was decided.

Even after it was decided, Blaise had his doubts about it. "If the redcoats look for this, they will slaughter us."

"That they will," Victor agreed, which made the Negro blink. Victor went on, "But if we essay anything that they anticipate, they are likely to slaughter us."

"Hmm." He'd made Blaise stop and think, anyhow. Then the black man delivered his verdict: "If we are going to do this, we had better do it quickly, lest a deserter betray the plan to the English."

That made excellent sense. Victor ordered the feint to go in at dawn the next morning, and the true attack to follow as soon as the redcoats seemed to have taken the bait. He also strengthened the picket line between his army and Cornwallis'. He didn't know whether he could keep deserters from slipping away, but he intended to try.

Both columns formed up in the chilly predawn darkness. Baron von Steuben volunteered to lead the attackers, replacing the late Major Hall. "Any cannon ball that hits this hard head will bounce off," he declared in gutturally accented English.

"Try not to make the experiment," Victor said. The German soldier of fortune nodded. Victor added one more piece of advice: "Strike hard and strike fast."

"I do it. The *Soldaten* do it also. They fear me more than any piffling redcoats," von Steuben said. Chances were he knew what he was talking about, too. A good drillmaster was supposed to inspire that kind of respectful fear in his men.

To Victor's ears, the feinting and attacking columns both made too much noise as they moved out. But he didn't hear any shouts of alarm from the English lines. Very often, what seemed obvious to a worried man was anything but to the people around him. Even more often, his failure to realize that alerted those other people to the idea that something funny was going on. *Don't give the game away ahead of time*, Victor told himself.

He waited to hear what would happen next. The feint went in when he expected it to. He'd urged the men to fight especially hard so they'd make the redcoats believe they truly meant to bull their way through. He was sure they understood the reason behind the order. He wasn't sure they would follow it. If anything, he feared them less likely to do so precisely because they understood why he asked it of them. Most of his men were veterans by now. They knew that, the more fiercely and ferociously they attacked earthworks, the better their chances of stepping in front of a cannon ball or a bullet or of meeting one of those fearsome English bayonets.

If they were veterans, wouldn't they take such mischances in stride? Redcoats would have. So would troops from the Continent—Baron von Steuben had taken such soldiering for granted till he got here. The Marquis de la Fayette still did, and got it from his Frenchmen. But Atlanteans were a different breed. They expected—no, they demanded—a solid return on their investment, regardless of whether they risked their time or their money or their lives.

English cannon thundered. Blaise coughed to draw Victor's notice. When Victor glanced his way, the Negro said, "The redcoats are going, 'Here come those Atlantean madmen again. Don't they ever learn their lessons?' "

"Heh," Victor Radcliff said uncomfortably. "Just wait a bit. Pretty soon, they'll find out how mad we are in truth."

"No." Blaise pointed at him. "Pretty soon *you* find out how mad we are in truth." Since that was what Victor was afraid of, he grimaced and shook his head and kept his mouth shut.

He wanted to go up and fight alongside the men in the striking force. Only one thing held him back: if Cornwallis' troops recognized him there, they would be sure that second column was the one they needed to concern themselves with. The general commanding started to swear.

"What now?" Blaise asked.

"Bugger me blind, but I should have gone in at the head of the feint," Victor said. "If anything would have made the Englishmen sure that was our principal column, my presence at its head was the very thing."

"And also the very thing to get you killed," Blaise observed. Atlanteans were more pragmatic than Europeans about such things: less likely to get themselves killed over pointless points of honor. Blaise was far more pragmatic than most white Atlanteans. He added, "Besides, the fellow leading it don't want you up there. If you are up there, the men pay attention to you, not to him."

Once more, Victor would have liked to find some way to tell him he was talking nonsense. Once more, he found himself unable. Major Porter was as much in charge of the feint as Baron von Steuben was in charge of the striking column. Both officers would do everything they could with what they had . . . and wouldn't want anyone else in position to joggle their elbow.

The feint went in. The racket of gunfire—and of shouts of rage and agony—grew and grew. So did the shouts of Englishmen rushing to their comrades' aid. By the noise they were making, they thought the Atlanteans were hitting the place where they'd bluffed before. After all, no one could be stupid enough to try the same thing twice in a row.

So de la Fayette had assured Victor, anyhow. It all sounded so lucid, so reasonable, so rational when the noble spelled it out. Then again, Frenchmen had a knack for sounding lucid, reasonable, rational. If they were as sensible as they seemed, why wasn't France in better shape?

Victor found himself cocking his head toward the left. He'd committed the feint. The redcoats were already responding to it. Baron von Steuben could get close to their line without their knowing it, as the luckless Major Hall had been doing when the heavens opened up.

"When?" Blaise asked.

"If I were up there with them, we'd go in—" Victor had wondered if he was nervous and fidgety and inclined to jump the gun. But he couldn't even get *now* out of his mouth before von Steuben put in the attack.

This cacophony made the other one small by comparison. Victor clenched his fists till his nails—which weren't long—bit into his callused palms. If they broke through . . . If they broke through, de la Fayette's Frenchmen would go in behind the striking column. They'd tear a hole in Cornwallis' line that you could throw a honker through.

And then what? Croydon? Victory? True victory at last? Cornwallis handing over his sword in token of surrender? Cornwallis admitting that the United States of Atlantis were here to stay?

Till this moment, the fight for Atlantean freedom had so consumed Victor, he'd had scant opportunity to wonder what would come afterwards. If Cornwallis and the redcoats had to sail away from Atlantis forever, where would they go? Back to England? Or west across the broad Hesperian Gulf to fight the rebels on the Terranovan mainland? Suppose they won there. How would the United States of Atlantis cope with being all but surrounded by the unloved and unloving former mother country? Victor had no idea.

There were worse problems to have. Losing the war against England instead of winning it, for instance. Not so long before, that had looked much too likely. Then, still unloved and unloving, the mother country would have set its boot on Atlantis' neck and stomped hard.

Which she might do yet. Victor knew he'd been building castles in the air. Any number of things could all too easily go wrong. He called to one of his young messengers—one who spoke fluent French. "My compliments to the Marquis de la Fayette, and please remind him to be ready to lead his men forward the instant the situation warrants."

"Right you are, General," the messenger agreed.

One of the usual slipshod Atlantean salutes, and away he went at a good clip. Victor smiled at his back. That kind of response would have earned the puppy stripes from Cornwallis—and, very possibly, from de la Fayette as well. Atlanteans did things their own way. It might not be pretty, but it worked . . . or it had so far.

Victor had talked himself hoarse making sure Baron von Steuben understood he was to send word back as soon as he thought it likely he would penetrate the red-coats' defenses. And the German officer did, but not quite the way the Atlantean commandant had expected. Instead of telling Victor what was going on in the middle of that cloudbank of black-powder smoke, von Steuben sent a runner straight back to de la Fayette.

That runner and Victor Radcliff's messenger must have reached the French noble at almost the same time. The first Victor knew about it was when de la Fayette's soldiers surged forward, musicians blaring out their foreign horn and drum calls.

For a heartbeat, Victor was mortally offended. Then he realized what must have happened. He also realized von Steuben had been absolutely right. If de la Fayette's troops were the ones who were going to move, de la Fayette was the man who most needed to know when they were to move. If Victor's laugh was rueful, it was a laugh even so. "Why doesn't anyone ever tell me anything?" he said.

"What's that?" Blaise asked.

"My own foolishness talking," Victor said, which probably made less of an answer than Blaise would have wanted. Victor climbed up onto his horse. His factotum also mounted. Urging his gelding forward, Victor went on, "If we are driving them, I will see it with my own eyes, by God!"

"And if by some mischance we are not driving them, you will ride straight into something you could have stayed away from." Blaise was always ready to see the cloud to a silver lining.

The firing ahead hadn't died out. The redcoats

were still plainly doing all they could to hold back the Atlanteans—and, now, de la Fayette's Frenchmen as well. But, as Victor rode past the woods that had sheltered his striking column till the moment it struck, he realized their best wouldn't be enough.

"By God!" he said again, and this time he sounded like a man who really meant it.

Baron von Steuben's men had punched a hole through the English line better than a furlong wide. Victor had hoped they might be able to break through so splendidly, but hadn't dared count on it. Counting on something ahead of time in war too often led but to disappointment.

And the Atlanteans had done what they were supposed to do after breaking through, too. They'd swung out to left and right and poured a fierce enfilading fire into the redcoats in the trenches to either side. Arrows on a map couldn't have more precisely obeyed the man who drew them. And if that wasn't von Steuben's doing, whose was it? The German deserved to be a colonel, if not a brigadier general.

De la Fayette's French professionals poured through the gap Atlantean ardor had torn. They too methodically volleyed at the Englishmen who tried to plug that gap. Victor was just riding into what had been the English position when the redcoats, every bit as competent as their French foes, realized they were playing a losing game and started falling back toward Croydon.

"On!" Victor shouted to his own men, and then, in French, *"Avant!"* He fell back into English to continue, "If we take the town from them, they've nowhere to go after that!" If de la Fayette or some of his officers wanted to translate his remarks for the benefit of the French soldiery, they were welcome to.

Croydon's outskirts lay only a couple of miles away. Whenever Victor rode to the crest of some little swell of ground, he could see the church steeples reaching toward the heavens. One of them was supposed to be the tallest steeple in all Atlantis, a claim furiously rejected in Hanover and New Hastings.

"I think we can do it." Was that Blaise's voice? Damned if it wasn't. If Blaise believed Croydon would fall, how could it do anything else?

Victor also began to believe his men would storm Croydon. And if they did ... when they did ... No one, yet, had thought to write a tune for the United States of Atlantis to use in place of "God Save the King." Maybe some minstrel needed to get busy in a hurry, because what stood between those united states and liberty?

Damn all Victor could see. His men were making for Croydon faster than the redcoats pulling out of their entrenchments and earthworks. If nothing slowed the Atlanteans and Frenchmen, they were less than half an hour from guaranteeing that the Union Jack would never fly over Atlantis again.

If nothing slowed them ... One more thought Victor Radcliff remembered a long, long time. No sooner had it crossed his mind than a band of cavalry—something more than a troop, but less than a regiment—thundered out of Croydon and straight toward the advancing Atlantean and French foot soldiers.

The riders wore buff and blue, not the red of English regulars. *Loyalists, then*, Victor thought with distaste. Like any cavalrymen, they carried sabers and carbines and long horse pistols. Most would have a second pistol stashed in a boot. Some might carry one or two more on their belts.

"Form line!" Victor shouted. "We can take them!"

Blaise pointed. "Isn't that—?"

"God damn him to hell!" Victor burst out. Sure as the devil, that was Habakkuk Biddiscombe—and the riders had to be Biddiscombe's Horsed Legion, which had been much spoken of but, till now, little seen. Victor wished he weren't seeing it at this moment, which did him no good whatever.

He wasn't the only one to recognize the defector, the

traitor, commanding the royalist Atlanteans. The cry of "No quarter!" went up from a dozen throats at once. Anyone who fought for and alongside Habakkuk Biddiscombe knew the chance he took. Muskets boomed. Here and there, legionaries slid from the saddle and horses went down.

But the horsemen who didn't fall came on. They knew exactly what they were doing, and why. They despised the soldiers who fought for the United States of Atlantis at least as much as those men loathed them. And now at last they had the chance to show their hated kinsmen and former friends what they could do.

"Death to Radcliff!" Biddiscombe roared. In an instant, every man he led took up the cry: "Death to Radcliff!"

They slammed into the front of the advancing Atlantean column: into a line that hadn't finished forming. They slammed into it and through it, shooting some soldiers and slashing at others with their swords. And, by their courage and ferocity, they stopped Victor Radcliff's army in its tracks.

"Kill them! Drive them out of the way!" Victor shouted furiously, drawing the gold-hilted sword the Atlantean Assembly had given him and urging his horse forward, toward the fight. "On to Croydon!"

Against a force of infantry that size, brushing them aside would have been a matter of moments—nothing that could have seriously delayed the assault on the redcoats' last sheltering place. But the horses of Biddiscombe's Horsed Legion gave the men on them a striking power out of all proportion to their numbers.

And so did the way they hated the men they faced. Victor might—did—reckon their cause and the way they upheld it altogether wrong. That didn't mean their contempt for death and retreat was any less than his might have been under like circumstances.

"Biddiscombe!" he called, brandishing his blade as he rode past his own men toward the fight. "I'm coming for you, Biddiscombe!"

"Oh, just shoot the son of a whore," Blaise said, which was bound to be good advice.

What were the redcoats doing behind Biddiscombe's Horsed Legion? Victor knew too well what *he* would be doing while such an outsized forlorn hope bought him time. Without a doubt, Cornwallis' men were doing the same thing: everything they could to hold their foes as far away from Croydon as possible.

After what seemed a very long time, the survivors from the Legion galloped back toward the town. They'd bought the redcoats—King George's fellow subjects, they would have said—enough of that precious, impalpable substance to form a line across the neck of the peninsula on which Croydon sat. And, whether from out of the town or from their abandoned fieldworks, the Englishmen had half a dozen cannon in the line.

"Don't like the looks of those," Blaise said.

"Nor do I," Victor agreed. No Atlantean artillery was anywhere close by. He didn't think the French had brought guns forward, either. Which meant . . . *We're going to catch it*, he thought sorrowfully.

The field guns spoke. Cannon balls and canister tore through the Atlanteans and Frenchmen. Two quick volleys from the dreadfully proficient foot soldiers followed. Men and pieces of men lay where they had fallen. The wounded staggered back when they could. When they couldn't, they thrashed and wailed and clutched at hale men, hoping to be helped away from the killing fire.

They got less help than they would have wanted. The Atlanteans were proficient in the craft of slaughter themselves by now, and gave back the redcoats' musketry as best they could. And more Frenchmen hurried forward to stiffen them should they require stiffening—and to shoot at the English any which way.

When the redcoats' cannon spoke again, one of their balls knocked a musketeer near Victor right out of his shoes. The musketeer howled—mercifully, not for long. At the start of the war, the Atlanteans never could have endured such carnage. Now they took it in stride, as sailors took the chance of being drowned. It was a hazard of the trade, no less and no more.

Regardless of how calm and brave they were, one thing seemed only too clear to Victor. "We shan't break into Croydon after all," he said bitterly. "God fling Habakkuk Biddiscombe into hell for ever and ever. May Satan fry him on a red-hot griddle for all eternity, and stab him with a fork every so often to see if he's done."

"Maybe it is happening even now," Blaise said. "Maybe he was killed in the fight at the front."

"Maybe he was. If God is merciful, he was," Victor said. "But then, if God were merciful, Biddiscombe would have died of the pox long ago."

With no hope of seizing Croydon, Victor reluctantly pulled his men out of musket range. The English guns kept banging away at them. But, by the same token, Atlantean riflemen picked off artillerists one after another.

Victor looked back over his shoulder. They'd forced the redcoats out of their lines, forced them to give up the field fortifications on which they'd expended so much time and labor. It was a victory: no doubt of that. If it wasn't quite the overwhelming victory he'd wanted when he set things in motion . . . well, what man this side of Alexander or Hannibal or Julius Caesar won such an overwhelming victory? For an amateur general with a formerly amateur army, he'd done pretty well.

Looking back over his shoulder also reminded him how close to sunset it was. His long-stretching shadow, and his horse's, should have told him as much already, but he'd had other things on his mind. He wondered if he had the nerve to fight a large night action, and regretfully decided he didn't.

"We'll camp here," he ordered, and then, to sweeten it as best he could, he added, "Here, on the ground we've won."

De la Fayette favored him with a salute. "You accomplished almost everything you intended, *Monsieur le*

Général," the French nobleman said. "It is given to few to do so much for their country."

"I thank you," Victor replied, returning the salute. "If only I could have done a little more."

That made the marquis smile. "A man who has much but wants more is likely to acquire it."

"I wanted it today," Victor said, and cursed Habakkuk Biddiscombe again.

Night brought only a nervous, halfhearted break in the hostilities. The redcoats also encamped on the field, not far out of gunshot range. Men from both sides went out to rescue the moaning wounded and plunder the silent dead—and if a few wounded were suddenly silenced in the process, so what? Englishmen and Atlanteans sometimes stumbled over one another in the darkness. They would grapple or open fire—except when both sides ran away at once.

The redcoats seemed busier than the exhausted Atlanteans. Victor didn't need long to realize why: they were digging in in front of Croydon. Rising earthworks partly hid their fires. They would have a much shorter line to hold now, even if they would also have far fewer men with whom to hold it.

When the sun rose again, Royal Navy ships were tied up at Croydon's piers. They were only frigates, but their guns outweighed and outranged anything the Atlanteans could bring against them. If Croydon fell, it would have to fall by siege.

XXII

"Damn the Englishmen!" Victor said when he'd ridden around the redcoats' new lines in front of Croydon. "God butter them and Satan futter them, they dig like skinks."

"*Comment?*" inquired the Marquis de la Fayette, who'd ridden the circuit with him. "Like what do they dig?"

"Like skinks," Victor repeated. De la Fayette's question puzzled him: the simile was common enough in Atlantis. Then he decided it might be common only in Atlantis. He cast about for a European equivalent, which he found after a moment: "Like moles, you might say."

"Ah. I see." The French nobleman did indeed look enlightened. But then he asked, "What are these skinks?"

"Why, lizards, of course. Peculiar lizards, though—I will say that," Victor Radcliff answered. "They're short and stout as lizards go. They have no eyes, but their front feet are broad and strong, and their tongues uncommonly long and clever. They dig through dirt after worms and bugs—only in summer in these northern lands, but year-around farther south, where the weather stays milder. They can be pests in gardens or on well-mown lawns, on account of the furrows they leave."

"They do sound like moles," de la Fayette said, "save

that they are of the reptile kind rather than being furry. But has Atlantis no true moles?"

"No more than we have any other viviparous quadrupeds except bats," Victor replied. "We have now the usual domestic beasts, and rats and mice plague our towns and houses. Deer and foxes course the woods, along with wild dogs and cats. Settlers brought all those beasts, though: this was a land of birds and scaly things before they came."

"And yet Terranova, beyond Atlantis, has an abundance of productions much like Europe's," de la Fayette said. "How could this be so?"

"The first man who learns the truth there will write his name in large letters amongst those of the leading savants of his day," Victor said. "But what that truth may be, I have not the faintest idea. I am more interested in learning how to winkle General Cornwallis out of Croydon."

"You do not believe we can storm this line?"

"Do you?" Victor didn't like answering a question with a question, but he wanted to find out what the Frenchman thought.

De la Fayette's shrug held a certain eloquence. "It would be . . . difficult."

Victor sighed. Steam puffed from his mouth and nostrils: the day was chilly. "They do have good engineers." The new English line before Croydon took advantage of every little swell of ground. It was also far enough outside the town to keep Atlantean and French field guns from bearing on the harbor. That meant the attackers couldn't keep the Royal Navy from resupplying Cornwallis. "Heaven only knows what kind of butcher's bill we'll pay to break in."

"One larger than we should desire, without doubt," de la Fayette said, and Victor could only nod glumly. The marquis added, "Our best course, then, appears to be to proceed by saps and parallels."

Formal European siege warfare had had little place in Atlantis. Victor and Cornwallis had invested Nouveau Redon, but they hadn't advanced towards it a line at a time. Cornwallis' clever engineers had stopped the spring instead, which made the defenders abandon the town for a sally with scant hope of success.

"That will take some time," Victor said.

"Are you urgently required elsewhere?" de la Fayette inquired.

"Well, no," Victor admitted. "But if the English choose to reinforce their garrison while we dig, we shall have wasted considerable effort."

"So we shall. What of it?" de la Fayette said. "We shall also have wasted considerable effort—and just as much time—if we merely encircle the English position. Better to do our utmost to force a surrender, *n'est-ce pas?*"

"Mm," Victor Radcliff said. "When you put it that way—"

"How else would you have me put it?" the marquis asked. "And, once we have demonstrated to the English commander that we are capable of making the approaches effecting a breach, how can he do anything but surrender?"

"Is that the custom in Europe?" Victor said.

"Most assuredly," de la Fayette replied. "Continuing the battle after a breach is made would be merely a pointless effusion of blood, don't you think?"

"If you say so," Victor replied. If de la Fayette thought that way, Cornwallis likely would, too: they fought in the same style. Victor thought there were times when he would keep fighting as long as he had one man left who could aim a musket. But he was only an Atlantean bumpkin—in the eyes of Europeans, just a short step better than a copperskin—so what did he know?

"I do say so," de la Fayette insisted.

"Saps and parallels, then," Victor said, and the Frenchman nodded.

Saps and parallels were part of a soldier's jargon. Even Victor Radcliff, who'd never used them or even seen them used, knew of them. And they were always mentioned that way: always saps and parallels, never parallels and saps.

In the field, though, the parallel always came first. People could argue about the chicken and the egg, but not about the sap and the parallel. One evening, under the profane direction of their engineers, French soldiers began digging a trench aligned with the stretch of enemy works the army would eventually assail. That was how the parallel got its name.

The Frenchmen threw up the dirt they excavated on the side where it would protect them from English fire. At that range—four or five hundred yards—only a lucky shot could hit anyone, but the game had its rules. And, when the redcoats realized what was going on, so many shots would fly through the air that some were bound to be lucky.

Realization came at sunrise the next morning. Cornwallis knew the same tricks as de la Fayette. They might have sprung from different kingdoms, but it was as if they'd attended the same college. As soon as Cornwallis saw that growing parapet protecting the first parallel, he did what any other commanding officer in his unpleasant position would have done: he started shooting at it with everything he could bring to bear.

Musketeers banged away. By the lead they expended, they might have been mining the stuff under Croydon. Most of the bullets either fell short or thumped into the dirt of the parapet. A few, more likely by luck than by design, just got over the top of the parapet and into the trench it warded. Wounded men went howling back toward the surgeons. One unfortunate fellow caught a musket ball in the side of the head and simply fell over, dead before he hit the ground.

English field guns also opened up on the parallel. The parapet swallowed some cannon balls, but others got through. Some skipped harmlessly between soldiers. That was uncommon luck; a cannon ball could knock down three or four men, and too often did.

Cornwallis stayed busy back in Croydon, too. His men

soon found or made mortars, as the Atlanteans had outside of Hanover. Mortars had no trouble at all throwing
their shells over the parapet and down into the parallel.
At least as often as not, that didn't matter. English fuses
were as unreliable as the ones Victor Radcliff's artillerists used. Sometimes the mortar bombs burst in the air.
Very often, they failed to burst at all.

Every once in a while, though, everything would go
as the artillerists wished it would all the time. Then the
shell would go off just when the gunners had in mind,
and the exploding powder would work a fearful slaughter. But it didn't happen often enough to keep men out
of the trench.

When the first parallel got long enough to satisfy de
la Fayette's engineers, they—or rather, French soldiers
(and now Atlanteans with them)—began digging a zig-
zag trench toward the English outworks: a sap. Because
of the way the sap ran, it was harder to protect than the
parallel had been. More mangled men went off to the surgeons. Some would get better after their ministrations—
although a good many of those, no doubt, would have
got better without those ministrations. Others would get
wounds that festered, and would slowly and painfully
waste away. So war was; so war had always been; so, as
far as Victor Radcliff could tell, war would ever be.

"Are the redcoats likely to sally?" Victor asked as the
sap snaked closer to the enemy line.

"I don't think so, not yet," de la Fayette answered.
"Look how much open ground they would have to cross
before they could interrupt us. Our musketeers and your
fine riflemen and the cannon would slaughter too many
of them to make it worthwhile. When we draw closer . . .
That may prove a different story."

Victor grunted. Like so many things de la Fayette said,
the Frenchman's explanation made such good sense,
Victor wondered why he hadn't thought of it himself.
Of course Cornwallis would wait till they'd dug another
parallel or two before trying to disrupt the excavations

with his foot soldiers. Victor would have done the same thing himself.

He rode back to a high point so he could survey Croydon and his harbor with his spyglass. The Royal Navy frigates were gone, but several tubby merchantmen had taken their place. Tiny in the distance even through his lenses, stevedores carried sacks of grain off the ships and into the town. Victor swore under his breath. Atlanteans and Frenchmen would have to break through the defenses in front of Croydon, for they would never starve the redcoats out.

"No big guns there, then. No nasty warships, neither," Blaise said when Victor gave him that bit of intelligence. He added, "Where did the Royal Navy go? When will it come back?"

"If I knew, I would tell you," Victor replied. "And, if you are about to ask me why the frigates set sail, I also know that not."

Blaise chuckled. "I could have done that well myself."

"So could any man here," Victor said. "Perchance, those frigates may return. Or first-rate ships of the line may take their place. Or, then again, the English may prove content with wallowing scows like the ones now tied up in Croydon. They give Cornwallis and his redcoats their necessary victuals and, no doubt, a copious supply of powder and lead."

"They have been shooting enough of it," Blaise agreed.

"Too much!" Victor said. "Damn me if they have not. Well, we did not think this war would be easy when we began it. Most Atlanteans, I daresay, failed to believe we could win it."

"You did not always believe that yourself," Blaise reminded him. "You went around preaching that we must not lose, that so long as we stayed in the fight England would tire of it sooner or later."

"I did?" Victor Radcliff had to think back to what

now seemed very distant days indeed. After a sheepish chuckle, he found himself nodding. "I did, sure enough. It may yet come to that, you know. Even if we beat them here, the English can mount another invasion—if they have the will to attempt it."

"What if they do?" the Negro asked.

Victor shrugged. "We fight on. We stay in the field. We refuse to own ourselves beaten, come what may. You see? The same song I sang before. We Radcliffs are a stubborn clan, say whatever else you will of us."

"Then you need someone stubborn enough to stay beside you," Blaise said, and tapped the chevrons on his arm. Smiling, Victor slapped him on the back.

The second parallel. As before, the soil went up on the side facing Croydon's defenses. This trench being closer to the redcoats' works, the Frenchmen and Atlanteans who manned it took more casualties. The English artillerists got as good with their mortars as anyone could with those balky weapons. The besiegers dug shelters into the sides of the trench, and dove into them when the shells came hissing down.

Then it rained—not so hard as it had on the day when Victor's attack went awry, but hard enough. The rain softened the dirt, which should have made digging easier ... but who wanted to dig when he sank ankle-deep in mud if he tried? The parapet in front of the trench displayed an alarming tendency to sag, too.

Firing from the English trenches slackened, but it didn't stop. The redcoats had had plenty of time to strengthen their works while their foes dug. Some of their men fired from shelters adequate to keep their powder dry. Some of their mortars still tossed hate into the air.

One shell splashed down into a puddle that doused its fuse. "Drown, you son of a bitch!" shouted the closest Atlantean infantryman. Within a day, half the Atlanteans were telling the story. So were a quarter of de la Fayette's French soldiers—it was easy enough to translate.

The rain changed to sleet, and the sleet changed to snow. The ground went from too soft to work with conveniently to too hard to work with conveniently, all in the space of a couple of days. Atlanteans and Frenchmen shivered in huts and tents. No doubt the redcoats were chilly, too, but they had Croydon's snug houses in which to lodge.

Watching smoke rise from chimneys in town, Victor said, "Sooner or later, they'll run short of firewood."

"Soon enough to do us any good?" Blaise asked.

"I don't know," Victor admitted. "How much wood did they have before the siege began? How cold will the winter be? How many of the Croydonites' chattels will the redcoats burn to keep from coming down with chilblains?"

"As many as they need to," Blaise said without hesitation.

"I shouldn't wonder," Victor said. Shivering Atlanteans would do the same—he was sure of that. Instead, they had plenty of timber close by. But wood freshly cut would smoke horribly when it went onto the fire. That wouldn't stop his men from using it, but the soot would make them look like Negroes if they kept on for very long.

"We need more picks, fewer shovels," de la Fayette said a couple of days later. "We are chipping at the ground more than digging through it."

"Well, so we are," Victor said. "Unless your blacksmiths feel like beating spades into picks—an eventuality of which the Good Book says nothing—I know not where we shall come by them."

"Off the countryside?" de la Fayette said hopefully.

"Good luck," Victor replied. "Maybe we can get a few. But unless we pay well for them, our own farmers will start shooting at us from ambush."

"They would not do that!" the marquis exclaimed.

"Ha!" Victor said, and then again, louder, *"Ha!"* That done, he proceeded to embellish on the theme: "Your Grace, chances are you know more about how they fight in Europe than I do. You'd better. But I promise you this—I know more about Atlantean farmers and what they're likely to do than you've ever imagined."

"It could be. Very probably, it is. French peasants, however, would not behave so," de la Fayette said.

"Next time I campaign in France, I'll remember that," Victor said. "For now, you need to remember you're campaigning in Atlantis."

"I am not likely to forget it," the French nobleman replied, tartly enough to suggest that, while he conceded he wasn't lost on the trackless prairies of northern Terranova beyond the Great River, he also didn't see himself as being so far away from those buffalo-thundering grasslands. After pausing just long enough to let that sink in, he continued, "One reminder is the weather. How soon can we resume our excavations, even if we obtain picks? Will we be able to do so at all before spring?"

"Well, I don't exactly know." Victor held up a hand before de la Fayette could speak. "Nobody exactly knows the weather—I understand that. But I don't even approximately know. I do not spring from this part of Atlantis, and I have not spent sufficient time up here to have a good feel for what's likely to come."

"Some of your men will, though?" de la Fayette suggested.

"Can't hurt to ask," Victor said, and instructed one of his messengers.

Grinning, the youngster said, "I'd make my own guesses, sir, but I'm from down in Freetown myself, so they wouldn't be worth an at—" He broke off, flushing to the roots of his hair. "They wouldn't be worth much, I mean. I'll go fetch somebody who was born around here." He dashed away as if his breeches were on fire.

Victor Radcliff stared sourly after him. *Wouldn't be worth an atlantean*, the messenger hadn't quite swallowed. When the Atlantean Assembly's own followers scorned the paper the Assembly issued . . . When such a thing happened, you knew that paper had lost more value than you wished it would have.

The messenger quickly returned with a sergeant who gave his name as Saul Andrews and who said, "I come from a farm about twenty miles from here. Never strayed far from it, neither, General, not till I picked up a musket and went to war with you." Sure enough, he used the flat vowels and muffled final *r*'s of a Croydon man.

"Good enough," Victor replied. "How long do you expect this harsh cold spell to last?"

Andrews glanced up at the sky. Whatever he saw there only made him shrug. "Well, now, sir, that's a mite hard to calculate," he said. "If it's a hard winter, it could stay this way till spring. I've seen it do that very thing. But if it's not so hard, we'll get some warm spells betwixt and between the freezes. Which I've also seen."

"If you had to guess—?" Victor prompted.

Sergeant Andrews shrugged. "The good Lord knows, but He ain't told me. Only thing I can say is, we got to wait and see."

"All right, Sergeant. You may go," Victor said, stifling a sigh. Andrews departed with almost as many signs of relief as the messenger had shown a few minutes earlier. Try as Victor would, he couldn't get angry at the man. Custis Cawthorne had tried using barometer and thermometer—both of which he'd had to make himself—to foretell the weather. And sometimes he'd been right, and sometimes he'd been wrong. Anyone who'd lived out in the open long enough to grow up could have done as well without fancy devices. So people delighted in telling Cawthorne, too, till he finally gave up and sold the meteorological instruments for what the glass and quicksilver would bring.

"He does not know?" De la Fayette's English was imperfect, but he'd got the gist.

"No, he doesn't." This time, Victor did sigh. "I don't suppose anyone else will, either. As he said, we just have to wait and see."

"Very well." By the way de la Fayette said it, it wasn't. But even a young, headstrong nobleman understood that a Power higher than he controlled the weather. "We shall just have to be ready to take advantage of the good and do our best to ride out the bad."

Victor Radcliff set a hand on his shoulder. "Welcome to life, your Grace."

In due course, the parallel advanced again. Then a blizzard froze the ground hard as iron, and digging perforce stopped. The wind howled down from the northwest. Snow swirled and danced. The redcoats' defensive works and their foes' saps and parallels vanished under a blanket of white.

Almost everything vanished, in fact. While the storm raged, Victor had trouble seeing out to the end of his arm. He wondered if he could turn that to his, and Atlantis', advantage. Cornwallis' men would have trouble seeing, too. Attackers might be able to get very close to their works before getting spotted. If anything went wrong as they approached, though . . .

Since he had trouble making up his mind, he held a council of war to see what his officers—and the French, most of whom needed translation—thought of the idea. As he might have guessed, they split pretty evenly.

"If anything goes wrong—even the least little thing— you've spilled the thundermug into the stewpot," one major said.

"If things go the way we want them to, we walk into Croydon," a captain countered. Both those notions had been in Victor's mind. His officers had as much trouble weighing them one against the other as he did.

"The glory of victory complete and absolute!" de la Fayette said enthusiastically. Whether his officers were or not, he was ready to attack.

He seemed so very ready, in fact, that he made "Baron" von Steuben stir. "We have in hand the game," the German veteran said. "With saps and parallels, sooner or later we are sure to win, or almost. An attack, even an attack in *Schnee*—ah, snow—and we all this risk. Why take the chance?"

"Only a snake could look at things in a more cold-blooded way," de la Fayette said—not quite the insult direct, but close. A touchy officer might have called him out for it.

Von Steuben only smiled and bowed. "Do not down your nose at snakes look, your Grace," he said. "There are in this world of them a great many, and most of them seem uncommonly well fed."

"I should rather fight like a man," de la Fayette said.

"No one says to on your belly crawl to the redcoats' lines and bite in the leg an English sergeant. This is more likely you than him to poison," von Steuben replied. The Atlantean officers laughed right away. After the joke was translated, so did most of the Frenchmen. Even de la Fayette smiled. Von Steuben went on, "Yes, you should like a man fight. But you should also like a smart man, not like some dumbhead, fight, is it not so?"

Plainly, de la Fayette wanted nothing more than to tell him it was not so. Just as plainly, the Frenchman couldn't, not unless he wanted to make a liar of himself. All but choking on the words, de la Fayette said, "It is so."

"Good. Very good." Von Steuben might have been patting a puppy on the head, not talking to his nominal superior. "You *can* things learn. Give yourself a chance longer to live, and you will more things learn."

De la Fayette looked more affronted than von Steuben had when the French noble—*the genuine French noble*, Victor reminded himself—called him cold-blooded. But all von Steuben had accused him of was being young. Time would cure that . . . unless he did something foolish enough to get himself killed before it could.

The council of war went on a while longer after the exchange between von Steuben and de la Fayette. As Victor soon saw, though, men on both sides of the question were only kicking it back and forth in the same track.

That left it up to him. Well, it had always been up to him, but now he had to look the fact square in the face. "We'll wait," he said. "We'll go on digging, as best we can. If matters develop differently from the way we now expect ... Well, in that case, chances are Croydon will see another blizzard before winter's out."

"You took that German *cochon*'s word over mine," de la Fayette said hotly as the council broke up.

"I will take good advice wherever I can find it," Victor replied. "He was right: failure would cost more than we can afford, whilst success is apt to come down without the attack, if rather more slowly."

"Are you a general or a bookkeeper?"

"I've been both," Victor said. "One is not the opposite of the other."

De la Fayette's response was funny, sad, and pungently obscene all at once: very French, in other words. Then he added, "I wish I could change your mind."

"A lot of people have said that down through the years," Victor answered, with a shrug far more resigned than the ones he'd got from Saul Andrews. "Not many of them have done it, though. Radcliffs are good at going straight ahead or stopping short, not so good at turning."

"Good at stopping short when you should go straight ahead," de la Fayette observed, and walked off with the last word if not with what he wanted.

Bright sunshine greeted Victor when he got up the next morning. Squinting against its glare off snow, he knew his men would have got slaughtered had they tried to storm the English works. Even had he agreed to the attack the night before, he would have had to call it off now. Sometimes what a man wanted or didn't want had nothing to do with anything: he simply had to make the best of the hand he got dealt.

Victor set his men to shoveling snow out of the entrenchments that worked toward the redcoats' lines. Once they'd thrown out enough so they could move around fairly freely, they started hacking away at the frozen ground. The parallel advanced again.

Cornwallis' soldiers shoveled snow out of their trenches, too. They made it as plain as they possibly could that they wouldn't give up without a fight. They went right on shooting at the diggers in the parallel. Every so often, they hit somebody. Being able to go back to Croydon when they weren't on duty, they had better quarters than the Atlanteans and Frenchmen investing their lines. English ships kept coming into port, too, which meant the redcoats were bound to be better supplied than their foes.

But the English soldiers remained shut up in one tiny corner of Atlantis. Cornwallis didn't seem to think they had the strength to break out against Victor's army. If they could be beaten here, they would have to try some massive new invasion to make the war go on. If ...

In due course, the French engineers pronounced themselves satisfied with the second parallel. A new sap angled toward the English line. With muskets and mortars, the redcoats showed how little they appreciated the compliment.

Then a fresh snowstorm shrieked down from the north. The digging had to stop for several days. Victor Radcliff swore and fumed, but he could do no more about the weather than Blaise or Sergeant Saul Andrews or any other mortal. All he could do was hope the storm blew itself out before long—and hope his troops stayed healthy long enough to let them attack the Englishmen. He could do no more about that than he could about the weather.

"At least the weather is cold," Victor said to Blaise. "There seem to be fewer sicknesses at this season than in warmer times."

"What about chest fever?" the Negro retorted. "What about catarrh? What about the—what do you call it?— the grippe?"

"Well, those are troublesome," Victor admitted. "But I was thinking of fluxes of the bowels, and of the plague, and even of smallpox and measles. They are seen more often in spring and summer—especially the first two."

"They probably stay frozen in this snow and ice, the

way meat does." Blaise rolled his eyes. "Who would have thought you could keep meat fresh as long as you froze it? In the country I come from, we have to smoke it or salt it or dry it or eat it right away. I never saw ice—I never imagined ice!—till you white men dragged me here."

"Kind of you to admit ice *is* good for something," Victor said. "You are not always so generous."

"If you could keep it in a box and use it for what it is good for, that would be fine," Blaise said. "When it lies all over the countryside and tries to freeze off your fingers and your toes and your prong, then that is too much." His shiver was melodramatic and sincere at the same time.

"We will be warmer once we break into Croydon," Victor said. "I have said the same to the men advancing the sap. I can think of nothing better calculated to inspire them to dig."

"It would inspire me, by the Lord Jehovah!" Blaise exclaimed. "But some of you white men like this weather. I have heard some of you say so. If you tell me now that these men are not mad, I will not believe you."

"I also think they are." Victor could take it no further than that, as he knew too well. Some Atlanteans—and some Frenchmen, too—did relish winter for its own sake. He liked cold weather himself: he liked coming in out of it, warming himself in front of a roaring fire, and sipping from a flagon of mulled wine or flip, the tasty concoction of rum and beer. Spending much time in it was a different story, as far as he was concerned.

Time dragged on. The sap moved closer to the redcoats' line, which meant they sent all the more musket balls and mortar shells and roundshot at the men digging it. The third parallel would be very close indeed. The sap that led out from it would break into the English works. After that, and after a clash and a show of resistance, General Cornwallis could yield with honor.

He could, yes. But would he? In a fight to the finish, his men had at least some hope of beating the Atlanteans and Frenchmen opposing them. Since he led the last English force in Atlantis, mightn't he feel obligated to fight as hard as he could? If he did win, he kept the war alive.

Every time Victor tried to decide what Cornwallis would do, he came up with a different answer. The English general certainly was conscious of his honor; Victor had seen that in the fight against the French settlers. Was he also conscious of the political demands his position imposed on him? How could he fail to be? And yet people weren't always sensible or clever—far from it. There was no sure way to judge till attackers swarmed into the breach.

Then the Atlantean commander found something new to worry about, for a courier from Hanover brought him a letter in a hand he found far too familiar. He'd never dreamt he would recognize Marcel Freycinet's script so readily. No matter what he'd dreamt, he did.

The letter was cheerful enough. Freycinet assured him that Louise was doing well, and that the slave and her owner both anticipated her safe passage through birthing time. *Take heart,* Monsieur le Général, *and be of good cheer*, Freycinet wrote. *Such things have happened since the days of Adam and Eve. You have nothing to be ashamed of; rather, pride yourself on your virility.*

Victor would have been happier to do that had any of the children Meg gave him lived to grow up. He could not wish for Louise's baby to die untimely . . . but neither could he wish his sole descendant to be sold on the auction block like a cow or a sheep. Nor could he buy the child himself, not when doing so would show his wife he'd been unfaithful.

That left . . . Victor burned *Monsieur* Freycinet's letter on the brazier in his tent. It left nothing he could see. Nothing at all. He'd been scrabbling for a way out since he first learned his bedwarmer was with child. He had yet to find one, scrabble as he would.

Since he couldn't do anything about what was going on far to the south, he threw his energy into the siege of Croydon. Even in the snow, he kept digging parties hacking away at the hard ground. A thaw came just after New Year's Day. As the last one had, it turned saps and parallels into morasses and made parapets slump.

No doubt the redcoats were similarly discommoded. But their works were already in place. They weren't trying to extend them and trying not to drown at the same time.

"Confound it, there has to be something between ground that's rock and ground that's soup!" Victor complained.

"What you want for it to be is summer again," Baron von Steuben said. "And soon enough it will be."

"It will be, yes, but not soon enough," Victor said.

"For fighting? Maybe not. For anything else . . . Summer comes sooner every year," the German said. "So does winter."

He wasn't much older than Victor was himself, which didn't mean he didn't have a point. Victor had noticed the same thing himself. Years used to stretch out deliciously ahead of him. Now each one seemed shorter than its predecessor. Before he had time to get to know it, it disappeared. And once time was gone, could even God call it back again?

Before long, Louise's light brown baby would be born. Before long, the boy—or would it be a girl?—would be sold. Marcel Freycinet would pocket considerably more than thirty pieces of silver. Everyone would be happy . . . except Victor, and probably the little child who was flesh of his flesh.

Baron von Steuben said something. Whatever it was, Victor missed it. "Crave pardon?" he murmured.

The German pointed out to sea. "Here come more English ships," he repeated. "May the woodworms eat them all below the waterline."

"That would be splendid," Victor agreed. "Devil take me if those be not first-rate ships of the line, too. From close in to shore, their guns may even reach the spot where we hope to breach Cornwallis' lines. A ball from a long twenty-four-pounder can do horrid things to a man."

"So can a ball from a musket," von Steuben said, which was true but had scant flavor to it. His hard, weathered features folded into a frown. "It does not seem as if they hope to tie up."

"So it doesn't," Victor replied. "I wonder why not."

"They have to be more stupid than you would expect, even from an Englishman," von Steuben said. Victor Radcliff wondered what kind of opinion General Cornwallis' held about the German soldiers of fortune from Hesse and Brunswick and other petty states who took King George's silver and fought for England. Similarly low? He wouldn't have been surprised.

He watched the men-of-war working their way toward Croydon against mostly contrary breezes. When all of them presented their broadsides to the town at the same time, a sudden mad hope caromed through him. He ducked back into his tent for the spyglass. Aiming the long brass tube out into the Atlantic, he drew out the slimmer part to bring the warships into focus. And when he saw them clear . . .

When he saw them clear, he began to caper like a fool, or like a man possessed. "They're French ships!" he shouted. "French, I tell you! French!"

"Was sagen Sie?" von Steuben demanded, though Victor didn't know how he could have made himself any clearer. A moment later, all the ships fired together. Tons of hot flying iron crashed down on Croydon.

XXIII

It had snowed again, blanketing the ground with white. While the flakes flew, the French ships refrained from bombarding Croydon. Maybe they didn't want to shoot at what they couldn't see. Victor Radcliff didn't know how much difference it made. They'd already gone a long way toward smashing the town, and started several fires.

And they'd captured three English merchantmen that tried to sneak into Croydon under cover of the snowfall. It hadn't screened them well enough. The French ships of the line might not have wanted to fire at Croydon through the swirling snow, but they weren't shy about shooting at the blockade-runners. All the merchantmen struck their colors in short order.

Somehow, the French warships must have won a battle against the Royal Navy out on the open sea. Victor could imagine nothing else that accounted for their presence here. That wasn't quite a miracle from On High, but it came closer than anything else he'd seen lately.

"General! General!" Several excited men shouted outside his tent. One outdid the rest: "An Englishman's coming out with a white flag!"

"God bless my soul!" Victor murmured. He hurried out to see for himself, Blaise at his heels.

The Atlanteans out there all pointed at once. Victor needed none of those outthrust index fingers. The enemy soldier's flag of truce might be scarcely visible against the snow on the ground, but his scarlet uniform tunic stood out like spilled blood.

Too much blood spilled already, Victor thought. "Bring him to me at once," he ordered aloud. "Show him every courtesy. Unless I should be very much mistaken, this war is about to end here." That was plenty to send his own soldiers dashing off toward the parallel closest to the enemy's works.

By the time they got there, men already in the parallel had taken charge of the redcoat. They offered him no abuse; they too could see he had but one likely reason for coming forth. By the time he'd made his way back through the trenches to Victor's tent, he had close to a company's worth of Atlanteans and Frenchmen escorting him.

"You are General Radcliff, sir?" he asked formally, after lowering the flag of truce and delivering a precise salute.

"None other," Victor said. "And you would be . . . ?"

"Captain Horace Grimsley, sir," the English officer replied. "General Cornwallis' compliments, and he has sent me to ask of you the terms you require for the cessation of hostilities between our two armies. Under the present unfortunate circumstances"—he couldn't help looking out to sea, where the French warships bobbed in the waves with their recent prizes—"he feels we have no reasonable expectation of successfully resisting the forces in arms against us."

"My compliments back to the general, Captain, and to yourself as well," Victor said. "By all means tell him that I am pleased to treat with you, and that the forces under his command have fought bravely and well."

"Thank you. He told me you would show yourself to be a gentleman." By the way Grimsley spoke, he hadn't believed a word of it. "And your terms would be . . . ?"

Victor had been thinking about them since the moment the French men-of-war appeared off Croydon. "Your men will stack their arms and surrender. Officers may keep their swords, in token of your brave resistance."

"A gentleman indeed," Captain Grimsley said under his breath.

"No surrendered soldier or officer will take up arms against the United States of Atlantis until he shall have been properly exchanged," Victor continued.

"Agreed," Grimsley said.

"Weapons excepted, men may keep one knapsack's worth of personal effects apiece," Victor said. "Property above that amount shall be reckoned spoils of war, and will be divided amongst Atlanteans and Frenchmen in a manner we shall determine. We shall undertake to preserve your men's lives and the aforesaid personal effects unharmed, so long as you continue to comply with the terms of the surrender."

"Agreed," Grimsley repeated. But then he asked, "By 'weapons,' sir, do you mean to include common eating knives, dirks, daggers, and bayonets?"

"Upon surrender, your men will no longer need their bayonets, which will prove a useful accession to our own stocks." Victor paused a moment to think. "They may retain knives with blades shorter than, hmm, twelve inches. Is that satisfactory to you?"

After his own brief consideration, Captain Grimsley nodded. "It will do."

"Very well." Victor Radcliff's tone hardened. "One thing more: our promise of safety and property does not apply to the individuals enrolled in what is commonly termed Biddiscombe's Horsed Legion. Those men are traitors against the United States of Atlantis, and shall be used accordingly."

"Oh, dear. General Cornwallis feared you would say something to that effect, sir," Grimsley replied. "He instructed me to tell you that singling them out for oppressive treatment is in no way acceptable to him."

"No, eh?" Victor growled. "Why the devil not?"

"Because they are King George's subjects, in the same way as his Majesty's other soldiers in and around Croydon."

"They're Atlanteans. They're traitors," Victor said.

"Were General Cornwallis now besieging rather than conversely, you would all be reckoned traitors against the king," Captain Grimsley reminded him.

"Maybe so. And do you think he wouldn't single out redcoats who'd chosen to fight for the Atlantean Assembly?" Victor said. "We have a good many of them in our ranks, including some of our best drillmasters."

"I shouldn't wonder at *that*," Grimsley said. To the English eye, Atlantean soldiers still fell woefully short on spit and polish: nothing Victor didn't already know. Cornwallis' plenipotentiary went on, "My principal will not permit any English subjects to be unjustly mistreated."

"They are Atlanteans," Victor said again. "They have given aid and comfort to the enemies of the United States of Atlantis. They have tried to kill us. By God, sir, they *have* killed us, most recently at the start of this siege. How can you—how can your commander—reckon them anything *but* traitors?"

"They are not traitors to the king. Until this war began, all Atlanteans were, and saw themselves as, his Majesty's subjects. How can you condemn these men for holding to their prior allegiance?"

"Aha!" Victor Radcliff aimed a finger at him as if it were a sharpshooter's rifle. "I have you now! I might be prepared to accept your claim for men who fought against us from the beginning. But you will know as well as I, sir, that Habakkuk Biddiscombe served in the army of the United States of Atlantis until, dissatisfied with his prospects amongst us, he suddenly discovered an undying loyalty to King George. He turned his coat, in other words. If that does not make him a traitor, I am hard pressed to imagine what would. The same holds true for most of his followers."

"General Cornwallis sees the matter differently,"

Grimsley said. "In his view, these men were but redis-covering their original allegiance."

"That's pretty," Victor said. "It means nothing, but it's pretty. You go tell him I want those men. If he should choose not to yield them, the siege will continue until we storm the breach. The cannonading from the ships off-shore will also continue. How long before famine does our work for us?"

Grimsley bit his lip. He had no answer for that. Nei-ther did Cornwallis, or he would not have asked for terms. At last, the English captain said, "May I beg a truce of twenty-four hours to take your words back to my superiors for their consideration?"

"Certainly," Victor said. "But unless their answer suits me, I fear the conflict must continue."

"I understand, sir. Please accept my assurances that I wish with all my heart circumstances were otherwise." With that, Captain Grimsley took his leave.

Naturally, the line the Atlanteans and Frenchmen held around Croydon ran from sea to sea. As naturally, some parts of it were held with greater force than others. The redcoats manned their line the same way. They concen-trated most of their strength against the saps and paral-lels that brought their foes up close to their works. And Victor Radcliff likewise kept most of his troops in and near those precious trenches. Anything else would have invited disaster.

Later, he realized he should have wondered when the redcoat asked for a truce stretching through the night. But that was later. At the time, the request seemed reasonable enough. Grimsley had refused a condition Victor saw as essential. Cornwallis and his leading officers might well need some time to decide whether to yield up the men who'd fought so fero-ciously on their side.

For that matter, Victor felt he needed his own council of war. "If they insist on our keeping Biddiscombe and his men prisoners of war like any other, how shall we respond?" he asked his officers. "Shall we allow it for the sake of the victory, or shall we say we must have the villains' heads?"

"Let the pigdogs go," Baron von Steuben said at once. "The surrender wins the war. That is the point of the business."

"We can win the war even if the redcoats don't surrender," an Atlantean retorted. "The redcoats wouldn't ask for terms if they weren't at the end of their rope."

"That's where Biddiscombe and his buggers ought to be—at the end of a rope." Another Atlantean officer twisted his head to one side, stuck out his tongue, and did his best to make his eyes bulge: a gruesomely excellent imitation of a hanged man.

The laugh that rose in the tent held a fierce, baying undertone. Victor wasn't the only one there who wanted Habakkuk Biddiscombe dead. But did he want Biddiscombe dead badly enough to make it an issue that might disrupt Cornwallis' surrender? Most of his officers certainly seemed to.

As councils of war had a way of doing, this one produced more heat than light. Several men had to get between a captain who favored flaying Biddiscombe and sprinkling salt on his bleeding flesh before hanging him and a major who thought letting him be treated as an Englishman was a reasonable price to pay for a surrender.

Wearily, Victor dismissed his subordinates. "What will you do, General?" one of them asked.

"Make up my mind come morning," he answered.

"Then why did you call the council?" the man said.

"To learn whether I might be able to make up my mind tonight," Victor told him. "But, as both sides have strong arguments in their favor, I need more time to decide what best serves us at this crucial hour."

His officers had to be content with that. Muttering, they went off to their own tents. Victor turned to Blaise. "The man in me wants to see Biddiscombe at the end of a rope," he said. "The general says I should do as von Steuben suggests and let him go for the sake of victory."

"Chances are you get the victory anyway," Blaise answered.

"I know," Victor said. "But there's also the chance that something may go wrong if I delay. I know not how badly those French ships worsted the Royal Navy. If an English fleet should suddenly appear off Croydon, all our work would of necessity commence again."

"Not all of it," the Negro said. "We have got close to the redcoats' line now. When we break in, what can they do?"

Victor Radcliff smiled. "Yes, there is that. You know as much of siege warfare these days as any Atlantean officer."

"More than a stupid nigger would, eh?" Blaise said, not without an edge to his voice.

"Do I maltreat you or reckon you less than a man because your skin is black?" Victor asked. He waited. At last, Blaise shook his head. "All right, then," Victor said. "Where, before you came to Atlantis, would you have learned of saps and parallels? It is not a matter of stupidity, my friend—only inexperience. Set me amongst your folk, and I should make the most useless of spearmen."

"Ah." Blaise considered that. "Yes, it could be. But you would be able to learn."

"I hope so. You have certainly learned a good deal here," Victor said.

"Not always things I want to learn," Blaise said.

"I shouldn't wonder." Victor followed the words with a yawn. He stepped out of the tent and looked over toward Croydon. Most windows in the town were dark or showed only the dim sunset glow of banked embers. Firelight did pour from two or three buildings. In one of those, Cornwallis and his officers were probably still hashing out what to do. Victor wished he could have been a fly on the wall at that conclave.

His breath smoked. His ears started to tingle. He would have been a chilly fly on the wall—he was glad to duck back under canvas. It wasn't warm inside the tent, but it was warmer.

"You'll sleep on it, then?" Blaise said.

"Yes, I'll sleep on it." Victor nodded. "Maybe I'll be wiser come morning. Or maybe I'll seem wiser, at any rate."

He pulled off his boots and shed his hat. Other than that, he lay down on the cot fully dressed. Even with two thick woolen blankets, he was glad for every extra bit of cloth between him and winter. Would he really be, or at least seem, wiser after the sun came up? He could hope so, anyhow. He closed his eyes. Before long, he slept.

"General! General!" Shouts pierced dreams of an earthquake. No, the world wasn't falling down around him. Someone was shaking—had shaken—him awake.

It was still dark. "What's gone wrong?" Victor asked blurrily. Something must have, or they would have left him alone till dawn.

"There's fighting, General, over in the northeast, on the far side of the line," answered the man who'd been doing the shaking.

"A pox!" Victor groped for his boots, found them, and tugged them on. The far side of Croydon from the encampment was also the weakest-held part of his lines. "Are the redcoats breaking out?" If they were going to do it anywhere, they were most likely to try there.

"Somebody sure as hell is," the Atlantean soldier said.

Victor hurried outside. He could hear muskets boom from that direction, and could see muzzle flashes piercing the night like fierce fireflies. Not all the booms came from muskets. Even at this distance, a trained ear like his could tell pistol shots from musketry. There were quite a few of them. . . .

He suddenly thumped his forehead with the heel of

his hand. "Biddiscombe!" he exclaimed, and it was as much a howl of self-reproach as a naming of the man likely leading that attack. "The Horsed Legion!"

What had been going on all night in Croydon? Why, General Cornwallis and his officers were trying to decide whether to throw Habakkuk Biddiscombe and his troop of horsemen over the side to keep the French ships and the Atlantean and French armies from pounding them to jelly. Captain Grimsley had insisted that Cornwallis would never abandon Biddiscombe's Horsed Legion. But if the redcoats would never abandon their local allies, why were they talking deep into the night about doing exactly that?

Why indeed?

Now, too late, Victor could read Habakkuk Biddiscombe's thoughts. If the English army changed its mind and decided to give him and his men to the rebel Atlanteans, they were all as good as dead. And if the redcoats refused to cough up the Horsed Legion and the rebel Atlanteans and the French broke into Croydon—which seemed all too likely—he and his followers were also as good as dead.

Breaking out offered more hope than either of those chances.

Or maybe Cornwallis had gone to Biddiscombe and said something like, *I wish things were otherwise, but they are as they are. I have no way to protect you. Flight seems your best hope. If you attempt it, I shall look the other way whilst you ready yourselves.*

Cornwallis was bound to deny any bargain like that. So was Habakkuk Biddiscombe. Victor doubted he would ever be able to prove a thing. But he could see the scene in his mind's eye all the same.

"What do we do, sir?" asked the soldier who'd wakened him.

"Try to stop them, of course," Victor snapped.

But some of them would break through—no, some of them had already broken through. Victor could see that by the places from which the gunfire was coming. They'd hit the weakest point in his line, all right. Was that good generalship? Was it fool luck? Or had someone gone over and told them where to strike? In a fight like this, with so much betrayal on both sides, could you be sure of anything?

Victor was sure of one thing. "From this moment on, those men are outlaws, to be run down like wild dogs. They will leave tracks in the snow. As soon as we have light by which to follow them, we shall hunt them to destruction."

"What if the whole English army goes after 'em?" the soldier said.

"Look at Croydon." Victor waved toward the town, which was quiet, and even darker now than it had been before he went to bed. "Not the slightest sign of that. No, it's Biddiscombe, trying to get away while the getting is good."

And Cornwallis, glad to rid himself of an embarrassment, he added, but only to himself. He couldn't prove that now. Odds were he would never be able to. Which didn't mean he didn't believe it, and didn't mean he didn't respect and even admire the English commander for so neatly disposing of his problem.

Captain Horace Grimsley gave Victor another of his precise salutes. "General Cornwallis' compliments as before, sir, and he bids me tell you no outstanding reason remains that he should not accept the terms of surrender you proposed yesterday."

"My compliments to your commander in return," Victor said. "You may also tell him we have slain or captured a good many members of Biddiscombe's Horsed Legion, and that we hope to be rid of every one of the villains before too long. It was . . . convenient for your principal that they chose to decamp under cover of darkness."

The English officer looked back at him with no expression whatever. "General Cornwallis wishes me to assure you that he had no prior knowledge of Colonel

Biddiscombe's intentions, and that neither he nor anyone else in our force assisted or abetted the Horsed Legion in any way."

"I bet he wants you to assure me of that!" Victor said.

"Do you presume to doubt his word, sir?" Grimsley asked coldly.

"Damned right I doubt it," Victor answered. "Whether I doubt it enough to throw away the truce and tell those French ships to start firing again ... That is another story. Once we've disarmed your lot, we'll be able to send more of our men after Biddiscombe. With the war as good as won, not so many people will care to help or hide him."

"It could be so," Captain Grimsley admitted. Then he said, "If you have truly cast off his Majesty King George's rule, shall we now commence to style you King Victor the First?"

"No," Victor said, and then again, louder, "*No!* We shall endeavor to make do without kings from here on out."

"Foolishness," Grimsley said.

"Perhaps it is. But it is our own foolishness, which is the point of the matter," Victor said. "And we reckon it a worse one to owe attachment to a sovereign across the broad sea, a sovereign who knows little of us and cares less, a sovereign in whose Parliament we are suffered to have no members. Better no sovereign at all, we think, than such a sovereign as that."

He wondered if he would get through to the redcoat. But Captain Grimsley only shrugged. "Sometimes it's better to have a king who pays you no heed than one who pays too much. Look at Frederick of Prussia—you can't walk into a backhouse there without paying a turd tax to some collector."

Victor smiled. All the same, he said, "Better not to have to worry that the next King of England will take after Frederick, then. And from this day forth, Captain.

no King of England, good, bad, or indifferent, shall tell us what to do."

"I cannot speak to that, sir," Grimsley said. "Have you the terms of surrender properly written out for me to convey them to General Cornwallis?"

"I do," Victor said. "You will note I have lined through the provision pertaining to Biddiscombe's Horsed Legion and initialed the deletion. I should be grateful if General Cornwallis did likewise, along with signing the document as I have done."

"Your courtesy is appreciated," Grimsley said. "If all proves satisfactory to the general, shall we set the formal ceremony of surrender for noon tomorrow? Should any questions arise before then, you may be certain I shall come out to confer with you concerning them."

"Noon tomorrow. That is agreeable to me." Victor held out his hand. After momentary hesitation, Captain Grimsley shook it.

The Englishman also saluted after the handclasp. "When I came here, I never dreamt it would end this way," he remarked.

"That is always true for one side in a war," Victor answered. "The United States of Atlantis no more wish to be England's enemies than we wished to be her subjects. As equals in the comity of nations, one day we may become friends."

"I suppose we may," Captain Grimsley said. "I doubt, however, whether it will be any day soon." Having won the last word if not the last battle, he took the surrender terms back into Croydon.

Victor Radcliff wore the best of his three general's coats and the better of his two tricorns. Under the tricorn, he'd even donned a powdered, pigtailed periwig for the occasion. His general's sash stretched from one shoulder to the other hip. On his belt swung the Atlantean Assembly's gold-hilted sword.

His men were drawn up in neat ranks outside of

Croydon. They looked as spruce and uniform as they could. After long service in the field, not all of them could boast clean breeches. Their green jackets were of many different shades. Most of them wore tricorns. A few, even in wintertime, had only farmers' straw hats. More than a few went bareheaded.

But they all had muskets, and most of them had bayonets. The long steel blades glittered in the cold sunlight. They might not be so elegant as their English counterparts, but they'd proved they could fight.

Across the way, the Marquis de la Fayette had assembled the soldiers he'd brought from France. They looked more nearly uniform than the Atlanteans did. They'd proved themselves in battle, too. Victor waved to de la Fayette. The Frenchman returned the gesture.

Inside Croydon, church bells began to ring the hour. Victor had a pocket watch, which ran fairly well when he remembered to wind it. At the moment, it was five minutes slow—or, possibly, Croydon's clocks were five minutes fast. One way or the other, it hardly mattered. General Cornwallis would have no doubt that noon had come.

And he didn't. The redcoats formed on the frozen meadow in front of the town hall. Then, flags flying and band playing—at first faint in the distance but soon louder and louder—they marched toward the assembled Atlanteans and Frenchmen.

"What tune are they playing?" Blaise asked in a low voice.

After cocking his head to one side and listening for a moment, Victor answered, "I think it's called 'The World Turned Upside Down.' "

"Is it?" The Negro grinned. "Well, good."

"Yes." Victor sometimes thought Blaise found white men's music as curious as anything else in Atlantis. The songs Blaise had brought from Africa had different rhythms—not less complex (in fact, perhaps more so), but undoubtedly different.

Then again, that also mattered little. Here came the English army. As the redcoats left their works and came out into the open between the ranks of the Atlanteans and the French, the band finished "The World Turned Upside Down" and started a new tune. Not the most musical of men, Victor needed a moment to recognize "God Save the King."

Some Atlantean patriots had tried writing new words to the old music. Victor had heard several different versions, none of which he liked. Maybe one day someone would come up with new words that really described what the United States of Atlantis stood for, what they *meant*. (And maybe that wouldn't happen for a while, because who could really say right now what this untested country stood for?) Or maybe a musician would find or make another tune better suited to this new free land in the middle of the sea.

One more thing Victor could worry about later, if he worried about it at all. He caught the Marquis de la Fayette's eye again. At his nod, both commanders rode forward to meet General Cornwallis, who was also on horseback.

A bugle at the head of the English army blared out a call. A leather-lunged sergeant echoed it in words: "All—halt!" The redcoats did. Then the sergeant bawled another command, one that had no equivalent in horn calls: "Stack—arms!"

Half a dozen muskets went into each neat stack. As the surrender terms had ordained, a bayonet topped each Brown Bess. A fair number of Atlantean soldiers still carried hunting guns that couldn't even take a bayonet. The longarms would definitely strengthen the new nation's arsenal.

As Victor and de la Fayette drew near, General Cornwallis saluted each of them in turn. The English commander was not far from Victor's age. He looked older, though, or perhaps only wearier.

"Good to see you again," Victor said.

"And you," Cornwallis replied. "You will, I trust, forgive me for saying I wish we were meeting once more under different circumstances."

"Of course." Victor nodded. "I do not believe you've made the acquaintance of the French commander." He turned to de la Fayette and switched languages: "*Monsieur le Marquis*, I have the honor of presenting to you the English general, Charles Cornwallis." Back to English: "General Cornwallis, here is the Marquis de la Fayette, who leads our ally's soldiers."

"A privilege to meet you, your Grace," Cornwallis said in accented but fluent French. "Your army played no small part in leading to ... to the result we see here today." He didn't care to come right out and say something like *in leading to our defeat*. Well, he could be forgiven that. What man living didn't try to put the best face he could on misfortune?

"I thank you for your kind words, General," de la Fayette said in English. Sitting his horse along with the middle-aged Atlantean and English commanders, he seemed even more outrageously young than he really was. Returning to French, he went on, "I have never seen English soldiers fight less than bravely."

"Kind of you to say so, sir—very kind indeed," Cornwallis murmured. He turned back to Victor. "When you winkled us out of Hanover: that's when things commenced to unravel, dammit."

"Yes, I think so, too," Victor said. "Hanover is our windpipe, so to speak. After we got your hands off it, we could breathe freely once more."

"Just so." Cornwallis stared out to sea at the line of ships flying King Louis' fleurs-de-lys. "And who could have dreamt the Royal Navy would let us down? That I might lose on land is one thing. But the navy has turned back all comers since the damned devil Dutchmen back in the last century."

The pirates of Avalon had also given the Royal Navy all it wanted and a little more besides. Victor remembered Red Rodney Radcliffe far more fondly than his own

clipped-e Radcliff great-grandfather had ever thought of
the pirate chieftain—he was sure of that. In days to come,
Red Rodney might yet be reckoned a symbol, a harbin-
ger, of Atlantean liberty. At the time, William Radcliff
had considered his own unloved and unloving cousin
nothing but a God-damned bandit. He'd been right, too.
Symbols and harbingers were best viewed at a distance
of a good many years.

Cornwallis' cough brought Victor back to the here-
and-now. The English general reached for his sword. "If
you want this—"

"No, no." Victor held up a hand. "As I said in the
terms of surrender, you and your officers are welcome
to your weapons. You certainly did nothing to disgrace
them." But he couldn't help adding, "Except, perhaps,
by seeking to harbor Habakkuk Biddiscombe and his
band of cutthroat traitors."

"One side's villain is the other's hero," Cornwallis
answered. "We were comrades in arms once, you and I,
against the marquis' kingdom. Had things gone differently, you would be the man blamed for turning his coat,
not Biddiscombe."

"Had things gone differently, Atlantis might be
joined to the Terranovan mainland, or even to the European," Victor said. "In either of those cases, we would
not be here discussing how things might have gone
differently."

Cornwallis' smile was sad. "I find myself in a poor position to disagree with you." As he spoke, his men went
on stacking their muskets. After surrendering them, the
redcoats stepped back into line. Beneath their professional impassivity, Victor saw fear. Without weapons,
they were at their enemies' mercy. He would have cared
for that no more than they did. But that cup, at least, had
passed from him.

Far off in the distance, gunshots rang out. Regardless of this surrender, men from Victor's cavalry went
on pursuing Biddiscombe's Horsed Legion. If Biddiscombe's men rode far enough and fast enough, some of

them might get away. Odds were some of them would. Victor hoped his own followers would beat those odds and hunt down every last one.

"How soon do you think we shall be sent back to England?" Cornwallis asked.

"Word of your surrender will have to cross the Atlantic," Victor said. "After that, it depends on how soon his Majesty's government sends ships hither to transport you, and on wind and wave. On wind and wave, your guess is as good as mine. On his Majesty's government, your guess should be better than mine."

"I suspect you credit me with more than I deserve," Cornwallis said. "That his Majesty's government works is not to be denied. *How* it works . . . is not always given to mortal men to know."

"When the ships come to repatriate you, they will be most welcome: that, I promise," Victor said. "And I hope they will also bring representatives of King George's mysterious government so we can come to terms with it once for all and take our recognized place amongst the nations of the earth."

"And also so that peace may be restored between the kingdoms of England and France," de la Fayette added in French. He'd followed the interchange in English between Victor and Cornwallis, but preferred to comment in his own language.

"Yes, that will also be necessary," Victor agreed, switching to French himself. "France's aid to our cause, both on land and at sea, was most significant."

"You would never have won without it," Cornwallis said.

"There again we stray into might-have-beens," Victor said. "Do you believe his Majesty's government would have been prepared to put up with twenty years of raids and ambushes? Would it not eventually have decided Atlantis was a running sore, more costly of men and sterling than it was worth, and gone off and left us to our own devices?"

"After twenty years of such annoyances, it might well have done so," Cornwallis answered. "But your own followers also might well have given up the war as a bad job long before that, had they seen no more immediate prospect of victory."

Since that had always been Victor's greatest fear about having to resort to guerrilla warfare, he couldn't very well call his beaten foe a liar. Instead, he gruffly repeated, "Might-have-beens," and let it go at that.

"One thing more," Cornwallis said, some anxiety in his voice: "Now that we pass into your hands, I trust you will be able to victual us until such time as we return to the mother country?"

"We'll manage." Victor knew he still sounded gruff. He half-explained why: "I fear it won't be boiled beef one day and roast capon the next. Our commissary cannot come close to that, even for our own men. But your troops will go no hungrier than we do ourselves—on that you have my solemn word."

Cornwallis glanced over toward the Atlantean ranks. "Your soldiers are leaner than mine, as a general rule, but I own that they are not famished. Very well, sir. If we must tighten our belts, so be it. I know that, when you give your promise, he to whom you give it may rely on it."

"They are good men, the Atlanteans: better even than I expected before I came here," de la Fayette said, again in French. "Meaning no disrespect to you, General Cornwallis, but your country was foolish in the extreme in not doing everything it could to retain their affection and loyalty."

"It could be that you have reason," Cornwallis replied in the same tongue. "Or it could be that nothing we might have done would have retained them. If a folk is determined to rise up, rise up it will, regardless of whether it has good cause."

Victor hadn't wanted to lead Atlantis into rebellion against England. But plenty of prominent Atlanteans had, among them men as eminent as Isaac Fenner and Custis Cawthorne. And England hadn't done everything it could to conciliate them—not even close.

All of which was water over the dam now. "No matter what we might have been, we *are* the United States of Atlantis," he said. "And we shall see—the world will see—what comes of that."

XXIV

*S*pring in Croydon. Some but not all of the robins had flown south for the winter. All the birds that had were back now, hopping and singing and digging worms from the thawed ground. General Cornwallis was amused when Victor Radcliff named them. "Not *my* notion of robins," the English general declared.

"Yes, I know," Victor answered equably; he'd heard the like from Englishmen before. "Soon enough, you'll have your own little redbreasts back again."

Even as he spoke, redcoats filed aboard the ships the Royal Navy had sent to bring them home from Atlantis. Many of them were thinner than they had been when they stacked their muskets. But none had starved. They might have been hungry, but he knew the difference between hunger and *hunger*.

So did Cornwallis. "You have met the obligation you set yourself," he said. "No one could have treated captured foes more fairly."

"For which I thank you," Victor said. "We have no wish to be your enemies, as I tell Englishmen whenever I find the chance. So long as your country no longer seeks to impose its will on ours, I hope and trust we can become friends."

"May it be so," Cornwallis answered. "But you must

work that out with the learned commissioners despatched from London, not with me. I have no authority to frame a peace; mine lies—or, I should say, lay—solely in the military sphere."

Victor wasn't sure how much authority in the political sphere he had himself. He'd begun talks with King George's peace commissioners, but he'd had to warn them that the Atlantean Assembly might supersede him at any moment. So far, the Assembly hadn't seen fit to do so. Back in Honker's Mill, everyone still seemed amazed the United States of Atlantis had emerged victorious. Victor cast no aspersions on the Conscript Fathers for that. He was more than a little amazed himself.

"Have I your leave to take ship?" Cornwallis asked formally.

"You know you do," Victor said. "This is not your first visit to Atlantis. I hope one day you may come back here in peacetime, the better to see how this new experiment in liberty progresses."

"I should like that, though I can make no promises," Cornwallis said. "As a soldier, I remain at his Majesty's beck and call—provided he cares to call on a soldier proved unlucky in war."

"Well, I am similarly at the service of the Atlantean Assembly," Victor said.

"True." Cornwallis' nod was glum. "But you are not similarly defeated."

He sketched a salute. Victor held out his hand. Cornwallis clasped it. Then, slinging a duffel bag over his shoulder, the English general strode toward the pier and marched down it with his men. Boarding the closest English ship, he made his way back to the poop. He would have a cabin there, probably next to the captain's. And, aboard ship, he would no longer get his nose rubbed in Atlantean egalitarianism. He was a good fellow, but Victor doubted he would miss it.

A horseman trotted up. "General Radcliff, sir?"

"Yes?" Victor nodded. "What is it?"

"Letter for you, sir." The courier handed it to him and rode away.

Victor eyed the letter as if it were a mortar shell with the fuse hissing and about to explode. He kept waiting for orders from the Atlantean Assembly, and kept dreading the kind of orders the Assembly might give.

He would go on waiting a while longer. The letter was not addressed in the preternaturally neat hand of the Assembly's secretary. Nor was it bedizened with the red-crested eagle the Assembly had taken to using on its seal.

That did not mean the missive bore good news. It also did not mean he failed to recognize the script in which it was addressed. He had his doubts about whether he wanted to hear from the Atlantean Assembly. If only he could forget he'd ever heard from Marcel Freycinet, he would have been the happiest man in the newly freed, ecstatically independent United States of Atlantis. So he told himself, anyhow.

Which didn't mean he hadn't heard from Freycinet. He flipped the seal off the letter with his thumb. It lay not far from his feet. As he unfolded the paper, a little brown sparrow hopped over and pecked at the wax. Finding it indigestible, the bird fluttered off.

Victor feared he would find the letter's contents just as indigestible. Freycinet wasted no time beating around the bush. *I congratulate you*, he wrote. *You are the father of a large, squalling baby boy. Louise is also doing well. She has asked that he be named Nicholas, to which I am pleased to assent. I pray God will allow him to remain healthy, and that he will continue to be an adornment for my household. I remain, sir, your most obedient servant in all regards....* His scribbled signature followed.

"A son," Victor muttered, refolding the sheet of paper. A son somewhere between mulatto and quadroon, born into slavery! Not the offspring he'd had in mind, which was putting it mildly. And if Marcel Freycinet chose, or needed, to sell the boy (to sell Nicholas Radcliff, only surviving son of Victor Radcliff—hailed as Liberator of Atlantis but unable to liberate his own offspring) . . . well, he would be within his rights.

Suddenly and agonizingly, Victor understood the Seventh Commandment in a way he never had before. God knew what He was doing when He thundered against adultery, all right. And why? Not least, surely, because adultery complicated men's lives, and women's, in ways nothing else could.

A bird called. It was only one of the robins whose Atlantean name General Cornwallis and other Englishmen so disdained. All the same, to Victor's ear it might have been a cuckoo. He'd hatched an egg in a nest not his own, and now he had to hope other birds would feed and care for the fledgling as it deserved.

Someone's soles scuffed on the dirt beside him. He looked up. There stood Blaise. The Negro pointed at the letter. "Is it from the Assembly?"

"No." Victor quickly tucked the folded sheet of paper into a breeches pocket. "Merely an admirer."

Blaise raised an eyebrow. "An admirer, you say? Have you met her? Is she pretty?"

"Not that sort of admirer." At the moment—especially at this moment—that was the last sort Victor wanted.

"What other kind is worth having?" Blaise asked. When away from Stella, he could still think like that, since he hadn't got Roxane with child—and since he didn't know Victor had impregnated Louise.

"I said nothing of whether this one was worth having," Victor answered, warming to his theme: "This is a fellow who, having read the reports of our final campaign in the papers in Hanover, is now convinced he could have taken charge of our army and the French and won more easily and quickly and with fewer casualties than we did. If only he wore gilded epaulets, he says, we should have gained our liberty year before last."

"Oh. One of *those*," Blaise said. The lie convinced him all the more readily because Victor had had several real letters in that vein. A startling number of men who'd never commanded soldiers—and who probably didn't know how to load a musket, much less clean one—were convinced the art of generalship suffered greatly because circumstance forced them to remain netmakers or potters or solicitors. Victor and Blaise were both convinced such men understood matters military in the same degree as a honker comprehended the calculus.

"I'm afraid so," Victor said.

"Well, if you waste the time and ink on an answer, by all means tell him I think he's a damn fool, too," Blaise said, and took himself off.

"If I do, I shall," Victor answered—a promise that meant nothing. He reached into his pocket and touched the letter from Freycinet. However much grief he felt, it remained a private grief. And the last thing he wanted—the very last thing—was that it should ever become public.

Dickering with the English commissioners helped keep Victor from brooding too much over things in his own life he could not help. Richard Oswald was a plain-spoken Scotsman who served as chief negotiator for the English Secretary of State, the Earl of Shelburne. His colleague, David Hartley, was a member of Parliament. He had a high forehead, a dyspeptic expression, and a shoulder-length periwig of the sort that had gone out of fashion when Louis XIV died, more than half a century before.

Most of the negotiations were straightforward enough. The English duo conceded that King George recognized the United States of Atlantis, separately and collectively, as free, sovereign, and independent states. He abandoned all claims to govern them and to own property in them.

Settling the borders of the new land was similarly simple. The only land frontier it had was the old one with Spanish Atlantis in the far south, and that remained unchanged. One of these days, Victor suspected, his country would take Spanish Atlantis for its own, either by conquest or by purchase. But that time was not yet here, and did not enter into the present discussions.

"There'd be more of a to-do over who owned what and who claimed what were you part of the Terranovan mainland," Oswald remarked in a burr just thick enough to make Victor pay close attention to every word he said. The comment reminded Victor of his byplay with Cornwallis at the surrender ceremony. Oswald went on, "As things are, though, ocean all around keeps us from fashin' ourselves unduly."

"So it does," Victor said, hoping he grasped what *fashin'* meant.

They disposed without much trouble of fishing rights and of the due rights of creditors on both sides to get the full amount they had been owed. Then they came to the sticky part: the rights remaining to Atlanteans who had stayed loyal to King George. That particularly grated on Victor because Habakkuk Biddiscombe and a handful of his men remained at large.

At last, David Hartley said, "Let them be outlaws, then. But what of the plight of the thousands of Atlanteans who never bore arms against your government but still groan under expulsions and confiscations? I fear I see no parallel between the two cases."

That gave Victor pause. How could he say the Englishman's complaint held no justice? Slowly, he answered, "If these one-time loyalists are willing to live peacefully in the United States of Atlantis, and to accept the new nation's independence, something may perhaps be done for them."

"Why do you allow no more than that?" Hartley pressed. "Let your Atlantean Assembly pass the proper law, and proclaim it throughout the land, and all will be as it should."

"If only it were so simple," Victor said, not without regret.

"Wherefore is it not?" Hartley asked.

"The Assembly chooses war and peace for all Atlantis. It treats with foreign powers. It coins specie. It arranges for the dealings of the Atlantean settlements—ah, states—one with another," Victor said. "But each state, within its own boundaries, retains its sovereignty. The Assembly has not the authority to command the several states to treat the loyalists within 'em thus and so. Did it make the attempt, the states' Assemblies and Parliaments and Legislatures would surely rise against it, reckoning its impositions as tyrannous as all Atlantis reckoned King George's."

"This is not government," Richard Oswald said. "This is lunacy let loose upon the world."

Although inclined to agree with him, Victor knew better than to admit as much. He spread his hands. "It is what we have, sir. I do not intend to touch off a civil war on the heels of the foreign war just past."

"Lunacy," Oswald repeated. He seemed more inclined to wash his hands of the United States of Atlantis than to spread them.

But his colleague said, "Perhaps there is a middle ground."

Oswald snorted. "Between madness and sanity? Give me leave to doubt."

"How would this be?" David Hartley said. "Let the Atlantean Assembly earnestly recommend to the governing bodies of the respective states that they provide for the restitution of estates, rights, and properties belonging to those who did not take up arms against the United States of Atlantis. This would be consistent not only with justice and equity but also with the spirit of conciliation which on the return of the blessings of peace should universally prevail."

Victor Radcliff suspected hotheads in the Atlantean Assembly would damn him for a soft-hearted backslider for making an arrangement like that. He also suspected the states' governing bodies might not care to heed the Atlantean Assembly's recommendations, no matter how earnest they were. But a mild occupation of French Atlantis had gone well on the whole, where a harsh one might have sparked festering rebellion. He didn't nod with any great enthusiasm, but nod he did. "Let it be so."

"Capital!" Hartley wrote swiftly. "I believe this conveys the gist of what I said. Is it acceptable to you?"

Victor read the proposed article. He nodded again. "It is."

"By the same token, then, there should be no further confiscations—nor prosecutions, either, for that matter—because of past loyalties," Richard Oswald said. "Any such proceedings now in train should also be stopped."

"I will agree to that, provided it also applies reciprocally," Victor replied. "England should not prosecute any Atlanteans in her territory for preferring the Assembly to the king."

Oswald looked as if he'd bitten into an unripe persimmon. But David Hartley nodded judiciously. "That seems only fair," he said. With his own countryman willing to yield the point, Oswald grumbled but did not say no.

Terms for the evacuation of English troops had already been worked out between Victor and General Cornwallis. It remained but to incorporate them into the treaty. The English also undertook not to destroy any archives or records. Quite a few documents had already gone up in flames, the better to protect informers and quiet collaborators. Well, the Atlanteans had burned their share of papers, too. But enough was enough.

"One other point remains," Victor said. "Operations of which we here know nothing may yet continue against Avalon, New Marseille, or the smaller towns of the west coast. In case it should happen that any place belonging to Atlantis shall have been conquered by English arms before word of this treaty arrives in those parts, let it be restored without difficulty and without compensation."

The English commissioners looked at each other. They both shrugged at the same time. "Agreed," Oswald said. Again, David Hartley wrote down the clause.

After he finished, he asked, "Is your west coast as savage as the savants say?"

"It is sparsely settled, though Avalon makes a fair-sized town," Victor answered. "The truly empty region is the interior between the Green Ridge Mountains and the Hesperian Gulf. Its day will come, I doubt not, but that day is not yet here."

"Will it come in our lifetime?" Hartley asked.

"I can hope so," Victor said. "I must admit, I don't particularly expect to see it."

"Shall we proceed?" Richard Oswald said. "Does anything more need to go into this treaty?" He waited. When neither his countryman nor Victor said anything, he went on, "Then let it go into effect when it is ratified by Parliament and by the Atlantean Assembly, said ratification to take place within six months unless some matter of surpassing exigency should intervene."

"Agreed," Victor said. He shook hands with both Englishmen.

"I shall give you a copy of the articles," David Hartley said.

"For which I thank you kindly," Victor replied. Amazing how defeat in the field inclined England toward sweet reason. He barely kept himself from clapping his hands in glee. No one now, not King George and not the Emperor of China, either, could claim the United States of Atlantis had no rightful place among the nations of the world!

Victor was lodged above a public house called the Pleasant Cod. The place had been open for business for upwards of a century; by now, very likely, every possible jest about its name had been made. That didn't keep new guests from making those same jokes over again. Only the glazed look in the taverner's eye kept Victor from exercising his wit at the Cod's expense.

He—or rather, the Atlantean Assembly—was paying for his lodging. One of the principal grievances Atlantis had against England was the uncouth English practice of quartering troops on the citizenry without so much as a by-your-leave—and without so much as a farthing's worth of payment. And if the taverner gouged him for the room . . . well, Atlantean paper still wasn't close to par with sterling.

Someone pounded on the door in the middle of the night. Victor needed a moment to come back to himself, then another to remember where he was and why he was there. He groped for the fine sword from the Atlantean Assembly. In these days of gunpowder, generals rarely bloodied their blades on the battlefield. But the sword would do fine for letting the air out of a robber or two.

Bang! Bang! Bang! Whoever was out in the hall really wanted to come in. People in other rooms swore at the racket. Victor had no trouble hearing every angry oath through the thin walls.

"Who's there, dammit?" he called, blade in his right hand, the latch in his left. He wasn't about to open it till he got an answer he liked.

He made the knocking stop, anyway. "Is that you, Victor?" a voice inquired. A familiar voice?

"No," he said harshly. "I am the Grand Vizier of the Shah of Persia." He would have assumed a Persian accent had he had the faintest notion of what one sounded like.

Someone else spouted gibberish in the hall. For all Victor knew, it might have been Persian. It was beyond a doubt Custis Cawthorne. Victor threw the door open. "I thought you were still in France!" he exclaimed.

"His ship put in at Pomphret Landing," Isaac Fenner said. "We've ridden together from there to Croydon to see you."

"Perhaps not quite so much of you as this," Cawthorne added. Victor looked down at himself in the dim light of the hallway lantern. All he had on were a linen undershirt and cotton drawers.

"I was asleep," he said with as much dignity as he could muster. "You might have waited till morning to come to call."

"That's right! You bloody well might have, you noisy

buggers!" someone else yelled from behind a closed door.

Victor ducked back into his room. After some fumbling, he found the candle stub that had lighted his way up the stairs. He lit it again at the lantern. Then he made a gesture of invitation. "Well, my friends, as long as you are here, by all means come in."

"Yes—go in and shut up!" that unhappy man shouted.

"We should have let it wait till morning," Cawthorne said as Victor shut the door behind them.

His little bit of candle wouldn't last long. Then they could either talk in the dark or go to bed. "Why didn't you?" he asked.

"Because what we came for is too important," Isaac Fenner answered stubbornly. The dim, flickering light only made his ears seem to stick out even more than they would have anyway.

"And that is . . . ?" Victor prompted.

"Why, to finish negotiating the treaty with the English commissioners . . . Confound it, what's so funny?"

"Only that I reached an accord with them this afternoon," Victor answered. "If the Atlantean Assembly should decide the said accord is not to its liking, it is welcome to change matters to make them more satisfactory. And, should it choose to do so, I shall retire once for all into private life with the greatest delight and relief imaginable."

Custis Cawthorne burst out laughing, too. "All this rushing might have been avoided with a faster start," he observed. "But then, that proves true more often than any of us commonly cares to contemplate."

Fenner, implacable as one of the Three Fates, held out his hand to Victor. "Kindly let me see this so-called agreement."

"No," Victor said.

Shadows swooped across Fenner's face as it sagged in surprise. "What?" he sputtered. "You dare refuse?"

"Too right, I do," Victor answered. "God may know what miserable hour of the night it is, but, not being inclined to fumble out my pocket watch, I haven't the faintest notion. I am certain the treaty will keep till daylight. For now, Isaac, shut up and go to bed."

"But—!" Fenner seemed about to explode.

"Isaac . . ." Custis Cawthorne spoke his friend's name in a voice full of gentle, amused melancholy.

"What is it?" Fenner, by contrast, snapped like the jaws of a steel trap.

"Shut up and go to bed. *I* intend to." As if to prove as much, Cawthorne shrugged out of his coat and began undoing the toggles on his tunic.

His colleague's face was a study in commingled amazement and fury. Fenner's red hair warned of his temper, as a light on a lee shore warned of dangerous rocks. But then the Bredestown Assemblyman also started to laugh. "All right, all right—just as you please. I see there are two beds in the room. Who shall have which?"

"This one is mine." Victor pointed to the unmade one, in which he'd been sleeping. "The two of you may share the other, this being the price you pay for disturbing me in so untimely a fashion."

Isaac Fenner looked ready to argue about that, too. Cawthorne, by contrast, took off his shoes. Grunting, he bent to reach under the bed Victor had designated. He picked up the chamber pot that sat there. "I trust you gentlemen will excuse me. . . ." he said, politely turning his back. When he'd finished, he presented the pot to Fenner. "Isaac?"

"Oh, very well." Fenner used the pot while Cawthorne lay down and made himself comfortable. Victor stretched out on his own bed. Blaise was in the servants' quarters downstairs. Chances were the Negro was asleep right this minute, too. Victor wished he could say the same.

"You'd better hurry up," he told Isaac Fenner. "This candle won't last much longer." Sure enough, it guttered and almost went out.

Fenner got into bed. The ropes supporting the mattress creaked under his weight. "Good night, sweetheart," Custis Cawthorne told him, as if men didn't sleep two or three or four to a bed all the time in taverns or inns.

"Good night—darling," Fenner retorted.

Victor blew out the candle. Blackness plunged down from the ceiling and swallowed the room whole. Victor didn't know about how his eminent Atlantean comrades fared after that: he went back to sleep himself too soon to have the chance to find out.

Down in the common room the next morning, Blaise looked grouchy. He usually drank tea, but a steaming mug of coffee sat in front of him now. He sipped from it as he attacked a ham steak and a plate of potatoes fried in lard. When Victor asked what the trouble was, his factotum sent him a wounded look.

"Some damnfool commotion in the nighttime," Blaise answered, swallowing more coffee. "Didn't you hear it? I thought it was plenty to wake the dead. I know it woke me, and I had a devil of a time getting back to sleep again afterwards."

"Oh," Victor said. "That."

"Yes, that. You know what it was?"

After a glance at the stairway, Victor nodded. "Here it comes now, as a matter of fact."

Blaise blinked as Isaac Fenner came down. He frankly gaped when Custis Cawthorne followed. "But he's in France," Blaise blurted.

"I thought so, too," Victor said. "In point of fact, though, he was in my room last night, wanting to see the treaty I hammered out with Oswald and Hartley yesterday. Well, actually, no: Isaac was the one who wanted to see it just then. Custis came with him, though."

The Atlantean dignitaries bore down on the table where Victor and Blaise sat. Without so much as a good-morning, Fenner said, "You have the terms with you?"

"I crave your pardon," Victor said. "I must have left them up in the room. After I break my fast, you may rest assured I shall let you examine them at your leisure."

That produced the desired effect: it incensed Fenner. "Devil fry you black as a griddle cake forgotten over the fire!" he shouted, loud enough to make everyone in the common room stare at him. "Why did you not have the consideration, the common courtesy, the—the plain wit, to bring them down with you? Think on how much time you might have saved, man! Just think!"

"Easy, Isaac, easy. You might do some thinking yourself, instead of bellowing like a branded calf." Custis Cawthorne set a hand on Fenner's arm. "Unless I find myself much mistaken, General Radcliff would end up holding your leg in his hand if he pulled it any harder."

"What?" Fenner gaped, goggle-eyed.

"I do have the treaty here, Isaac," Victor said. The serving girl chose that moment to come up and ask him what he wanted. He got to prolong Fenner's agony by hashing over the virtues and vices of ham, sausages, and bacon. Having finally picked sausages and sent the girl back to the kitchen, Victor produced the draft. "Here is what the Englishmen and I have arrived at. Why don't you and Custis sit down and look it over and order something to put ballast in your bellies?"

"A capital notion," Cawthorne said. "Capital." He proceeded to follow Victor's suggestion. Isaac Fenner stood there till the older man tugged at his sleeve. "You wanted to see this. Now that you can, aren't you going to?"

"Errr—" Fenner had to take a deep breath to stop making the noise. He sat down most abruptly. Almost as if against his will, he started reading over Cawthorne's shoulder. Then he tugged the paper away from the other man, so that it lay on the table between them.

The serving girl came back with Victor's breakfast. She smiled at Fenner and Cawthorne. "What would you gents care for?"

"I don't care for this fifth article—not even slightly," Fenner said.

"She means for breakfast, Isaac," Custis Cawthorne said. "As for me, I'll take the ham and potatoes, and a mug of ale to wash 'em down."

"Breakfast." By the way Fenner said it, the possibility had slipped his mind. "Hmm . . . What Custis chose will suit me well enough, too."

Victor wouldn't have given better than three to two that Fenner had even heard what Custis Cawthorne chose for breakfast. The answer was enough to make the serving girl go away, though, which was what the Bredestown Assemblyman had in mind. Fenner's forefinger descended on the treaty. "This fifth article—" he began again.

"England wanted us to compel the states to undo their measures against the loyalists," Victor said.

"Good luck!" Cawthorne exclaimed. "We'd be fighting half a dozen wars at once if we tried."

"Just what I told 'em," Victor said. "They do have something of a point, after all—loyalists who did not bear arms against the Atlantean Assembly may become good citizens in the circumstances now prevailing. No certainty of it, but they may. And so—what's the phrase Hartley used?—'earnestly recommending' that the states go easy struck me as a reasonable compromise."

"Why should we compromise?" Fenner said. "We won!"

Patiently, Victor answered, "The firmer the peace we make with England now, the smaller the chance we'll have to fight another war in ten years' time, or twenty. God has not sent me word from On High that we are bound to win then. Has He been more generous with you?"

"When I was a boy, Croydon folk would have thrown you in the stocks for a jape like that," Cawthorne said. "They might do it yet, were the fellow so exercising his wit some abandoned vagabond rather than the hero of Atlantis' liberation."

"People here *are* touchy about God," Blaise agreed. "Even touchier than they are most places, I mean."

"They are certain they are right. Being thus certain, they are equally sure they have the right—nay, more: the duty—to impose their views on everyone they can," Cawthorne said.

A crack like that might have won *him* time in the stocks were he less prominent and less notorious. His breakfast, and Isaac Fenner's, interrupted perusal of the treaty. After a while, Fenner said, "This is good." Again, he sounded surprised.

"A full belly strengthens the spirit." Custis Cawthorne seemed to listen to himself. "Not bad. Not bad at all. I must remember that one."

Fenner was still eyeing the draft of the treaty. "It will be some time before we can pay our debts at par with sterling," he said sadly.

Victor also knew the parlous state of the Atlantean Assembly's paper—who didn't? But he answered, "Would you rather I had told the English commissioners we intend to repudiate those debts? They lodge down the street. I will introduce them to you later this morning. If you intend to convey that message, you may do so yourself."

"No, no," Fenner said. "Now that we are a nation, we must be able to hold up our heads amongst our fellow nations. Even so, putting our house in order will prove more difficult than many of us would wish."

"Never fear. We can always find some cozening trick or another to befool our creditors," Cawthorne said. "France has proved that year after year."

"How *was* France?" Victor asked him.

"Most enjoyable, at the level where I traveled," Cawthorne said. "If you have the means to live well—or have friends with the means to let you live well—you can live better in and around Paris than anywhere else on earth. But the peasantry? Dear God in heaven! Upon my oath, the grievances the French peasants have against their king and nobles make ours against England seem light as a feather drifting on the breeze by comparison."

"Then let them rise, too," Fenner said. "Freedom is no less contagious than smallpox, and no inoculation wards against it."

"Would you say the same, Mr. Fenner, to a Negro

slave picking indigo or growing rice in the south of Atlantis?" Blaise asked.

Custis Cawthorne chuckled softly to himself. Fenner sent him an irritated look. "Speaking for myself, I have no great use for slavery," he replied. "I hope one day to see it vanish from the United States of Atlantis, as it has already vanished or grown weak in so much of the north here. For the time being, however, it—"

"Makes the slaveholders piles of filthy lucre," Cawthorne broke in.

"Not how I should have phrased it," Fenner said.

Why not? Victor wondered. His son could be sold at any time, for no better reason than to line Marcel Freycinet's pockets. That made him look at holding Negroes and copperskins in perpetual servitude in a whole new light.

But Fenner hadn't finished: "One day before too many years have passed, I expect property in slaves to grow hopelessly uneconomic when measured against property in, say, machinery. And when that day comes, slaveholding in Atlantis will be at an end."

"How many years?" Blaise pressed, as if wondering how patient he should—or could—be.

"I should be surprised if it came to pass in fewer than twenty years," Isaac Fenner answered. "I should also be surprised if slavery still persisted a lifetime from now."

Blaise made a noise down deep in his throat. That did not please him. No—it did not satisfy him. *Isaac thinks my son Nicholas will grow to manhood a slave*, Victor thought. *He thinks my son may live out his whole life as a chattel.* Put in those terms, Fenner's reasoned and reasonable estimate didn't satisfy him, either. But what could he do about it? Freeing slaves was far more explosive than compensating loyalists.

"Can I bring you anything else, gents?" the serving girl asked.

Custis Cawthorne shoved his mug across the table toward her. "If you fill this up again, I shall thank you sweetly for it."

"And you'll pay for it, too," she said, and walked off swinging her hips.

"One way or another, we always end up paying for it," Cawthorne said with a sigh.

Fenner wasn't watching the girl; he was still methodically going through the treaty. When at last he looked up, Victor asked, "Does it suit you?"

"We might have squeezed better terms from them here and there." Fenner tapped the document with the nail on his right index finger. "But, if you have already made the bargain . . ."

"I have," Victor said. "They may possibly reconsider: I daresay there are certain small advantages they still hope to wring from us. If you reckon the game worth the candle, I do not object—too much—to your proposing further negotiation to them."

Isaac Fenner tapped the treaty again. By his expression, up till Victor's reply he'd thought only of what the United States of Atlantis might get from England, not of what England might still want from the new nation. "If the agreement as it stands suits you and suits them, we might be wiser to leave it unchanged," he said.

"So we might," Cawthorne said, "not that that necessarily stops anyone."

Victor hadn't thought it would stop Fenner. If it did, he wasn't about to complain. If he did complain, after all, wouldn't he fall into the common error himself?

XXV

$\mathcal{V}$ictor had wondered whether the English commissioners would want anything to do with Isaac Fenner and Custis Cawthorne. After all, he'd already reached agreement with King George's officials. And, had he brought Fenner alone, the Englishmen might well not have cared to treat with him.

But Cawthorne made all the difference. Richard Oswald and David Hartley were as delighted to meet him as if he were a young, beautiful, loose-living actress. Oswald used a pair of spectacles of Cawthorne's design, so that he could read with the lower halves of the lenses while still seeing clearly at a distance through the uppers.

"Ingenious! Most extraordinarily ingenious!" the Scot exclaimed. "How ever did you come to think of it?"

"What gave me the idea, actually, was a badly ground set of reading glasses, in which part of the lenses were of improper curvature," Cawthorne answered. "I thought, if what had chanced by accident were to be done better, and on purpose. . . . Once the notion was in place, bringing it to fruition proved easy enough."

"Remarkable," Oswald said. "It takes an uncommon mind to recognize the importance of the commonplace and obvious."

Curtis Cawthorne preened. The only thing he enjoyed more than hearing himself praised was hearing himself praised by someone with the discernment to understand and to state exactly why he deserved all those accolades.

Because the commissioners so admired Cawthorne, they even put up with Fenner's urge to fiddle with the treaty. As far as Victor could see, none of the changes from either side made a halfpenny's worth of difference. A few commas went in; a few others disappeared. Several adjectives and a sprinkling of adverbs were exchanged for others of almost identical import. Fenner seemed happier. The Englishmen didn't seem dismayed or, more important, irate.

The one phrase David Hartley declined to change was "earnestly recommend" in the fifth article. Fenner proposed several alternatives. Hartley rejected each in turn. "I do not believe that has quite the meaning his Majesty's government wishes to convey," he would say, and the Atlantean would try again.

Finally, Victor took Fenner aside. "He likes the wording of that article as it is," Radcliff said. "He is particularly pleased with it because he created the formula himself."

"Ah!" Fenner said, as if a great light had dawned. "I had not fully grasped that he was suffering from pride of authorship."

Although Victor might not have phrased it just so, he found himself nodding. "That is the condition"—he didn't want to say *disease*—"controlling him."

"Very well, then." By Fenner's tone and expression, it wasn't. Victor followed him into the meeting room with some apprehension. But Fenner was smiling by the time he sat down across the table from the English commissioners. "Mr. Hartley, General Radcliff has persuaded me that your language will serve. I shall earnestly recommend"—his smile got wider—"to the Atlantean Assembly that it should abide by this article as it does by all the rest."

"That is handsomely said, Mr. Fenner," Hartley replied. "I am pleased to accept it in the spirit in which it is offered. And I also thank you for your good offices, General Radcliff."

"My pleasure, sir," Victor replied. He still wasn't sure he liked the way Isaac Fenner was smiling. The Atlantean Assembly could earnestly recommend as much as it pleased. That didn't necessarily mean the Atlantean states would pay any attention to it. Fenner had to know as much, too. But he said nothing of it to David Hartley. Maybe he had the makings of a diplomat after all.

"With that matter settled, have we any more outstanding?" Richard Oswald asked, as he had with the draft he and Hartley arranged with Victor. Nobody said anything. Oswald nodded decisively, like an auctioneer bringing down the hammer on.... *On a slave*, Victor thought, and wished he hadn't. Before he could dive deeper into his own worries, Oswald went on, "Then let us affix our signatures and seals to the document. Mr. Hartley and I will deliver our copy to London, whilst you take yours to Honker's Mill."

His manner was altogether matter-of-fact, which only made the comparison more odious. London was the greatest city in the world, perhaps the greatest in the history of the world. Honker's Mill ... wasn't. A touch of asperity in his voice, Isaac Fenner said, "Now that peace has been restored, New Hastings will become the capital of the United States of Atlantis."

"How nice," Oswald murmured. New Hastings wasn't the greatest city in the history of the world, either. Maybe one day it would be, or Hanover if it wasn't so lucky, but neither came anywhere close yet. Not even the most ardent—the most rabid—Atlantean patriot could claim otherwise.

"Signatures. Seals," Custis Cawthorne said—and not one word about New Hastings' honor.

Men from both sides solemnly initialed the changed adjectives and adverbs on the treaty. They let the altered commas go. Maybe, one day, some historians would note the ones that had been deleted and learnedly guess which ones had been added after the first draft was done. For the time being, nobody thought they were worth getting excited about.

Richard Oswald and David Hartley signed for England. They splashed hot wax down on both copies and pressed their signet rings into it. Then the Atlanteans followed suit: first Victor, then Isaac Fenner, and finally Custis Cawthorne. One by one, the Atlanteans also used their seals.

"It is accomplished," Hartley said as the wax hardened. "Your land is separated from ours." Jeremiah could have sounded no gloomier. Even Job would have been hard-pressed.

"Now it is truly our own, to do with as we will!" Isaac Fenner, by contrast, exulted. Victor wondered how that balance between gloom and exultation would tip in years to come. Only the coming of those years would tell.

Company by company, regiment by regiment, the Atlantean soldiers who'd taken service for the duration of the war against England went home. The United States of Atlantis would retain a small professional army—one modeled on that of the mother country—but most of the greencoats wanted nothing more than to go back to their farms and shops, and to their families.

And French ships put in at Croydon to return de la Fayette and the survivors from his army to their native land. French sergeants cursed more musically than their English or Atlantean counterparts, but they were no less sincere. Ordinary French soldiers seemed as ready to go anywhere they were told and do anything they were told as a like number of redcoats would have.

De la Fayette clasped Victor's hand. "You may be sure, *Monsieur le Général*, it was a great honor to serve beside you and to help bring freedom to your land." The French noble grinned impishly. "And I also very much enjoyed giving England one in the eye."

"The fight would have been much harder and much

longer without you, your Grace," Victor answered truthfully. "Your army's courage and its skill taught us a great deal, and your fleet slammed the cork into Cornwallis' bottle." He paused a moment, then added, "And, had you not come here, I should not have made a friend I value."

"I feel the same way." De la Fayette squeezed his hand again. He too hesitated before continuing in a low voice: "Now that Atlantis has shown the world what freedom means, perhaps my country will also discover it before long."

Victor remembered Custis Cawthorne's comments on the current state of France. What Cawthorne could say among his fellow Atlanteans, Victor didn't feel comfortable repeating to a French nobleman, even one of liberal ideas like de la Fayette. He contented himself with replying, "Come what may, in your land and in mine, I hope we meet again."

"As do I—and may it be so!" The marquis' smile was sweet and sad and knowing beyond his years. "If this is to come to pass, I think I shall have to come back here. Atlantean affairs will likely leave you far too busy to cross the sea and visit me in France."

"Maybe so—but then again, maybe not," Victor said. "I am going back to my farm. I never wanted to be anything more than a private citizen. Now that the war is over, I intend to seize the chance and go back to what I was."

"Well, *mon ami*, I wish you good fortune in your endeavor." Yes, de la Fayette's smile looked knowing indeed. "But fame, once it takes up a man, often is not so eager to let him go again."

That had also worried Victor. He gave the best answer he could: "If I am willing—no: eager, by God!—to let fame go, I hope the beast will prove willing to take its claws out of me."

"A man should always hope," de la Fayette agreed. Victor Radcliff was old enough to be his father. The marquis had no business sounding like the more experienced of the two of them. But he brought it off with grace and without much effort, as he brought off so many things.

"You don't believe I can do it." Victor turned that into an accusation.

De la Fayette's shrug was a small masterpiece of its kind. "What a man can do . . . What fate will do . . . Who but *le bon Dieu* can say how they fit together? As, for example, the matter of your paternity."

"What about it? How did you know about it?" That was the last thing Victor wanted anyone to know about. And it was the last thing he wanted to talk about, even if they were unlikely to be overheard.

This time, de la Fayette's shrug just looked . . . French. "*Monsieur* Freycinet communicated the news to me. Rest assured, he understands the need for discretion, and he relies on mine, as you may."

"Mmm," Victor said. Freycinet could afford to rely on that. Victor couldn't. Might the man from the south have told anyone else? Radcliff didn't want to contemplate that.

With a sigh, de la Fayette said, "It is a great pity when what should be a time of joy brings you no happiness."

Calling it a pity, to Victor's way of thinking, made a formidable understatement. He forced a shrug of his own: a poor thing next to those of de la Fayette, but it would have to serve. "Nothing to be done about it," he said.

"I know," the marquis agreed sympathetically. "Not even amending your laws would change the predicament, I fear. If you led a single life . . . But you do not, and no woman can look kindly upon her man after he sires a child on another."

"No," Victor said, wishing the marquis would shut up. Nothing de la Fayette said hadn't crossed his own mind. He and Meg had got on well for many years, but she wouldn't be one to take something like this in stride. How many women would? Precious few. Victor didn't need the Frenchman to point that out for him.

Someone aboard the nearest French ship called de la

Fayette. The marquis grabbed Victor's hand one more time. "I must go," he said, and kissed Radcliff on both cheeks. He hurried down the pier, over the gangplank, and onto the ship. He waved from the deck before heading back toward the poop.

Victor also waved. Little by little, Atlantis was being left to her own devices. The prospect excited Isaac Fenner. Despite all the fighting Victor had done to produce exactly this result, he still wasn't sure whether it excited him or frightened him more.

Writing to Meg, which once was always a pleasure, had become a trial since Victor learned Louise would bear his child. He wasn't used to concealing himself from his wife. He'd always been able to speak his mind to her. No more, or not fully.

If she ever found out about his dark descendant, she would speak her mind to him. He had no doubts on that score.

Worrying about what would happen when he got home kept him in Croydon longer than he would have lingered with a clear conscience. His aides could have handled the release of what was left of the army that had bested the redcoats. They knew it, too. He caught the quizzical looks they gave him when he rode out to the shrinking encampments outside of town.

He hoped none of them knew about his predicament. He'd done his best to keep it secret, but Custis Cawthorne had plenty of pungent things to say about secrets and all the things that could go wrong with them.

His lingering meant he was in Croydon when a courier rode into town at a full gallop, his horse kicking up great clouds of dust till he reined in. "What is it?" Victor asked anxiously—good news seldom needed to travel so fast. He hoped there hadn't been a bad fire somewhere, or a smallpox outbreak.

This time, the courier surprised him. The man threw back his head and howled like a wolf. Then he said, "We've caught Habakkuk Biddiscombe, General!"

Everybody who heard that clapped and cheered. "Have we?" Victor breathed.

"Sure have," the courier said. "I haven't seen him myself, but word is he's a sorry starveling thing. And he'll get sorrier pretty goddamn quick, won't he?"

More cheers declared that the people of Croydon liked the idea. Victor wondered how much he liked it himself. After Biddiscombe went over to England, Victor had wanted nothing more than to see him dead. He wondered why killing the traitor in cold blood seemed so much less appealing.

Appealing or not, it would have to be done. If he'd wanted to avoid it, he would have let General Cornwallis take Biddiscombe and the men of the Horsed Legion away with him when he went back to England. At the time, he'd made a point of allowing no such thing.

"Where is he?" Victor asked.

"Up in Kirkwall, about fifty miles north of here," the courier said. "Do you want them to string him up there? They'll do it in a heartbeat—you can count on that."

"No," Victor said, not without a certain amount of reluctance. "Even a traitor deserves a trial."

The courier shrugged. "Seems a waste of time, if you want to know what I think." Like most Atlanteans, he assumed people did want to know what he thought. After another shrug, he went on, "I'll need me a fresh horse to head north. Almost ran the legs off of this here poor beast."

"You'll have one," Victor assured him. "Are all the cutthroats captured with Biddiscombe, or do some remain at large?"

"Most of 'em're caught or killed," the man answered. "A few got away. Odds are they'll chase 'em down pretty soon."

"I hope so," Victor said. "The sooner they do, the sooner Atlantis will know perfect peace at last."

"Perfect peace," the courier echoed. "That'd be something, wouldn't it?"

"So it would," Victor said solemnly. Sure enough,

with Habakkuk Biddiscombe gone from the stage, the United States of Atlantis might come to know perfect peace, at least for a little while. He wondered when—or if—his family ever would.

But Biddiscombe's capture did let him write to his wife. *My dear Meg, I am sorry past words to have to tell you my departure from Croydon is once more delayed. I am not sorry, however, to tell you why—Habakkuk Biddiscombe is run to earth at last. Until such time as he should receive the justice he deserves, I find myself compelled to stay here. And, until such time as I can get away, I remain, fondly, your . . . Victor.*

His goose quill fairly raced across the page. The letter held a good deal of truth. He would have written one much like it had he never bedded Louise. He might even have set down the very same words. Unfortunately, he knew the difference between what might have been and what was. Had he never bedded Louise, he would have meant all the words he wrote. Now he was at least partly relieved to stay in Croydon. If Meg had heard the truth . . .

Sooner or later, he would have to go home and find out. For now, later would do.

Atlantean horsemen brought Habakkuk Biddiscombe and half a dozen men from the Horsed Legion into Croydon three days later. The leading traitor and his followers were all skinny and dirty and dressed in clothes that had seen hard wear. Their hands were bound to the reins; their feet had been tied together under their horses' barrels. Some of them, Biddiscombe included, had already taken a beating or two.

The people of Croydon crowded the streets to stare at the traitors, to jeer at them, and to pelt them with clods of dirt and rotten vegetables. Only when stones began to fly did the prisoners' guards raise weapons in warning to leave off. Even that was more to protect themselves than to save Biddiscombe and his friends.

Croydon's jail was a solid brick building, with iron

bars across the narrow windows. Victor Radcliff wondered if it was strong enough to hold out the crowd. He stood on the front steps and held up his hands. "Have no fear!" he shouted. "They will get what they have earned. Let them get it through lawful means!"

"Tear them to pieces!" someone squalled.

"Paint them with pitch and set them afire!" That was a woman. More than a few people of both sexes cheered the suggestion.

Victor shook his head. "If they are to die, let them die quickly. Are we not better served to leave harsh, wicked punishments to England?"

"No!" The cry came from a dismaying number of throats. One man added, "Cut the ballocks off 'em before you kill 'em!" He won himself another cheer.

"You will have to kill me before you murder them," Victor declared.

For a bad moment, he thought the mob would try just that. He set his hand on the hilt of the Atlantean Assembly's sword. If he went down, he'd go down fighting. To either side of him, Atlantean horsemen raised pistols, while Croydon constables pointed ancient blunderbusses at the angry crowd. The blunderbusses, with their flaring muzzles, had barrels packed end to end with musket balls and scrap metal. At close range, they could be murderous . . . if they didn't blow up and kill the men who wielded them.

The sight of weapons aimed their way killed the crowd's ardor. People at the front edged back. People at the back slipped away. Victor had hoped that would happen, but he hadn't been sure it would.

"You see, General?" one of the horsemen said as he slowly lowered his pistol. "You should have let us settle the bastards up in Kirkwall. Then we wouldn't have had all this foofaraw."

"No." Not without some regret, Victor shook his head. "Laws have to rule. More: laws have to be seen to rule. Let Biddiscombe and the men who rode with him have their trial. You know what the likely result will be. Once the matter is settled with all the propriety we can give it, that will be time enough for their just deserts."

"Past time. Long past time," the Atlantean cavalry-man said stubbornly.

"We can afford what we spend here." Out of the corner of his eye, Victor glanced at the crowd, which continued to thin. "Can we go inside now without seeming cowards?"

"Reckon so, but why would you want to?"

"To speak to Biddiscombe," Victor answered. "He was one of us not so long ago, remember."

"So much the worse for him," the horseman said. "If he'd stayed on the side where he belonged, we wouldn't've had near so much trouble throwing out the God-damned redcoats."

"That is true," Victor said. "Biddiscombe, of course, purposed our having more trouble still."

"Devil take him. And Old Scratch will—soon."

"I shouldn't wonder." Victor did go inside then. The jail smelled of sour food, unwashed bodies, and chamber pots full to overflowing. Much of Croydon smelled that way, but the odors seemed concentrated in here.

"Hello, General." The jailer, a man with a face like a boot (and a man who hadn't missed many meals), knuckled his forelock as if he were a servant instead of the master of this little domain. "Which of the scoundrels d'you care to see?"

"Biddiscombe himself," Victor answered.

"Thought you might. Heh, heh." That chuckle would have sent ice snaking up any prisoner's spine. "Come along with me. We've got him in the snug cell by his lonesome, so he can't go trying any mischief."

The snug cell had a redwood door as thick as the side timbers on a first-rate ship of the line. The pair of locks that held it closed were both bigger than Victor's clenched fist. The jailer opened a tiny door set into the enormous one. An iron grating let people peer into the cell. The jailer gestured invitingly.

Victor looked through. The window that gave the cell

its only light was more than a man's height above the ground. Even if it hadn't been barred, it was much too small for even the most emaciated prisoner to squeeze through. Habakkuk Biddiscombe had got thin, but not that thin.

He lay on a miserable straw pallet. Along with a water pitcher, a cup with the handle broken off, and a thundermug, that pallet comprised the furnishings in the dark, gloomy cell. Biddiscombe's head swung toward the opening in the door. "Who's there?" he asked.

"Victor Radcliff."

"I might have known." Biddiscombe stiffly got to his feet. Yes, he'd taken a thumping when the Atlantean cavalry caught him—and maybe afterwards as well. "Come to gloat, have you?"

"I hope not," Victor said. "You would have done better to stay with your own side."

"That's how it worked out, all right. But who could have guessed ahead of time?" The traitor peered through the grating. "And you would have done better to listen to me more."

"It could be so," Victor said. "You aren't the only man I didn't always heed, though. The others didn't turn their coats to pay me back."

"Well, the more fools they." Habakkuk Biddiscombe kept the courage of his convictions, even if he had nothing else.

"How well did Cornwallis listen to you?" Victor inquired.

"He would have done better if he'd listened more." Biddiscombe hadn't lost his self-regard, either. "In that case, maybe you'd be stuck in this stinking cell instead of me."

"He wasn't going to hand you over. You might have done better staying where you were."

Habakkuk Biddiscombe laughed raucously. "Likely tell! If he'd made up his mind to protect us come what might, he wouldn't've needed to call a council of war.

And the damned Englishmen wouldn't've taken so long making up their miserable minds, either. No, they were going to hand us over to you, all right, sure as Jesus walked on water. They wouldn't've lost any sleep over it. After all, we were nothing but Atlanteans—one step up from niggers, and a short step, too."

And what would Blaise have said about that? Something interesting and memorable, Victor was sure. "If the redcoats felt that way about the loyalists who fought beside them, why did you stay on?"

"Because I wanted your guts for garters, General Victor High and Mighty Grand Panjandrum Radcliff, and that looked like my best chance to get 'em." Biddiscombe didn't bother hiding his venom. And why should he? Things could get no worse for him than they were already.

"If it makes you any happier, I felt the same way about you after you raised Biddiscombe's Horsed Legion," Victor said.

"It doesn't, not so much as a fart's worth," Biddiscombe replied. "Only one of us was going to get what he wanted, and I wish to heaven it were me." He scowled through the grating. "If you were any kind of gentleman, you'd pass me a pistol so I could end this on my own."

Victor shook his head. "The trial will go forward. The hounds baying outside wanted to end it on their own, too."

"Ah, but my way would finish it fast, and with luck it wouldn't hurt so bloody much," Biddiscombe said.

"When properly done, hanging slays quickly and cleanly," Victor said.

"Why bother with a trial when you already know the verdict?" jeered the man on the other side of the grate.

"So all the evidence comes forth. So the future can know you for the traitor you are," Victor answered.

Biddiscombe's mouth twisted. "A traitor is a man unlucky enough to end on the losing side. Past that, the word has no meaning."

"Not quite," Victor said.

"No? How not?" his onetime cavalry officer returned.

"A traitor is a man unlucky enough to *choose* the losing side in the middle of the war," Victor said. "You might have chosen otherwise. You would have done better if you had. And you will pay for what you chose."

Habakkuk Biddiscombe's sweeping gesture took in the whole of his sorry cell. "Am I not already paying?"

"You are," Victor said, and walked away.

Victor declined to serve on the three-officer panel that decided Biddiscombe's fate. "I doubt my ability to be just," he said. He doubted any Atlantean's ability to be just to Biddiscombe, but that was the turncoat's hard luck. At least Biddiscombe's blood would not directly soil his hands.

He was summoned to testify against Biddiscombe. The accused did have counsel, a Croydon barrister named Josias Rich. Outside the small meeting room in the town hall that served as a courtroom, Rich told Victor, "I do this not in the belief in the man's innocence, nor for the sake of my own advancement, God knows— people I thought my friends commence to cut me in the streets. I do it for the sake of Atlantis' honor. Even a dog should have someone to speak for it before it is put down."

"Your views do you credit, and I agree," Victor said. Josias Rich—whose worn linen and down-at-the-heels shoes belied his name—looked surprised and pleased.

In due course, a sergeant serving as bailiff called Victor into the room. He took his oath on a stout Bible. The judges elicited from him that Habakkuk Biddiscombe had commanded cavalry in the Atlantean army, had gone over to the English and formed Biddiscombe's Horsed Legion, and had led the Horsed Legion in combat against the forces of the United States of Atlantis.

Biddiscombe (who was burdened by manacles and by a ball and chain attached to his ankle) had muttered to Josias Rich all through Victor's testimony. The barrister rose. "Did Biddiscombe fight well and bravely while serving under your overall command, General?" he asked.

"He did," Victor said.

"Might he have continued to serve Atlantis well and bravely had you been more inclined to recognize and applaud his military merits?" Rich asked.

"I have no way to know that," Victor replied.

"What is your opinion?"

"My opinion is that, had I judged him worthy of more recognition and applause, I would have given them to him."

Rich tried again: "Do you now regret not having given them to him?"

"I regret that any man who once fought for us should have decided to cast his fate with King George, whatever his reasons may have been," Victor said carefully.

"In retrospect, do you wish now that you had been more inclined to heed his suggestions as to the Atlantean army's conduct of its campaign against the redcoats?"

"Do I think he might have been right, do you mean, sir?"

"Well—yes," Josias Rich said.

"Here and there, he might have been," Victor said. "But that is hard to say with any certainty now, looking back on it. And it would have been all the harder to say trying to look forward into an unsure future."

"Thank you, General." Rich sat down.

One of the captains who would decide Biddiscombe's fate asked, "Did other officers who sometimes disagreed with your orders remain loyal to the cause of the United States of Atlantis?"

"They did," Victor said. And there, in two words, was the essence of Biddiscombe's treason.

The panel excused Victor after that. He left the little room with nothing but relief. Baron von Steuben waited outside. "Bad?" the German asked sympathetically.

"Well . . ." Victor didn't need to think long before nodding. "Yes. Plenty bad."

"Treason is a filthy business," von Steuben said. "Common where I come from—so many little kingdoms and duchies and principalities, so many divided loyalties—but filthy all the same. Here you have but one country. If God loves Atlantis, no reason for treason again."

"May He grant it be so," Victor agreed.

The sergeant stepped out into the hallway. "Your turn, sir," he said to von Steuben, who sighed and shrugged and followed him in.

The trial was more than a drumhead, but less than something a civilian would have wanted to face. The panel of judges called several more witnesses. Even so, they'd heard enough to satisfy themselves by the middle of the afternoon. And they delivered their verdict only an hour or so later: Habakkuk Biddiscombe was guilty of treason against the United States of Atlantis, and should suffer the penalty of death by hanging.

Naturally, the news didn't need long to reach Victor, who sat in a tavern across the Croydon Meadow (on which a few sheep grazed) from the town hall drinking porter and eating a sausage and pickled cabbage stuffed into a long roll. He sighed and nodded to the man who'd brought word to him. "Well, no one expected anything else," he said.

"No, indeed," the man said. "You ask me, hanging's too good for him. He should take a while to go so he has time to think about what he did to deserve it."

Victor shook his head. "He'll have plenty of time to think on that before the trap falls. If we once start putting men to death cruelly, how do we stop?"

"You must be a better Christian than I am, General," the man said. Victor was far from sure he meant it as praise.

Blaise had his own mug of beer and cabbage-shrouded sausage. "What will you do if Biddiscombe begs you for mercy?" he asked after the news-bringer had gone on his way.

As commanding general, Victor had the authority to set aside any court-martial's verdict. He had it, but he didn't think he wanted to use it. "Not much room for doubt about what he did, or about what treason deserves," he said, and let it go at that.

Trials for the men captured with Biddiscombe went even faster than the leader's. All of them were convicted and sentenced to death by hanging except one. No witnesses came forward to show he had actually fought against the Atlantean army. The officers who made up his court convicted him of aiding fugitives from justice, but nothing more. They sentenced him to thirty lashes well laid on, the punishment to be carried out immediately.

A whipping post stood in the middle of the Croydon Meadow. Excited townsfolk chased away the sheep, the better to enjoy the spectacle. The guilty man got a strip of leather to bite down on, as if he'd gone to the surgeons after a battle wound. The man with the whip had a French accent. Maybe he'd had practice whipping slaves south of the Stour. Victor wished he hadn't thought of that; it made him imagine his own son under the lash.

Crack! Crack! The strokes sounded like gunshots. Despite the thick strap, the guilty man soon screamed after each one. The crowd cheered almost loud enough to drown him out. After the last stroke, they loosed his shackles. He slumped to the ground at the base of the post like a dead man. Then a doctor came forward to smear ointment on his raw, bloodied back, and he started screaming all over again.

Croydon didn't have a permanent gallows. Carpenters who would have been building furniture or houses or ships gleefully took time off to knock one together not far from the whipping post. The sheep were probably offended, but no one cared. Long enough to hang all the convicted traitors at once, the gallows dominated Croydon Meadow.

Ravens tumbled in the air overhead as guards with bayoneted muskets brought Biddiscombe and his confederates from the jail to the execution site. Victor Radcliff wondered how the birds knew. Biddiscombe had not appealed his sentence; he must have known it was hopeless. Two of the men from the Horsed Legion had. Victor turned them down. Men who took up arms against the United States of Atlantis had to understand what they could look forward to.

Habakkuk Biddiscombe climbed the thirteen steps to the platform as if his beloved awaited him at the top. He took his place on the trap and looked out at the crowd howling for his death. "Devil take you all!" he shouted. The Croydonites howled louder. The hangman put a hood over Biddiscombe's head.

There was a brief delay while a parson and a Catholic priest consoled some of the condemned men. The parson approached Biddiscombe. He shook his head. Even though he was hooded, the motion was unmistakable to Victor—and to the parson. Clicking his tongue between his teeth, the man withdrew.

The hangmen positioned the victims, then looked at one another. Some signal must have passed between them, for all the traps dropped at the same time. Most of the hanged men, Biddiscombe among them, died quickly. One jerked for a few minutes before stilling forever. The crowd applauded. The hangmen bowed. People left the meadow in a happy mood. Some stayed to bid for pieces of the rope. A raven perched on the gallows, waiting.

Nothing held Victor in Croydon any longer. He could go home. He could, and he would. He'd never dreaded going into battle more.

XXVI

$\mathcal{M}$eg hugged and kissed Victor. Stella hugged and kissed Blaise. So did their children. It was the happiest homecoming anyone—any two—coming back from the wars could have wanted. Victor and Meg, Blaise and Stella, drank rum. The Negroes' children drank sugared and spiced beer. Joy reigned unconstrained.

Blaise told stories in which Victor was a hero. Not to be outdone, Victor told stories in which Blaise saved the day. They both stretched the stories a little. Victor knew he didn't stretch his too much. He didn't think Blaise stretched his too much, but nobody could properly judge stories about himself.

They ate ham and fried chicken and potatoes and pickled cabbage and cinnamon-spicy baked apples till they could hardly walk. After supper, Blaise and Stella and their children went off to their smaller cottage next to the Radcliffs' farmhouse.

And Meg Radcliff looked Victor in the eye and said, "You son of a bitch."

He opened his mouth. Then he closed it again. After that opening, how was he supposed to answer? Helplessly, he spread his hands. "You know." He'd thought those were the two worst words that could possibly come out of his mouth. And he'd been right, too.

"Don't I just!" his wife answered bitterly. "You were supposed to ride a horse while you were on campaign, Victor, not some damned colored wench. And how many other trollops were there that I don't know anything about?"

"None. Not a one." Victor lied without hesitation or compunction.

Meg laughed at him—not the sort of laugh she'd given him before they were alone. "Do you suppose I hatched out of a honker's egg? You just happened to lie down with this one bitch, and she just happened to get up with child."

"That is what happened." Having begun to lie, Victor had to go on. Except for what had happened with Louise, Meg couldn't prove anything, anyhow. What she suspected . . . she had a right to suspect. But she couldn't prove it.

"Ha!" It wasn't a laugh—it was a sound she threw in his face.

"Meg . . ."

She wasn't going to listen to him yet. Maybe eventually—maybe not, too. Certainly not yet. "So tell me," she said, "have you got yourself a nigger son now, or a daughter?" She wouldn't have used that word if Blaise or Stella might have heard it. But she seized any weapon she could get her hands on to hurl at her husband.

"A son," Victor answered dully. "How is it you don't know that?"

"Because I had only one letter from dear *Monsieur* Freycinet," she snapped. "It was addressed to you, of course, but I opened it because I thought it might be important. And so it was, but not the way I looked for. He *had* to inform you that *sweet* Louise was having your baby."

Damn Monsieur *Freycinet*, Victor thought. The planter had been much too thorough. He'd sent one letter to where he guessed Victor was, and another to the place where Victor was bound to get it sooner or later. And Victor was indeed getting it, though not in the way Marcel Freycinet would have had in mind.

"A son." Meg breathed out hard through her nose.

"Yes, a son. A son who is dear *Monsieur* Freycinet's property. A son who is a slave, and likely will be all his days," Victor said. "If you think I haven't flayed myself about this, you are much mistaken."

"You fool, you're flaying yourself because you made her belly swell," Meg snarled. "I want to flay you because you bedded her in the first place. The hero of the Atlantean War for Liberty! Huzzah!"

Victor hung his head. "I deserve all your reproaches."

"And more besides," Meg agreed. "Why, Victor? Why?" But before he could answer she held up a hand. "Spare me any more falsehoods. I know why. I know too well—because you are a man, and she was there, and I was not. Heaven help me, though, I did not think you were that kind of man. Which only goes to show how little I knew, eh?"

"What can I say?" Victor asked miserably.

"I know not. What *can* you say? What would you have done if you could? Not just leave Louise in her present situation, I gather?"

"No," Victor said. "I offered to buy her and set her free here north of the Stour, where slavery is as near dead as makes no difference. I offered a price for ... for the boy, as well. Freycinet declined to sell her or the boy."

"God *is* merciful!" his wife exclaimed. "That would have blown a hole in our accounts, not so? Did you think I would not notice?"

"No. I thought you would," Victor said.

"And ... ?" The word hung in the air.

"What difference does it make now? I might have been able to explain it. Or if not, that would have been no worse than this."

"There!" his wife said in something like triumph. "That's the first truth you've told since you came home, unless I'm much mistaken."

She wasn't, and Victor didn't have the nerve to claim she was. "I'm sorry," he muttered under his breath.

"You're sorry you got caught. You're sorry your hussy caught. Are you sorry you went in unto her, as the Good Book says? Not likely!"

"What would you have me do?" Victor asked.

He thought she would say something like *Cut it off and throw it in the fire.* By the look in her eye, she wasn't far from that. But what she did answer was, "I never dreamt in all my born days that I would say such a thing as this, but right now I wish with all my heart you were more like Blaise. He would never mistreat Stella so—never!"

Victor didn't remember Blaise declining to swive Roxane, the slave girl who was so nearly white. The only difference between general and factotum—between one man and another—was that the factotum's companion hadn't conceived.

The general had no intention of betraying the factotum. One man, one friend, did not do that to another. But Meg's words caught him by surprise. Some of what went through his mind must have shown on his face.

Blood drained from Meg's cheeks. "No," she whispered. "He didn't! He couldn't! He wouldn't have!" Victor didn't claim that Blaise did or could or would have. He also didn't leap to his factotum's defense—not that Meg would have believed him if he had. He just stood there. That was bad enough, or worse than bad enough, all by itself. If Cornwallis had been able to blast holes in his defenses so easily, the Atlantean cause would have foundered in short order. Meg shook her head in what had to be horror. "God save me! You truly are all alike!"

"Don't tell Stella," Victor said.

"I have not the heart to do any such cruel thing," Meg said. "The truth will come out, though. Sooner or later, it will." She paused. "Did he get a byblow on his harlot?"

"Not so far as I know," Victor answered. "And, so far as I know, he has no notion that I did."

"I wish I had no notion that you did!" Meg exclaimed.

Then she hesitated. "Or do I? Is it not better that the truth has come forth?"

"I know not," Victor said, "but I do know how much I wish *Monsieur* Freycinet had never told me I have a colored son."

"And, surely, you wish even more that he had never told *me* you were to have a colored child," Meg said. "The one thing you have not said is that you wish you had never used this Louise for your bedstraw. Am I to gather that the reason you have not said it is because it is not true?"

Victor had no idea how to answer that. What man ever regretted doing that which made him a man? He might—he would!—regret discovery. He might—he would!—regret unexpected offspring. But regret lying down with a pretty woman and getting up afterwards with a smile? No, not likely. And yet . . .

"I wish I had not hurt you by doing what I did," he said—and he meant it all the way down to his toes.

Not that it helped. "You would do better to wish me made of stone, then," his wife said. "I trusted you, Victor. Fool that I was, I did. Now I see I must have been a fool indeed. If you took this Louise on that journey, then you must have taken a Nell or a Joanna or a Sue or an Anne or a Bess or a Kate on all your others. And then you would come home and say how much you missed me!"

He'd feared he was wasting his breath when he insisted he'd fallen from virtue, fallen from fidelity, with Louise alone. How hideously right he'd been! "I always did miss you," he said, and he meant that, too.

"Not enough!" Meg retorted. "Besides, why would you. What did you have from me you could not get for a few shillings from any tavern wench with a hot cleft?"

That shot, like so many of hers, came too close to the center of the target. Unlike some of the others, it wasn't quite a bull's-eye. "What did I have from you? Yourself. With Louise"—Victor still wouldn't admit to any others, no matter how right about them Meg was—"it was a matter of a moment, forgotten as soon as it was over. With you, I always knew we were in harness together so long as we both should live, and I never wanted it any other way. I love you, Meg."

"Forgotten as soon as it was over? She left you something to remember her by, though, didn't she? And nothing but luck she didn't give you the pox to remember her by, too, and for you to bring home to me," Meg said. "You love me, you say? You love me till you ride off far enough so you can see me no more, and then you go your merry way!"

"That is not so," Victor said, painfully aware how likely it was to seem so to a woman who discovered herself scorned.

But Meg was shooting bigger guns. "What is not so? That you love me whilst I am within sight? For beyond doubt you cease to do so once I sink below the horizon. Then the whores rise!"

"I have been away since the beginning of the war," Victor said.

"So you have. And how would you have liked it had I entertained gentlemen callers the way that black bitch entertained you? Do you suppose I have not been lonely of nights?"

He winced. "I should have liked that not one bit, as you must know. But ... it is different for a man, as you also must know."

"Much too well!" Meg said. "Which makes me believe God is truly a man, for were He She we should operate under some other, more equitable, dispensation."

"Whatever you would have me do to show my contrition ..."

"Ride south and shoot them both, and that brothel-keeper Freycinet with them, and sink all the bodies in the swamp?" his wife suggested.

"I doubt I could escape uncaught," Victor said, which was putting it mildly. "And it is not the baby's fault."

"No. It isn't." Meg started to cry then. "Not his fault he lives and cries and makes messes in his drawers, while

all of mine lie in the cold ground. Not his fault at all."
The tears ran down her cheeks. "Damn you!"

Victor had wondered if she might let him buy Nicholas and bring the colored boy north for some free colored couple in these parts to raise. He didn't bring it up now—the answer seemed much too obvious. Maybe she would change her mind once her temper, like any tempest, at last receded.

On the other hand, maybe she wouldn't.

When they went upstairs to bed, she said, "If you lay so much as a finger on me, I will scream the house down."

"Meg—"

"I will," she insisted. "Better than you deserve, too." She started crying again. "And if I don't yield myself to you, what will you do? Go out and scatter your seed among more strange women." She eyed him on the stairs. "I could win a bill of divorcement against you. Not much plainer proof of adultery than a child, is there?"

"No," he said, the cold wind of fear blowing in his ears. She *could* win a divorce. And if she did, he would never be able to hold up his head in polite society again. Wherever he went, he would always be *the man who. . . .* And, behind his back, he would always be *the man with the nigger bastard*. Conversation would stop whenever he walked into a room, then pick up again on a different note. How could you go on like that? "I . . . hope you don't." He forced the words out through stiff lips.

"I don't want to," she answered. "Not only for the scandal's sake, either. I want to love you, Victor. I want you to love me. I want to be able to believe you love me."

"Whatever I can do to bring that about, I will." After a moment, Victor added, "It will be harder if I may not touch you."

"One day, maybe. One night, maybe. Not today. Not tonight," Meg said. "As things are right now, I could not stand it."

"All right," Victor said—he could hardly say anything

else. They went up the rest of the stairs together and a million miles apart.

Victor stood by the edge of the pond, eyeing the ducks and geese. They swam toward him, gabbling eagerly—they hoped he would throw them grain. And he did, and smiled to see how eagerly they fed. There were more of them than he'd thought there might be. The farm as a whole was in better shape than he'd expected. Meg had done a splendid job.

And he'd repaid her with a bastard boy. Worse—much worse—she knew it, too.

Blaise ambled up alongside of him. The Negro looked less happy with the world than he had when he was riding up to the farmhouse with Victor a few days before. Victor understood that down to the ground. He was none too happy himself.

Blaise eyed a goose as if he wanted to wring its neck. "Women," he said—a one-word sentence as old as men.

"What's wrong?" Victor asked. Maybe someone else's troubles would help take his mind off his own.

"Some kind of way, Stella done found out about that girl I had, that Roxane, when I went down with you to meet de la Fayette," Blaise answered. "My life's been a misery ever since."

"Oh, dear," Victor said. Even if Blaise didn't, he had a good idea about how that might have happened. His wife might have told him she wouldn't say anything to Stella, but. . . .

"Had Meg got wind of you and Louise?" Blaise asked. "Is that why you were biting people's heads off while we besieged Croydon?"

"Was I?" Victor said. "I tried not to."

"You did pretty well most of the time," Blaise said, by which he had to mean Victor hadn't done well enough often enough. He went on, "No wonder you didn't care to talk about it, though. A woman who finds out her man's put it where it don't belong . . ." He shook his head. "She's trouble."

"I found that out," Victor said. The part of the truth his factotum had grasped was the part that wouldn't get in the way between the two of them. It was also the part that Victor didn't much mind getting out. Meg might say what she would, but only the most censorious condemned a man who slept with other women when he was away from home for years at a stretch. A white man who sired a little black bastard on one of them, though, was much easier to scorn.

"Expect Meg was the one who tattled to Stella, then," Blaise said resignedly. "Women are like that, dammit. I suppose I should be grateful she waited till after we got back—Stella wasn't waiting for me with a hatchet, anyhow."

"That's something," Victor agreed.

"How do you go and sweeten up your wife after she finds out about something like this?" Blaise asked. "Back in Africa, I never had to worry about it."

Did he mean he'd never strayed or he'd never got caught? If he wanted to explain further, he would. If he didn't care to, it didn't much matter. The question did. "If you find a way, I hope you'll be kind enough to pass it on to me," Victor answered. "So far, I am still seeking one myself. 'Seek, and ye shall find,' the Bible says, but it tells me nothing of where or when, worse luck."

"I try to make her happy as I can, every way I know how," Blaise said. "But it's harder when she won't let me lie down with her. If she did, maybe I could horn it out of her. Now—" He shook his head and spread his hands, lighter palms uppermost.

"If misery truly loves company, you should know you aren't the only one in the same predicament," Victor told him.

"Damned if I know whether misery loves company or not. It's still misery, isn't it?" Without waiting for an answer, Blaise pulled a metal flask out of his back pocket. "Here's to misery," he said, and swigged. Then he handed Victor the flask. "Takes the edge off your troubles, you might say."

"To misery," Victor echoed. Barrel-tree rum ran fiery down his throat. If you drank enough, the potent stuff would do more than take the edge off your troubles. Of course, it would give you new troubles, and worse ones, in short order, but plenty of people didn't worry about that. Their calculation was that, if they drank enough, they could forget the new troubles, too. If you didn't care that you lay stuporous in a muddy, filth-filled gutter, it wasn't a trouble for you . . . was it?

"My children are angry at me, too," Blaise went on in sorrowful tones as Victor gave back the flask. "They don't hardly know why, but they are. Long as their mama is, that's good enough for them." He took another nip, a smaller one this time.

Victor didn't answer. Blaise wasn't tactless enough to say he was lucky because he had no children of his own; the Negro knew how Victor and Meg had kept trying and failing to start a family. He didn't know, and with luck would never find out, how Victor had succeeded at last, if not in a way he either expected or wanted.

Something else occurred to Victor, something he hadn't thought of before. He wondered if the rum had knocked it loose. If tiny Nicholas—would he be styled Nicholas Radcliff? entitled to a family name?—grew to be a man, what would he think of his father? *I hope he doesn't hate me*, Victor thought. A moment later, he added *too much* to himself. He didn't see how a slave could help hating his father some if the man who'd begotten him was free himself.

"Sooner or later, things will work out," Blaise said: an assertion that, to Victor's mind, would have been all the better for proof. His factotum went on, "We'll have to watch ourselves from here on out, though. You get caught once, that's bad. You get caught twice . . ." He slashed the edge of his palm across his throat.

"I fear you have the right of it," Victor said with a sigh.

A goose waddled up to him, stretched itself up to its full height, and honked imperiously. It was a barnyard bird, of stock brought over from Europe, but the call still reminded him of the deeper ones that came from honkers. Plainly, the enormous flightless birds had some kinship with geese. Why geese lived all over the world, why the rapidly fading honkers dwelt only on this land in the midst of the sea, Victor had no more idea than did the most learned European natural philosopher. But then, honkers were far from God's sole strange creations here.

He fed the goose grain. Before lowering its head to peck up the barley, it sent back a black, beady-eyed stare, as if to say, *Well, you took long enough.* A mallard came over to try to filch some of the treat. The goose honked again, furiously, and flapped its wings. The mallard scuttled away.

"Any rum left in that flask?" Victor said suddenly.

Blaise shook it. It sloshed. Blaise handed it to him. He drank. After he swallowed, he coughed. "You all right?" Blaise asked.

"On account of the rum? Yes," Victor said. "Everything else? Everything else—is pretty rum." He wondered if the Negro knew that turn of phrase.

By the look on Blaise's face—half grin, half grimace—he did, and wished he didn't. But he nodded. "Can't live without women," he said, "and can't live with 'em, neither." To celebrate the propounding of that great and profound truth, he and Victor made sure the flask didn't slosh any more.

A month went by, and then another week. Victor did not lay a hand on Meg in all that time. He did lay a hand on himself, several times. Doctors and preachers unanimously inveighed against the practice. Preachers called it the sin of Onan. Doctors said it sapped the body's vital energies. Victor didn't care. It kept him from wanting to haul off and clout Meg. It also might have kept him from jumping out a top-floor window and hoping he landed on his head.

He and his wife stayed polite to each other where any-

one else could see or hear them. So did Blaise and Stella.
If Blaise hadn't told him, Victor wouldn't have known
anything was wrong between them. He hoped he and
Meg showed an equally good façade.

The two of them had an extra mug of flip apiece with
supper before they went upstairs on a hot, muggy summer evening. Meg lit the candle on her nightstand. "I
hope you sleep well," Victor said as he put on his thin-
nest, coolest nightshirt.

He waited for her to scorch him. These past five weeks,
she'd done it more often when they were alone than he
could count. She started to say something. Whatever it
was, she swallowed it before it got out. After a moment,
she brought out something that had to be different:
"Victor?"

Only his name; nothing more. No, something more—
a tone of voice he hadn't heard from her in private since
he'd come back from Croydon. "What is it?" he asked
cautiously.

She looked at the candle flame, not at him. "Would
you care to try?" she asked in return, her voice very
low.

"Would I care to try what?" For a moment, Victor
honestly didn't know what she was talking about. Then
realization smote, and he felt like a fool. "Try *that*?" He
was very glad his own voice didn't—quite—break in
surprise. "Are you sure?"

"As sure as I need to be," Meg answered, which was
less sure than Victor wanted her to be. She went on,
"If we are going to braze this back together, we should
begin again, not so?"

She made it sound about as romantic as using a pre-
scription from an apothecary. Victor didn't care how it
sounded. "Yes!" he said eagerly, and then, "Pray blow
out the candle."

Meg surprised him by shaking her head. "If you see
me, if you cannot help but see me, you will have a harder
time imagining I am . . . someone else . . . than you would
in the dark." Her chin came up defiantly.

Victor started to tell her he wouldn't do anything like that. This time, he was the one who reconsidered. She wouldn't believe him—and why should she? So all he said was, "However you please."

They lay down together. Meg didn't flinch when he began to caress her, but she didn't move toward him or embrace him, either, the way she would have before she learned about Louise. She'd enjoyed his lovemaking ... up until then. He'd always enjoyed hers, too. He hadn't strayed when she was close by. How astonishing was it that that turned out not to be good enough?

He went slowly and carefully, literally feeling his way along. After a while, she did begin to kiss and caress him in return. He didn't pride himself on warming her up, and not just because they both would have been sweating even if they'd lain apart. She did it with the attitude of someone remembering she was supposed to, not with a kindled woman's wanton enthusiasm.

Afterwards, Victor asked, "Was it all right?"

"It was." Meg seemed surprised to admit even so much. "You ... took considerable pains, and I noticed, and I thank you for it."

"It seemed the least I could do," Victor said.

"Yes, it did," Meg agreed, which made him gnaw at the inside of his lower lip as she continued, "But how was I to know ahead of time whether you would do even so little?"

"I love you," Victor said.

"I believe it—as long as I'm in sight. When I'm not, you think that what I don't know won't hurt me, and so you please yourself," his wife said. "We've been over that ground before."

"We have indeed," said Victor, who didn't want to go over it again.

Meg overrode him: "But what you forget is, sometimes I find out what I didn't know, and then it does hurt. It hurts all the worse, in fact." She'd been having her say much more often than usual since learning of Louise— and Nicholas. She talked of going over the same ground.

As things were, she held the moral high ground, and used it as adroitly as a professional soldier would have used the literal kind.

"I *am* sorry for the pain I caused you," Victor said. "I know not what more I can do to show you that. . . ."

She didn't answer for a little while. Then, thoughtfully, she said, "After what just passed between us, I also know not what more you might do. You loved me as if you love me, if you take my meaning."

"I think so," Victor said, nodding. "Dare I ask if I be forgiven, then?"

"In part, surely—else you should not have touched me so," Meg said. "Altogether? Not yet. Not for some time, I fear. I shall find myself wondering about you, worrying about you, whenever you go more than an hour's ride from here. More than an hour's ride from me, I should say."

"Then I had better not go any farther than that, eh?" Victor said.

"An excellent notion." His wife blew out the candle at last.

The messenger wore the green coat of an Atlantean cavalryman. With a flourish suggesting he'd played in an amateur theatrical or two in his time, he handed Victor Radcliff a letter sealed with the Atlantean Assembly's red-crested eagle. "Congratulations, General!" he said in a loud, ringing voice that also made Victor guess he'd been on the stage.

"Er—thank you," Victor answered. "But for what?"

Still in those ringing tones, the man said, "Why, for being chosen one of the first two Consuls who will lead the United States of Atlantis now that no one can doubt our freedom from King George's wicked rule."

Ever since departing from Honker's Mill and returning to the much larger (and more euphonious) New Hastings, the Atlantean Assembly had argued about how the new nation should be run. Victor had followed the often-acrimonious wrangling from what he'd thought was a safe distance.

Taking as their model the Roman Republic, the Assemblymen had decided to let executive authority rest in the hands of two Consuls, each with the power to veto the other's actions. Roman Consuls served only one year at a time, though; their Atlantean counterparts would have two-year terms. The Assembly had also rechristened itself the Senate, even if hardly anyone used the new name yet. It would select the Consuls. Under the rules it had agreed upon, one man could serve up to three consecutive terms, and a total of five in his lifetime.

"Who shall my colleague be?" Victor asked. The letter was bound to tell him, but the messenger seemed well informed. And, if he didn't care for the answer he got, he had every intention of declining the Assembly's invitation (*no, the Senate's*, he reminded himself).

"Why, Isaac Fenner, of course," the messenger said, as if no one else was even imaginable. But Victor had imagined plenty of other possible candidates: anyone from Custis Cawthorne to Michel du Guesclin. Still, he could easily see how Fenner would have got the nod.

And he found himself nodding, too. "Isaac should be a good man to work with," he said, hoping he would still feel that way two years hence.

He broke the seal. The letter was addressed in the fantastically neat script belonging to the Atlantean Assembly's secretary—the Senate's secretary now. That same worthy had indited the contents. In much more formal language, the letter told Victor what he'd already heard from the messenger.

He was still reading through it when Blaise walked over and Meg came out of the house to see what was going on. Victor told them. Blaise shook his hand. Meg hugged him and kissed him on the cheek. She went back inside, returning a moment later with a mug of rum punch, which she handed to the messenger.

The horseman doffed his tricorn. "Much obliged,

ma'am." He gulped the punch and smacked his lips. "Ahhh! Much obliged indeed—that's tasty stuff."

"You shall be one of the first Consuls," Meg said to Victor. "Schoolboys yet unborn will have to learn your name and deeds or get a whipping, as if you were William the Conqueror or Queen Elizabeth."

"You make me think I should say no!" he exclaimed. Blaise and the messenger laughed. Meg . . . didn't.

Blaise went back to his cottage to tell Stella and the children. They came out to congratulate Victor. In public, all seemed well between Stella and Blaise. But Blaise hadn't said anything about her letting him make love to her again. Even though Blaise hadn't got Roxane with child, Stella seemed less forgiving than Meg.

Victor's wife ducked into the house once more. When she came out again, she gave the messenger another mug of rum punch and a sandwich of roast duck between two thick slices of brown bread. The duck was from night before last, and wouldn't stay good much longer. Even so, the messenger wasn't inclined to complain. Just the opposite—he dipped his head and said, "By all that's holy, ma'am, I wish I'd had call to come here sooner!"

"You rode a long way, and you brought good news," Meg said. Her gaze swung toward Victor. "I suppose it is good news, anyhow."

The messenger only grinned—he didn't follow that. Victor smiled uncomfortably—he did. Blaise and Stella and perhaps even their children understood . . . some of it, at any rate. But none of them let on.

"Well, General Radcliff—uh, Consul Radcliff, I guess I should say—will you write me an answer I can take back toward New Hastings?" the messenger asked.

"I shall do that very thing," Victor said. "Come inside with me, why don't you? Everyone come inside—we'll get out of the sun."

After finding a sheet of paper and inking a quill, Victor wrote quickly: *To the Conscript Fathers of the Senate of the United States of Atlantis, greetings. Gentlemen, I am honored beyond my deserts to be selected Consul, and gratefully accept the office, which I shall fulfill to the best of my abilities, poor though they may be. I am also proud to share the Consulship with the most distinguished Isaac Fenner, and look forward to working with him closely and cordially. I remain your most obedient servant and the servant of our common country. . . .* He signed his name and added his seal.

He sanded the letter dry, shook away the sand, folded the paper, and used a ribbon and his seal again to make sure it stayed secure. On the outside, he wrote *To the Senate of the United States of Atlantis, convened at New Hastings.* His hand was no match for that of the Senate's secretary, but was tolerably legible.

"You did tell 'em yes, I take it?" the messenger said as Victor gave him the reply. "I need to know that much, in case something happens to the paper."

"Yes, I told them yes," Victor answered.

After two mugs of rum punch, the messenger thought that made a fine joke. "Yes, yes," he said. "Yes, *yes . . . Yes*, yes . . . *Yes, yes!*" He kept trying to find the funniest way to stress it, and laughed harder after each new try.

He rode off down the dirt track that would take him east and south, back toward New Hastings. Victor wouldn't have been amazed had he trotted west instead, and ended up in the foothills of the Green Ridge Mountains. But no.

"Well, I won't have to chase after him and put him on the right road," Blaise said, so Victor wasn't the only one who'd had his doubts.

After congratulating Victor again, the Negro and his family went back to their own cottage. That left the new consul alone with his wife. When Meg said, "New Hastings," she might have been talking about the tallest dunghill for miles around.

"New Hastings," Victor agreed in a very different tone of voice.

"I had not planned on leaving the farm for so long, but I had better come along with you," she said in a voice that warned she would tolerate no dissent. "You go there to keep an eye on the country, and I shall go there to keep an eye on you."

Sed quis custodiet ipsos custodes? For once, Victor had an answer to Juvenal's ancient and cynical question. He knew exactly who would watch at least one of Atlantis' watchmen. He let out a soft chuckle.

"And what do you find funny now?" Meg asked ominously. Victor explained. To his relief, Meg at least smiled. She was an educated woman, even if she hadn't used her Latin much since her school days (for that matter, neither had Victor). After a moment, though, she said, "But Juvenal wasn't talking about the Roman Senate and Consuls when he wrote that, was he?"

"No, I don't believe he was," Victor said, and not another word. Juvenal *had* been talking about brothel guards. If Meg didn't recall that, Victor wasn't about to remind her.

"Between you and Isaac, the country will be in good hands," she said, mercifully letting the quotation drop. "Between my right and my left, so will you."

"Fair enough," Victor agreed. And, at least for the time being, it was.

NEW IN HARDCOVER

FROM

NEW YORK TIMES BESTSELLING AUTHOR
HARRY TURTLEDOVE

LIBERATING ATLANTIS

Frederick Radcliff is a descendant of the family that founded Atlantis's first settlement, and his grandfather Victor led the army against England to win the nation's independence. But he is also a black slave, unable to prove his lineage, and forced to labor on a cotton plantation in the southern region of the country.

Frederick feels the color of his skin shouldn't keep him from having the same freedoms his ancestors fought and died for. So he becomes the leader of a revolutionary army of slaves determined to free all of his brethren across Atlantis...

"The maven of alternate history."
—*San Diego Union-Tribune*

Available wherever books are sold or at
penguin.com

ALSO AVAILABLE

FROM

NEW YORK TIMES BESTSELLING AUTHOR
HARRY TURTLEDOVE

OPENING ATLANTIS

Atlantis lies between Europe and the East Coast of
Terranova. For many years, this land of opportunity
lured dreamers from around the globe with its
natural resources, offering a new beginning for
those willing to brave the wonders of the
unexplored territory.

It is a new world indeed: ripe for discovery, for
plunder, and eventually for colonization—but will
its settlers destroy the very wonders they had
journeyed to Atlantis to find?

**"The unchallenged master of alternative
history touches on a common myth in his
latest retelling of the history of the world."**
—*Library Journal*

Available wherever books are sold or at
penguin.com

THE ULTIMATE IN
SCIENCE FICTION AND FANTASY!

From magical tales of distant worlds to stories of
technological advances beyond the grasp of man, Penguin has
everything you need to stretch your imagination to its limits.

penguin.com

ACE
Get the latest information on favorites like
William Gibson, T.A. Barron, Brian Jacques,
Ursula K. Le Guin, Sharon Shinn, Charlaine Harris,
Patricia Briggs, and Marjorie M. Liu,
as well as updates on the best new authors.

ROC
Escape with Jim Butcher, Harry Turtledove, Anne Bishop,
S.M. Stirling, Simon R. Green, E.E. Knight, Kat Richardson,
Rachel Caine, and many others—plus news on the
latest and hottest in science fiction and fantasy.

DAW
Patrick Rothfuss, Mercedes Lackey, Kristen Britain,
Tanya Huff, Tad Williams, C.J. Cherryh, and many more—
DAW has something to satisfy the cravings of any
science fiction and fantasy lover.
Also visit dawbooks.com.

*Get the best of science fiction and fantasy
at your fingertips!*